HIDE AND PEAK

SPECIAL EDITION

A RIGGS ROMANCE
BOOK 2

VICTORIA WILDER

Edited by NiceGirlNaughtyEdits

Cover by Melissa Doughty - Mel. D. Designs

Copyright © 2022 by Victoria Wilder

To the person who kissed you so well that it jilted your universe, shook fate, made your tummy flip, overheated your senses, and ensured you never forgot what it felt like. This one's for him or her.

And don't worry, there's more than just kissing in this book.

A NOTE TO READERS

This book contains adult material. It is an open-door romance, meaning multiple descriptive sex scenes exist. There are discussions of infertility, violence described in graphic detail, the death of a parent, and profanity is spoken throughout.

PROLOGUE

There is nothing better than block parties where pizza frittes and stale beer waft through the air. The scents not only make your mouth water, but also spark your memory bank, offering feelings of nostalgia for years to come. Maybe when you need it. Or least, when you don't expect it. Funny how nostalgia works.

The section of the Bronx where I grew up was littered with transplants from every passionate, hand-talking country you could imagine. And in the summer, we'd play in the street, sneak our parent's booze into Gatorade bottles, and listen to the old-timers argue about who made the best homemade liquors.

I realized as I grew older, block parties took place whenever enough adults wanted to kick back and not sweat inside. Air conditioning was for the rich and most homes only had a window unit in one room. Not to mention, most of the adults in this neighborhood would rather drink together and swap stories on sidewalks and front steps.

It was a melting pot, and that meant lots of clashing cultures, but somehow our snippet of life worked, and everyone managed to get along. Functioning as a big extended family. The Irish lived three blocks over. The Portuguese families mingled with the Greeks. And the Puerto Rican brothers, who, I still believe, were lovers and not brothers, taught me how to dance to more than just the tarantella. The owner of the bodega on the corner, Thiago, was Dominican. The best diner on the block was run by a Sicilian family, whose oldest son, according to my father, stole my innocence, but in all honesty, I handed over my virginity to that magnificent sex toy the moment my senior prom was over.

The Fourth of July was the biggest of the block parties. Every person in our surrounding blocks was proud to be from whatever country they migrated from, but on the Fourth of July, we were all proud Americans. Owning a piece of their dreams to start fresh, provide for their families, and be a part of the greatest city in the world. Fireworks started at noon, went on throughout the night, and well into the morning hours.

And while I lie here, thinking about all the amazing things that make up my life in this six-block radius, it was the people who surrounded our family who made life more special. Loud and overbearing, likely arguing, but there was always food cooking, conversations that flowed into tangents, and a sense of safety that was irreplaceable. Except for right now. Where are they all right now?

There is nothing safe about this moment. The ringing in my ears is making everything else loudly silent. I can only blink slowly and make out the figures in the farthest part of my family's duplex. I feel a dripping down my face. The smell of birch or maybe black licorice, permeates around me. The tall figures are now standing above me. They spat on my face.

Lion, tiger, bear.

A shooting pain hits my lower stomach. Once, twice, three, maybe four times.

A deep, accented voice vibrates in my head. "I made your father a promise a long time ago, Su-ka. He crosses me, and every single person he cares about will suffer for it. I gotta say, I didn't think I'd be collecting on that promise, but here we are."

Lion. Tiger. Bear.

My breathing is quicker now. I can't take a full breath. I watch as my father is dragged into the room. I can only see his lower body, and he's yelling my name. "Gia! *Il mio piccolo fiore limone.* No, no! I have no reason to betray your trust. I have nothing to tell. Please no," he cries. "Kill me, leave my daughter. Please, please," he yells again. "Lemon blossom, you are strong. I love..." His voice cuts out, and my heart stutters.

Lion.

I can't say anything. My body feels heavy, but hearing my father plead for my life has me confused and angry. I've never heard him ask for anything. My father is a force. Large in stature, but even bigger in a room. A booming voice, spacious hand gestures. He's never sounded so small, so scared. I'm not an idiot. I know the kinds of people he works with, but I never thought past the idea of it being dangerous. Dangerous is a word that's cautionary if you've never experienced or witnessed any type of violence. It never carried the weight it should have. Now that I'm lying here, unable to feel anything and watching my father cry and plead for my life, I realize I've miscalculated the heaviness of the word.

I hear a loud bang like a can of coins being violently shaken.

Tiger.

Everything after that is hazy. It's like the sounds of people speaking when you're underwater. Deep and muffled, with no pitch or clarity. I see a foot cocked back and ready to kick me.

Bear.

I say a short prayer to whatever deity is listening. Whichever god or goddess wouldn't mind intervening on a whim. My surroundings darken. The sounds are all gone in an instant. Everything that hurts in my stomach and head is erased. I don't move. And I'm not sure if it's to make them think I'm dead or if I really am.

I crack an eyelid open slightly, as much as it will allow, because I'm certain that the left one is swollen shut. Getting pummeled in the face will do that. And that's when I realize I should have kept it closed. The man who raised me, who gave up so much to ensure I was cared for, is bleeding out in front of me only a few feet away. I can't move to help him, but even if I did, the way his eyes are looking at me now is no longer filled with pride or joy. There is no life or love left in them. Instead, I stare at my pops, and I make a promise that I'll survive this. For him.

What feels like hours later, I hear yelling and banging. Numbers and names are shouted from voices I don't recognize. A hand touches my neck. *Goddess*. It searches for movement. "Sargeant, we're going to need a bus. I feel a pulse on this one."

Her raspy voice barks back, "Fuck, this is a mess. Meet the medics at the curb, keep it off the radio. Go. Now! If there's an audience, I want the lines up and everyone pushed as far back as possible."

I see hurried feet moving. "Hang in there, darlin'. We got you."

I mumble, "Lion. Tiger. Bear."

"I can't understand you, honey. Let's go. Here, I need you guys in here now!" the voice yells urgently.

I try to yell for my father, but nothing comes out except a cough.

I miss him already.

Then everything goes black.

PART I
FINDING HER

CHAPTER 1

Giselle

THE DOUBLE DOORS SLAM OPEN, THE WIND FROM THE COOL evening outside exaggerating the entrance of a group of men. A loud bravado of what must be a handful of them spills into the bar. It's impossible not to look up. They're the perfect illusion of sex appeal and confidence, but an illusion nonetheless. As a collective, they're stare-worthy. But when you focus more closely, it's all a lie. Delusions of grandeur. Mediocrity at its finest. Dressed well and boozed up.

It's after 10 p.m.. Two are half in the bag. One is laughing at his own story about the time he was hit on by his buddy's mom, and the other is already scouting the room for girls. Once they settle themselves at the end of the bar, I watch as they elbow each other and nudge their chin toward me. I hope it's just their eagerness to order, but I've been tending bar long enough to know that these guys are ready to flirt and try to achieve the ultimate hurdle of taking the hot bartender home for a ride.

No thanks. Not interested.

I'm likely to pour some drafts of our IPA and then a round of Patrón to really balance out their night. But maybe one of them will surprise me with something interesting—a Negroni or maybe even just a club soda.

But before I can ask for their order, the doors slam open again. Only this time, the man that enters demands my attention. Fully and uninterrupted. And if it were even possible for me to look away right now, I'd probably glance around and find that I'm not the only one paying attention.

There are plenty of good-looking men in this city. Some of the prettiest I'd wager, but this stranger's appeal is more than the sexy dark hair that contrasts with his white thermal. The tight shirt showcasing his tall, thick frame. It's not even the handsome face and cut jawline that has me catching my breath either. Nope. It's the badass, don't-fuck-with-me swagger that has now parted the damn room as if he were Moses and the drunks dry-humping on the dance floor were the Red Sea.

Instantly, he has me wanting to conquer his big dick energy, and then straddle him like a well-trained bull-rider. Beyond eight seconds. Multiple times, and well beyond sunrise.

"Bulleit Bourbon neat."

I stare as he lowers himself onto the stool, dragging his elbows onto the bar.

Dropping the glass in front of him, I spin the bottle in

my hands a full two turns before pulling it high for an exact two fingers pour.

He hasn't looked at me. He simply stares at the glass in front of him. Lost in his thoughts and unaware of my very blatant and aggressive eye-fucking. Oh, how I love toying with this kind of guy. Most people would leave him be and back away from the *fuck off* vibes he's volleying around, but not me. I'm just bored enough tonight to make my mission about seeing him smile. I'd bet good money that he's even hotter when he does. Sometimes they're not, but this stranger looks like he may have a pretty smile. One that's worth the effort it takes to earn it.

"I wouldn't have pegged you for the kind of man who would be so predictable." The grumpy asshole grunts at me, and I'll be honest, I only thought old Italian men who played bocce ball with my pops made those sounds *at* people. Albeit, none of those guys sounded like a voice-over actor really making the sound "hmm" his bitch. This man did, though. And he did it without even trying. There are no dry seats in this house. Achievement unlocked, because that grunt or growl was like a beautiful lark singing a song to my downtown valley. And this kitty was purring right back.

Let's play.

"You could have picked something with the same brawn, but far less typical. Better aromas and flavor. I always expect more out of the sexy silent ones, honey."

He finally looks up at me. Fucking hell, he's intimidating. There aren't many people that have had this kind of effect on me. I want his attention; I'm craving it. I wait for him to respond. But, instead of words, you know, as most people use, he locks eyes with me, raises his brow, and juts his chin in my direction as his signal for me to continue.

Okay, education time, handsome.

"I would have been more impressed with something like a Cognac. It'll still make your panties pucker, but you're getting a full-body flavor that's going to hit your nose before your palette. Still burns the same and does the job, but it comes from grapes, while Scotch is made from malted barley. Now that isn't a bad thing by any stretch, but it's just an entirely different process. With Cognac, you taste it. All of it. You'll taste the earth it came from, the barrel it aged in, and it can only be made in the region from which it's named in France. Which also means it can't be replicated elsewhere. It's limited and specific. If you want the whole package, then you go with Cognac. If you want to fall in line with the hipsters or rub elbows with the Wall Street guys, then order a basic-bitch Scotch."

He stares at me. I wait for his next move. His Bourbon is midair, in a slope halfway between the bar top and his mouth. I tend to have that effect on people. Render them speechless. Sometimes it's from my brilliant thoughts. Other times, I've just blown their mind between my knowledge and Bronx-born accent. The tits too. My tits are fantastic, so if you put them all together, it's a brain-buster for most guys.

I purse my lips, then smile at the big guy. "What's the matter? Pussy got your tongue?"

That gets him out of it. He throws back the glass. Only this time, a slight change. He uses words.

"Pour me a Cognac." And as I turn to grab the bottle from behind me, I hear him mumble, "Pixie."

I do my best to fight back my growing smile. Pulling my lower lip into my mouth, I revel in the warm excitement that coats my limbs from hearing a mere five words from my stranger. And to boot, he's taking my drink suggestion. I wouldn't have guessed him to be the kind of guy who's so quick to change something as personal as a drink order. I preen a little as I turn and pour.

Once it's sitting in front of him, I make myself busy with juicing a full lime for the margarita order I'm filling. He doesn't answer me right away. The silence has me peeking over. He folds a corner of his napkin that sits beneath the glass, keeping his hands busy as he relishes whatever thoughts he may be working over.

"Whaddya think?" I ask, nodding to his drink as he takes his second sip.

He tilts his glass again, taking another sip, but right before the rim of the glass hits his bottom lip, I see it. A small twitch that kicks up the corner of his mouth. It's not the jackpot, but it's a start.

"You mean to tell me that the only way I'm getting your number tonight is if I can either tell you a quan-drama formula," the blue collared shirt slurs, having taken way too long to process this after hitting on me. His voice kicking up at the end makes it a question, and I almost laugh.

"The quadratic formula," I interrupt to correct him as I move on to making a dirty martini. I know I'm being an asshole, but this finger-gun slinger is too much fun to simply turn down with a quick "no thanks" or "I'm not interested."

The guy came in, attitude blazing, laughing at the punchline to the joke he was telling his friends, and zeroed in on me immediately. I don't really have a type, but this guy is *not* someone I'd lean into. Not to mention, I'm working this shift at my cousin's bar as a favor. It's also a way to make some extra cash before I finally sink every penny of my savings into my own business. Going home with one of these overachiever advertising executives or Columbia undergrads is not on the agenda.

"Yea, that," the twenty-something gawks. He nudges his buddy's arm and laughs. "Or if I tell you why the sky is blue?"

He is pretty. I'll give him that. I bet he picks up his fair share of beautiful women and rarely gets turned down. Maybe if I were just drinking here, I would have considered it. But not tonight. Especially not when a muscled, grunting sex fantasy is breathing confidently at the other end of the bar. He's trying not to, but I see him paying attention to this exchange.

If they made men like *that* in this city, I'd be in a whole hell of a lot more trouble than I usually am. Nope, that beautiful man is not from here. Too much "I don't give a fuck energy" mixed with something lonely or even lost. He's easily the most intriguing person to walk in here or into the same room as me in a very long time.

"So, basically, your answer is no. No, I can't have your number."

I smile at him as I rinse and then dry the tumbler in

my hand. "It's a no. Unless you can answer one of those for me, Sparky."

Instead of swearing at me or sulking off, he and his friends start laughing and buy a round of shots. After they each close out their tabs, my friendly drunk says, "Well, this sucks."

A grunting laugh reverberates from the far end of the bar, where my sexy stranger leans over his drink.

"You're still the hottest bartender I've ever seen. I'll come back with those answers, gorgeous," the drunk guy yells as I make my way back to the only man here who has my interest.

I pour myself a glass of water and drop a lemon wedge into it. "Drinking alone tonight?"

Ignoring my question, he asks, "Would you have given that guy your number if he knew your answers?" The timber of his voice gives me a jolt of energy. It's low and slow. The kind of tone that can be commanding and firm. A man who takes his time with words, not like most of the people I know. In this city, we move fast. Everyone is quick to answer, fast-talking, and over-eager to hear the sound of their own voices.

"I could tell you why the sky is blue if you really don't know," he says.

"I already know the answer. It's not why I asked. I love the idea of someone else knowing. For someone to be curious enough to care about something they see every day. To appreciate the beauty, and the science of chaos behind it."

"So you're a romantic, then? My sister is the same way."

"You stop that right now, sir. Don't say mean things like that. I am no such thing." I lean forward on the bar, tossing my hair behind me. "I believe in the right now. That people say what they mean," I tell him, part joking and part serious about his comment. I'm rough enough around the edges to never be considered a romantic.

"That doesn't mean you aren't a romantic." He starts to smile at me as he speaks. It's just a twinge, but wow, is it pretty. "It wasn't an accusation, either. It was more of an observation. People don't say things like that unless they have a romanticized outlook on life or at least parts of it. You believe in fate, too?"

He coughs out a small laugh at the frown I'm giving him. And I notice the white scar that cuts right above his lip.

"Do you?" I ask in response.

"I don't think I can. It means all the shitty stuff that happens was meant to happen. And I can't wrap my head around that. I don't want to," he says as he folds the corners of the cocktail napkin under his now empty glass again.

"Maybe fate is a thing, but not like it is in movies. Maybe there's a whole outline for each of us, but tons of variations. Like a choose-your-own-adventure book. Do you remember those?"

He just stares at me like I've said something prolific, or maybe just plain silly, but really, it's how my mind works, splitting off into tangents. Just like the concept behind those books.

"There are multiple choices. We choose what we

want, but the different outlines are still there, already written out as guidelines or pathways."

"Or anchors," he adds thoughtfully.

I smile at the thought. "I like the idea of fate, so yes, I suppose I believe in it. But that doesn't make me a romantic."

He raises his eyebrow, challenging my last thought.

"Just open minded. Not a romantic, just a harbinger of possibility." I laugh. "Another round?"

He nods. The tiniest curve of a smile still dances on his lips, but his mood has shifted. Something changed, and it has him thinking about something heavier.

As I pour him a new glass, I search his face for that flirtatious humor we had a few minutes ago. I cringe at the reality that I might be the world's worst bartender. I'm supposed to let people talk. Have them leave here feeling lighter or at least buzzed enough to erase something weighing them down. Right now, it looks like my sexy brute has hoisted that weight back onto his shoulders.

I grab my phone, scroll down and select something new to play over the sound system. A few seconds later, the sound of a keyboard and hi-hat rhythm in what feels like a lazy, half-time beat moves around the room. Then, Bob Marley's singing that everything's gonna be alright. It permeates the negative air that's plagued the room. I even wish I were on a beach listening to this right now. With this stranger, especially.

He looks up at me, the corner of his sexy-ass mouth tipping up. I smile back. My valiant effort to reprise my role as a helpful and stereotypical bartender is a success. "Tell me something good, big guy."

He thinks about it for a minute, then says, "Cheesy grits with crispy bacon and a perfectly poached egg. Shave a little fresh parmesan over top." Mimicking the movement of sprinkling parm over a plate, he continues. "More than good. Almost perfection," and as he's saying it, my mouth waters.

"You're a foodie?"

A full smile takes over his face. Dammit, the man is beautiful. There is some kind of heartbreak warfare attached to those lips. And my fucking panties are currently singed to my skin. A new-age chastity belt that won't unlock until this man smiles directly into my crotch, ready to devour it like the food he's describing.

"A bit. I've always loved to eat." I laugh, because I'm immature like that, and my mind's currently in the gutter. But he continues, "I had to find new things to fill my time over the last few months. I figured out that I can cook pretty well. Love it, in fact. Almost as much as I love to eat."

"I bet you do," I say. "Profession or obsession?"

"Maybe just a way to work out aggression," he says, taking a sip of his drink and piquing my curiosity.

"There are lots of creative ways to do that. But I like the idea of doing it with food." I smirk. "If you cook, then I'm in. There's not much I don't like. I've never had grits before. Just no bacon." I smile wide as I pour two beers from the tap for my remaining two customers a few seats down.

"Tasting it is far better than words." The funk he was in is now forgotten, and all of a sudden, heat flashes across my cheeks. "Wait, why no bacon?"

"Vegetarian." I point to myself.

"I knew there had to be something." He lifts his hand up as if he's surrendering. "I'm not going to dive into the magic you're missing out on." He's shaking his head at me, teasing me about his disdain for my lack of meat-eating.

I shrug my shoulders. The smile he pulled out of me just a few minutes ago is still going strong. "My pops says to me all the time"—I tweak my voice to make it lower and give it the proper Italian accent—"You are-a Toscana. Oh, Madonna. We are meat-eaters." I pull my fingertips together, raising my hand in the air and rocking at the wrist.

He laughs at my impersonation of my father. "Sounds like he knows what he's talking about," he says.

"I don't have a big reason, really. I just don't love it. And I read that you can live a longer life if you remove animals from your diet. So I went for it."

"A longer life, but I don't know about a happier one. Bacon and burgers, oh! And smoked duck. It's practically a religion in my family. I cook it best, and there isn't a Sunday dinner without something grilled, smoked, or fried."

"You can do any one of those things to vegetables."

The last couple of customers close out their tabs. Two regulars who've been in a few times over the past handful of years that I've helped my cousin out here. "Tell your old man he still owes me a game of horseshoes at the next block party."

I smile wide. "Larry, *you* talk to him about horseshoes and bocce rematches. I'll stay out of it."

He laughs at me. "Have a good night, kiddo." He taps the bar and walks out, giving my sexy stranger a once-over as he goes.

I pull out two shot glasses and a bottle of chilled limoncello from the cooler; there's no label since it's my cousin's batch. Pouring two shots, I push one in front of my sexy stranger. I raise mine up.

"What's this? It looks radioactive."

"Limoncello. And a little thank you for walking into my bar tonight."

"I should be the one thanking you. Best decision I've made in a long time." His eyes lock onto mine as he raises his glass and says, "To a long life."

"A una bella vita." *To a beautiful life.*

CHAPTER 2

Henry

"ONE EYE IS GREEN, AND THE OTHER IS HALF GREEN AND half blue. I've never seen that before." She smiles as she leans on the bar, closer to me. "Beautiful," she whispers.

I'm thinking the same thing, but for an entirely different reason. This woman is cute and sexy, and I don't mind her staring. Mesmerized by an imperfection. The imperfection that has forced my life into an entirely different orbit. It's the first time in months that my eyes haven't been the source of my anger and complete frustration. She's the kind of person whose singled-out, focused attention feels like an achievement. A feeling I didn't know existed until right now. Talking to her, feeling her eyes wander around and discover parts of me, it's quickly becoming more than a desire, maybe even a weakness.

I didn't see her when I came into the bar. I was too lost in my own thoughts to notice a pretty girl, never mind a beautiful woman. Listening to her talk with everyone from the douchey drunks to her waitstaff, I couldn't stop paying attention.

"Tell me your name," I demand as I drain the last sip from my Cognac.

Ignoring me, she smiles and says, "Tell me what you're thinking. You have a very insistent look in your beautiful eyes that is making me think it's something either really good or gorgeously naughty."

How much I don't want tonight to end is the least dirty of them.

"I'm not thinking of anything right now. I just want to know your name," I say and move my right hand closer to her arms that are folded on the bartop. The truth is, I'm thinking I'd like to taste her lips and see if her tongue will feel as good as I'm expecting. She finishes pouring out a shot and then looks at me as if she just remembered something.

"Stay Puft."

I pause at her outburst. "What?" I laugh.

"Stay Puft Marshmallow Man. That's what Dr. Ray Stanz thinks about in the movie Ghostbusters when he's told not to think of anything. And then a giant marshmallow man traipses down 5th Avenue..."

I stare at her, brow furrowed. I know I didn't drink enough yet to have missed any part of our conversation. Maybe she's crazy after all. A woman who looks that good, and has a personality to match, had to have something *off*. Maybe this is her flashing red light flaw.

She watches as I brush my fingers on her forearm and goosebumps emerge along her smooth skin. The place closed ten minutes ago, and the young barback is cleaning up around us while the two waitresses are counting their tips at the other end of the bar. I'm not usually the guy to hit on bartenders or wait around until after last call, but this woman has me under some kind of trance. I don't want to leave her yet.

"Dan Aykroyd has two different colored eyes. He plays Ray in Ghostbusters. That's what I thought about when I noticed your half-green, half-blue eye. And we're in New York, and you're this big, beautiful man that just barreled into my bar."

Okay, not crazy after all. Just... remarkable. I realize it's why I can't seem to leave. I'm anchored to this moment with her.

"Your bar?"

"Well, my bar tonight. It's my cousin's bar, but tonight it's mine," she says as she gives her staff, who are clearly trying to eavesdrop on our discussion, an exaggerated eye squint and scowl.

For the next two hours, we talk. All of it should seem trivial—a distraction. But for the first time in a while, I'm feeling good. Like myself again. A version of me that hasn't surfaced for a long time. Maybe even long before the accident.

"I could watch Seinfeld for hours and never get tired of it. It's my multitasking show. That, and Law & Order: SVU."

"Both New York-based, but very different vibes," I say.

"They're fantastic and you can binge 'em, or just have them on while switching over your summer to winter wardrobe. Almost like background music. They're timelessly enjoyable," she says. And I picture her doing it. Sitting in a pile of clothes in the middle of the floor, watching Kramer fly through Jerry's front door. Her laughing. She's got a great laugh. The kind I'm finding has me smiling as a response.

"I always thought Benson and Stabler should have ended up together," I say.

She smiles at that. "Well then, who's the romantic now?"

"They go through a ton together and then Stabler just leaves the show. Such a letdown."

A minute ticks by, both of us smiling in the wake of our TV discussion.

"What's the catch, big guy?" But before I can say anything, she asks, "Married?"

I smile and slowly shake my head. "Not yet."

She smiles at the response. "The M-word scares most men from the vicinity if a woman dares to speak it, and you say, 'not yet.'"

"I'm not most men. And why cower from something I eventually want?"

"No, you are definitely not most men." She stares at my mouth and then back into my eyes.

"I'm not in any rush, but I want that." I take a deep breath, steeling my nerves a bit because, really, who says this kind of thing to a stranger in a bar? "The all-consuming feeling. The part where you decide to live life with someone instead of just on your own. Having a partner who knows you, and then wants to keep learning everything about you along the way."

When she smiles at me this time, it hits me right in

the chest. "I like that. I don't know if I've witnessed it, but I like the picture you paint of it."

"Just like those blue skies?" I ask, lifting a brow.

"You know they're not really blue, right?" she says. "It's just how we see it." She shifts her eyes toward me, realizing something. "You were eavesdropping."

"Just paying attention."

"Good. I wanted your attention."

How can words from a stranger have me reacting like this? I'm not one to smile often, even when life was going my way. I can't remember the last time I felt happy enough to smile so easily. The feeling I have when I'm talking to her is addictive. I've never shared as much about myself with a person I knew so little about before. Maybe anyone, for that matter.

"It's late," she says in a hushed voice. After last call, I waited to close out my tab. I didn't want to leave, and she seemed to be on the same page.

"It is," I say as I look up from her legs to her face.

She proceeded to lock up after the last waitress counted out, and then we moved to one of the high-top tables. She kicked off her shoes and draped her legs in my lap. It felt... comfortable. Not a typical feeling I have with many women. Especially ones that I've just met. But I can't say I've ever met someone like her before. I don't just want to take her home and fuck her. I mean, I definitely want to do that, but I like being around her. Talking to her. She's the only person who's made me forget about my own bullshit. I feel light around her. Weightless seems like the wrong word, but something like it. Careless, but in a good way. I should ease back, but I can't seem to do it.

My fingers drag up and down her calves lazily.

"That's your move, big guy? To agree with me? And not, 'you're coming home with me' or 'let's get outta here?'" she asks in a teasing tone. "Fucking hell, I thought you would have had more game than this."

I sit up in my seat, and in one fast movement, I pull her chair closer to mine. The sound of it dragging on the floor disrupts the relaxed mood we've curated. And without waiting for approval, I lift her off her seat and into my lap. She sucks in a breath and then lets out a nervous laugh.

"This isn't my game. I don't have an agenda. I simply take what I want. And, right now, I want to taste your mouth," I say, moving my hands to frame her face and brush my thumbs along her pretty lips.

Tracing her top lip, it's one curved line with no dip or bow. Thinner than the bottom, but together they're asking to be adored. "I want to hear what small sounds you make when I lick this lip. And tug this one between my teeth."

I take a minute to really look at her. See what that admission does to her. Thick lashes frame her warm brown eyes, smudged black with whatever makeup she had on from the day. There's a single handful of freckles along the bridge of her nose, with a tiny diamond stud pierced on the right side. She's adorable and sultry, mixed in a curvy, petite package that I'm crushing on, hard.

One long, curving line of black ink starts from her shoulder down to her wrist with a small white and light pink blossom every few inches. It's delicate. A type of tattoo I've never seen before, and it makes her all the more alluring.

"I like this," I tell her as I drag my fingers around the tiny flowers, following the vine.

"I drew it. Not on myself, but it's my design. I love the idea of being able to put art along my body." She shifts closer to me. "If life were a little different, maybe I would have been a tattoo artist instead of an actuary that moonlights as a bartender." She laughs, but I don't. The idea of wanting to become something other than what you worked for seems like the most foreign concept to me. And yet, I'm being forced to do it while she's fantasizing about it.

"And this one." She turns her neck, and I see a vine that runs along her hairline when she lifts her dark hair and pushes it over her shoulder.

I caress more of her skin. Soft and warm. I see a shiver ripple through her, and her neck flushes pink. "What are these?" I ask as I explore the tiny white flowers. Each one with flecks of purple and yellow toward the center.

"Lemon blossoms," she says quietly. I trace my finger along them again.

"You have any?" she asks as I keep drawing along her neck and behind her ear.

I shift to show her. "I do. Mountains start on my shoulder, and I plan to move them down my arm. And then one on my chest." She lets her hair fall from her grip. Raising her brows, she silently asks about the design on my chest. "An outline of wings. For the Air Force."

"Active duty?"

I shake my head.

"So, not a career boy, then?" she says playfully.

I point to my imperfect eye. The one she called beautiful. "Not anymore."

"Blank slate," she says softly.

"Not by choice. Not really sure where I go from here."

She smiles, and I can tell she wants to say more. She watches my face as my fingers trail the vine along her arm again. "Well, flyboy, you should already know this. But I'll say it because maybe you need the reminder. Sometimes you just need to look up and check out the blue skies. Maybe they'll help clear your mind a bit. Give you a better idea. Start a new path."

"You make it sound so easy. Just to pick something and start again."

She leans back as she sits in my lap and traces my hair line from my forehead down to behind my ear. I shut my eyes in response. The warmth of her close to me is calming and the motion of her fingers brushing along my skin and into my hair melts away the negative. "Find something you love to do that has nothing to do with what you did before. Start there and see where it takes you."

My mouth twitches, lips curling without effort. I open my eyes, meeting her gaze as she rakes her attention around my face, from my eyes to my lips and back. "Did you just full circle our conversation back to choosing our own adventure?"

But without answering, she moves her hips in toward mine, grinding into my lap, and the movement shoots any remaining reserve I had out that front door. The thoughts about life and careers are long gone. As I pull her closer, she leans in and playfully bites my lower lip.

"Fuck," I whisper, drawing out the word as she pulls back. My brain can't register much else other than the sexiness of that move.

I do the same to her, dragging my teeth along her plush bottom lip and licking it slightly with the tip of my tongue. She lets out a soft moan, and it urges me on. There's no way of holding back after that. Our lips collide furiously. When her tongue glides against mine, every lingering thought is erased. My sole focus and moment's purpose is to be kissing this woman. She tastes like lemons dipped in sugar—tart *and sweet.*

Wrapping one hand behind her neck, I push my fingers into her hair to tilt her head where I want her. She moves with me easily. My other arm circles her hips, just above her ass. I drag her even closer, closing any gap left between us. It's been hours of coy smiles and flirtatious conversation. This, right here, is one helluva payoff.

I walked into this bar to drink away the uncertainty. Forget about the path my life is no longer taking. Be a stranger in a strange city. Find myself in the luxury of having no obligations and being completely alone.

But right now, I've never wanted to get lost with someone else more in my life. I'm certain of it.

CHAPTER 3

Giselle

You kiss by the book. It's not a line that would have stuck with me if I read Romeo and Juliet. Which I haven't. To be honest, the idea of kissing, according to the way a book instructs, seems like a boring-ass kiss. Assumptive. Unoriginal. But when Claire Danes breathily said it to Leo DiCaprio in the movie version of Shakespeare's story, I nearly had a coronary from too much blood draining from my heart and into my lady bits. Both of them were beautiful. An innocent, puffy-lipped virgin and a heroic fuckboy in training. They were nothing short of perfect sexual chemistry in motion. My perspective about that one line changed utterly, simply by the way it was delivered. But I suppose that was the point—the delivery.

I've never thought too long about kissing someone. I take what I want, and offer what I desire, but kissing was never as epic as Claire proclaimed to Leo. With anyone. Except right now, this sexy stranger that I've known for less than a handful of hours has nearly dismantled everything I've ever assumed about a kiss.

I always approached kissing as a warm-up. An appetizer for the main course to follow. But not right now. Right now, I'm thinking this man kisses my lips and invades my mouth in a way that is fucking poetic. Claire Danes or Juliet, or even Shakespeare himself, did a shit job of describing what it feels like to be kissed the way I was apparently meant to be.

"Why do your lips..." He rubs my swollen bottom lip with his thumb, seemingly in awe. And I feel just the same. "This mouth feels so fucking good against mine?" He stares at my mouth and then looks back up into my eyes. I can't help but smile. Back and forth, he grazes my lips ever so slowly. I taste the tip of his thumb, making him groan. The low hum that he's making. The approval and praise of it, mixed with the low octave, feels like I've been tea-bagged with pure fucking eroticism.

My phone vibrates on the table behind me. I want to yell at it to shut up so this magic we're coated in doesn't fade. It's *too* good.

Then it buzzes again.

There are very few people who would be texting me right now. After 2 a.m., it usually means someone's looking to hook up.

Another buzz.

"Need to get that?" he asks, still lazily moving his thumb around my lips.

I reluctantly stand up off his lap, but before I leave him completely, I quickly kiss and nip his lips one more time. It pulls a smile out of him. He was really fucking sexy when he came in tonight, with his severe and some-what grumpy exterior, but this man smiling is an entirely new high for me. A new kink, because I'm almost certain that smile has the ability to disarm me in every way.

The phone buzzes again as I pick it up.

Three missed calls and text messages from my pops. That's not good.

> POPS
>
> Need you to stay away from the house
>
> Love you, kid

I call him back. My guess is he's had too much fun playing horseshoes with the guys tonight, decided to collect on the sexual innuendos that Lenora from across the street throws his way on the regular, and doesn't want me to be traumatized. Maybe even decided to polish off the new batch of limoncello my cousin made.

No answer. I stare at the texts one more time. The last one isn't something he'd usually say to me.

"Everything okay?"

I nod.

"Let me walk you home," he offers, standing up and dragging me back into his arms. "Tell me your name. I still don't know your name."

"Gia."

He kisses me lightly. Almost a ghosting of his lips against mine. "I'm Henry."

"I live in the Bronx. You're not going to want to walk all the way there."

"I'll make sure you get to your train, then." He pauses

for a minute and moves his hands from my face and neck down to my shoulders and arms. "Give me your number so I can make sure you got home okay."

I don't answer. Instead, I think about what would be better. I don't want to just text him. I want to see him again.

I lock up the bar, set the alarm, and we make our way to the subway station. Before I head down the stairs, I decide I'd rather see him tomorrow night than just give him my number.

"Meet me in Bryant Park tomorrow night. They do old movies on the lawn. I'll bring the blanket and booze. You bring the food," I tell him.

He nods and smiles. I didn't think it was possible to like him more, but I do.

"Kiss me like that again tomorrow night, and you'll get my number," I tell him. I lean in and press a soft kiss to his throat. Right where his Adam's apple protrudes and bobs as he swallows roughly. His neck is smooth in contrast to the scruff that lines his jaw and cheeks. I take another sniff, trying to lock it into my memory. He smells delicious. Aftershave and leather mixed with that clean scent of right before it snows. It sounds ridiculous, but I want to nuzzle into him. Or lick him.

With a laugh, he asks, "Did you just sniff me?"

I lift a shoulder as I walk away and move down the steps of the subway.

"What movie is it? At Bryant Park?"

I turn back, looking up at him from the bottom of the subway steps. "Ghostbusters."

CHAPTER 4

Henry

"WHAT HAS YOU SMILING THIS EARLY ON A SUNDAY morning?" my sister asks from her living room couch. I tried to be quiet when I came in, but that didn't matter. I should have known better. Everly is up earlier than I am most days.

Ignoring her, I grab a cup from her dish rack and fill it with tap water. So thirsty. The sun is just barely up right now, but I'm wired after walking the length of the city back to her apartment.

"Henry! Answer me. I don't think I've seen you smile in, like, a year," she says with a laugh. Pointing to the coffeepot as she pours another cup, I nod, letting her know I'll take a cup too. My sister is the best of us. There isn't a damn thing she wouldn't do for the rest of my family or me. Something is both comforting and stressful about that. Knowing that a person wants nothing more than to see you happy. No expectations or exchange necessary. She radiates pure warmth. She keeps us honest in the ways that matter the most: looking out for each other and ensuring that there's someone to help you breathe when life gets too heavy.

That's why I came to New York. Instead of heading back home to Strutt's Peak right away. I've never felt the need to escape from there. It's the one place that grounds me. My friends and the rest of my family were all there, but I just couldn't stomach going back for one very glaring reason. Going back to tell everyone that I failed at the one thing I wanted to do for my entire life seemed like a self-torture I wasn't ready to dive into just yet. I needed to get my head right before settling into my life. When I left, I left thinking I was going to be someone entirely different, but it didn't turn out that way. I went back to spend time with my brothers. They were both struggling in their own ways, so I did what I always do; I tried to be the hero. It bit me in the ass and then fucked me sideways. So, now I'm here. Licking wounds. Trying to do some soul searching and figure out my next moves.

She clears her throat, "Hello," waving at me as she passes me the cup of coffee she poured.

I laugh. "Sorry. A lot on my mind."

"Ahhhhhhh, no. No way are you getting away with that. You either had one helluva subway ride, or you met someone."

"Can it be both?" I squint as I ask, knowing that she won't let up until I've spilled.

She barks out a laugh just as she swallows a sip of coffee. "Hah! Yes, it can be both. Now tell me everything and don't leave out any details." She tucks her feet under her on the couch across from where I sit. "Well, leave out anything that might gross me out." She flips her hand in the air.

"I'll talk about the girl in a minute, but I had another idea. Something you might want to entertain."

"I'm listening."

"What would you say to coming back to Strutt's and diving into the business with me?"

She pauses for a minute to really think about what I'm saying. "Seriously?" she asks.

I give her a nod. "I did a lot of walking and just thought about what would make sense now that," I trail off the thought. "—the Air Force. Being a pilot is the only thing I've ever wanted, but that's off the table now, and regardless of whether or not I like it, that's my reality. So I'm thinking, why not dig into our legacy? See if we can really do some good with it. Either that or I stay in New York and try something entirely out of left field."

I shift in the chair, suddenly feeling more confident with both of those ideas. Both are a fresh start. That's what I need. Something to feel good about again. A goal. Goals, I understand. I'm great with a purpose and a goal. The in-between I'm in right now is a damn nightmare.

"There's no way I could ever imagine you in this city, Hen," she says. And I laugh a bit because she's right. I'd never last here very long. Not enough open space. Breathing room. Although if that gorgeous pixie asked me to stay, I'd probably find a reason to do it. I smile, thinking about her. I need to see her again.

"There's so much that Dad hasn't been able to do yet with the business. Things that we've all talked about hypothetically with him for years. It could be so much more than storefront and equipment rentals. Don't you think?" She nods, smiling. I know I've got her attention now. I see her wheels spinning. "I'm going to talk to him when I'm back and pitch the concept of building out winter adventures."

She takes a minute, sipping her coffee. I can see her trying the idea on and picturing it. I've had more time to think about it, and I want to give her the same to consider what it could mean for all of us. It's also a big change from what she's in New York doing right now.

"I'm so burnt out, stressing about getting a call back from one of these fashion houses, or even a somewhat respected designer to gain an apprenticeship with, and it feels like I'm in a losing battle. I've already been tempted to pack it up and come home, so you don't have to sell me too hard on this. I just never wanted to quit, but if this is something I could really dig into..."

She stares at the wall, lost in her thoughts for a minute.

"I love New York, but I've never really called it home. Not when I know what big blue skies look like without having to find the nearest roof deck to see them." She leans on her fist and says, "And Daddy's there. Nowhere feels like home when he's this far away."

She's a true daddy's girl. The only girl. She's also the most lovable of all of us. But the truth is, we all play our roles. My brother Michael is quiet and stoic, but passionate about everything he does. It's infectious. Law is the youngest. Always carefree, doing things over the top. But it earns him a fuck load of smiles and approvals.

And then there's me. The oldest, with a penchant for calculated risks. I thrive on doing things I shouldn't. Like flying. Leaving home. Choosing to join the Air Force when I knew the risks. Flying for a living could have meant safer choices, but the safe choice isn't usually the one I want, and I wanted to be the best. The adrenaline I got from flying, becoming the best there is, and creating my own name for myself is a high I never anticipated.

In Strutt's Peak, being a Riggs has expectations. My father is well-known and respected. He's built up his business in such a way that he's brought in tourists. His business has helped build up other businesses. Everyone knows Asher Riggs. But they only know us as his kids. I've only ever wanted to be a pilot. I've talked about it since I graduated from high-school years ago.

And now, I can barely do that. At least not in the way I was trained. Enlisting in the Air Force meant I'd trained to be the best. I didn't want to just be a pilot. I wanted to wreck goals and records. Be part of the elite. My peak-level reflexes and reaction time made me the top of my class, and in special training too. And it was all for nothing.

What do you become when the thing that defined you, the goal you've had for your entire adult life, is no longer on the table?

Ev and I spend the morning exchanging ideas that could become realities back in Strutt's. Ones that we've pitched over the years to our father but that he couldn't execute without help. We talk about what it could look like going back home and really doing this. How to make the move look less like nepotism and more like a fresh perspective for a business that hasn't reached its potential yet.

Riggs Outdoor is already a place worth checking out when tourists come into town—renting equipment, taking lessons for skiing, snowboarding, and snowmobiling. It takes up a massive space on Main Street in our town, but it could do so much more in the warmer season. Expand even further during the peak winter months.

I'm excited thinking about it. An excitement that I didn't think I was still capable of having until I met a beautiful woman who managed to turn me inside out in just one night.

I haven't felt this good in a while. That lighter feeling when you'd much rather smile at a stranger than stare straight ahead. A concept that really isn't optimal in New York City.

Just after 7 p.m., I walk up the hot subway steps from the 6 train and into Bryant Park. I ditched the long-sleeved thermal for a t-shirt. It's hot tonight. The massive lawn of the park is peppered with people on blankets and chairs, facing a huge screen that plays advertisements. No one pays attention. People are still waiting for food and talking with friends. I realize quickly that finding her in this sea of people is going to be a bit of a nightmare.

I spend the first hour of the movie walking around the lawn, looking every bit like the tourist that I am. Every time I think I see her, it turns out it's just a curvy brunette meeting girlfriends. It's never her.

The high that I was on from earlier today plummets

by the time the credits roll. I'm sweating from the night's humidity and the constant searching.

Maybe it was just a random night and an amazing kiss. That I should leave it at that. A small swoop of fate woke up a part of me that I hadn't realized I let shut down. The excitement of learning something new and feeling something again didn't turn into feeling sorry for myself.

But I've never been someone to let loose ends go untied, so when I show up at the bar again, my emotions make a bit of a leap of hope that maybe she thought the same thing that I did. Come back here if she couldn't find me. Either that or she purposely didn't show, and I'm about to be the creepy stalker guy.

"Sir! Sir, I'm sorry, but you can't go in there," a man shouts in my direction. As I turn around, I notice a huddle of people to the right of the bar. Behind them are a few police cars.

"Is the place open?"

"Closed. Under investigation," he says.

But before I can ask anything else, another man comes up behind him, flashing a badge and asking me if I know the owner.

"I'm from out of town. I met a girl here last night, the bartender, actually." I smile. "I was hoping I'd see her again if I came back here tonight."

The look that the plainclothes officer gives to the other one in uniform is what should tip me off first. Or at least prepare me for what comes next. A reporter and cameraman interrupt our discussion, and I step away. The sinking feeling I have in my gut is what keeps me there. Another officer comes along to ask me questions about when I was at the bar last night. Things like what time I left and where I went from here.

It's not until I hear the line of reporters that have set up on the sidewalk talking about a homicide that I finally start to understand what could have happened. I look around, hoping that I see her. Maybe she wasn't involved in the situation that's overtaking the sidewalk. But the sick feeling I have is outweighing the hope.

"Sir, you said you came looking for the bartender from last night?" the only female officer I've seen asks, as she saddles up next to me. "Gia Neri, twenty-two years old, brunette?"

I nod. Not wanting to hear what she has to say, but listening, regardless. *I didn't even know her last name.*

"I'm sorry to be the one to tell you this, but she's not going to be here, sir." The officer looks around, maybe thinking that I'm going to pass out at this news. Because I do feel like I'm going to pass out, my fingers and legs tingling. And a wave of sickness rolls through me. There's no way the woman I met last night is dead. No way.

"She was involved in a home invasion. I'm so sorry, but she didn't make it," the officer says. I stare at the officer. I can only blink.

Everything else after that seems like a blur. The trip to the station. The statement I had to make formally. The walk back to my sister's apartment. The way I found myself crying into Everly's shoulder as I told her what I found out. The weeks that followed had me calling the police station and investigating officers every day. I showed up to Bryant Park every evening and just watched. Waited.

Maybe they were wrong. I stayed a month later than I had planned. I helped Everly pack up her apartment. When I was able to focus, we'd plan tasks around the business with regular calls to our dad for feedback and approvals. But every night, I'd ride the subway. Walk for blocks. The big-ness of the city always felt like nothing there could be final. I looked, but never found her.

Even after we went back to Strutt's Peak. After Everly moved home and we started working with our dad, I would return to the city. Quick trips. Sometimes for a night, other times for just a few hours. I'm not sure why or what I thought I'd find. I read her obituary. Attended her services. Even stopped by her gravesite. But I still felt like it wasn't final. It was only one night with her.

A handful of hours, and I couldn't let it go. Let *her* go.

CHAPTER 5

Giselle

3 YEARS LATER...

"Hey, fuckwad, she said no thank you. Read the room."

I can never mind my own business when douchebaggery is hard at work. You can move to a thousand different towns and change a million little things about yourself, but one thing is always there and remains the same. It's the one constant that you'll always find. There will be douchebags no matter where you go. Some women, some men, but you can always recognize them when you hear them—flaunting something mundane, peacocking even though there's nothing to show, or being so narcissistic that they'd rather call you a name than smile and move on. Case in point, the tall guy with a scowl is not catching the obvious "go away" signals from the gorgeous brunette to his right.

He huffs and turns away. "You're not even that hot. Bitch."

"Ah, the sound of a toddler man not getting what he wants gives me such a lady boner. There's such satisfaction in popping an over-inflated ego."

"Thank you. I don't get why some men don't understand that ordering me a drink isn't a free pass to touch me or an instant phone number handout." She smiles and raises her hand to call the bartender back.

"That wasn't a man. That was someone dressed like one, but a man doesn't act like that, at least not the ones worthy of the title."

"I'm Everly. And I owe you a drink."

"Giselle. And I'll take a dirty martini. You know, I don't blame the guy for trying. Gorgeous dress. Designer or local?"

"Local. Very local. Mine, actually." I raise my eyebrows because I wasn't expecting her to say that. "It was my final project in school. I try to wear it when the occasion arises. I kind of love it, too."

The dress being praised is nothing too flashy, but it hits her curves just right. Thick black material with a deep V cut in the front, showing off just enough decolletage to be sexy, not stereotypically slutty, but still wholly fucker-iffic. It's just short enough to show her toned legs. Her long chestnut hair is pulled back, and her earrings are simple. *Stunner.*

"You made that?"

She nods.

"Wow. I'd absolutely buy it in a second."

She stares at me for a few seconds, gauging if I'm

being genuine or just being polite, making small talk. "Well, I have some pieces like it, that I don't know if I have a reason or the courage to wear if you ever wanted to see. It's a hobby more than anything." She shifts, and if I wasn't looking so intently, I'd have missed the slight undercurrent of her discomfort. "Are you here with someone or just out for the night?"

"You changed the subject, but I'd love to see your other pieces. I hate buying things that everyone else might have. And I never need a reason to dress in what I want, so I might just be your perfect customer." I wink, and that gets a megawatt smile.

"I can see that. I like your shoes, by the way. I haven't had a pair of converse in forever." She surveys what I'm wearing more closely. My style is a little eclectic. I like mixing things together that don't really classically jive— breaking the unspoken rules of proper attire or matching, for that matter. I've made some changes over the years to suit the personality I'm growing into, and I'll admit, I like it. "The leather with the lace has a whole vibe that you can definitely pull off."

Everly is easy to talk to. It also helps that she's overly sweet, and I love a good compliment. I smile at her, grab a napkin from the bar, and swipe a pen from behind the bartender's ear.

"Here's my number. I'd love to see those dresses sometime."

"Are you here for skiing, or–?"

Another guy in a pair of jeans and a sweater squeezes in between us, flashing a smile. Very attractive. Not really my type, but I'm not sure what that means these days. His blindingly white teeth shock me a little, and it makes me bark a laugh. I look over to Everly and raise an eyebrow.

Toothy looks between the two of us. "I'm sorry if I'm interrupting, but I had to come over here and talk to you."

I love a good line, but I like a guy to sweat a bit if I can. "Oh yeah, why?"

I smile at Everly. Toothy is taken off guard by my response. He must not have to do much work when it comes to getting any around here.

"Honestly? You're hot and you look like you'd be a good time."

Everly just laughs to herself as she obviously overhears what's going on just a foot or so away from her. The bartender comes around with two dirty martinis, extra olives, and places them in front of my new friend. She peeks around Toothy's shoulder, silently asking if I want an escape. What she doesn't know about me yet is that I rarely need rescuing, because I don't give a flying ass hair if I hurt some guy's feelings. Nobody bats an eyelash when a guy is an asshole, and I've lived plenty of versions of myself to realize I'm not an apologizer or a handle-with-care kind of person.

"Listen..." I pause, waiting for Toothy's name.

"Blane." *Of course, his name is Blane.*

"Listen, Blane. I appreciate that you had the confidence to come up here and interrupt my conversation with my girl and tell me that I look like a nice piece. Which, I am, but you'll have to do much better with your material to hold the attention of any woman who won't be satisfied with a lazy lay."

And with that, I move around Toothy Blane, grab Everly's arm, which is bent at the elbow for me to loop through, and we make our way to somewhere less congested with mediocrity.

We carry on our conversation for another hour and it's the first time I feel like I've met someone that any version of me would want to have in my life. Someone that could really be a friend, which is something I haven't allowed myself to have in years.

She tells me about her family and how they own and run one of Colorado's biggest outdoor sports companies. About her plans to grow the business with her father and older brother, but for now, she's working with the sales team to learn everything she can. Her two younger brothers are in college, one in Boston, and the other not far from here in Boulder, finishing his undergrad.

"What or who put its hooks in you to get you to Strutt's Peak?" she asks.

Truth first, lies later.

"Its name." She smiles, but waits for me to elaborate. "The place is named after an old English dude who discovered tons of important things, but the most beautiful of those things is the reason why we see blue skies."

"Rayleigh's Scattering," we say in unison, smiling at one another.

"Then, when you actually see how breathtaking it is... the blue-ness of the skies. The massiveness of this place. It feels, more than anything," I pause, a little lost on the tangent, "like a fresh start, a new adventure."

This was my third town in the witness protection program, or WITSEC, if you want to be official about it.

When my assigned U.S. Marshall finally realized it would be easier if I picked my next location instead of being plopped somewhere I didn't want to be, I looked around the Midwest, the section of the U.S. that I needed to be folded into, and zeroed in on Colorado. The funny thing about having a memory like mine is that sometimes those memories need to be jogged a bit. When I saw Strutt's Peak in the tiniest print, I remembered.

It was the one question I had gotten wrong in my geography class that sent my grade down a fraction, shoving me down as salutatorian instead of the valedictorian spot I deserved.

She tilts her head to take in what I'm saying. But before I can let her see the emotion behind the words, I say, "And I wanted to find a tourist location that wasn't too over-hyped with a need for a tattoo shop."

I tell her about Griff, the current owner of the only tattoo shop in town, who she knows, of course. Small town and all. The timing of him wanting to relocate and sell his business mixed with my arrival just seemed like a sign that I found where I was supposed to be.

The part I left out was that my only options were out west, far away from my old life, and this was my third stop. The other two were awful and I may have had enough verbal sparring with locals in those places that my intended low-profile wasn't very low after only a couple of weeks. This place, however, I've been here a month now, and I like it. Enough that I want to stay.

"I love the artwork on your arms. So pretty." She traces the vines and flower patterns up my forearm. Brushing right past the old design and only seeing what's new. The only one I left untouched, unchanged, is the small vine of white lemon blossoms that trail, from my hairline to behind my ear. I couldn't change those; it's the one thing that's the same on the outside, that reminds me of my pops.

He always called me "mio piccolo fiore di limone" (his little lemon blossom).

A loud group comes into the restaurant, and it pulls both of our attention. "So, can I assume you don't have any other plans tonight, or are you meeting someone?"

"My only plans were to grab a few drinks, a grilled cheese, and maybe some decent dick." She coughs after taking a sip of her drink and starts laughing.

"Oh my gosh, Giselle. I think I love you." She studies me for a minute. "You can still do all of those things, but come with me to my brother's dinner party first. I think he's going to tell us that he's proposed to his girlfriend." She rolls her eyes.

"Do we like her, or...?"

"I don't hate her or anything, but... I think I just always imagined when my brothers got married that I'd end up being super close to the women they chose. We're all really tight and I thought it just meant that I'd gain sisters. Denise is kind of cold and always has a way of turning conversations back into something she's done or seen or knows. I love my brother, and I see the way she talks to him too sometimes and it..." she cuts herself off, shaking her head.

"Got it."

Smiling at me again, she says, "Giselle, I feel like it's a little bit of fate that we met."

"Fate is apparently a fickle bitch, so let's just say it's a fabulous circumstance."

"You're going to love my family. My dad, especially. You were bound to meet him eventually. He's like the unofficial mayor of Strutt's Peak. I guarantee he already knows who you are and about your plans to take over Griff's shop on Main."

I follow Everly into the heart of the restaurant. Her effervescent personality is a relief, almost like a full breath after a dive into the deep end of a pool. I hadn't realized how much I crave being around people. Building relationships, even if it can't be completely truthful. It's not like it's going to harm anything. Having relationships isn't off-limits. Just the level of details I share need to be monitored. It doesn't make me a liar, just mindful. I need to take a deep breath, remind myself I can do this. It's not against the rules. I need to be smart.

Don't focus on the past, only on the present. And limit the lies.

CHAPTER 6

Henry

"Please do not tell me how I should be feeling, Henry. This isn't how I wanted to do things, and you know it. I want to have a party to announce the engagement, not a cheap dinner and drinks with just your family."

Count to three. Breathe in. Breathe Out. Tonight is supposed to be happy, and I'm barely out the door of our place and already pissed off. Denise can't seem to understand why it's important to me to make a big deal about asking her to marry me and that I want to tell my family before her friends and clients.

I take another deep breath through my nose and look at my fiancée. "Denise, we can still have a party and invite everyone you want, but first, I want to tell my family that we're going to be married and that you're going to be a Riggs. We called your parents. They already know, so I wanted to tell my family over a toast and some good food."

She rolls her eyes. "I'm not changing my name, Henry. It'll be hyphenated. Yes, I know this is important to you. I'll just power through it."

I don't want to dissect what that means.

"Your father is going to be happy you're finally settling down. Officially keeping roots in Strutt's. Maybe this will push him toward the idea of you as CEO. I know they encouraged you to start dating after the Air Force. That they want this for you."

"That's not—" I huff in frustration. "The family business has nothing to do with us being engaged. And I've told you that I have no interest in taking full ownership. I like what I'm doing right now." I push my hand into my pocket, pinching my thigh, so I don't fly off the handle with the direction this conversation is going. "Let's not talk about this. I don't want to be in a bad mood when I tell my family about a huge life decision like this."

She is right about them encouraging me to date. It took me a long time to look at women again. At least for anything more than just a quick, meaningless lay. Everly was the one who encouraged me to try. She knew how broken I had been after we moved her back from New York.

It took a year before I went on a date. And then a couple more months until I met Denise at the Summer Farmers' Market. By then, my family's business was starting to really take off, and I was finally on a high. At first, we were friends. I'd see her around town and then we ended up working out at the same gym. Then she asked me out.

She gives me the space that I need, and I do the same for her.

My father is waiting for us at the host station, and my two brothers are behind him, talking to a few professional snowboarders who are in town to kick off the winter season.

"There they are," my youngest brother, Law, yells out.

The three snowboarders, who I know well from when I took them out last season on a memorable end-of-snow adventure, start yelling at the same time, "Bro! Henry, my man!"

"If it isn't the biggest badass I know. Damn, Henry, it's been a minute. How you been, bro?" my buddy Sean calls out.

"I didn't realize you were back already. You're like two weeks too early. We haven't even had a good dump of fresh powder yet." I laugh.

Aside from being my friends, they're also high-profile clients, and each of them has their own set of fans on the other side of the world. I'm never too busy for hellos to the people who make an effort and have done right by me. I see out of the corner of my eye that my father is taking the reins on chatting with Denise, so she won't be huffing behind my back for ignoring her for a few minutes.

We say our goodbyes and promise a night out for drinks while they're in town. It's pretty clear that we've caused a loud enough commotion that the patrons of the restaurant keep trying to see the celebrities. That happens in this town; you have the same faces all year long, but in the peak season, there's a roster of celebrities and athletes that come in to enjoy the winter sports. It's the business my father built, and how I'm helping him cultivate it, that brings that level of money and attention to this place. I'm proud of it. The business, the vision for it, and the town's natural resources are what afford it all to happen.

"Asher, you have to try it. It's all about the turmeric right now. There are all of these healing properties..." Denise carries on her conversation with my father, and I can tell by the perma-smile on Dad's face that he's already stopped listening.

"Dad." Shaking hands, he grips my other shoulder and squeezes. Then plants a kiss on my cheek. It's his way of greeting and telling me he's proud of me without needing to say it out loud. I give him a nod in thanks for occupying my fiancée.

"Your sister is already here. Somewhere," he says, looking around. "She texted me about an hour ago saying she wanted to make sure David had set us up with a great table for the night. Ah! There he is now. David." My father nods at our long-time family friend and neighbor. Most of this town knows David as the top sommelier of this place, who can pair food with a wine like none other. And while all of that is true, there's more to him than that. He also owns the ranch next door to where we grew up. Many acres next door, but we are neighbors none-theless. That term goes a long way in Strutt's Peak. Stronger than family, in some cases.

What many don't know about David is that he and my father are business partners. They bought the restaurant we're in together, and a handful of others, just a few years ago. Both of them could retire if they wanted, but they each have grown kids and say all the time how they'd be bored golfing or playing around all day.

My mother isn't in the picture; she left us a long time ago. My father never said a bad thing about her, but I knew it killed a part of him that she wasn't here for us. Even with the lack of an example, I never had a skewed reality of wanting to find the right woman, get married, and start a family of my own. Hell, my brothers, sister, and my father are such a huge part of my life that starting and growing a family has always been something I've wanted. Just as much, if not more, than a successful career.

I didn't want to start again. Starting over was hard enough. I hated that Denise gave me an ultimatum, but I knew the idea of finding the kind of partner I fantasized about wasn't going to happen. I'd found *her* already. I knew I did. And *she* wasn't an option. She was gone. No matter how hard I had looked for her.

Which is why I also knew if I didn't try to move forward, then I'd end up alone. And I wanted to share my life. So with Denise, I kept saying yes. My sister, hell, even my brothers convinced me that it was time to live outside of work. So I did. She's smart, beautiful, and she goes after what she wants. We're similar in a lot of ways, which some would argue is a bad thing, but for me, it works.

So, when she jilted me by saying we needed to make a change, move on, or move forward, I said let's try forward.

That was two nights ago. Yesterday, we picked out a ring. Today, we tell the people that I love that we're going to get married.

CHAPTER 7

Giselle

I SPLASH WATER UP MY ARMS, FLICKING THE EXCESS ONTO my neck. Just enough to wake me up a bit, knock some reality back into my situation. I just need to get my bearings. I've just made a new friend. I haven't had one of these in a while. It's been a lonely three years trying to figure out how to be someone new, and now I'm ready to fold some new people into that. Hooking up with random men fills that void only for so long. I don't think I realized how much I just needed a friend. I can do this.

As I stare in the mirror, it's hard to recognize myself sometimes. I'm not who I once was. I'm new here. My name, my attitude, my accent, everything I once knew, has been forcefully forgotten. Evicted from my brain and filed away back east. I've come around finally to the idea that anything before is now dead, and everything after is the life I'm left with to create and not fuck up. At least I'm alive. That's the whole point, right? I'm alive. So let's start living.

I gather my wits, nod at myself in the mirror, and walk back into the dining room of the picturesque restaurant. Time to meet my new friend's family. I'm nervous and not much makes me feel this way. The idea of being the new person in a group setting means talking about myself. I need to remember the balance of how much of what I say can be truth versus the lie.

It took a gondola to get here. The downtown area of Strutt's Peak is at the base of the mountains, and that's where I've set up my new life. But the great spots in this town are woven throughout the slopes. The gondola is like a trolley system, but instead of a train car, it's a bunch of moving pods suspended hundreds of feet off the ground that taxi the townies and tourists up and down the mountains. It's as frightening as jaywalking in midtown Manhattan at rush hour. But holy spumoni is it beautiful.

I take in the large windows that frame the mountains I can barely see at this time of night, snapshotting the faces eating around the room. Redhead with the gold hoops moaning around a bite of risotto, mustache-guy sipping his water across the table from the receptionist who works at the town clerk's office. Her name is Marie. She's a cat person. She didn't tell me this directly, but her desk knick-knacks were very aggressive. I count thirteen people with chicken dishes, eighteen having pasta, three still reviewing their menus, and about twenty-two cutting, biting, or wiping their mouths from their juicy filets. There is nobody eating the grilled cheese, but then again, it's too late for kids to be out to dinner and most families likely don't come here with little monsters.

"Oh my goddess," I whisper to myself as I make my way back from the restroom. My steps falter slightly. And something in the air shifts. Something noticeable, like a window is open and a cool breeze just danced through. It's an awareness that I can't describe, just a sense of knowing, but not wanting to believe it.

The man who's back is to me sits tall and straight. He's big and bulky. Dark hair cut tight and faded into a thicker length on top. Nicely dressed. Something about how he's sipping his drink from a Cognac glass hollows out my stomach. As I curve around the table, his side profile with his sharp jawline and beautiful lips tells me that my instincts aren't wrong.

Fuck, this can't be right. It can't be, shouldn't be *him*.

I want to run right to him. Throw my arms around him and tell him that I looked for him. But as my feet take me closer and I register what I'm walking into, I realize I can't do that. I feel the itch to run away instead, and two seconds earlier, maybe I could have, but when I catch Everly's eye, I remember who I'm supposed to be.

I keep my eyes everywhere but where I want to look as I come into full view of the party. The face that I so desperately want to see and study, I can feel on me now. I want to look, but I can't just yet. I'm not ready for that. So, instead, I find my spot next to Everly. I pep talk myself internally all over again.

Take a breath, don't give anything away. Take a sip of that water. Look around the table.

I freeze. I'm able to swallow the sip of water, but the

glass never meets the table. It's suspended in the air like my brain has malfunctioned and it can't process what to do next.

Three years later, and even if I didn't have an incredible memory, I would have still remembered my flyboy down to a T, with his broad shoulders, those beautiful lips with its tiny white scar, and his handsome face. Those arms that look bigger than I remember. Like they're trying to escape the suit jacket they're being suffocated in, and I remember what it felt like to be engulfed in them. Grabbed with those hands. The way his fingers felt coasting up and down my legs as we talked. Flirted.

A chill runs through me. And I finally put the glass down. Meeting his stare.

His cleanly shaven face is still just as beautiful. He looked better with the tight beard. It was award-winning scruff. But this is okay too. That man's facial hair is what fantasies are built on. I still sometimes think about how great of a ride that scruff would have been. My thighs actually tingle just thinking about it.

Stop staring!

All eyes are on me, and the interruption I just made by coming to their table. His toast cut short. I can tell he's trying to place me, or perhaps he's just annoyed that I'm a stranger crashing his family dinner. I watch his Adam's apple bob down and back up again. His mouth pressed in a straight line, which is making his mood unreadable until he raises his eyebrows in a hopeful question. I sit there and say nothing. I school my reaction and just keep a friendly smile. As if I were someone new.

He shifts and looks around the table, maybe remembering what he's doing too. I watch as the woman to his right snakes her hand from beneath the table, draping over his fist. Laying claim. *Shit*. When I look back up, I'm met with a scowl. He looks angry. My hands start to sweat at the sight. The last time he saw me, I was an entirely different person. Not in a *I've made massive strides in being better* different person. Nope, I was someone else. I look different, sound different. Hopefully enough.

He doesn't recognize me.

He can't. He's just pissed I've crashed his party. That's all.

If he calls me out, then I have to move again.

Dammit! Just when I started thinking of this as my home. Just when I've made a friend whom I actually like. I don't want to leave.

Especially not now. Not when I've found him.

CHAPTER 8

Henry

IT'S HER. IT HAS TO BE. I CAN'T STOP STARING. MY instincts are going off like fireworks. I know it's her. My body knows it's her. Like some kind of brute force I've run into at full speed. I feel like I've been punched. Hit in the gut. Slapped. Stunned. Stung. As soon as I caught sight of her, I cut off what I had started saying. That was at least a minute ago now and the abrupt stop and now prolonged silence causes everyone to follow my line of sight. And it's directed right at her. She won't look at me.

My father clears his throat.

Everly pushes out her chair to stand. "Giselle! Everyone, I want you to meet my friend," my sister announces. "She's new in town, just about to take over the tattoo shop on Main."

"No kidding," our father says as he puts his drink down and angles his attention toward her, but not before shooting a quick look my way. He'll cover this awkwardness, but he's going to have questions. Believe me, Dad, I have plenty too.

"I didn't realize Griff found someone to take over. I thought he was ready to just sell the space and not the actual business."

She smiles. A big, full-faced smile that reaches her mocha-colored eyes. "Well, he hasn't said yes yet. He told me that I have to prove myself first before he's willing to hand it all over," she says, then leans over to whisper not so quietly, cupping her hand over her mouth, "but I think I've got him in the bag. A few more sessions with his regulars and he'll recognize I'm the right choice."

She looks around the table, stealing a peek my way, and then moves on. "Thank you for letting me crash your party. Everly and I were having too much fun warding off a bunch of eager douchebags and toasting their pitiful efforts. We didn't want the night to end."

Yeah, I remember that feeling.

"So, she invited me along to celebrate." She finally meets my eyes this time and gives me a small, closed-mouth smile. I'm not sure if she's saying thank you or hello. Either way, it's not enough.

My family laughs as Everly tells the rest of my family how her new "friend" saved her at the bar. It takes me a few minutes to register the pissed-off voice that is getting louder and more aggressive next to me. Denise. Denise! *Shit.*

"Henry. You're staring."

As I look at Denise, I'm not sure what to say. It's not even clear what I'm thinking other than I need to talk that woman. How is she here right now? And of all places and of all days? It has to be some kind of joke, or it better be, because laughing is far better than what I want to do right now.

"Are you going to move this along, or am I the one making this announcement, Henry?" I'm on the verge of grabbing Giselle, or whatever her name is, by the arm and out of this place. Demanding answers.

I ignore Denise. "What did you say your name was?" Her gaze meets mine again, her eyebrows raised, likely from the way I shouted across the table and interrupted the conversations taking place. I watch as she swallows her drink, carefully setting it down in front of her. I notice details; I may not see perfectly, but the little things are the ones I'm very good at remembering and recognizing. The slope of her nose. The way she sipped her drink. Pressing her lips to the glass before she tips it, her tongue peeking out to taste before the rest flowed into her waiting mouth. The way she won't look at me for more than a beat.

She pauses for just a moment, steadying her reserve, or readying her lie. Then, tilting her chin up, she meets my gaze.

"Giselle." *Liar.* "But my friends call me G."

Everly smiles at her new friend. Law takes a swig of his Scotch and soda, eye-fucking the party crasher. *I don't think so, baby brother.* Michael picks the label from his bottle of IPA, likely feeling the anxiety rolling off of me and into the room. My dad looks at me curiously, readying to clean up a situation that is starting to feel messy.

Bringing attention back to *her*, my dad says, "Well, G,

you are welcome to join us anytime. I'm interested in knowing how you even found Griff's shop. His place isn't really a tourist stop I imagine out of towners buzz about."

Law interrupts, "You ski or snowboard, Giselle?"

She glances around, as if someone is going to give her the answer, smiling as she replies. "Nope."

The table basically drops their utensils at that, because rarely will someone relocate to Strutt's and not have a need to be on the snow.

She takes a sip of her drink, then adds, "I slay."

Everly giggles and lifts her glass to cheers with G. "Where have you been all my life?"

"Like, you sled? I don't get it. Like a sleigh ride?" Law looks at her, dumbfounded.

"Sure. That sounds fun. If there's some boozy hot drinks in there too, then I could really get on board with that."

Law looks around the table, trying to decipher if she's kidding, but I have a feeling that she's serious. She's not a skier or a snowboarder. She's a bartender. And a liar.

"Wait, what about snowshoeing or cross-country?" Law asks.

"Not for me. Not unless you're pulling me while I sip on something hot and spiked. Or if there's something hot and spiked I could sit on." She winks.

I can blink back. It takes every muscle in my body not to fall over in a fit of laughter the same way the rest of my family is doing right now.

My dad shakes his head, laughing to himself. "You come to my house for dinner next Sunday. I've got some great hot toddy recipes you and Everly can try, and I want to hear all about your new shop. But..." Turning toward my end of the table, he says, "Right now, though, I think we need to bring our attention to the purpose of this special dinner tonight." He tips his head to me as my cue. "Son?"

I clear my throat and stand. "I know you've all guessed why we've invited you to dinner here, and not just grilling at Dad's, like usual." I swallow around the lump in my throat, but nothing but dry air makes its way down. As I take a breath, I hope this struggle isn't as visible as it feels. When I let it out, I see her watching me intently. Her eyes sparkling, not only because they're beautiful, which they are. Some of the most beautiful I've ever seen on a woman, but they're shining, holding back tears. And she's working hard at it. Schooling any type of emotion from registering across her face, but tears are funny like that; they don't just go away. They have to fall eventually.

I didn't imagine this moment feeling this way. Like air was being rationed. Like I was about to make some kind of colossal mistake. Like I've just messed up. How could I have known? I looked. *Fuck!* I searched for her. I can feel my pulse kicking against my skin. My heart beating so fast that I can actually hear it.

I've always looked forward to being able to tell my family I was engaged to be married. The idea of living life with someone that you enjoy, maybe even feel like you can't live without. I always wanted it. The romanticized idea of it keeps people single, though. So I put away that vision of love and partnership and instead focused on what was in front of me. That was Denise. But now, she's not the only person here anymore.

I feel off. I feel like I'm moving backward. Away, and right out of this moment. Instead, in this moment that is supposed to be happy and thrilling, I'm dreading saying the words out loud.

"Henry and I are getting married!" Denise announces, holding up her left hand and showing off the ring she picked out.

I watch as G leans over toward Everly and then gets up to leave. The pixie grabs her clutch from the floor and smiles at my dad as she tries to excuse herself.

"Henry?" Denise says while squeezing my arm, drawing my attention back. The questioning look on her face guts me. She has no idea what's just happened. Denise doesn't deserve this. A partner that wants to leave and take it all back. The ring, the last two years, all of it. It's not the kind of treatment anyone deserves. I know that. But I need to talk to someone else right now.

I bring Denise's hand to my mouth and kiss it. Remembering we have two years together and that it should outweigh just one night, years ago. It should, but it doesn't. Everyone stands up and moves toward us, hollering congratulations, throwing around hugs, and clapping handshakes. My eyes shift to see if the party crasher returned. But she hasn't. It's been longer than a quick bathroom break, and I can't let her leave.

Everly pulls me into a hug. "Congratulations, Hen," she whispers, "I know I shouldn't say this, but you're not looking as happy as you should be right now. You okay?"

I answer her question with another. "Where'd your friend go?"

She rears back to look at me. "What? Oh! I'm sorry. I didn't think it'd be a big deal for her to join us. I just fell in love with her, ya know." *Yeah, I know.* "She was so much fun." Everly glances over my shoulder, then looks at me with a slight frown. "She just needed to use the bathroom. You mad?"

"Not mad," I tell her. And it's the truth. Honestly, I don't know what I am right now. But it's not mad. I need a minute. "I'll be right back," I say over my shoulder as I start moving toward the restrooms. But before I turn down the hall, wildly long blonde hair catches my eye. Shifting her weight back and forth in front of the coat check.

Away from the crowd, where I can take my time looking, and out from the shock of seeing who should be a ghost, I know it's her. She's the woman who stole a part of me one night, for only a few hours, in a bar three years ago. The woman who stood me up. A woman who is supposed to be dead.

I move quickly as soon as she pulls her coat from the attendant, plucking the black leather out of her hands. She startles. She didn't expect me to follow her. Without saying a word, I hold up her coat. She turns around, slipping one arm into each sleeve.

"Mr. Riggs, do you need your coat, sir?"

"No, he's staying," G answers for me. In a rushed breath, she says, "I apologize for crashing your party." But before I can say anything to her, she moves from where I'm still gripping onto her coat. Without turning around to face me, she adds, "Have a beautiful life, Henry." And then she's rushing out of the restaurant.

I rub my chest. Like I've been shoved after hearing her say my name. She's real. She's alive. And as much as I feel drawn to her, she doesn't know me. Because if she did, then she'd know there's no way I'm just going to let her leave.

Especially now that I've found her.

CHAPTER 9

Giselle

IT SMELLS LIKE SNOW WHEN I STEP OUTSIDE. I TAKE A DEEP breath and try to calm my erratic heartbeat. I'm about to have a panic attack. I didn't expect to see him. How could I have known? I didn't prepare for the idea that if I ever did see him again, that he'd have an entire life happening. *So stupid!* For someone who can memorize faces and moments with almost uncomfortable clarity, to never think a man I met one night, an entire lifetime ago now, would have built a life of his own. A life he's about to start sharing with someone else. I feel sick.

"You can't be here," a deep voice says from behind me.

"No shit, Sherlock. That's why I'm leaving," I bite back. I'm so much better when I'm short and bitchy with people. Less emotion. Especially right now. It'll keep me from drowning. The softer side of me wants to run right into his arms. Someone familiar, someone from before. Or maybe it's just him. "You don't need to follow me."

He jogs up next to me. Loud, hurried steps. I've only made it about twenty feet from the restaurant. I'm still at least a city block away from the gondola station. I need to get there. Get away. Get home and then figure out what the hell I do next.

"I didn't—" he cuts off and then steps in front of me, blocking my way. "That's not what I meant." He runs his hand through his hair, clearly exasperated. "How are you here?"

I push my hands farther into my leather jacket pockets. His hair is a bit longer now. A little wave to the strands on top. I can't see the blues and greens of his eyes in this light, but I remember how beautifully they swirled. How much I liked them focused on me for those few hours. Being this close to him makes a chill run through my body.

"I don't know what you're talking about," I say and move around him. *Just get to the gondola station.*

"Don't give me that bullshit. It's too late to play the *I don't remember you* game."

Breathe in and out. Twenty more feet, and I'll be able to get onto the gondola, ride down the mountain, and talk to my handler. I can't think when he's near me. I haven't even sent a text out yet. And I should. I'm supposed to text if I'm in any kind of danger. The only problem is, I don't think I'm in danger. Not with him.

"Fuck, Gia. Stop!"

And that does stop me. He moves right behind me, close enough so that I feel the warmth of his body, but he isn't touching me. *God, why do I want him to touch me?* My chest feels heavy and I'm breathing harder. I know it's not the elevation; I've already gotten used to the thinner air up here. No, my breath is labored because of him.

"I know it's you. I'd have to be blind not to recognize you. And even then, I probably still would have. Now I just need to know how. How are you here?"

I steady myself and then turn around to face him. Nothing would have prepared me for the way this man is looking back at me. His eyes wide, and pleading, hoping for some kind of explanation for why I'm here.

"No."

His brow furrows. "What do you mean, no?" A piece of hair moves out of place and falls just to the right of his widow's peak as he shakes his head.

I don't realize what I'm doing until I brush the hair away with the tips of my fingers. He doesn't flinch. I push the pieces back into place, and because I'm a masochist of sorts, I drag my fingers lightly down his temple, tracing along his hairline. He leans into my touch and his eyes shut for just a moment. An exaggerated blink that gives me just enough time to look around his beautiful face. I linger on the scar above his lip. I remember those lips. The way they felt kissing mine that night. I can almost still feel them, even after years, and through the chaos. How easy it was to be near him.

"No, I never expected to see you. No, I can't tell you more. No, I never stopped—" I cut myself off from saying any more. There's nothing good that will come from telling him that I've never stopped thinking about him. That it's almost unhealthy how much I do. How thinking of him is my safe space. When I have days that I want to only think about the bad, the darkness, that I use memories to pull myself out of it. He's my only memory not connected to my pops, my neighborhood, the people who knew me as the loud smartass.

"You need to tell me what's going on."

I think about doing exactly that, telling him what happened. Telling him how I ended up here. But then something tells me to hold back. *Keep quiet. It's not just yourself that you need to keep safe. It's everyone who is tied to you as well.*

"There're a few ways we can play this right now, Pixie. And none of them includes you leaving town. So don't even think about trying."

That tone would normally make me flinch, but with him, I want to lean in. Maybe even poke a bit. "You're not trying to boss me around now, are you, flyboy?"

I must catch him off guard with that, because he sniffs out a small laugh.

His already deep voice drops an octave lower when he responds. "If I was giving you direction and telling you what to do, believe me, you'd know."

I swallow the threat, and warmth rolls through me. I don't want to admit it, but damn, I kind of liked that.

"I'm just trying to figure out how a dead woman just showed up and crashed into my life? A woman that I looked for even after I went to her wake and funeral, because for some reason I didn't want to believe that the universe could be so cruel. Giving me only one night with her when I knew, *I knew*, I was supposed to have more," he says so easily. I swallow the emotion that's trying so hard to creep forward. He can't be serious. I mean, who says this?! By all accounts, I'm just a stranger. We're strangers to each other. *Aren't we?*

He crowds into my personal space, putting us toe to toe, leaving only inches between our bodies. I've never stood so close to a person, and not been touching. Yet, I feel like I'm being held. Suffocated by his proximity and not at all interested in breathing if it means moving away. I want to be smothered, but then again, the man doing this to me just announced that he's going to marry someone. And that someone isn't me. And *that* dose of reality is what snaps me out of this. Whatever *this* is.

He looks up at the sky, a white puff of air leaving his mouth in a frustrated-sounding huff. He rubs the back of his neck, letting the silence thicken. "Why do I want to just forget about everyone back there and go wherever you're going?"

I take a small step back. And then another. He looks down at my feet moving away. Two more steps back and I hear the ding of the gondola approaching the station. My ride is here, and I need to get the hell away from him. For a roster of reasons now. One very glaring one in particular that has nothing to do with my situation and everything to do with his.

"Get back to your fiancée, Henry."

I don't hear him say anything else. I don't want to either. I've already made up my mind. I need to put space between us. Immediately. I turn on my heel and I don't dare look back, keeping my pace steady.

It's not until nearly thirty minutes later, after the gondola ride down the mountain and the brisk walk to my loft, that I let out a long breath, followed by a "FUCK! Fuckity, fuck fuck fuck," hopefully loud enough for the universe to hear. She really slapped a bitch tonight.

I pull out my phone and send out a text. One that I've dreaded ever having to send.

CHAPTER 10

Henry

"WHERE DID YOU GO?" HER EYES ARE SEARCHING MINE FOR an explanation. The problem is, I don't have one that's going to make her feel better. In fact, if I tell her where I went or who I followed, it's going to make all of what I'm about to do much worse. "After we made the announcement, I turned around, and you were gone. Then, you were quiet for the rest of dinner when you came back. And now you've been sitting at the kitchen counter without saying a word."

It takes me a minute to say this. I hate that I'm going to hurt her. But staying is no longer an option. Denise searches my eyes, and she has every right to feel anxious. This is going to sting.

"I don't want to get married."

She doesn't move, just stares at me for what feels like a full minute.

"Elaborate. Right now, Henry." She shifts her weight,

readying herself for this conversation. Denise is a fighter. We're alike in that way, so I know for a fact this isn't going to be a calm discussion. "You don't want to get married? After we just announced to your family that we're getting married!?" She throws her arms out, slapping her sides on the way down.

"There isn't anything I'm going to say that's going to make you feel better right now. And I feel like shit doing this. But I know I can't marry you, Denise."

"So it's not that you don't want to get married. You don't want to get married to *me*. At least be specific when you're about to destroy someone."

I take a deep breath and stand up, so I can move closer to her. I care about her; we have history together. We share a dog, a home, a life. I feel like a piece of shit. I know if that pixie hadn't walked back into my life tonight, this conversation wouldn't be happening right now. But I respect Denise, and I don't want to hurt her by staying and thinking that would be the right thing to do. It wouldn't, for either of us. So that means I need to get out now, before it can get messy. And it will. I know it will.

"What's changed? Between now and earlier this evening, what could have possibly changed, Henry?" she asks with anger laced throughout the words.

Everything.

I lean back on the counter behind me, taking in my partner. My friend. She's been the person to get me back to a normal that didn't feel chaotic, but regimented. "We make sense, Denise. If you ask anybody, you and I are a power couple, but I don't think I realized until tonight that it's not enough for me. I thought it was, but..." I don't finish the thought because I also don't want to hurt her by telling her the whirlwind who just barreled into my universe, the one who makes no sense at all, is the catalyst to the immediacy of this decision. I think, no matter what, I would have come to this conclusion about Denise and me eventually, whether it would be in a month from now or five years after we tied the knot. But it doesn't change the fact that at this moment, I'm leaving because what I want is not only alive but living in my town.

"Denise, you had to give me an ultimatum. That, in and of itself, should have tipped me off that I'm not the right person for you. And vice versa."

There's even more beyond that, because I understand ultimatums. Sometimes people can't get out of their own way, but that's not me. I'm not a lazy partner. I'm happy in my career. The role that I've cultivated inside of my family's business is exactly what I want right now, but Denise can't seem to let go of the fact I don't want more. She's always been a bit of a debutant, a rich upbringing coupled with her socialite-level status has awarded her to come across as a bit intimidating. I always liked that about her, but over the past few months, her need to fuel negative gossip in town has become more noticeable. It makes me wonder if she's unhappy underneath it all, or if this is just a side I never allowed myself to see.

Either way, I don't like it. And as much as she loves being associated with my family and people, knowing that she's a part of the "inner circle" of the Riggs family, she really doesn't enjoy or want to spend much time with them. They're always going to be important to me, so that means spending time with my brothers, having dinners with my dad, and working late with my sister. None of that interests her.

She takes a sip of her drink as her eyes well up with tears. Her voice lowers as she speaks again, sounding shaky. "Why? I mean, what's changed?"

"We have," I tell her honestly. I lean against the counter, mimicking her stance. "We're not the same people, and I don't think we want the same things."

"That's what's supposed to happen. You grow with people, Henry. Is there someone else? Oh my gosh, are you cheating on me?"

I wince. The urgency to end this is because I will never be in a position that would label me as a cheater. "No. I'm not cheating on you." I level with her, look around her face and try to soften my reaction to her question. It's a fair one. "I think we fight more than we get along. We're not married, and we fight like we're already sick and tired of each other. I don't want that kind of relationship."

She cuts me off, "Henry, that's what couples do. They fight." The problem is, maybe I just don't want to fight with *her*.

She stalks away from me and into the living room.

"Denise, don't walk away."

She keeps moving toward the stairs to our bedroom. But before she gets to the first step, I yell, "I'm going to move my stuff out. Milo and I will stay at my sister's place while we figure out what we want to do with the townhouse."

She turns slowly to face me.

"Milo stays with me. I'm keeping the condo too."

I tilt my head back, giving myself a minute to breathe and not just react. Maybe also to ask the universe for some strength right now, and remember I'm the one with the shitty timing. I'm breaking it off.

"That's not how this works, Denise. We're not married. I had this place before we were ever together. And Milo is my dog."

She raises her eyebrows, and I know precisely the wrath that's about to follow. "You're going to give me this place, Henry, in exchange for dealing with canceling all our wedding plans that have been set into motion because, let's be honest, it's going to fall to me to do anyway. I have to tell people I know that this diamond ring that appeared on my left finger for only a few short days is no longer there because you wanted take-backs. And Milo is just as much my fur-baby as he is yours. But since you technically had him before we started dating, then we can figure out visitation."

"Again, Denise. This isn't how this works. I'm not visiting him. I want him with me."

"Then we figure out a shared schedule," she says. And though it's not ideal, she's right; he's been ours.

The clinking of metal tags pulls our attention to Milo, who's just coming down from our bedroom. He knew we were talking about him. Smart pup.

"Hey, buddy boy, c'mere." His long floppy ears slap as he shakes his body again before moving closer. His red-brown hair makes him look like a cross between a fox and a bear. Still, a puppy at only two years old. I brought Milo home a week before I had my first date with Denise, so he's known her just as long, but he's mine. I wouldn't just let him go with her.

"We'll share. Take him every other week. If one of us needs to travel, we'll just figure it out along the way. It's not a clean break, Denise. Are you going to be okay with that?"

She wipes underneath her eyes and presses the palms of her hands on her cheeks. Nodding, she says, "This is how it's going to work, Henry." She puts her hands on her hips, and immediately, I realize she needs to be in control of the rest of this discussion or she's going to fall apart. And if it's one thing I know about her, she won't let me see her get emotional, not anymore. "I'm taking the townhouse. We will share Milo's time, but I want him during holidays like Christmas and Thanksgiving."

"I never had any intention of hurting you, but I know I still have." I take a deep breath and hate what I'm about to do. "You can have the townhouse. I'll take Milo with me after I pack my things, and then we can work out a schedule." I lean down and scratch behind his ears. "I'd like for us to agree that the minute we think about getting a pet sitter or if he is being neglected in any way that we give him to the other." The truth is, she treats the dog better than most people, so I know he'll be cared for when he's with her. But at some point, she won't want to be tied to me any longer, and when that happens, I want my dog.

"Fine." She crosses her arms. "And I'm keeping the ring."

I just shake my head at her and fight back a smile, because if I wanted to show off my genuine emotions right now, it would be a version of myself I've locked away. The part of me that only comes out when it's warranted. This woman is raking me over the coals. It's almost impressive if I wasn't the one on the receiving end.

She's hurt. I did that, and I'll own it.

Three hours later, and I've packed up most of the belongings that I consider genuinely mine. The actual townhouse not included. It's late, but Denise went to a friend's house for the night, and I decided that I didn't want to be here when she came home in the morning.

Most of my clothes fit into duffle bags, and all my suits I've draped in the cab of my truck. I put on Milo's harness and secure him in the passenger seat. I've left most of the things we've bought together, like electronics and furniture. None of it important. Just things. And the only feeling I have in leaving all of it is relief. But when it came to the kitchen, I packed every pot and pan. Every knife and utensil. Everything I cook with, from the rice cooker to the meat thermometer, the cast-iron skillet to the pasta roller, and the set of cutting boards to the different-sized spatulas. It all comes with me.

This is the second time in my adult life I thought would end up one way, but took a drastic turn in another direction. Only this time, it's on my terms, and while I feel sad and guilty to be ending a relationship, there's a part of me that feels like this is exactly the right call. I have no plan, other than to listen to my gut and figure it out as it goes.

CHAPTER 11

Giselle

"Kid, I need you to tell me if it's a problem."

"I'm telling you that, right *now*, I don't know. My gut is telling me that it's not..." I hesitate to say more because I know it's going to be a problem. Just not the way Bea is thinking. "I like it here. It's the first place that feels like a home. I don't want to give this up. Plus, my shop is primed. I can probably open it next month. Griff is ready to sign the papers."

"But?" Bea leads the conversation to where I don't want it to go. But for her, I owe her truth. Always the truth with Bea.

"But I met him. I met him *that* night. At the bar. Before."

"And? I know how that night panned out for you, so I'm going to assume you didn't sleep with him." She looks at me like I'm bullshitting her when I shake my head.

"I didn't sleep with him, but we talked. Most of the

night, we talked, and we had this attraction that was so..." I look up at the ceiling and groan. "Ugh, it was so swoony, and I kissed him. Or he kissed me, I can't remember." *Yes, I can. He kissed me, and it was everything, but that's more detail than Bea needs right now.*

"Okay. So, when he approached you, what did you tell him?"

"Not much. I couldn't deny that I was, well, me. Unknowingly, I crashed his engagement party. So really, he shouldn't think about me again. He confronted me and I didn't really confirm or deny anything. Maybe there's a level of curiosity, because I'm clearly lying about my name, I sound different, and I've obviously changed my appearance. Maybe he doesn't *want* to know anything and forget about me, especially if he's blissfully happy with his fiancée."

"Is he?"

"Is he, what?" I ask.

"Blissfully happy."

"I don't know. I don't see why he wouldn't be"

I continue blending my charcoal gray eyeshadow and add a bit more to the edges to darken it up. Bea sits on the end of my bed, eating her pistachios and fingering through files.

Blissfully happy. Who the fuck is blissfully happy, anyway? The words themselves are the most significant example of over-promising and under-delivering. With that thought, the wind picks up, and the long linen curtains hanging from the windows overlooking the main drag of downtown Strutt's Peak fan out and into the room. It cools my skin, which has gotten a bit overheated.

Talking about this has me nervous, the possibility of what it could mean. I know that I want to stay here; it feels like it's where I'm supposed to be.

This town is its own version of perfection. The views from just about every spot I've been are incredible. I can only imagine how stunning it all looks once it snows. Right now, we're living the best late summer life where not a single day is humid. And hot for this town is when the temp spikes to the high seventies. As soon as the evening hits, though, it gets chilly.

It's such a welcome change compared to sweaty, humid summers on the East Coast, where late August means we dip into the nineties and stay there well into September. Subway grates and congested sidewalks would help it swell into the hundreds. I don't miss the heat, but I do miss the small details of New York, the easiness of getting around the city, and the way the seasons changing meant something new and exciting was coming. Fall brought the promise of cozy food festivals. Winter brought Christmas at its absolute finest, from decorations to celebrations that lined every neighborhood. Spring brought the promise of warmth and summer, while summer in the city meant parks and outdoor movies. I never got to enjoy the last summer I was there. Never made it to the outdoor movie.

"Well, kiddo," Bea says, snapping my attention back to what she was asking. "I can tell you right now that if it becomes an issue, then I'll need to know about it. If he makes it a problem, you text the burner. I'll come any time you need. It may seem insignificant, but all it takes is one person to know more than they need to know, and this starts to unravel. I've seen it. Lived it." She finishes chewing her nuts and stands up. "I'll do some more background work." She fingers through her file. "He was Air Force. Top guy, too. Fairly decorated. Boys like that tend to follow rules."

I outline my eyes with a black gel liner for the perfect wingtip. The secret is always in the tiny brush and the confidence of the movement. If you second guess it, it'll look less pointed. It's the same with thin lines for tattoos. Confidence in the movements mixed with the right level of pressure.

"What else does it say about him?" I nod toward her stack of files.

She flicks her eyes up to me. We look at each other in the reflection of the mirror. "No."

I just laugh at her and try to brush off the fact that I'm as curious about Henry Riggs as he is about me.

"No. Don't get involved with someone like that. He knew you. And while I'll bet he won't make problems for you right now, I can't guarantee he won't ever, if you decide to mess around. People are unpredictable after sex is involved. Not to mention, he's in the news a bit. Granted, it's minimal gossip sites and local, but you don't need to be caught up in any of that."

She stops talking, and that has me looking back at her. I know she wants to keep me safe, and I want that too, more than anyone.

"You need to hear me on this, G. Be careful with that family. They're well-known, connected, so be smart. Keep your stories about your past as close to the truth as you can. And for the love of all things sane, do not fall into bed with any of them. Literally or financially. You need to keep them at an arm's length."

I nod. I can do that. And I can be smart about being friends with Everly. She's the least gossiped about out of all the Riggs family.

"Now, I have some transcripts and photos that you need to look at for me pertaining to your case. If anything jogs a thought or memory, write it in the margins and we can talk about it."

"Yeah, yeah. I know the drill," I say as I line my lips with a nude-colored liner.

As part of an ongoing case and the kind of memory I've been cursed with, I'm their best option for finding who is responsible for the night that my life changed.

"My hunch is still telling me that it's the Russian crew your dad had done some off-track betting with, but a hunch is nothing more than a feeling. And I can't lock any bad guys up with either of those." She moves toward my living room, and I follow her to the front door. "I'll be back in a month. I mean it, kid, if anything feels off, you text or call. You've only been here for a bit. Don't get too attached yet. We don't know what the tourist situation will bring come the winter months."

Knock. Knock.

Bea looks at me and raises an eyebrow. "I thought you were meeting your date at the bar?" She tsks. "You know better."

The light double tap knock happens again, and I realize I'm going to have to lie to whomever is on the other side about who Bea is to me.

"Go ahead. It's a bit surprising we haven't had to do this yet."

I open the door, and I'm immediately anxious when I see Everly standing in front of me with a bottle of tequila in one hand and a bag of limes in another. *Shit*. She smiles her big bright smile, completely unknowing of the nerves rushing through me.

"G, I know we were just going to meet at the bar, but I feel like it's our first double date. Well, my first blind date, to be honest, and I need some liquid courage." She looks behind me, spotting Bea. "Oh! Hi. I'm sorry, I should have texted you first."

"No big deal. You can surprise me with tequila any time you want." I signal for her to follow me inside. "I was just finishing up getting ready."

My apartment is still in disarray between the boxes that I haven't unpacked and all the clothes I've been trying on for tonight. It's not very big, but it's renovated, and everything is new and freshly painted. The one-bedroom loft is two levels, has an open floor plan, and overlooks Main Street. In this town, that means it's in the heart of the hustle and bustle. My tattoo shop is just a block down to the right, so it's convenient and just steps away from the firehouse and police station. All of which are good to have nearby, if I ever need them.

"I'm so sorry if I'm interrupting." She walks over to Bea and extends her hand. "I'm Everly."

"You're stunning! My gosh, Giselle. Your taste has upgraded." Everly starts laughing and looks over at me as I try to work through the complicated nature of this entire situation. I haven't really discussed my sexual preferences with Everly, so this may be even more awkward.

"Oh no, I'm not her girl tonight. She and I are doubling. With who? Were they construction guys from your shop?"

I nod. "Contractors. Brothers, I think."

"Lucky guys, you girls are gorgeous. I'm Giselle's Aunt Bea." My eyes widen at her. *Aunt?* I'll go with it, but a heads-up would have been helpful. I also cringe that I'm spouting another lie to Everly. I like the idea of having a real friend. Someone who I can connect with, where my lies are limited.

"Oh my gosh! G, you didn't tell me you had family visiting. It's so nice to meet you." Everly leans in and hugs her. Bea isn't sure what to do with that at first. Bea tends to be a little rough around the edges. Minimal touching.

"Yeah, well, I'm on my way out anyway. I was just passing through. I wanted to see that Giselle was settled in her new apartment. I have to get back. Work is always calling." Bea pulls out her cigarette case and taps one as she walks to my door. She leans in for a hug, which I'm not expecting, but I welcome it nonetheless. "Be good, kid."

"See you soon, Bea." I smile at my handler. And though she's not really my aunt, she's the closest thing I have to family these days.

As soon as Bea shuts the door, I grab the tequila and bag of limes from Everly's hands and plop them on the counter. I start looking through a box in the corner for some shot glasses. I have a few somewhere.

I smile as I remove the clear plastic from the rounded top. "You brought the good tequila. Thank goodness."

She stares at me, a little worry painted between her perfectly curated eyebrows. "I'm sorry. I really should have called first."

I shrug my shoulders at her, passing it off as no big deal. I'm not used to having anyone interrupt my meetings with Bea, so it's a first for me. But I love that I have someone to worry about interrupting now.

After cutting a lime, I pour two shot glasses of tequila, and pass one along to my friend.

"Cheers. Here's hoping the big dick energy I'm getting from these guys isn't just a bluff." I raise the glass higher. "May their swagger support a gagger." We toss them back, Everly coughing and then laughing.

"You're going to get me in trouble. I just know it."

"My darling Ev, a little bit of trouble is exactly what we need."

CHAPTER 12

Henry

TROUBLE JUST WALKED INTO THE BAR WITH MY SISTER ON one arm and a pink sparkling wand in the other.

Law lets out a barking laugh at the spectacle. "Why is our sister wearing a feather boa, and her sexy-ass friend throwing glitter on people?"

I open my mouth to respond, but then take in the sight, and all words escape me. This is the kind of bar that tends to be more of a dive than a tourist trap. Glitter and feathers aren't the usual vibe, but I watch the men lean away from the bar to look at the two women who are about to break all of those unwritten rules. It's clear that if G glitter bombs any of these guys, they'll revel in it. I know I would.

Summer nights in Strutt's Peak are limited and coveted, so when it finally comes around, you can take roll call at just about any restaurant or bar in town.

Tonight is no different. Every place we went was packed, and this is our last stop.

Any time I came back from college, and then from training, the summertime was what got me out of my funk. The easiness of the days that led into late nights with women, betting on yard games with friends, and outdoor sports—anything that meant competing with my brothers. Everly was always not far behind in the competition too. Summer has always been my favorite time. Even now, while winter is my peak season at work, summers are for planning, even relaxing. Like tonight was meant to be. So when Law demanded that I go out with him and Michael, it was easy to say yes. I didn't need to check in with a partner, work wasn't demanding too much attention, and I'd be lying if I said I wasn't hoping I'd see *her* out.

Now as I watch the blonde who has been on my mind parade around the bar, gaining the attention of every man and woman, I almost regret coming. I know I'm not going to be able to stay away. Quietly observing is going to be a bigger challenge than I had thought. But, I do love a good challenge.

Michael clears his throat. "So I think I want to build out the climbing program. There's a ton of high schoolers that are always asking for more hiking time when I'm home, and I'm realizing we're missing out."

I knew Michael wanted to talk business tonight. He would never so easily agree to going out unless it was to warm me up and talk shop. I'm surprised it took three bar stops to finally bring it up. He's usually a straight shooter, which makes me think he really wants this.

"Are you sure you want to dive in like this? It's going to be more than just summer and seasonal work," I warn him.

"I'm coming back home to be a part of this. Build out more of what you and Everly have already started. I want the summer sports." He leans back and holds up his hand, stopping me from saying what he knows is coming. "I know. I know. I earn this, but I'm telling you. Help me talk Dad into building out climbing with an indoor wall space and it'll be a year-round money maker. Plus, it'll allow anyone who's local to really work out and hone in on strength and technique in the off season."

While Riggs Outdoor is an all-season sports business, the winter sports are what I've been growing. From expanding into new equipment options, to types of guided adventures like heli-skiing and fat biking. It's my role to stay in front of trends to pull in tourists, sell the experience, and ensure they have everything they need to have a good time and be safe while doing it. Michael's interests lie in spring and summer sports; they always have. Hiking is a form of therapy beyond just a sport he loves. He also is naturally great at fishing and guided tours. You name a summer mountain sport, and Michael does it and does it well. It makes sense that he wants to take that aspect of our family business and move it forward.

"You know I'll support anything you want. I trust you," I tell him.

"Why isn't it that easy with me?" Law asks, and I ignore.

"It's not about you, man," Michael says to him.

I'm not in the mood to unpack our drama tonight. I came out to enjoy some time with my brothers and not hash out heavy shit with them. Law and I can do surface level these days, but anything more than that, I avoid.

"I figured you'd talk about it if you wanted or needed to, but I need to make sure you're okay," Michael says. And I've been waiting for someone to. I'm surprised it hasn't happened sooner. "So are you?"

I nod yes. "I'm okay, but I feel shitty for hurting her. Letting us get to this place where we were talking about marriage, announcing it to people, when I think I knew deep down it wasn't right." I look over at the bar again. At the person who keeps managing to turn my world on its axis. "The moment I thought about what I really wanted" —I take a deep breath, because this is as much of the truth I can share right now—"I knew it wasn't a life with Denise. It's not a clean break. I mean, I'm going to see her, because of Milo. She wants shared custody."

Law barks a laugh. "That's fucking stupid."

I send him a glare. "It's what has to happen. At least for right now."

Michael claps my shoulder, gives it a squeeze, and says, "As long as you're happy, that's what matters to me."

I polish off my beer. "I need another drink. You guys want another?"

"Let's snag a nightcap at Dad's," Law shouts. "He just got that smoker. I want to try an Old Fashioned smoked."

I nod, looking back. "I'll close the tab."

My father started the family business shortly before I was born. He met my mother, fell in love with her, and Strutt's Peak, though I'm not sure which order is the most accurate, and then all of a sudden, I was on the way. He came here to try something on his own, to not be forced into being a bonafide cowboy with his family's business, so failure here wasn't an option. When he found a storefront, he just said, "I'm going to do this." He was a kid, barely eighteen. The craziest part was that it was a brilliant move. At the time, there were no big chain stores, and ordering equipment online meant making a phone call, not pulling up a website on your phone, and having something delivered within the next two business days.

Tourists flock to Strutt's for the mountains, snow, and every kind of adventure you can think of when those things combine. Everly and I have plans to make it an empire, and I'm fairly certain when Michael is folded into the mix, we may just be able to accomplish it.

I make my way to the front and a woman's scream knocks me out of focus. I dart my attention over to the bar and, it is, of course, who I thought it was, but she's not in distress. She's flirting. That's what she does. She's either shit-talking or flirting. Those are her personalities: an epic bitch-slap or a charming smile. I've seen her a handful of times since I've known she was alive and well, and those are her two modes, both of which push my buttons.

"That's absolutely the right type of lubricant," she yells and laughs at the two men leaning against the bar top. Everyone around her laughing in chorus.

She flirts with everyone and, whether or not it means she takes them home, it doesn't matter. She has that ability to attract people. It's magnetic. She's new by Strutt's Peak's standards, and the rumor mill loves a precocious bad girl. Small towns are filled with big mouths and even bigger imaginations. So you add the beautiful tattooed transplant into the mix and it's the gossip train's aphrodisiac. And yet, people are drawn to her. When she's not at her shop, she's inadvertently helping someone.

"We're heading out, Lou," I say as I saddle up to the bar.

"Lou, baby!" I hear G croon from the other end.

He laughs. "Give me a minute, Henry. Let me help the girls out first."

I nod and watch as Everly and G kick back a shot of tequila and then suck on limes. The only reason my sister would be doing shots right before last call is if she's more than half in the bag.

I watch as Ev jumps down from the bar stool, moving away from G to chat with one of our distributors. I can see my sister flexing her negotiation muscles, which makes me proud. However, the loud blonde still sitting on the bar keeps my attention. I'm pretty sure that the two guys beside her only have one endgame of taking her home tonight, as most would. The problem is, they look like a couple of scumbags. Over-eager tourists looking to get laid. My guess is they're here for business, maybe a company excursion. I know these types; they likely have someone back at home, but while they're away, they play. They keep touching her, and it's pissing me off. The last squeeze of her thigh has me moving their way.

"I'd love to see where these tattoos lead. The flowers back here are hot. You're a colorful little thing, aren't you..." Such a douchey line. I can't help but laugh to myself as I get closer. She better not go home with these two dipshits. She's way out of their league.

The blonde guy steps away from Giselle and turns his head toward me. "Hey, man, something funny?"

Giselle leans back and hops off the bar. "Must have been your creative line, sweetie. Henry doesn't laugh at much, so I'd take it as a compliment, Thor." She pats him on the chest. "Isn't that right, Hanky? You usually only grunt and grumble at people. That, just then, was a legitimate chuckle. You must be feeling *really* good this evening."

She peers behind me, looking to see who I might be here with, and I can guess she hasn't heard about Denise yet. News travels fast here, but only if you're a townie. She's too new to get the details from Lenny or anyone else that likes to circulate stories. I'm surprised Ev hasn't said anything, but why would she? Everly doesn't know who G is to me.

Lou steps toward me after helping the girls. "Henry, what can I get you, man? Oh, you want to close out. Hang on."

I call him back just before he hits the register. "I'll take one more before you close it. Cognac rocks."

I turn my head to stare right at Giselle and catch her eyes. She blinks. Her mouth opens slightly, and that's when I know that I've caught her off guard. She knows what I'm telling her. I remember. And so do you.

If I had blinked, I would have missed the side of her mouth kick up, but instead of rewarding me with a smile, she turns to the dipshits again.

I take a sip of my drink, sign the slip, and lean on the bar to finish up. And to eavesdrop.

"Gentlemen, it's been a pleasure drinking on your dime, but I'm afraid this is where our night ends. You see, Henry over here is getting married soon, and I promised him and his fiancée a threesome before they tie it off." I choke on my sip, the glass jerking in my grips and splashing over my hand. Giselle grabs a napkin, dabs it on my lip, winks at me, and smiles.

"How's that Cognac, Hen?"

Everly walks up a moment later and snakes her arm around G's waist. "What'd I miss?"

"Well, I was just telling these fine gentlemen that I have to bid them a good evening because Henry and his fiancée are collecting on their threesome tonight."

Most people would laugh or even be taken aback by that. Not Everly. Leave it up to my fucking sister not to bat an eyelash and instead she just replies with, "Oh, that's tonight? Totally forgot. Gentlemen, thank you for the drinks. I hope we'll see you out again."

And like a damn idiot, the tall blonde guy, who is nothing like Thor, if I'm being honest, is also not picking up the rejection and decides to ask, "Why don't we do this again sometime?"

Instead of responding, G huffs and whispers, "Madonna mia," under her breath and waves the bartender back over. "The drinks were so good tonight, Lou. Please be sure to put my and Everly's drinks on Henry's tab. We're about ready to head out."

"You got it, G." He looks up toward me. "You good with that, Henry?"

As if I had a choice. The moment this woman entered my life, I was out of choices because I was hooked. I didn't think it would happen that way. The stunning effect of finding a person that, for some reason, you crave to be near. Equal parts attraction and curiosity. Heat and warmth. The strange notion of listening to some ridiculous instinct that isn't visible or likely sane, but doing it anyway.

I nod at Lou, "All good."

"Yo yo yo! You girls coming to Dad's for a nightcap?!" Law calls out as he thrusts himself into the mix.

"Fuck yeah, we are, Law-baby," G pipes in over Everly, already saying yes.

"I just texted him, so he knows we're coming," Michael says behind me.

The funny thing is, I'm not ready for the night to end either, and now that she's folded into it, I'm trying my damndest not to look as happy as I am that she's tagging along.

"You're extra broody right now. Nerves? Worried about having to perform for two women? I have very low expectations. Wait, is it bigger than a baby's arm?" G keeps prodding as we make our way out. I know she's trying to get me to crack.

I can't help it as a small laugh falls past my lips. And she looks like she just won the lottery, the way her eyes widen and a coy smile crawls across her mouth. Because she's the only one who saw it.

CHAPTER 13

Giselle

"Why are you staring?" Everly asks from the couch.

"I'm not staring. I'm concentrating."

"On what? I asked you about your shop."

"What?" I ask.

"What is going on with you? We didn't drink that much!"

"I'm doing kegals. I need to concentrate when I do them. Some women are like"—I lift my voice to a higher pitch—"You can do them wherever you want. It's so easy." I flap my arm to my side, annoyed. "I need to focus on the clenching," I say when I look back at my friend.

She's giggling. "G, my face hurts from laughing so much tonight."

"The shop is great. I mean, it will be great. It needs a bit of a makeover, but I seriously can't believe I have my own space," I say and wave my hands, shaking them out in front of me. "I can't think too much about it, I don't want to psych myself out."

"Those guys, by the way..." Everly scrunches her nose when she says it. "Boring."

"Oh my gosh, sooooo boring." We laugh, and the easiness of it makes my heart feel lighter. Everly leans over, looking across the massive living room and into the kitchen of her dad's house, as if she's on the lookout for someone. "The threesome thing. It wasn't the time to correct you, but they broke up."

The kegals cease, my stomach doing a very serious Olympic-style back handspring with a bunch of pikes and twists. My face feels hot. I might have just started sweating. *Shit. Shit!* "What do you mean, they broke up? Like, they were getting married, and then just decided they didn't want to anymore?"

"That's exactly what I mean. They broke up," Everly whisper-shouts back to me as she pours limoncello into the shaker. "I don't have all the details. My brother hasn't really been over-sharing lately. Henry moved his things in the night of the engagement dinner, and he's been living with us for the past week."

"He's living with you?" I whisper-shout back at her, trying and failing to hide my shock at the timing.

"Yep! Brought the dog and everything. But I guess they're sharing custody of Milo," she says with an eye roll.

I make a stink face at that idea. I didn't even know he had a dog, and for some reason, knowing it now makes me like him a fraction more.

"I know," Ev says and returns the same expression. "So anyway, looks like the threesome definitely won't be happening." She starts laughing at her own joke. "But you're all clear for a twosome, if you were interested. I mean, ew, but..." she trails off and shrugs her shoulder.

I ignore the twosome comment. I shouldn't be happy about this news. But holy shit-nuts, does this make me happy. So happy, in fact, that I can't contain a smile. So, here we are, ready to toast some delicious limoncello at two-thirty in the morning, and I'm beyond excited that the oldest Riggs son is now freshly single. I can't stop smiling. It must be the drinks, because I'm usually way better at schooling emotions. And I should have battened it down, since now Everly is looking at me curiously. *Shit*.

"G, do you like him? I was only kidding, but seriously, are you into my brother? Is that why you look like the joker right now?"

"What? Don't look at me like that. Absolutely not. He's not my type at all." *Fucking lies.*

She smiles at me like I'm not fooling her one bit. "What is your type?"

"I am an equal sexual opportunist. Just depends on my mood. I don't want to be thrown into a category based on who I like. I find personalities attractive. Sometimes those are attached to women and not just men. Sure, there are certain features that give me an extra tingle and just make everything downtown a little more humid..."

Everly leans back, listening, waiting for me to continue.

"Lately, though, I'm really feeling like I'm in my Viking phase. Longer blonde hair. Muscular but lean. I'm liking when they get to the point and tell me how they're feeling, ya know. " I smile, very obviously talking about someone who is the polar fucking opposite as the dark-haired brute with thick, muscular thighs and an ass I have every intention of at least nonchalantly grazing my hand across by the end of the night. "I wonder how long it will take for Henry to get back into dating." *Hopefully forever.*

"I don't see it happening any time soon." She shakes her head as she grabs a gummy worm from my pouch. "I was happy when he started dating again. Really happy. It was time for him to move on, but I always kind of thought he was settling when it came to Denise."

"Wildebeest," I say over a bite of sour blue raspberry worm.

"Wildebeest," Ev answers. We fist bump. Something about Denise just screamed, *Wildebeest*, and yet she wasn't humpbacked or had horns or a beard. It's all about personality. "Like it worked enough for him, but he wasn't madly in love. It just seemed... okay. And who wants to settle for just okay, ya know? But what the hell do I know?"

I toss back the rest of the drink, one that makes me feel a little nostalgic. Whew! This batch of limoncello is strong. "Ev, who made this?"

"Henry."

That surprises me. And that surprise is like a flashing light all around my face. I'm the literal fucking worst right now at keeping my face on lock, because Everly is just smiling at me again. I toss a gummy worm into my mouth and look around to make sure nobody's started to creep into our space. "Well, it's delicious. A bit stronger than what I usually like. I'll need to make a batch."

"Wait, where did you get these gummy worms?"

"I always have a stash in my bag. Limoncello called for something gummy or sour, so voila, sour gummy worms!"

The youngest and the most charming of the Riggs boys sidles up next to me at the bar, leaning on his elbows. He nudges my hip. "So, my new favorite shit-stirrer, I hear you're starting renovations soon on the shop." He grabs the half-eaten gummy worm out of my hand and pops it into his mouth.

"Law, my darling, you've heard correctly. Care to come and help me rip out some gross as hell wallpaper or swing a sledge to some counters?"

He smirks. "Fuck yea, I will."

I hear a heavy breath being huffed out from behind us, and if that didn't tip me off, it would have been the deep clearing of his voice. "Who the hell is letting you swing a sledgehammer?"

I turn around, and maybe it's the fact that I haven't seen him more than a handful of times since I've been in this town, but I'm still struck by the level of hotness this man radiates. It really isn't fair that he was blessed with a bulky, strong stature that somehow makes him even more delectable. To most, he's intimidating, but to me, he looks like home base. A place I want to run to, be safe within, and nuzzle. Run my nose along his body and just capture the scent of what a real man smells like because I remember that smell, and it practically makes my toes curl.

Sex appeal fucking seeps from his pores. I don't want to be attracted to him, but holy spumoni, I could lick him from toes to nose and I'd probably feel my clit flippity-flap as if it was waving in the wind. I thought maybe it's his green eyes with the little bit of mingling blue. I've decided that those fuckers don't sparkle. Nope, they have some kind of voodoo power. I swear the shades of green move like a kaleidoscope of forests and olives, and then that little twinkle of blue just glimmers, especially when those eyes lock on me for too long.

And that's just the physical attraction. I can't even allow myself to remember what it was like to talk to him for hours. But since I'm feeling all sorts of buzzed right now, I'm going to allow just a smidge... It felt like the coziest blanket in the safest place on the coldest day.

Fuck, I'm drunk. That's my only excuse for letting my mind go down this rabbit hole of a Henry Riggs pep rally. Because he's off-limits. *Harden my heart, swallow my tears,* like that 80s song recommends.

So instead, I'll make him uncomfortable with some sexual innuendos, get him to back off at bit, and then throw him into the friendzone. *Way easier, right?*

"Listen, Hanky, you should know I don't seek permission. For anything. But if you want to come by, I'd be happy to show you how to swing a sledgehammer." I give him a broad, obnoxious smile. As he shifts his stance, my eyes travel down, and look at the very impressive bulge in his pants. *Oh, Mister Riggs, is that a giant dick in your pants, or just extra turned on when I talk to you?*

He blinks at me. Watching as I objectify him, very blatantly at this point.

Law interrupts our silent little showdown. "Are you two flirting?"

Henry turns his head slowly to Law. It's kind of frightening. Like Law just poked the bear, and the bear is about to rip his head clean off his body.

But the perceptive idiot just continues. "Listen, if you're flirting, I could see it. You two are like polar opposites, and there's something to be said for that. I'm just a little caught off guard. Ev, are you catching this? I'm intrigued. Disappointed, because you know, G, you're fire, but still I'm intrigued."

Everly chimes in, "Law, read the room, and be quiet."

He scoffs. "Fine, whatever. Everyone is so uptight. Dad. Dad? Dad!"

"Right here. I'm just about to toss some cheese on these late-night burgers," Asher yells back. I don't know how we managed to find ourselves here for burgers and booze well after midnight, but I'm not mad about it. "G, you're sure you only want grilled cheese?"

"YES! I'll help," I yell. "Plus, I like tossing things." I wink at Henry. And because I can't help myself, as I walk by, I ghost my hand across his ass. *Yahtzee!*

A couple of hours later, I'm tucked into one of Asher's guest rooms, underneath what might be the softest comforter, surrounded by pillows, and practically hugged by the Riggs Outdoors branded guest pajamas. *Who has guest pajamas? Asher Riggs, apparently. Friggin' magical.*

I feel so welcome here. A group of people I didn't know just a week ago have folded me into their lives. It's wonderful and terrible all at once. Wonderful in the fact that my new best friend is incredible, and it feels like I've known her for my entire life. Her family is hilarious, warm, and fun. All of it is just so easy with them, well, except for one glaring, six-foot-something beauty. He's the most complicated situation, and I have no clue how I'm going to navigate it. How do I stay away from someone I want nothing more than to be around?

Tonight I realized three very important things: I have undoubtedly found my people, I should never throw glitter on a woman named Ruth DeMaio, no matter how much she might have looked like she "needed it," and I have to come up with a real plan on how to keep my mind off of Henry Riggs.

CHAPTER 14

Henry

"THERE HAS TO BE ANOTHER WAY TO APPROACH THIS. WE compete against other tourist towns in Colorado, but that doesn't mean we have to do what they're doing in order to keep up. We all know people will go to Aspen or Breckenridge to snowboard or ski, and then maybe hit up Strutt's if they get another go of winter sports while the powder is still falling, but we're never going to be someone's first stop unless we offer something different."

"Henry, you don't have to convince me. I'm supporting you on this," Everly says as she types out a text. "You need to take some of the new board members out and get them hooked. If you say Snowcat, they're not going to understand the feeling of finding fresh, private snow trails, or how the adrenaline hits as soon as you land mountainside on a helicopter. You have to show them. Take them out, plan the entire adventure the way you'd want it.

That's the only way they're going to approve the ad spend we need to turnover more customers."

"You don't want to do traditional ad spends for that either. You'll want to host some social media influencers on a trip out here. Have them post about it, vlog the new excursions. But you need to pick people that have the right audiences."

I look in the rearview mirror at Law, since what he's suggesting is a route we hadn't considered. "What's the spend going to be on something like that?" I ask.

"I can work something up. It'll depend on your target. Think about three different groups of people you'd consider an ideal tourist. Then, from there, we look at who those types of people are following on social media. My recommendation would be to couple that spend alongside a big winter sports brand, say that we already carry, and coordinate a campaign where they shoot photography and stuff here too."

"Baby brother, you looking for a job?" Everly says, as we both look at each other. The current marketing consultant we have didn't even broach the topic of partnerships or social media influencers. We're paying for ideas that we don't have the experience to come up with on our own, and our kid brother just eclipsed a seasoned marketer.

"Nah. Not yet. I'm going to Don Draper the shit out of the Boston advertising scene first. Then I'll be primed to do some damage back here."

Everly and I both laugh. "You do realize, Don Draper wasn't the brains behind the operation. He was the dude getting drunk and cheating while his secretary was the brains," Everly says.

"You didn't watch the show, obviously. But you make a fair point," he says.

"Also, that entire advertising universe being portrayed was during a time when men were just…"

Law cuts her off, "Okay, that was the worst example. All I'm saying is I want to be a badass on my own for a bit and then be able to bring something great to the family table."

I smile at that and catch him looking back at me in the rearview. I keep my emotions in check with him, so when he catches a sense of approval from me, I know he basks in it. "You've got a lot to learn, little brother."

"Except the part where I just schooled your ass on how to capture a better audience with your ad and marketing spend. Hell, I'm still an intern and I just influenced the shit out of your winter marketing program. So, you're welcome. I'll send you my bill."

Everly gives me the side-eye. Telling me to lay off of it, before he and I end up fighting.

"G, wants us to grab a few more drop cloths and paint rollers on our way over."

"Already got 'em," I mumble out. It wasn't crazy to think ahead and assume that G would need more paint supplies if she was enlisting our help in painting her shop. We've all been working for the past few weeks to help her get it in good shape for her grand opening. My family volunteered whenever they had free time, and tonight she offered pizza and beer in exchange for the final touches. Michael and Dad were going to help her with some lighting fixtures and the rest of us were tasked with painting before the furniture was delivered.

"I'm really hoping she's wearing those overall short things again. Ev, your friend is hot as fuck. DAMMIT!"

I slammed on my brakes to shut him up. He's right, she's insanely hot. Even her new look, with the blonde hair and all the tattoos. You add that to the way she laughs and can tell a person off at the drop of a hat. It's an instant hard-on for me. He can agree, but I don't like him calling it out.

"I hit my nose on the goddamn headrest. Shit, Ev, am I bleeding? Ease up, man," Law whines.

Everly gives me another side-eye and turns back to her phone, but not before smiling. She sees it. I know she does, but I'm not about to confirm her suspicions. Especially when, really, I'm supposed to be staying away.

Instructed to steer clear.

As soon as I park my truck out front of Hideaway Ink and take a look through the big front windows, my mouth salivates. Yeah, she's wearing those overall shorts, only this time, instead of a white tank underneath, she's got on some kind of black sports bra thing. Cropped short enough that I can see a patch of skin from beneath her breasts and down the side of her stomach. I could easily imagine tasting that piece of real estate in a slow path of discovery. Take a lap around her hips and torso, nibbling my way from the curve of her breasts to the swell of her ass.

As soon as she sees us pull up, she climbs down from

the ladder, and I salivate as I watch her thick thighs move down the rungs.

"You guys are the absolute best!" she calls out as she opens the front door. "I honestly don't know how I'm going to repay the favor."

Bend over and let me show you. Though, also not part of the deal I made. *The fucking deal that might just kill me slowly.* I keep my mouth shut. I pull out the supplies from the back of my truck and move inside, past her, without saying a word.

"You could pay me back by squeezing me in for a tattoo appointment," Everly says.

"Oh, please." G waves her off as she goes back up the ladder to finish painting some trim. "You never need an appointment with me. You tell me what you're thinking, and we'll make it happen. I'm your girl."

"I already have a girl," I say in response. Without thinking, I blurt it out.

G stares coldly at me, and if I had blinked, I would have missed the way her eyebrows furrowed when I said it. I regret saying it the second she schools her reaction and plasters a fake, bullshitting smile in response.

"Yeah, Henry's got someone he goes to in New York. Goes there enough that he's made it a consistent thing. So, G, I've got some thoughts on a design for my back," Law says from back of the space, pouring out a can of black paint into the roller dish. "G, you want this black on the back wall? On both sides of the opening, right?"

"Yes, please. You can get it on the ceiling too. I'm going to do the ceiling black as well. I want to get some murals up there over time since that's where most customers are staring when they're being worked on."

"Everly, you have to see the insane light we just put in back in the office. When it's lit, it looks like an oversized flower," Dad says from the doorway.

"Hi, Daddy. I forgot you and Michael came early," Everly says. I don't miss her whisper to him a thank you for helping out her friend.

I start taping up around the front window, trying to keep my attention set on the task in front of me and not the tempting pixie on the ladder behind me. I can hear the muffled conversation between my brothers and dad in the back of the shop, talking about how great the renovations came out, from the floors to the clean design.

Griff's shop was old school. A stereotype in a lot of ways for what a tattoo shop is assumed to look like. A dark space that always smelled like cigarette smoke and was covered wall to wall with photos of every tattoo he had ever done. It had a nostalgic vibe, but that wasn't what G had in mind. She was about to turn this place into a modern style art gallery, where ink and skin were her tools and canvas. And what she had done was incredible. I had looked at her work. Her posts on social media and some of the oversized images she had blown up to hang in the space. They weren't on skin, but the artwork was her original designs. They were detailed and bright. So clear and detailed, they looked like photos and not tattoos.

"Show me."

I turn around and find G standing a foot away with her arms crossed.

I chuckle at her stance. "Show you what?"

"Your tattoos. The ones that *your girl* did. Show me."

I turn back around and pull the blue tape taut against the glass, trying to ignore her request. "You've already seen them. Remember?"

You remember, Pixie.

"I want to see the new ones. Show. Me."

If she wants to see, fine. It's not like I was planning to keep it to myself. Dropping the tape to the ground, I look over her shoulder and see that my family is cracking open beers and just biting into the pizza. Out of earshot and not paying attention to us up here.

I look G in the eyes and silently challenge her to keep them there. She seems annoyed and for some reason, that makes me smile. Her getting fired up does things to me. And I know that sounds awful, but when she's riled and animated, she's unpredictable. And I like it.

Her eyes stay on mine as I lift my shirt away from my waist. Up my left ribcage and then higher. I pull my arm out of the sleeve. She doesn't break our gaze until my shirt is raised high enough to prop on my shoulder. Baring the design that started from my upper back and has since moved over my shoulder, across my collarbone, down the left side of my chest, over my heart, and down the side of my torso. She's fighting to keep her eyes trained on my face, almost as if she's not ready to look down. As if, somehow, she might know what awaits her. She loses the battle, though, as her gaze falls. Her cheeks turning pink as she moves her eyes down my body. Canvassing the artwork and my skin. She moves closer and stands on the tips of her toes. She's much shorter than I am, but barefoot, she's living up to the nickname I've given her.

Haven't seen it yet, Pixie.

"This looks incredible." Her eyes trail along my shoulder. "Clean lines. Really beautiful design. I like the graphic-style mountainscape. The way the color is minimal. It doesn't take away from the black shading, and the—"

There it is.

She looks up at me, stopping her train of thought. Her eyes water slightly, just enough so they shimmer. Being this close to her, looking so closely at me, has relit something within me that I've tried to tamp down. I want her hands to trace the places she's looking.

"The Air Force tattoo is different." She brings her fingers to my skin, and I'm brimming with tension, a buzz of adrenaline to be felt by her. Her fingers caress across the words that are wrapped in a circle, following their path so lightly that it leaves an eruption of goosebumps along my arms. Words that we toasted. Words that I promised her I would uphold, even if that meant she'd never know it. *A una bella vita* (to a beautiful life).

"I met a woman one night in a bar. We talked about nothing. And it was..." I shake my head. "It felt like everything."

My eyes search her face, studying the features all over again. Big brown eyes surrounded by thick lashes, a perfect nose with the hint of a scar from where a nose ring once was, her full upper lip the shape of a half moon. Beautiful.

"I didn't know that feeling was possible. To connect

like that. To just know you had met someone that was going to change you." I pull my arm back through my shirt, tugging it down over my chest.

"He couldn't stop going to New York to look for her," Everly chimes in from behind us. Knocking us both out of the bubble I had just built.

Giselle clears her throat and shifts her stance back, adding some space between our bodies. "What happened?" I look her in the eyes, asking, pleading why she would even ask that. Because she knows exactly what happened. She knows more details than I do.

"It was so awful. He meets this incredible woman. I mean, you should have seen him the next day. He was different. Smiling at nothing. Anyway, it was so sad. She had been killed in a home invasion. It was all over the news," Everly says, whispering the part about her being killed, as if saying it softer will lessen the impact. I turn around back toward the window. I'm not interested in this conversation any longer. My emotions are far from in-check. I'm frustrated at being interrupted, pissed off at the situation I'm in right now. I need some air.

"I still can't believe it and it's been years. He still goes back," Everly adds. *Shut up, Ev.*

"Why? I mean, if she's gone, why?" G asks, but I don't answer.

My dad shouts from the back of the shop, "Henry, you got any more drop cloths in your truck?"

"Yea, I'll grab 'em." I head out the front door. I need to catch my breath a bit. My skin is hot. I'm angry at myself for having felt the need to say any of that to her. Tip my hand at all. Dangle something in front of her that she can't have.

I hear the door swing back open behind me. But, instead of turning around, I move faster to the cab. I'm not interested in hashing out any of this right now. She asked to see my tattoos, so I showed her. I knew as soon as she saw it, she would need to know more. I should have kept my mouth shut about the rest.

"Is all of that true?"

I open the door to my truck and lean in. No sign of the drop cloths, so I turn around and look in the truck's bed, but as soon as I move to close the door, G is standing there. I had every intention of keeping away from her. Observe from a distance. But being this close to her, all of those plans fall away.

She should smell like paint and turpentine, but I catch the faintest scent of lemon as the wind picks up. It's like a drug, the smell of her. I want to drag my nose down her neck. Breathe her in.

"Yes," I say, stepping closer, knowing that the closer the proximity, the easier it'll be to touch her. And while I shouldn't. While I've been cautioned to keep my distance, it feels wrong to step away.

"Yes, it's true." I crowd her, closing the gap. Backing her into the truck so that her back hits the seat, and she has nowhere left to go. She stares at my chest. I can see her confidence wavering. She doesn't want to look up at me. She doesn't want to see how she's hurt me. That whatever happened to her that night didn't just destroy her world. That there are repercussions that she had no idea about. One of them is right in front of her.

"I'm not going to lie to you. Even though they told me you were dead, I couldn't bring myself to stop thinking that maybe they had gotten it wrong. That it didn't feel like you were gone."

The wind kicks up again, only this time, it brings a cooler breeze that splits the warmth of the summer evening. I brush my fingers across her forehead, moving away the hair that's blowing into her face. My hand brushes across her cheek and glides into her hair. I run my thumb back and forth slowly along her cheekbone. I remember what it felt like to kiss this woman. Intoxicating. Purposeful. Addictive. I bring my mouth closer to hers to see if she'll let me have another taste.

Her eyes flutter closed. "You're dangerously close to taking something that does not belong to you, Henry."

I don't dare move back, instead rubbing my thumb along her lower lip. "That's where you're wrong, Pixie." I lick my lips and the invigorating tension between us becomes overwhelming. "I never take anything that doesn't belong to me, but we both know this mouth. These lips. They're as good as mine."

She swallows roughly and stares at my mouth hovering mere centimeters from hers. But I don't take a taste. Not yet.

The vibrating in my back pocket is loud enough to break the moment.

"Your ass is buzzing," she says in a whisper with a smile kicking up the sides of her mouth. *Damn that mouth.*

I pull back and grab my phone.

AGENT HARPER

> It doesn't look like you're following
> protocol, Riggs.

And just like that, I remember why moments like this can't happen. Finding myself alone with her will only end in breaking the rules. I made a deal. Make sure she's safe and she can stay. Or else she's gone again.

CHAPTER 15

Giselle

"You can't even see it anymore. Shit, G, I don't know how you did it, but wow. This is good."

"Thanks, Mac, I really like how it came out. If you want me to add some color, we can do that, but why don't you see if you like the black and shading first. Live with it for a couple of days and then let me know."

Mac has become a good friend of mine. As a retired MMA fighter, you'd think he'd be rough around the edges, or just a full-time asshole, especially with the level of swagger that he emanates. It's intimidating, but he's a sweetheart. The man does a great job of putting people in their place if they need it, but really, he's a lover or teacher, less of the fighter. He may have held a title for a decade, but this man was born to build people up, and show them how to move around a mat.

"She's officially erased from my life," Mac says on a sigh. The hopeless romantic got his ex-wife's name across his chest in massive roman lettering when things were good. Then they weren't. It's been more than a few years now since she left, and he was finally ready to erase the reminder.

"I know I did it, but damn, I'm good," I say as I start wrapping it.

"A little bit of good and a bit of evil. Couldn't have imagined it, but the way it's designed. It's badass, G."

"Spread the word. Keep your shirt off." I smile back at him. "You know, for advertising purposes."

"What do I owe this time?" he asks as he stands and moves toward the door. The shop opened a week ago now, and I've been booked solid. Mac is my last one for the night.

"Nothing. I'll take some private lessons, so I don't keep getting paired with the new high school kids in classes. And seriously, take your shirt off when you're around some of the guys training. I want their business." I wink.

"I'm not going to argue. I know it won't get me anywhere." He pulls his flannel on and laces up his boots. It was a good three hours in the chair, which meant he needed to be comfortable. "Do me a favor and work on getting some more girls over to the gym, okay? I want to do that self-defense class more regularly."

I salute him in response. "On it. Bring women."

He laughs at me. He's one of the easy ones. Always willing to smile.

"You done for the night?" Mac asks. I look at the clock and it's still early. Since it's summer, the sun is going strong at 6 p.m. I have plenty of time to get to the hot springs as planned.

"Why, you going to ask me for a drink?"

"G, you're sexy as fuck, but you'd destroy me. I know you're not looking for anything long-term. So, I think we're good as friends, yeah?"

I jut out my lip and pout. "We are. Friends have drinks."

"I'm still a man and I know having a few drinks, just me and you, would end up being more. We need a buffer."

"Fine, fine. And you're right. That was a long while touching and staring at that chest. You may be retired, but your body didn't catch the memo." He's stupidly hot, a bit older than me, but we flirt enough to know that if you add some alcohol, we'd end up hooking up.

I prefer sex only. No relationships. I have no interest. But a sexy retired MMA fighter could be an excellent distraction from a certain bulky Riggs brother. Too bad Mac's the kind of man that you take off the market, not just sample.

"Mac, you're a good guy." He waits with me as I move around the shop to lock up.

"Don't tell anyone that. I'm saying *we* shouldn't cross that casual sex line, not that I don't want all the casual hooking up I can get."

The man has no clue, he's click-bait hot. "How long has she been out of the picture now?" I ask.

"Not long enough. But I'm ready to see what I missed when I was being the faithful one." He laughs. We walk a couple of doors down to where his truck is parked out front. I give him a few instructions on the aftercare of his tattoo and wave him off as he drives away.

The best part of living in downtown Strutt's Peak is the lofts above the shops on Main. What's even better is owning one of those shops. Hideaway Ink is *my* tattoo shop. I still can't believe it sometimes.

The name came from my specialty. Hiding. Covering up and redoing older tattoos or reworking imperfections into a new type of art. A passion that developed quickly when I apprenticed in the first town I was dropped into for witness protection. I watched, drew, and studied non-stop. I dove into a new obsession, so I didn't have to think or reflect on anything else.

Tattooing and all the components it takes to be at the top of your game in this business, developing my skill set, it's what brought me to a better place emotionally. The beauty is that I can make a living from it too. A therapy and passion turned into a business is something I never would have imagined for myself. A silver lining. Nah, better. Platinum lining.

The colors and flowers that cascade down from my shoulders to my wrists cover the olive branches that had been started back when I was in New York. Unless you look closely, you would never know something else was there before. Something old turned into something brighter and new.

I wouldn't have hooked up with Mac. Maybe flirted a little more heavily, but I am keeping my meaningless sexual encounters to people that have zero connection to this town. I'm not interested in making anything else more complicated. But I am going to do what I can to get one man in particular out of my system. The opportunities are endless when living in a tourist town. A filthy little perk.

I change into my bathing suit and throw a loose, short black skirt and my favorite neon cropped tank over it. I've wanted to dip into the hot springs since the weather warmed up, but I haven't had a chance. Between the shop finally becoming mine, planning out renovations, and joining Strutt's town business division, there hasn't been a moment to enjoy the weather. I plan to change that tonight.

An hour later, and I'm in pure, steamy heaven.

Relaxed and feeling like any stress that's been creeping in lately is finally draining out of my body. I feel lighter, and for a few quiet moments, I stay present and away from the heaviness of my past. I don't like to celebrate anything from my old life. It makes me feel like I'll just fall into a depression if I thought too hard for too long, but today is different. Today would have been my pops' birthday.

The handsome lug would have been seventy, and I can only imagine how he would have celebrated. Likely, it'd be a big stogie. Some watered-down Campari with a splash of gin and maybe a trip to Coney Island, so he could snag a few too many funnel cakes.

My pops, no matter how hard it's been not to have him, I'm thankful I had the time with him that I did. And *that* is worth celebrating.

"What are you drinking, troublemaker?"

I tilt my head up to look at who is audacious enough to bother me right now. And, sure as shit, Law Riggs pushes his way into my private hot spring. He gives me his megawatt smile, and it's impossible not to smile back. Even if I didn't want company. He's the most charming person in this town. Always ready with a teasing compliment and a bright, genuine smile.

"Just enjoying some quiet time. Until you showed up." I close my eyes and tilt my head back, leaning against the side of the spring. It's warm and apparently incredible for skin, but I love it most because it's something I would have never thought I'd be able to do. "All the hot girls are a few springs over. I assume you're out here to find someone to fuck around with later?"

"What if I already found someone I wanted to fuck around with later?" he says, immediately responding to my question.

That gets my attention. We joke around. Flirt, even. Flirting is just how I am with people. But Law hasn't ever been this bold. We've teased each other a bit, but this Riggs brother isn't the one that hits my places just right. I look at Law like a friend. I can appreciate his good looks, but he's not it. Not enough bulk, too happy, too little of the resting dick face I've come to search for.

"Then I'd ask you, where'd she go?" I smile and look over at him. Challenging him.

"I'm just fucking with you, G. I mean, that bikini is insane. I'd have to be blind not to appreciate it, and everything it's barely covering up, but you're my pseudo-sister now. And I don't think Everly would approve of us messing around. Though, I wouldn't mind you teaching me a thing or two..." He quirks his eyebrow. Making it a dare.

"Law, baby, there's so much I can teach you." He slides over to where I'm sitting and pulls the drink from my hand, taking a sip.

"Negroni?" he asks.

I lift my shoulder to shrug. "Campari makes me sentimental."

"Of all the things I know about you, G, which isn't much, being sentimental is not one I would have guessed."

I scoff exaggeratedly. And we both burst out laughing. Mine more of a giggle, and if his voice wasn't so deep, he'd be giggling too. A few of his lighter curls flop down over his forehead, and he looks, even more so, the part of the younger man. He'll be a damn fine man in a handful of years, but he still seems so much like a kid. It's the lightness about him. It makes being around him easy. The Riggs family does that, makes things effortless and content. It makes me want to be around them. The love they have for each other, it's always so obvious. I envy it and try to absorb what I can from it whenever I'm with them.

A few more drinks and all the pruned fingers later, Law and I are taking bets on which girls are going home with which guys in the springs on the other side of us.

"What are the chances you can flirt it up with that tall young Clooney over there so I can swoop in and take that redhead off his hands?" He nudges me.

"I'd say very good." I laugh into my drink. We both get up and grab our bags. They clink as we move, his filled with Coronas and mine with my gin and Campari. I do a double take at the small spring just behind us, and my breath catches for a minute. It always does when I see *him*. Especially now, when I don't expect it. I haven't seen him since he showed me his tattoo, then touched my lips like he was trying to memorize them without giving in to what he wanted.

Henry sits tall but relaxed, his arms draped along the mud wall of the spring as if he's emerged from the earth like some sort of god. And he looks like one. The broad chest and thick arms swelled and dipped with muscle from his shoulders to forearms. Neck to pecs. A tattoo, that has somewhat knocked me sideways, peeks out just enough so that I can't help but stare. Of all the things I want to pay attention to, it's the ink that makes my stomach swoop. The idea of why he would do that makes me feel lightheaded, nervous.

The lights that were put up around the springs for nighttime are just bright enough to see around the area, but still dim enough that I can't read his face. I can tell his attention is on us, though. Watching me as we move. Henry isn't even close, and he's flooded my senses. The air is cool tonight, but my body is heated. Partly from the hot spring and negronis, and the other from that man's attention.

"Henry, we're moving down a bit. Want to join?" Law yells out.

He stands from the water as a response. And it's as if the world slows down. A slow-motion reel of a hard-worked body erecting from the murky, healing waters. I'm assaulted with so much tanned skin packed with muscle, that all the knowledge stored in my overactive brain recedes like the tide. I'm borderline stupid right now. My mouth hangs slightly open as he saunters my way. And that's what he does, he saunters. His board shorts suctioned to his massive, toned thighs, and I catch a thick outline of his dick right through his pants. I'm equal parts annoyed and relieved because, at some point, I want a glimpse of that dick. It's on my very real bucket list, written in a permanent marker.

Maybe that's the solution. That's how I can get him out of my system. Kill the sexual tension and just say fuck it. Or, fuck me. Then move on. Keep it surface level. My mind just runs over and over again, as if it were on a reel of the way water cascades down his abs and disappears either into those board shorts or cuts right and left into the divots of his V-line. Like well flagged lanes directing towards his party-time highway.

"Eyes up here, G." I flick my eyes up fast to his face. I'm caught, but really, who wouldn't be looking? It's where my eyes go first. Note to men of the universe, if you're wearing gym shorts, sweatpants, or a wet swimsuit, most people who are sexually attracted to your type, will look. And anyone who doesn't, well, their loss. I'll study on their behalf.

That's the problem, though. Looking up means I'm going to see his face. His lip marked with that white scar that I remember tracing with my tongue. The look in his eyes as he dragged his fingers up and down my legs. It's a feeling that I've never felt again, until last week, with his hands on my face, in my hair, tracing my mouth. Regardless of how many arms I've been in, since or before, nothing seems to compare to the memory of Henry Riggs in my bar, stealing my breath that night.

I sleep around. I have a healthy-ish sex life, and I enjoy being intimate with other people. I like the closeness, and the orgasms, obviously. But kissing other people never feels quite right. So, I "Pretty Woman" them, and try to avoid kissing altogether. It happens, of course, every now and then, but I don't seek it out. I'm never staring at someone's lips, thinking, "please crash into me." Usually, I'm thinking about how will that mouth work me into an orgasm.

"G, that was the dirtiest eye-fuck I've seen in a long time. Dang, girl!" Law laughs.

"I'm human, boys. Hanky, stop flexing your dick at me, and I'll keep my eyes above your equator," I laugh out as he glares back at me.

"Yo! Riggs!" Henry and Law look toward the crowd. The largest of the hot springs tends to attract the tourists. But tonight, it seems like the townies are the only ones here. While many towns have community gardens in the summertime, Strutt's Peak residents tend to the landscape and add amenities to the hot springs.

Massive boulders and dark gray rocks edge along each hot spring with some foliage. The main pool is the best lit and prettiest. With some underwater lights floating and string lights hung around and over, it's easy to see the gorgeous bodies that are enjoying the summer evening. The larger pool also smells much nicer because lavender, lemongrass, and rosemary are planted along the perimeter. During the day, the water in the main hot spring is an off-white, blueish color, but at night, it's black, much like the sky above right now, freckled with stars.

Law shimmies up to the redhead he was eyeing earlier without even a "see ya later." As much as it would be smart to distract myself, and flirt with someone else, I don't want to tonight. The idea of getting Henry out of my system still sounds like more fun than it should be, which means it's time for me to go. So, with my cheeks flushed, I decide to listen to my reasonable brain for once, and not my hungry kitty.

"I'm going to take off."

His strong hand grabs my elbow and forearm. Gah! Why does him touching me feel so fucking good? "You okay to drive?" It sounds like a growl, all deep voiced and low, like he doesn't want to embarrass me by asking too loudly.

I pull my arm out of Henry's grip, making my way back to the parking area.

Without looking, feeling him following behind me, I say over my shoulder, "I'm fine. You don't need to follow me."

"You're not fine. You've been drinking. You're even more drunk than I thought, if you really think I'll allow you to drive home."

I spin around to look at him, stopping us both in our tracks. "*Allow?* Oh, please."

"You think I didn't see how much you and Law threw back tonight? You're not getting in a car unless you're a passenger."

His gaze trails down, stopping on my mouth for a second, before continuing down my throat and pausing at my chest. His eyes linger there longer than a glance.

"My tits are pretty, aren't they?" I push them out a

little more. "Now who's looking?" I see his nostrils flare a little.

He ignores me and says, "I'm taking you home."

"That's very forward of you, Henry, but I think I'm good for tonight. My vibrator is all charged up and ready for me."

With a quirked brow, I keep heading toward the parked cars. Why does it feel so good to throw little digs his way? He is right about drinking, but I wouldn't be stupid enough to drive. I can quickly call a car to get me. Walking up to my trunk, I click it open, dropping my towel and shoes on the ground in front of it and throwing my bag in. I turn around to quickly pull on my cover-up skirt and neon tank. Henry stands tall, arms crossed, a few feet from me.

"I'm not going to drive. You mistake my very honest and smart mouth for being flighty or stupid. I know I've been drinking," I say as I pull my tank down over my tits. Then I shimmy my short black skirt up over my legs and situate it around my waist.

"I'd never think about calling you stupid. I'm going home now anyway," he says. I watch him swallow as his eyes track my movements. Reaching up under my skirt, I drag my bikini bottoms down my legs. "Um, it's easy for me to drop you at your place. And it would..." He stops his sentence as I turn and bend over to pick the now discarded bikini bottoms off the ground. I throw them into my trunk and slip on my flip-flops. Once I click the lock and alarm, I find Henry rubbing the back of his neck.

"Let's go, big guy. I'm still thirsty," I say, moving toward his truck.

"We're not going out for another drink."

"I have plenty of things for you to sip on. You're coming in for a drink at my place. Don't fight me on it. It's been a long day, and I need to turn off," I say and laugh at my next thought. "Or maybe turn on." I wiggle my eyebrows. "Feel like getting turned on with me, Hanky?"

He ignores the question, but I'm almost positive I hear him say, "Already there," under his breath.

Fifteen minutes later, we make our way down Main Street and, without too much overthinking, we trek up to my apartment. My stomach clenches at the thought of what being alone, without an audience, might be like. I know I'm playing with fire here. Common sense isn't showing up, pushing me to stop this progression, so I move forward. What's wrong with some flirting? What would be so wrong with scratching the Henry itch and pushing him right into the "been there, done that" category. Sure, the man makes me feel warm and safe. And yes, talking to him that night was just as incredible as learning his mouth, but what if we just keep it sexual now? One and done.

I take a cleansing breath as I open the door to my apartment and brush off the goosebumps that ripple down my arms as he stands close behind me. I slip into the new me, the one who can freely have sex with a beautiful man. Trust that we can make this simple and leave it in the past. I can do that. It's brilliant. Get dirty, make a clean break, and then move on.

CHAPTER 16

Henry

THE FUCK AM I DOING? I KNOW SHE DIDN'T NEED TO BE walked to her door. I knew agreeing to a drink was asking to test the willpower I'm not sure I have a full handle on right now. And yet, here I am, walking into her apartment.

One drink. Alone together. Maybe I'll ease her mind a little and tell her that I'd never divulge her secret. Put her in any danger. Hell, I've been commissioned to help make sure she and others like her stay safe, for fuck's sake. The problem is, she isn't supposed to know that part. Agent Harper is supposed to be her only visible handler. But there are always more U.S. Marshalls assigned. Plain-clothes civilians who support, placed specifically to check-in and keep the person in WITSEC unaware. With cases like hers, or so I'm told, where the death toll was more like a massacre than just a murder, the check-ins need to be frequent. *Just a murder.* The thought of it makes me ache for her loss.

Those were the exact words used to describe the chaos that surrounded my pixie when Agent Harper paid me a visit. The day after a dead woman walked into my life, blowing up just about every plan I had set into motion, stirring up emotions in my gut that I had long since resigned would stay buried along with her. That's the problem, though, she's not mine. No matter how much I want it, want her, she can't be.

"You're ex-military, top of your class, and I've done my homework, Riggs. Now it's up to you to decide what happens next," the agent, who I learned was Agent Bea Harper after she flashed her credentials in my face, says. She takes a drag of her clove cigarette. "I can't have my folks in WITSEC have any connection to their old life. And you made quite a stir back in New York with the constant calls and stop-ins. The agent assigned to her case knew you by first name. Said you even attended her service. So now, this place can't work unless I make it work. This is me asking if you want to help me make it work?"

She caught me at my truck, right after my morning run. Sweat-soaked and clear-headed, even after the upheaval the night before had caused. Breaking off an engagement, moving out of my home, realizing I was right and she was alive, it didn't hit me hard. It hit me just right. Knocked me sideways, but I feel relieved. Ready.

"How would I do that? Help you make it work?"

"You work with me. Be my eyes on the ground here. Help me place new people where necessary even if they're short term. There's a lot of funding approvals that have to happen and the speed at which it happens doesn't jive with the immediacy that some of these folks need. I need people I can trust who are going to be silent eyes, and quick to move if I need it. It's off the books, but I'll make sure you get compensated."

"I don't need the money."

"What do you need, then?"

I mull the thought around. And it keeps coming back to the woman who has now taken up residence in my mind in just under a day.

"I need to know what happened to her."

"I can offer you high-level detail, but the rest she'll have to tell you. It's confidential and there are some rules I don't bend. You care about her and that's... nice, but I need to cover her ass and make sure you're not a problem. This is the only way to do that and let her stay here. You may not need the money, but you'll get paid for your time anyway."

"So if I say no?" I ask, already knowing what she's going to say. My stomach tight at the reality of this situation.

"Then she's relocated. Erased from here. I'm not in the business of finding people; my job is to hide them. It might sound harsh, but it's her life on the line. You have twelve hours to get back to me—"

I cut her off. I don't need to hear any more. "I'll do it."

She quirks her brow at my quick decision. "You obviously will have some kind of a relationship with her. Your sister and her have become close, but that's where the connection ends for you. This isn't a green light for you two to rekindle whatever you had started in New York."

I nod. "Will she and I be doing check-ins?"

Harpers drops the butt of her clove and stamps it out. "No, Riggs. She needs to live her life. As quietly as possible, which for her, is going to be a challenge already. She will not know about your involvement with WITSEC. And you will maintain a professional distance. That, or I relocate her. It's the only offer I'm willing to serve up. I refuse to let feelings and coincidences put my people in danger. And, Riggs, there's danger in this."

"Understood."

"I'm not going to go into the reasons why if you do this, things with Giselle will remain platonic." I try not to wince at the very clear line she just drew in the sand. "She already knows this, but you need to be sure as well that she remains out of the spotlight when she attends your family's events. Leave it up to that kid to make friends with low key celebrities." She scoffs. "Keep your interaction with her minimal. She's going to want to do the same. She alerted me of you and of how you met." Harper levels her attention, making sure I hear her, and then points a finger at me. "So do us all a favor, and keep your distance."

I'm not a man that likes to be pointed at, but instead of hauling an insult, I swallow the sandpaper that's coating my throat. The situation I've been backed into pisses me off, but I'm reasonable enough to know, if I don't want G disappearing again, that this is the only way. Not to mention, she's just restarted her life. How could I say no, knowing she'd have to give it up and start from scratch somewhere far from here? Far from me.

"You have my cooperation. In all of it," I grit out.

"Good. Thought you might. You flyboys are some of the best, most loyal I've worked with. Your superiors had only good things to say about your dedication. Shame what happened." I don't respond to that. Quite frankly, my life is none of her business, and I'm annoyed that she has the authority to know about any of it. "Great to have you onboard. I'll be in touch." She turns on her heel and walks off. As if she didn't just throw an anvil on my life. A wet blanket draped over all the possibilities I had let escape into my mind.

"Are you coming in? Or are you just going to lurk in the stairwell, like a creep?" G says as the door swings open. She slings her bag onto a bench by the door, tossing her keys in a bowl. Shoes discarded too. It's a fast and careless deposit of belongings. Like she can't get into her space fast enough. Get comfortable.

I should go. She's home safe. But my feet move forward, and instead of leaving like I should, I waltz through the front door without pause. I ignore the fact that it's exactly what Agent Harper demanded I *not* do. Tempt the urge to be more than a memory for her. Keep myself a spectator and not a player in her story. Instead, enough Corona's at the hot springs, watching her flirt with my brother in that bikini, and I'm here.

I can keep this simple. I'm here for a drink. Defuse some of the worry she may be carrying. *That's it.*

When I finally look around, G's apartment is exactly what I would have expected. Splashes of color and texture, tapestries on walls, oversized pillows around the living room floor, all mismatched, plants on every surface, and some oversized palm-tree-looking ones with monster leaves in the corner. The loft itself is massive, with exposed brick and ceilings that would normally make a space like this feel modern and cold, but she's warmed it up. She has that way about her. Color. Warmth. It feels good to be near it, near her.

There's a hammock swing hanging from the rafters in the corner in front of a wall of windows. A front seat to Strutt's, overlooking the city-like feel of downtown. Next to it is a pile of notebooks. Some splayed open are filled with color. Next to them are at least six mismatched cups stuffed full with colored pencils of all different sizes.

"You can look. I don't mind you being nosy, Hanky," she says as she moves toward the kitchen.

"You know my name, Pixie," I say as I make my way to her creative space. "Let's use it."

"Ha!" She peers back from the freezer. "That I do. Not a fan of nicknames, and yet, you've so freely given me one.

"I'll stop if it bothers you."

"No way, Hanky. You can call me an-y-thing you want," she drawls out.

I just smile to myself as I watch her. Because as much as I hate the nickname, I'm liking that she's calling me something different. Just for her. Even if it's ridiculous.

She drops ice cubes into two glasses and smiles at what she's doing. I wonder how she can be so easily content. After the chaos she's been through. If she's really as strong as she portrays. I can handle intense situations, and disengage myself from feeling where necessary, but going through something like losing family so tragically, I know for a fact, it would cripple me.

She knows I'm studying her again. She stands tall as she glances back at me over her shoulder. Everything about her interests me. She moves with so much confidence. It comes easily to her. I'm learning that it's just how she is. I'm drinking in my fill. Quenching a thirst while enough alcohol flows through my bloodstream, tipping the needle of what's considered platonic, towing the line, and plain old breaking the rules. And the way I can't seem to stop looking at the way her waist curves and leads to a round ass perched on top of her thick, full thighs, it's cutting dangerously across those lines.

"Put something on. It's too quiet in here."

I look at the record player she's set up next to two prominent speakers and four crates filled with records. She walks into the living space with the two ice-filled glasses balanced in one hand and a bottle of Titos in the other.

"I'm not drinking vodka, G."

"Too much of a panty pucker for ya?"

She laughs.

"Geez, you don't have to be so growly about it, Hanky. Let me see what else I have." She huffs and struts back into the kitchen.

I stop my perusal of music and watch the sway of her hips. A melodic movement like a swinging metronome. I'm never this dumbstruck over a woman's body. I need to knock it off, so instead I find a record I haven't heard in a while. The lead singer from Kings of Leon echoes throughout the room with his falsetto and rhythm guitar. He croons away on speakers placed throughout the space, suggestively saying that he could use somebody. And my eyes connect with hers as soon as he repeats it. We're both thinking the same thing. *Great suggestion.*

As she says, "Nice choice," my breath catches. It's not the first time, hell, it's happened often, but it's the first time that I can keep her eyes locked onto mine. Challenge her not to look away. The sexiest thing in the world has to be eye contact with the right person. It's the first time that I *want* her to be the woman from the bar, but even more so, I want to be the man who was in the bar that night. I was a blank slate then, flailing, but I was less pissed off at the world. Which is funny because when I stepped foot in that bar, I was angry at the path my life was on. Now I look at her, and I think, how stupid of me. That path led me right to her.

She looks away, focusing on finding me a drink in the refrigerator. "I have a stray Corona, but no limes."

"How about a Cognac?"

She freezes and doesn't look up. I hear her say softly, maybe intended only for herself, "Not so predictable anymore, apparently."

I walk toward the kitchen, and my approach has her moving away, as she says, "Nope." Cracking the Corona open, she slides it across the countertop. The silence in the room is waiting to be broken. I don't mind quiet. I can usually find out a lot about a person or understand a situation better when there's a bout of silence.

Her cheeks are flushed as she takes a sip of her vodka. She sighs and then must make up her mind about something, because she follows it up with a breathy, "Okay." She moves past me and back into the living room.

Silence can make a person realize the full depth of the situation they're in, and right now, we're alone together. And while I shouldn't be here, there is also nowhere else I want to be. A baser instinct that I'm following. Or maybe it's just my cock, urging the rest of me to stop ignoring the sex appeal that's pouring off this woman and to do something about it. I also haven't forgotten that she's not wearing anything under that short black skirt either.

I take a long pull of the beer. "I'm not going to cause you any trouble," I tell her.

She doesn't say anything to that, or react at all. Instead, she continues her path to the oversized green armchair, kicks off her sandals, and sits as she pours another shot of vodka into her ice-filled glass. Instead of taking a sip, she sucks on a lemon wedge and plunks it into her drink. The entire room smells like lemons mixed with something sweet. My eyes fixate on her mouth. Her tongue peeks out and meets the glass a fraction of a second before it reaches her lips.

She keeps her eyes on me as I lean my back against the counter, across the room from where she sits, her legs casually draped over one arm of the chair. She looks too comfortable, while I'm standing here stiff as a board, trying to figure out if I've just walked into a situation I'm not strong enough to move away from.

I take another long pull of my beer, to which she

smirks. Suddenly, I'm uncomfortable in this silence. I can usually school my emotions, but the uneasiness of being alone with her now, and the obvious attraction that I have to her, has to be coming off of me in waves.

"What if I want a little trouble, flyboy?"

I sniff out a laugh to myself. This has to be some kind of test.

I look around the room for a red light. Some kind of signal that I'm being recorded, because this shit right here has to be psychological warfare at its finest. When the woman you've obsessed over isn't just alive, but is sitting in front of you, begging for trouble, and you're not allowed to do a damn thing about it.

She sits up, takes one more sip from her glass, and puts it down on the oversized coffee table in front of her. Smiling at me, she drags her fingers over the top of each thigh. My eyes dart from her legs to her face and back again. Watching those pretty hands with long, decorated nails moving much too sensually along her bare skin.

"So you've become the kind of man to just stand there and tell me what you're not going to do," she says playfully.

I lick my bottom lip, trying to buy time with how I want to play this.

"Pixie, you have no idea what kind of man I am." My facial expression is schooled not to move, but every vein in my body pumps over time. I wait for her to continue that path up her legs. I may be on a leash, but I'm not about to back down from this challenge. I'll happily watch. Wait her out and see if she's got the courage to keep pushing me.

"You seem to be the kind that waits for approval. The kind that looks for direction. The type that would rather follow the rules than play with something you're not supposed to." Her eyes explore me from top to bottom, the same way I'm surveying every inch of her.

The massive ceiling fan isn't doing much to cool the room off, and sweat is starting to gather low on my back. I don't respond, because I know what she's doing. She wants to push, see how far she can take this before I snap. So, I smile at her.

"I think the best thing to do is just get it out of our system. Enjoy a little bit of sweaty fun tonight. We can keep it a secret or blame it on the drinks or whatever, but you've been looking at me all night like you're just dying for a taste," she says with a raspiness to her voice that has my nerves tingling. "I won't tell if you won't."

My mouth salivates. The idea of sinking into her, any way that she'll request, has me ready like an eager asshole. One who is all but seconds from breaking the rules I've been given. But the thing is, she's trying to make this all about sex. *Only* about sex. And with her, the way she makes me think, the feelings she's been pulling from me, it's more than that from where I stand. And I'm not about to let her set the pace.

I take the last sip of my beer and put it down behind me, resting against the counter. Instead of saying yes and having this night with her, which a part of me wants to do *very* badly, I need more from her. Forget the agreement with WITSEC; hell, even put her safety to the side for a second. I'm not about to say yes and fuck her. She'll put us into a box that she can handle. I'd never risk her or cheapen my feelings for her for a fast fuck.

Air Force training was more than flying. It was about analyzing the situation and making quick, analytical decisions. The ability to rein in emotion being just as important as take-off or landing. And right now, I'm both pissed off and turned on. My training is a flex that I have to use, as it's taking all of my willpower not to concede and fuck her senseless.

G sits back in the chair and drags her skirt higher, toward her hips.

Don't you dare, Pixie.

Her thick, toned thighs are just asking to be grabbed, slapped, and licked. I want to bite a path from her hips to the curve of her ass and then dip my mouth down to bite and slap them so goddamn hard. But instead of any of that, I lean back and just watch her. Talk my dick down.

She pulls her knees apart slowly, bunching up the already pushed high skirt. Then, leaning back, she moves her left leg over the chair's left arm, and then her right leg over the chair's right arm. She sits there, legs wide open, baring her pussy to me shamelessly.

Well, *fuck me.*

My pulse ticks faster, and I can't help but bite my cheek. Infringe some kind of pain in order to snap me out of her spell and keep my feet planted in place. She's forward, aggressive, and gives zero fucks about what anyone has to say to or about her. Fearless and confident, the perfect combination. I rub my thumb across my upper lip. And swallow. Tasting a bit of copper from biting too hard.

The lighting in the room is dim, but it doesn't matter. Her swollen pussy is completely bare, visibly wet, and less than ten feet away. I wasn't built for this level of discipline, to withstand her words and body inviting me to do my best, or perhaps my worst. Honestly, I don't know anyone who could resist this. She sits patiently, tilts her head to the side, sizing up my next move, and runs her tongue along her bottom lip.

"It's not going to lick itself, Henry," she says.

And that's all it takes for me to snap. My cock hears her loud and clear. Too ready to be pulled off the bench and into a warmer, wetter place that looks exactly like the gorgeous cunt in front of me.

Any commonsense or reserve I had about this situation with her is fucking dust in the wind, and in five quick strides, I make my way across the room. With intent, I drop to my knees in front of her and wrap my hands under her thighs.

An audible gasp escapes her. I don't think she actually expected me to break.

I jerk her closer to the edge of the chair, tilting her ass upwards. My mouth hovers centimeters above her pussy, and it's taking everything I've ever held in the way of willpower not to dive in face first and devour the ever-living hell out of her. She pushed me too far and now I need a taste. It's no longer a want, but an actual need. The smell of her makes my mouth water. Everything about her screams irresistible right now, the crease of her hip, the pathway from her thighs to the curve of her pussy lips. All of it smooth, warm, and waiting for attention.

"Holy fuck," she groans out. Her breath is ragged.

I pull my eyes away from what I so desperately want in every way possible and look into hers. The woman is beautiful. In a class entirely her own when it comes to sex appeal, but there's something gut-wrenchingly perverse and glorious about her being dominated in this moment. I savor the sight and commit it to memory. The problem with savoring is that it can allow reality to creep back in, along with a bit of self-control. I know that this moment starts and ends here. It's going to destroy me, but I don't see any other way.

Her sultry voice rasps out my name. "Henry."

That does it. I'm fucking human, after all, and the woman I've searched for, craved, and thought was no longer a possibility, is literally in my grasp, legs open, dripping with arousal for me.

Just one taste.

I jerk her up higher, stick out my tongue wide and flat, and begin a savoring drag at the start of her ass crack, up through her slit, finally tasting the excitement spilling out of her. But instead of stopping, my tongue stays flat and moves slow enough to part the lips of her pussy so I can lap up the excitement that's coating her. There's nothing more delicious than the taste of this woman. When I finally reach her clit and pulse my tongue slightly, it gives her the tiniest jolt of pleasure. And she moans. Sounding equally turned on and frustrated. Before I pull away from her completely, I move my mouth back, flick her clit with my tongue once, twice, three times, and then suck on it. Just for a beat. Just long enough to drag out one last tiny moan. Then I pull back and lick my bottom lip, tasting the salty sweetness.

"I won't cause you any trouble. Don't go looking for it," I say as I lean away. I don't wipe my mouth. I leave the remaining taste of her on my upper lip and chin. Smeared on the scruff that's grown out. I drag my thumb through her slowly, giving myself a moment to settle down and feel the slick that I've just spread so well. Back and forth, lightening the pressure as I graze her clit over and over.

Breathless, she stutters, "Wh-what?"

She meets my gaze. "First, I have no intention of getting you out of my system. So don't fucking say that to me again. And second, you taste even better than I imagined. And, Pixie, I've got a great imagination. Now close your fucking legs and stay out of trouble."

I back away, placing her thighs that I've had in my hands back down onto the chair. She stares at me and only blinks. Speechless, or maybe pissed off. Perhaps both, but I'm not about to stay and test any more wills this evening.

When I turn back around, I'm met with a glare that could set lesser men sterile. Instead of moving or feeling any type of modesty, she sits there, legs still wide open, and watches me as I get up to leave. I adjust my angry cock, take a massive breath, and without another word, I walk out the door.

That's the end of it. I'll watch her from a distance. I won't allow myself moments alone where I know I won't have the ability to keep my hands off, smell her, or taste her again. I remind myself that it's for her. That this woman, who is probably one of the most incredible I've ever met, can live the new life that she's started. And I can make sure she's safe. I won't let her downgrade what's between us by making it just about sex, because for me, it will always mean more.

I'll pretend like tonight never happened, just like our night in the bar. If I can see her, watch her, make sure she's looked after, then that'll have to be enough.

CHAPTER 17

Henry

"You're a stubborn shit!" I yell toward my youngest brother as we take the sharp turn. The wind whips at my face. The cold slicing the small openings of my mask and where my snow glasses won't cover. I feel my body chill at the memory. Every other inch of me is protected from the weather. I take the left trail, knowing that there's no way Law would take the right. Michael would, since he's more experienced out here, but he's not careless like Law.

I follow the fresh tracks, and that's when I see him off to my right, up ahead. I push harder; there's no way I'm going to lose this bet with my seventeen-year-old kid brother. The snow started falling harder, close to white-out conditions, but we know this trail.

The bet was simple; whoever made it to the bottom first gets to ask out Shelley Farley. She's been flirting with me for years, as we went to school together, but it wasn't until this winter home for the holidays that I really noticed her. She's *my age, but Law has it in his mind that she'll say yes if he asks her out. I'll give it to the kid. He has balls, always has. When it comes to girls, he's never shy. I've been so focused for the past five years, it's been physically impossible for me to even look at a girl for more than a quick fuck when we were able to get off base.*

I think about the conversation that got us here. "You know who's looking really good lately is Shelley," I say as we sit in my dad's movie theater room, talking to my brothers and sister.

"No fucking way. Dibs," Law says back to me as he throws popcorn in the air to catch with his mouth, missing most of it.

I look at Michael, and then at Everly, like I've missed something. "What do you mean, dibs? You can't call dibs on a girl."

"I can. And I just did. Dibs. I'm asking her out," he says.

"That's not... Dude, c'mon. I'm home for like two more weeks. I want to take her out. See if there's something there," I tell him.

I graduated from the Air Force Academy last spring, and it's taken every resource, handshake, and connection to get where I am. Not to mention, the hard work and long hours of flight time. I went through five and a half grueling months of SOFREP in Nevada. The Air Force Weapons School is only meant for the best. Altitude chamber training, simulations, and even the academy itself were easy in comparison to the last handful of months. This is why, if you make it, then you're respected, elite, untouchable. I earned my patch, and I wear it proudly. I'm the best. It's that simple. And now I want a couple of weeks to sink into a hot woman before I have to go back to base.

"I'll race you for her," he suggests.

"No."

"Fine, then dibs," he says, while popping a handful of popcorn into his obnoxious mouth. "I'm just sayin', she's going to want to go with the younger one that doesn't have to lie about where he is and ask permission to wipe his own ass."

"What the fuck does that mean, you prick?"

"Just means you're military. You need permission to do everything. Like right now, I called dibs, and you're actually backing off. Jesus, when did you get like this, Hen?"

Those few words have me fuming. My temper is one thing that I work to keep under my belt. I have to when I'm playing my role as a pilot, but especially here, because with my siblings, that's not who I want to be. I'll do my best never to let that part of me show.

"Fine. Let's go," I tell him as I walk toward the garage of our family ranch. "Down the black diamond on the ridge side. Whoever makes it to the Sugar Shack first gets a crack at Shelley." Even as I'm saying it, I cringe at the idea of wagering over a woman. But fuck, it's been a minute since I've been around a woman I found attractive. And she's pretty spectacular. Long red hair. Legs for days. Worth it.

I jerk awake. Cold sweat covers my torso up to the hair that's grown a bit longer, hitting the back of my neck. I shuffle to the bathroom and lean over the sink, staring in the mirror. Still angry. Frustrated. The reflection that stares back reminds me of my stupid, careless choices. And that I still haven't outgrown them. What was I thinking last night?

I touch the scar above my lip. A reminder of what a choice can leave behind.

Along with an icy-blue imperfection in my eye that made all of my hard work obsolete.

I tell myself to be thankful I still have it. That I can see out of it, even if it's not at perfect capacity. But it doesn't change the part where I'm still resentful.

I wake up with this memory often enough that I could never forget what a few stupid decisions meant for the trajectory of my life. Doctors were able to correct my vision enough so I could still pilot privately, but it wasn't possible to correct the damage enough to be in the Air Force the way I was trained to be. A fighter pilot who wore the Special Weapons patch with pride. Now it sits in a case like a trophy. A memory, not in use. I still wince at the failure of not being able to serve. To have been trained well, only to be benched. I knew the moment it happened. The sound. The pain that came screeching in. Almost as loud as Law screaming in my face.

"There's so much blood. Holy fuck! Henry, be okay. Please, please, be okay," he shouted in my face. But I wasn't okay. I was in surgery for hours. The broken femur was the longest recovery time, but the shard of sunglasses that protruded from my eye is what cost me the most. It cost me my career. What I considered my life's work. My identity. Gone.

A loud *thwap* on the bathroom door knocks me back out of the memories. Out of the self-loathing I've become so good at dishing out in palatable portions. Enough to remind me that I had something I worked my ass off for once. And then fucked it up, over a woman and a bet. Stupid. I couldn't be stupid like that again. And last night, I was.

"Hen, we're leaving in ten minutes. You almost ready?" Michael yells from outside my bedroom door. "Law and Dad are in the truck. I need to grab some of the gear I stored in your garage."

"Yeah, no problem. Be there in a minute," I yell back. I splash water on my face and try to change the course of my thoughts. What I'm doing now is challenging. I'm good at it. It helps my family. We're building our legacy, and I can make parts of it my own. I've already started. *"Find something you love to do that has nothing to do with what you did before. Start there and see where it takes you."*

An hour later, and we've managed to discuss and outline the blueprint plans for our newest business asset. The indoor facility for Riggs Outdoor. It's a concept that's been a bit of a passion project of Michael's. He's wanted some kind of climbing facility to utilize during the off-season without having to drive an hour to the nearest one.

"There's enough space here for exactly what you described, Michael. And honestly, I think we can do even more. There's no reason why this couldn't be an indoor space for all types of athletes who are looking to train in their personal off season," my dad says.

"What about your buddy Mac?" Law says, looking toward Michael.

"What about him?" I snap back, still buzzing with animosity that didn't leave me after I woke up and showered.

"Jesus, what's got your panties all bunched today?" he barks back with a laugh. But he's right, I've been short with him all morning. Between the way I watched him come onto G at the hot springs. And then the fresh reminder of his role in my accident, thanks to last night's dream. The truth is, as much as I beat myself up about my choice in that stupid bet, he was there. I blame him too.

"I was just thinking that maybe he'd be into working with us. Upgrade his MMA gym space. There's more than enough room here, don't you think?" He looks around, and I follow his line of vision. "And it'll bring in a new crowd. There's an element of wanting to try new things if you can actually see them." He shrugs his shoulder.

"Us? Thought you were going to,"—I put my fingers in air quotes—"'Don Draper *the shit* out of the advertising world' or whatever company was dumb enough to hire you."

"You know what, Henry? Fuck off." He knocks my shoulder as he walks by me.

"Watch it," I yell back, pointing my finger in his direction.

"Or what, huh? You going to do something about it or just continue to treat me like I'm stupid, or keep pretending like I barely exist?"

"You said it, not me," I say.

I see my dad coming over to where we're squared off at each other. "Both of you. That's enough."

Law ignores him and moves closer. Chest puffed out and ready to say something I'm sure he's been working on for a while. My pulse ticks up, and I'm not in the mood to hold back today. There's no filter or deep breath I'm willing to put into effect.

"You fucking blame me for everything. EVERY-

THING," he shouts. "I've had enough of you talking to me like I'm some kind of joke all the time."

"You are a fucking joke," I yell back. I point my finger at his chest, and he swats it away. Michael comes up next to me, readying to interject if he needs to. I watch as Law's eyes well up with tears. Any other day, and I would back down from this, but for some reason today, I want to make him feel like shit. I need to pass it off to someone else for a change. And he's my target.

"Henry, that's enough, man," Michael says in a low tone next to me.

"No way. He's a big boy now, he can hear it. Isn't that right, Law? You want to play at the big boy table, then here it is. You never take anything seriously. Everything is a game or a joke to you. But guess what? I don't think you're funny. I don't think it's fucking funny that you're the reason that I was forced to retire from a career I barely even started." My dad moves to hold him back from getting any closer to me. "Everyone coddled you when that accident happened, but the truth is, it's your fucking fault that I lost my vision. I didn't crash into myself on that mountain. I didn't jam a fucking shard of my sunglasses into my own eye." I breathe out heavily through my nose, nostrils flaring. "Nope. That was all you, brother."

But I'm not done. There's so much negative energy vibrating through me right now and he poked the bear. He's going to hear all of it.

"And now you want to be a part of this, but only as an idea man, right?" I huff a sarcastic laugh. "You're not willing to do the work. You want to coast in, sprinkle in your bullshit, and then leave to go live your own life. Well, newsflash, you may be a part of this family, but you're not a part of the business. And if it were up to me, you wouldn't step a single toe into it, because I have no interest in doing all the work and then you show up just to destroy it. Because that's what you do, baby brother, you fuck things up and everyone thinks, 'Oh, that's just Law.' Well, not this time. You don't get a pass here. You don't get a say here."

Law jerks his arm out of my dad's grip, pushes at my chest, and whispers, "Fuck you." Then he storms out of the empty warehouse.

"Asshole," Michael says in my face and then moves to go after him.

I look over at my dad. His disappointing glare cuts me at the knee. "If that was your version of therapy, then shame on you. That accident is as much your fault as it is his. He didn't deserve that. He goes back to school in a few weeks to finish out his semester. He doesn't need to feel shitty at the end of his college career. Find a way to fix this before then."

I ignore all of it. Fuck that. I need to get away from this, and out of here for a while.

CHAPTER 18

Giselle

"Deputy, I promise, the glitter was purely meant to be fun. Not an assault by any stretch." I give the old bat in front of me the evilest eye I can muster.

"I still want to press charges," Ruth DeMaio says without even letting me finish.

I came outside to start my day with some fresh air and a glimpse up at the blue sky that was nothing short of perfection this morning. I'm still shook by what I'd like to refer to as "The Lick-Luster incident." That man's tongue with just one swipe has done things to my body and imagination that I didn't even know were possible. Even now, just thinking about his slow glide, I'm feeling fuzzy and slick. But it was cut short, the damn tease, and my lady bits might revolt. I can't even think about why he said he wouldn't do anything more with me.

My cleansing breath is now feeling hot and suffocating. The screech of a whiny voice starts yammering in my ear. Now, that early morning refresher feels like I'm swallowing a mouthful of hot garbage because this Ruth DeMaio lady is insistent on getting in my face today. *She really did need a pinch of glitter that night.*

"Ruth," the hot-ass deputy who waltzed up to my shop with her says, with a twinge of annoyance. "It's been a number of days since this occurred. There was no physical damage, and I can't find a single witness that is willing to say anything against Miss Heart."

"Please, call me Giselle, or G." I smile widely.

"It's a waste of breath. He won't be interested, ya floozy," Ruth chimes in.

"You know what lady," I shout back.

Before I can unleash on her, the deputy pipes in and squashes the possible disaster that knocked on my door. That's all I need, someone pressing charges; WITSEC will relocate me in a heartbeat. "Ruth, that's enough. You're not pressing charges. Giselle, please apologize, and then we can all move on with our day."

I watch as Everly approaches this shitshow happening in front of my shop. "Callen, what's going on?"

"Hey, Ev, it's Deputy Muldowney at the moment."

She nods and then looks wide-eyed at me, as if I've done something wrong.

"Ruth, is everything okay?" she asks.

You have to love small towns where everyone is a part of everyone else's business. In this case, I kind of love that my new bestie, also my accomplice, is about to play nice with the bitch-face plaintiff.

"Oh, for Christ's sake. You were there too. That's it, just, just," she stutters and waves her arms at me. "I still have glitter in my hair and I'm not the kind of woman to wear glitter. Keep yourself in check in this town, missy. It's not some trashy place like you're used to," she bites out.

This woman really messed with the wrong person today.

"Yeah? What kind of place is that, queen? Tell me, because I'd love to hear how you're about to marginalize me because of my appearance or attitude. Please dish out for me all the ways that you feel superior right now, when all you're doing is making yourself appear small and intimidated. People like you in small towns do not scare me. You empower me to prove your presumptuous, close-minded ass wrong."

As much as I want to tell her to go gnaw on a bag of dicks, I won't. The police officer and Everly don't need to see me with the gloves off.

Of course now, the police officer, the loudmouth, and the new girl have attracted an audience. All of my business neighbors are out front, busying themselves with some sort of outdoor task so they can spy on what's happening.

"Muldowney, you're not getting my vote for Sheriff when it comes time. So don't count on it." She turns sharply on her croc-clad feet and speed walks back to whatever crack from hell she scurried out of.

"Not a problem, ma'am," the deputy responds back.

Everly's biting her lip, trying her best not to burst out laughing. I can't look at her, or I will too. This entire situation, all because of glitter. Granted, I shouldn't have thrown it, but involving the police seems a bit overboard.

I also know, for a fact, that woman voted at the last town council meeting to push out the tattoo shop in favor of a chain bookstore. She was unanimously outnumbered. One thing small towns tend to hate more than outsiders is chain brands putting small businesses out of business.

"Ladies." The officer smiles a devastatingly charming smile and says, "I'm going to provide you both with a verbal warning." He bites back a laugh. "Tread lightly with Ruth. She's grouchy, but there's no universe where sprinkling glitter on her was a good idea."

"Callen, totally my fault. G is new, and I should have stopped the situation," she flirts back. "Now that we got that out of the way, you coming over for dinner on Sunday? It's been a minute since you were there."

"Can't this week. I'm on duty, but the next Sunday I'm off, I'll be there."

"Deal. Tell your Dad I said hi," she says.

He clears his throat and smiles. "Yours too." He puts his hat back on his head and slides aviators back on. Anyone within a visible distance likely salivated at the sight, because holy smokeshow. "G, pleasure meeting you. Stay out of trouble."

"I can't make promises, officer. But nice meeting you too."

Everly and I stand shoulder to shoulder, watching Deputy Callen Muldowney back out of his parking spot. As soon as he pulls down the road, she says, "I have been friends with that man for the majority of my life and I'm still awestruck at the level of handsome he turned into."

"It's the whole package. The face. That ass. I mean, he

has handcuffs." I laugh. "Why haven't you ever, you know, with him?"

She smiles. "Oh believe me, I've tried." I give her a curious eye. And it clicks before she can say it.

"Let me guess, he's more attracted to your brothers than you?"

"Spot on. Though, I doubt he'd look at my brothers like anything more. We all grew up as a big family. His Dad and mine have business investments together. We did holidays, birthdays together, the whole nine. But yeah, Callen is damn fine." We start walking toward my shop door as she adds, "And he's a good man. I wouldn't be surprised if he ends up Sherriff, when the current one is ready to retire."

CHAPTER 19

Henry

THE SMELL OF SOMETHING BURNING IN THE OVEN GREETS me as soon as I open the front door to my dad's house. No smoke, just the nose-pinching stench of someone who fucked up dinner. It was my fault for getting in later than I expected. I always cook, but I needed a breather. So, I got out of dodge to pull my shit together. Hopped on a plane and flew where I needed. It's not the first time, hell, not even the fifth time, I've flown myself to New York City. The part about this trip that didn't make sense, though, is that I went there to forget what happened with G. To scrub her taste from my tongue and the vision of her laid out like a meal, from my mind. Every other time that I've traveled to that city, I was always trying to think about her, remember details, play back the conversation. The dichotomy of the situation is exhausting to rationalize.

So now, I'm eager to see my family, even if they might

not be too thrilled to see me. Aside from dinner, I'm here to apologize. It's long overdue.

"Dude, you look like shit," Law yells my way as I step through the back door. Dick.

"You burn dinner?" I reply.

He laughs. "Nope. That'd be Giselle."

I hadn't thought that she would be here.

"She convinced Dad to go meatless tonight and said she'd cook since you weren't coming." He lowers his voice. "I'm going to be honest here; I think it looks better charred. I still have no idea what it was. So, we ordered instead."

I still don't know what to say to my brother, but I need to start somewhere. I don't want a lifetime with him that's filled with anger and resentment. I've seen what that can do to families.

"Can we talk later?"

His eyebrows shoot up, so clearly, he wasn't expecting it. And the surprise on his face guts me a bit. I've been punishing him and pushing him away because of our accident for way too long. He smiles and nods as I follow him into the main room.

"Ab-so-fucking-lutely not. There are few places I refuse to tattoo. I mean, not many, but an asshole is one of them," Giselle says, hands flying as she speaks to Everly.

"G baby, I thought most women loved assholes." Law laughs and looks around at Michael and Everly, thinking they're going to tag into his joke.

And without so much as a breath, G responds to him

by saying, "I prefer nice boys, but if you think that's true, then just ask your brother. He must know."

I stifle a laugh and try my hardest not to smirk, but it creeps out. She slung that dig pretty well.

"Gettin' all those girls, huh, Hanky?"

And they're both right. Women do like assholes. At least in my experience. I was moody as fuck on my last trip and had plenty of women I could have taken back to the hotel with me. Fuck them the way I'd like to fuck her and maybe feel less keyed up. But I wasn't interested in any of them. My mind was elsewhere. Still trying to forget the way G's thighs felt in my hands. How she squeaked and trembled when my tongue finally touched, tickled, and tasted her pussy. That taste I can't seem to stop thinking about. The need of wanting to savor it again knocks into me as I look her up and down.

"You tell me, Jizz?"

The look on her face is priceless. A mix of shock and a smirk she can't fight. "Oh, *fuck no.*" She shakes her head and points her finger at me. "That is not a nickname. And you'd better cover your jewels and ears if I ever hear it again, Hanky."

While everyone around us starts laughing, I mouth out the word "an-y-thing" to her, mimicking her phrase from the night at her loft.

She narrows her eyes, giving me a placating, tightlipped smile. "As far as assholes, I refuse to tattoo you, Hanky. So"—she shrugs her shoulders—"case and point. I refuse to tattoo assholes." She takes a sip of her drink and winks at me.

"I hear you cooked. Smells like it too."

She stares back at me. I can see the annoyance all over her face, practically radiating from her body.

"You've never had my cooking, so shut it. You're not a professional, sweetheart."

"You really showed us this time, huh?" I laugh out. "I never hear you complain that I'm hogging the kitchen when you're getting a custom dish every Sunday." I lift a brow, and she rolls her eyes.

"Did I hear you brought a German Chocolate cake?" Michael asks as he joins us at the dining table.

G's brow furrows as she says, "Fucking show off," under her breath.

I laugh.

"It's so good," Michael says.

"I always ask him to make German chocolate cake for my birthday," Law pipes in. "Usually, he tells me to fuck off, but then I get one anyway. It's been a few years." He looks at me, and I know how long I've carried on about our accident. I feel like a shithead all over again. "I can't wait to eat a slice from the one you brought tonight."

"His desserts are even better than his main dishes," Law tells G, as if she hasn't been eating what I've been cooking lately.

"Totally disagree. I love those brownies he makes, but it's always the grits that get me," Everly chimes in. I look over at G, remembering something I said to her years ago about "telling her something good."

"You really should have been a chef. You missed your calling, man," Law says over a bite of pizza.

They say this to me at least once a month, but I never thought of cooking or baking in that way. It's always been an anchor for me. A way to focus on something and get out of my head. To play with flavors, try new ways to cook things that are familiar, and share it with the people I care about most.

Michael pulls me out of my thoughts when he asks, "Where'd you disappear to, by the way? I thought you were going to talk to Mac about the gym space. When I mentioned it, he had no idea what I was talking about."

He takes out two heaping scoops of salad, and then starts separating the vegetables.

"You going to eat those olives?" I ask.

"You know I'm not. They're all yours," he says. His eyes search mine for a response to his question.

"You pitch him the idea?" I ask.

"Well, yeah. I couldn't just stand there and not get into it after I asked."

"And?" I say back to him.

Michael shifts uncomfortably, straightens out his cutlery so that each side has the balanced number of items. He pushes his glass forward, so it's set properly, and then rotates his plate, so the design is dead center to where he's seated. "He likes it. Wants to talk numbers a bit more, but he was into the idea."

I give him a smile and clap him on the back. "You didn't need me. Let's talk numbers with him tomorrow."

Michael smiles. The nerves gone, anxiety quelled for the moment, and he's proud of himself. As he should be. He sells himself short, but he's a damn fine businessman in addition to the outdoor sports guy he's known around town as. The climber. The guy who can scale rock walls like he's some kind of superhero.

"New York," I say quietly to him.

"You were in New York?" Everly pipes in from across the table.

G's eyes dart over to mine. Curiously.

I look back to my sister. "It's not what you think. I just needed to stop in and tie up a few loose ends."

The problem is, I really don't know why I went there this time. It's on autopilot in my brain to go there as an escape.

Everly eyes me, knowing that whenever I went to Manhattan, it was to search. Ask questions and find out more about what happened. It always led to dead ends, the same conclusion that I just couldn't let lie. That the woman I met that night was dead. And now, as I look at her sitting across the table, quietly questioning my motives for going to her city, I realize they were right. That woman is gone, but the woman across from me is alive. Safe. And I need to help make sure she stays that way.

"I hear New York is nicer in the wintertime. All that snow and hoopla at Rockefeller," G pipes in over a mouthful of cheese pizza. "A total spectacle, but stunning nonetheless."

What is she doing?

"Winter here is better. But I like the late summers in that city. That time of year holds some good memories for me," I say.

She takes a sip of her water. "Hmm. You're definitely more of a mountain guy than a city boy. You must stand out like a sore thumb. All those suits and polished men," she says, poking and trying to get under my skin. It's not working, but it's amusing to watch her try. "Men like that are punctual and never leave anyone high and dry." The dig has me coughing on my sip of beer.

But I can play too. "Polished is nice, but I prefer to leave them sprawled and wet," I say back without even thinking about who else is around us.

My dad barks out a laugh. Michael stares at me mid-bite. Law cups his hand and makes a hooting noise.

"Why is this so much fun to watch?" Law looks at Everly, shaking his head. "Ev, why are they so entertaining? I feel like I'm intruding, but I can't look away."

I take a bite of my bacon pizza and just stare back at G. She's pissed. But I'm ready to take whatever she wants to dish out. I'm half hard thinking about her lashing out at me.

"Nothing to look at, just a tiny little ego trying to keep up with big clit energy."

Everly laughs around her mouthful of food as Giselle levels me with a sarcastically laced smile. "I need to head out. I have a bachelorette party coming through in about an hour to get matching ink. Should be fun." She moves toward my dad's chair and kisses his cheek. "Thanks for dinner, Ash. I'm sorry I ruined the casserole."

"All good. Try again soon?"

She nods sweetly, then goes over to Law's chair and sits on his lap sideways, whispers something in his ear, and they both laugh. She looks back at me when she gets up and then flips me off. "Be careful, please, and call me after," Everly says as they hug.

"I'll text you. I think this bunch of girls are going to be wild. I might tag on and see what kind of trouble I can get into with them." She winks at Everly, and the idea of her getting into trouble makes me uneasy. Trouble for her, I'm learning, can be anywhere from blowing glitter in people's faces to dancing on bars. I don't want to think about what she'll want to do or who she'll find to finish the job I started.

She says goodbye to everyone but me. The fact that I'm the only one who knows her for real. The only person who deserves a goodbye is skipped over. My neck is hot, hands feeling jittery, and I'm doing my best not to over-analyze the type of trouble she's on a mission to find later.

I realize I've been staring at the door she just walked through for longer than normal. My dad clears his throat to gain my attention. "You doing okay, son?"

I nod.

"Any luck in New York? Find anything new?" he asks, knowing the whole story. They all do. It wasn't something I could or even wanted to hide.

"It's done. I won't be going back," I say.

And that's enough to get everyone to stop their moving. Everly cleaning her plate, Michael standing to help. But I'm not interested in talking about it anymore.

"How about some cake and Setback?" I ask, looking at Law. Then to Michael and Everly. It's my olive branch, and really, I think I need the time with them as much as I need to make sure Law knows I don't hate him.

"Yeah," Law breathes out. "I'm in."

"You guys really want to try to beat me again? I was barely trying the last time, and I schooled you," Michael asks as he shuffles the deck. The smirk on his face is the signal that the shit-talking can commence.

"I'll agree with Michael. It was pretty embarrassing, if you ask me," Dad chimes in from the kitchen.

"Nobody asked you, Dad," Law belts back.

Everly points at Michael and yells, "We wanted to forfeit! We were all dying! You kept farting, and none of us could breathe."

"That was Henry's fault! He made those roasted chestnuts. How was I supposed to know it was going to ruin my stomach like that? Ended up working in my favor."

"Dad, you joining?"

He shakes his head while he pulls on his coat. "Not tonight. I'm going to check on the horses, maybe go for a ride."

"Love you, Daddy," Everly yells.

"Love you too, pumpkin." He gives me a look at the door. A knowing nod that I'm planning to set things right. My grudge has gone on long enough.

I clear my throat. I don't care that Michael and Everly are going to hear this, because they've witnessed all of it and deserve to hear it too.

"I'm sorry." That's the best way to start. Law's smile falls away slowly, and his eyes tear up immediately. "I've been punishing you for something that you didn't deserve. I don't have to tell any of you how much leaving the Air Force affected me. But I put all my anger on you." I keep my eyes on my baby brother. "And that wasn't fair. It wasn't right. And I'm still doing it."

Law's voice breaks when he says, "Hen, I'm still so

sorry. I fucking hate myself for being involved in any part of you losing somethin' you worked so hard for."

"And I'm telling you, I forgive you. But it was an accident. I know that. And I had no business making you feel like you should hate yourself for it. You don't deserve that, either. And this is me telling you that it's done."

Law wipes tears before they have a chance to fall, blowing out an exaggerated breath. I get up from the table and give him a hug. One that's years overdue. I know it's not an instant fix, but it's a start. We hold on a bit longer, an extra couple of back slaps, too. He mumbles, "Love you, Hen."

"You too, man."

When we break apart, I find both Michael and Everly smiling. I give them a nod.

"Alright, suckers." Law claps his hands. "Who's ready to lose?"

Three hours, two games of Setback, and one entire German chocolate cake later, and I find myself sitting in my truck across the street from Hideaway Ink. I don't know what I'm doing here, but I needed to be sure she was okay. And if I'm being honest, I didn't want her finding her version of trouble with someone else. So here I am, watching from my front seat, across the street, and through the front window of her shop. I watch as a group of five women laugh and talk with their hands as G works her tattoo pen across the lower back of the sixth.

Tap, tap, tap.

The sound startles me, and I'm met with a scowling Agent Bea Harper at my driver's side window.

"The fuck you doing here, Riggs?" She doesn't mince words and cuts right to it.

"Just what you've asked me to do. Keeping an eye out."

"Bullshit. She's working right now. Leave it alone," she says, and then turns away from my truck.

I move fast out of the driver's seat and slam the door behind me. Four paces catch me up to her. "What's that supposed to mean?"

She huffs and glances at me over her shoulder. "Exactly what I said, Riggs. You are to keep an eye out for suspicious interest. You have a list of names and faces you are being paid to be aware of and alert me. ME," she shouts in my face. "If they pass through Strutt's. That's all."

We both stop walking and continue the conversation around the corner of Main Street and out of eyesight or earshot. We are only meant to be acquaintances. She's posed as Giselle's Aunt Bea. And I am only supposed to know her that way, not as civilian support for WITSEC.

"Listen, Riggs." She lights a clove cigarette and takes a pull. "You think you know her, but you don't. The woman has been through hell and back. She doesn't need a reminder of her life before. So, leave it alone."

I bow my head. I don't know what the fuck I'm doing here either. I know better.

"Now, do yourself a favor and stop. Keep this agreement we have working, got it? I don't want messy. I don't want to be called because someone can tie her to you.

Maybe it doesn't happen now, but you start something, then it snowballs, and she's recognized by the parties we're trying to keep her hidden from. Then, it'll be a problem. For everyone in this town. I need you to be responsible here, or I relocate her."

I nod again. She stalks off after giving me a warning look.

"See ya around, Harper." I walk away, pissed off at myself for even being here. And then being called out on it. Pissed off at the authority that's calling the shots in my life. Her life. I left town to clear my head, sort out the lines I need to stop myself from crossing with G, and then all it takes to undo it is her talking about finding trouble. The jealousy that ran through me the moment I thought "trouble" meant fucking around with someone other than me. Maybe she should be relocated. But as soon as I think it, I turn the corner and catch a glimpse of her smiling in the shop.

"If life were a little different, maybe I would have been a tattoo artist..." She got her do-over, even if she never wanted it.

It's impossible not to watch her talk passionately. She makes people laugh and feel good about themselves. She's a natural at being unforgettable. She looks like she may have found some happiness again.

"Are you fucking serrrrrrrriouss?"

"He better not be at that strip club with my brother. I'm gonna kill him," the drunk dressed like a bride slurs outside of the tattoo shop. A second woman consoles her by taking selfies and saying something like, "It's just tits... who cares if he sees other women's boobs."

"I love how this came out. She completely covered the initials. You can't see any of it." Two more women chat and admire the work Giselle has just finished. "Are we waiting for Eliza, or is she meeting us at the bar?"

One of them says, "She's staying behind. She wanted a piercing too."

I wait a few minutes for them to collect themselves. An older couple who just came from the diner on the corner passes by before I walk closer to the shop.

As I look through the window, I see Giselle speaking closely with another woman with long black hair. Their body language seems flirtatious. Small touches that have nothing to do with tattoos or piercings. It stirs something within me. Seeing her with someone that way makes me anxious. That's my cue to leave or find my own distraction. But I don't leave. My feet stay planted.

I watch Giselle throw her head back in a loud laugh that I can hear through the glass. I smile in response. It's a knee-jerk reaction when I hear the way she giggles or barks out a sarcastic laugh. When she stands up to walk around the chair that she uses for piercings, she sees me.

I can tell by the way her footing stutters that she wasn't expecting to see me outside the window, like a fucking creeper. I watch her and it's something I can't seem to stop—agreement or not.

She smiles and looks down, shaking her head, silently saying, "Of course you're here."

Moving back to the chair, she continues to talk with the dark-haired woman. She takes her time setting up her station with what she needs. Moments later, G pierces the woman's septum. She hands the woman a mirror and stands in front of her, blocking me from view. Giselle leans forward and whispers something into the woman's ear. I can't see the response, but I can read people and situations very well. And I know that I'm a minute away from seeing something that'll piss me off. I know when to tap out. Seeing her with someone else isn't going to put my head right.

I make up my mind to leave. Already thinking about what, or who, I can do to tamp this feeling I get every time I see her with someone else. But just as I do, G turns and walks to her front door. She looks me in the eye the whole way there. I don't move from the left corner of the window, her gaze pinning me in place. She keeps her eyes on mine and turns the lock. The sound of the click is enough to let me know I've worn out my voyeuristic stay.

She moves to close the black velvet curtains. I turn away, but a tap at the glass makes me turn back. She mouths, "Wanna watch?"

The right side of her mouth tips up, giving me the fastest snapshot of a smirk. But before she turns around, she bites her lip and looks at me with her big brown eyes. Silently asking again. Then she turns back to the woman in the chair.

What the fuck do I do with that? I'm not about to play into this situation. She's a smart woman, and she's either trying to piss me off or make me break. I won't fuck her, so she's going to make it as uncomfortable as possible. There's no way I could watch her with someone else. I want her. Plain and simple, but I can't have her. So now it's time I leave. Put distance between temptation and a selfish decision.

I rake my hands through my hair and lean against the chilled brick wall that connects Hideaway Ink from the vacant storefront next door.

A moment later, I hear a large slam and crash. The clanking of metal hitting the floor and wall. Without thinking, I'm sprinting around the back of the building. I manage to tweak my ankle on something as I cut the turn to the door. I turn the handle, but I'm met with silence. I see a tray of her equipment on the floor, knocked over. No sounds. The quiet is almost deafening.

Instead of calling out for her, I move down the short hallway. I take a deep pull of air from my nose to calm my nerves and push out a breath. I pull the knife tucked above my boot, strapped to my calf. I can see the front of the shop from where I stand, only the dim counter lights illuminated. To my left is the bathroom, and it's vacant. Up to the right is a large room for storage that G also uses as her office. There's no door, so as I approach, I can hear muffled voices, and the moving of a chair.

"I can't believe you've never been," a woman's voice says.

"Never. But I love beignets," Giselle says.

"You taste like them. Sugar and something else. I can't place it. But your lips are so sweet."

Are you fucking kidding me right now? I'm worried she's in harm's way and they're talking about desserts, and kissing. Part of me wants to say it's lemons. Lemons and sugar are what she tastes like. But I don't want anyone else to know that. To experience her mouth like I have.

G speaks up. "There's a huge fair I used to go to every

September, and the beignets were my favorite thing to have when we went."

"New Orleans is really the only place you can get a true beignet. My brother has a place down there," the woman hesitates, pausing before continuing. "You could meet me down there sometime. It might be fun."

I peek around the corner now that there's a lull in the conversation. Giselle sits on top of her desk as the woman with the long dark hair stands in front of her. Close. So close that my body tenses. I rub my palm down my thigh to wipe the sweat and grip the knife in case I need to move quickly, eyeing the door I came through. I know she's seen people. Slept with them. It's been three years. She's made it known that she likes men and women. Hell, I'm sure she's had relationships here and there, but I've never witnessed it up close. Now I'm experiencing a small twinge of how she felt, seeing me with Denise. If roles were reversed, I would have spiraled. But then again, maybe it didn't faze her the way it would have me.

I watch Giselle roughly grab the person in front of her by the nape, lick her upper lip slowly, and then kiss along the column of her neck. So goddamn slowly. It's achingly sensual. I can hear my pulse in my ears. I'm keyed up with anger and slightly turned on, wishing it were me instead. Being licked by that mouth. Savored.

I'm frozen in place.

My mouth is dry. I have a sick feeling in the pit of my stomach. I've lost all ability to remain stoic. The jealousy is written all over my face. I'm sure of it. But before I can think to turn away, Giselle flicks her eyes open, looking right at me as she continues to devour the brunette's neck, pacing toward her collarbone. She snakes her legs around the other woman's ass, bringing her closer. She pulls her mouth back, eyes on me, without a flinch or sense of surprise. And smiles.

That fucking pixie smiles.

Like she knows exactly what she's doing right now, and it's equal parts cruel and eye-opening. It's as if a war has officially been declared. That sinking feeling of not knowing her at all; the woman I met or the romanticized version of her would have never done that, not this way. This wasn't meant to be playful; this was intended to sting. A figurative line in the sand. And maybe it was necessary. Maybe I wouldn't have been strong enough to do it. Hell, look at where I am right now and the anger swirling in my belly.

"You looking to join us, Henry?"

Her voice knocks me out of my internal tirade. The black-haired woman turns around fast and glances between me and Giselle. "Seriously?" she shouts. "Who the hell is that?" G hops off of her desk, wiping the corners of her mouth, as if she's just had a snack.

"This is Henry. Henry, this is," she pauses. I guarantee she knows this woman's name. She knew I'd come in if I thought she was in trouble. Despite not knowing I've been assigned as her backup, she knows the type of man I am. If she were in trouble, I would come.

"Eliza, my fucking name is Eliza. And I'm not interested in whatever this is all about," the woman says in a huff and rushes out of the room and out the door. If I wasn't as jealous as I am right now, I would have felt sorry for the girl.

Giselle pulls her hair back into a knot at the nape of her neck, turns to me, and says, "That was disappointing. Totally misread it." Nothing else. Just an aloof statement coated in nonchalance.

"Un-fucking-believable," I say under my breath. I turn away and walk toward the back door, slamming it wide open and stalking into the back alley.

"Oh, come on, Henry. Don't be like that. Why are you upset? You saw me in here with her. You knew what you were walking into when you chose to come through that door," she yells from behind me.

I hear her close the door and run up closer to me. "Are you mad because I was kissing her, or are you mad because you didn't have the balls to join in?"

I stop walking, and she catches up to me. Closing my eyes, I quickly try to sort out what I'm feeling and what I could possibly want to say to her. As I take a breath, I look at her. She's standing a foot away from me, studying my face, searching my eyes for some kind of response, so she knows how to play this right now. How much more she needs to poke to officially drive me away.

But instead, I walk right toward her. Forcing her to shuffle her feet backwards until she hits the brick wall. I crowd her. Breathe in close to her in a way that's primal. I want to smell her and remember it, because I know it's going to be the last time.

CHAPTER 20

Giselle

I CAN'T CATCH MY BREATH. I'M STRUGGLING NOT TO borrow it from him. Press my mouth to his and hope he can breathe the air I need into my lungs so I don't black out. The cold brick wall to my back is the only thing keeping me standing and alert. He's so close, my blood is pumping so fast I feel like I might pass out, because everything I'm going to say is a lie from here on out.

He looks at me with seriousness dancing across every feature and says, "We're adults. You're allowed to do whatever you want. With whomever you want. But keep me out of it. You want to fuck every tourist who rolls through here, do it. I don't want to see it. You wanted to fuck me out of your system and now you're acting like a child who didn't get her own way." It makes me flinch, because that's not what I really want.

I search his eyes for some sign of empathy. He has to know this isn't easy for me. I feel so much for him, but I can't do anything about it. I'm fucking paralyzed, being pulled between what I want, and what I can have. And I can't have him.

He leans forward, boxing me in between his arms. "I've never wanted anything as much as I want you. I've fucking tried to forget about you countless times. I did my best to move my life forward. You were gone, and I forced myself to move on, but"—he drags in air through his nose, something to ease the energy that's radiating off of him—"now you're here. And it's so fucking complicated."

How can he say this to me? I'm not prepared for these feelings he's so easily throwing. Leaning my head back against the brick, I steady myself for what I need to say. I look up at the dark blue, almost black sky to keep the tears from falling. I need to hold it together.

"This can't happen. I don't want..." I say as I struggle to keep my chin from shaking.

"Liar," he whispers back.

"Henry, you need to forget about what we were before," I whisper back. Anything louder, and I'll crumble.

He moves even closer. "I can't," he says as he pounds his fist against his chest, over the tattoo, over his heart. "It won't let me."

The air is punched out of me. Whatever remained in my lungs left with that confession. Tears streak down my face. There's no reason to try to hold them back anymore; the emotions that made them fall have swirled around so vigorously that keeping them away is impossible. But I can't fall apart right now. I keep my eyes trained on his, telling myself that falling anymore will only end in something I truly can't handle. I don't want to leave, but this dance we keep doing is only hurting us both.

I put my hands on his chest and push him away. I need space if I'm going to get through this. My only option is to push him away enough that the blurred lines of who we are and what we want from one another become crystal clear. We are only acquaintances, and the only way to remain there is for him to want nothing to do with me. To stop searching for the woman with the bright disposition and carefree, charming wit. To stop looking for the parts of me that are no longer the same. The thought makes my breath shudder. For him to stop. I hate it. But it has to happen.

His proximity is daunting. He's still too close. I want to snake my arms around his middle and hold on. I want the illusion of safety that he emanates to be a permanent fixture on my skin. But I'm not living a life of wants anymore, only one of survival, and some version of palatable contentment.

"Look at me," Henry says softly. His version of soft, at least. A gravelly whisper that manages to roll from my ears down my neck and arms. I can only stare at his chest. I bite back my emotions. Bristle at the tender feelings that linger and make this clear. That it's not going to happen for us. Tell him a lie. That I don't want him. Make him hear me.

He brushes his thumb below my chin, forcing me to raise my attention. "Look at me, Pixie."

When I finally do, he looks around my face. The pain in what I need to say to him is written all over it.

"Don't," he says.

But I ignore the request. "Too much connects us." He drops his hand, his fingers gone from my chin. But I continue through the longing that missing touch created. "Your sister. This town. Our past. I thought we could have a bit of fun and then call ourselves friends."

"So that's it. You want to be friends? How's that supposed to work?" he spits back at me, almost as if the idea of friendship is offensive. And maybe it is, after the words he just said to me. I hate this so much.

"You didn't let me finish." I tip my head back more, meeting his glare. And even now, as I try to harden myself to meet his energy, I'm so drawn to him that my hands and fingers feel the absence of touching him, only grasping at the empty air around me. I study the scar above his lip, the beauty of a green iris with a splash of blue, and the perpendicular lines on his brow that remind me of the hard shell he had on the first time I saw him.

I steady myself, push out my chest, and make myself bigger, because right now I need the illusion of the upper hand if I'm going to come out of this conversation without scars of my own.

"Friendship, I take seriously. I won't fake it with you, but I'm also not going anywhere if I can help it. I'm in this town, so I'll be spending time with Everly, and your family. You don't have to like it, but we have to navigate it. This gray territory we've been in won't work. Friends is apparently offensive to you, so how about enemies?"

He shuffles himself closer again. I keep eye contact. Those blues and greens are an aching combination of anger and defeat. His mouth inches so close to mine that

I can feel the pull. A stupid gravitational force that the universe somehow built between us. It almost hurts not to close the space, and he knows it. He waits, a breath away, to see if I'll break. And hell do I want to. But something in the way I'm quietly pleading with him to spare me here must register, because he leans in and brushes his lips on my forehead instead.

"Done," he says. Then he turns and walks away just as abruptly. I don't know what I was expecting, but it wasn't that.

I hate the position I'm in. I hate that I can't fall into the man I want. But that's the thing I've learned about hate. It can be redirected. It's a feeling that I've grown content with and, more so, I find it comforting. I know how to hate. I know how to dance around truths, and I'll learn how to hate the man I've held on to.

PART II

HATING HER

.

CHAPTER 21

Giselle

IT'S BEEN NINE YEARS. NINE YEARS SINCE I FIRST SET FOOT in Strutt's Peak. I sit in these downtown business meetings, practically breaking out in a sweat, trying to hold back from flipping off at least one person each week. The one who's talking right now is my least favorite in this town. I still sprinkle gold glitter on her whenever she's not looking. Typically, when she's sulking at the counter in the diner, it's the perfect time to walk by, drop a pinch, and sleep better at the fact that the crotchety-est of them all has a little bit of sparkle. I chalk it up to small-town boredom. Everly calls it instigating. Agree to disagree, I tell her.

"You can't tell me that a shop like hers doesn't bring a certain *element* to our town. Just the other day, there were more than twenty motorcycles parked out all along Main Street. Taking up every single spot," the shrillest of voices carries on. Imagine a chicken clucking and then add words. My ears should be bleeding right now.

Small towns aren't always happy shop owners and family-friendly diners. This town is pretty badass, but we still have our fair share of locals that love nothing more than to see the half empty side of life. Ruth DeMaio is one of them. My glittery little stink-face. I can't with this woman sometimes. It's been nine years since I've been here and every season, like clockwork, this pain in the ass complains about something "I've done" to bring an "element" to our town. It doesn't matter how wide open the space is here, there will always be someone too close-minded and judgmental lurking around to take a dump all over it.

She uses the Q&A session every week at our downtown business association to complain about one of us. She's an equal opportunity hater. It's not just me. Her sister Lenny, while she loves to gossip, is not a total asshat like Ruth. I've actually grown to love Lenny. Not to mention, she's Gracie's mom and Gracie is my brand of amazing. She needed a job to save for prom and spending money when she was in high school, and we clicked. That girl could run my tattoo shop if she wanted. Hell, she practically does while she's home from college these days.

Last week, Ruth, in all of her sour gummy worm face glory, managed to ask Vinny at the Flower Shop if he could, and I quote, "not get the sidewalk so wet when he waters the plants in the morning. It causes her dog to then track debris back into her home." That was my favorite, because Vinny simply told her, "No." Nothing more, not even in a frustrated tone. A simple no, followed by squeezing his stress ball. He says it's for his arthritis. I know it's because he communicates with one-word answers to most people, and that level of reserve bottles up. Eventually, it has to go somewhere. I feel bad for the ball.

The door slams open, and I know who it is without even looking. There's always at least one Riggs that attends these meetings. Usually, it's *him*. After all these years, I still get a little zing every time he's close in proximity.

"Ruth," I interrupt.

"You call me Ms. DeMaio," she barks back. I look up at the ceiling and suck in a breath for strength. This bitch is on my last nerve today.

"Ms. DeMaio, I'm going to cut you off right there and just ask you one question."

She looks at me and stops talking. Finally.

"Did you know the motorcycle club that came into town brought in relatively enough return to more than six businesses that line Main Street when some of them were being tattooed in my studio?"

Oh, she better be ready for this. Her stink face is about to get real nasty.

"That *element* you are referring to are good people. They came all the way from California to get tattooed by me. The club's owner had open heart surgery last year, and he decided he wanted to cover his scar with artwork. Reminding him that even the hard stuff can be beautiful. So, his entire squad got the same ink, out of camaraderie and respect."

I look at her with a smirk.

"Imagine a community of people that cares about each other so much that they'll share markings on their bodies out of respect, and a sense of belonging."

She looks around, noticing that all eyes are on her now. "That's nice, but it still congested every single spot downtown."

Vinny speaks up, "You don't drive, Ruth."

Snickers from around the room ring out.

I'm not done yet, because there's nothing that pisses me off more than someone judging people, or making assumptions based on appearance, or their choice for self-expression. Normally, I could give two enthusiastic middle fingers to people who like to look at my tattoos sideways, but not when it comes to those who are paying top dollar to wear my art.

Leo, who owns the boutique clothing store three doors down from my shop, chimes in, "I had my best sales day that day, Ruth. Nearly triple what I make this time of year." He shoots me a wink.

"I sold out of my barbeque sauce and had to place new orders for those cute heart sunglasses when those boys stopped on through my shop," Rhonda says. She runs the most trafficked store, Strutt's Sentiments. It's a catchall for tchotchkes and random original things you can only find when you come to Strutt's.

Ruth pipes in, "That's. Well, I don't—" She's left with little to say. "It wasn't a nice look for our community," she says, getting the last word in.

"Ruth, I think that's enough now," Henry bites out from the back of the room.

The entire family is regaled in Strutt's, so when one of them shows up, everyone sits a little taller. She smiles at Henry and blushes. It's what most women do when they see him. When any Riggs decides to grace the town with their presence, that happens. They're practically royalty here. And for good reason. They bring in an insane amount of money from tourists seeking out their brand and the outdoor sporting adventures they offer. Not to mention, they're all insanely hot. Hot goes a long way. Anyone who says otherwise hasn't witnessed true, boob-sweat, stutter-inducing hotness. And Henry, Everly, Michael and Law are hot. Asher too; don't get me started on that silver-fox. But more than that, they give a shit about everyone here. The meeting wraps up a few minutes later, and all of us who own a place on Main Street talk a bit longer about the approaching tourist season. Ideas around the Annual Riggs Tree Lighting Event in December, The Hot Toddy Stroll, and even the collective agreement on the times that all outdoor heaters will run so that we don't have to salt the sidewalks as frequently.

It's taken time, but I'm one of them now.

A townie.

When I first took over the tattoo shop, I wasn't liked. I thought it was because I was an outsider who looked different and spoke her mind. But it was really about someone new coming in, making changes to a way that had been comfortable.

It took a while for anyone to really take time to talk with me. Get to know me. Asher helped, but it was on me to really build out the shop, to start making a name for myself so that people would seek me out. That I'd bring business in that would support the shops around me too. And not just from our county or state. I've been bringing in business from all over the Midwest and west coast. Hideaway Ink has become a tourist destination of sorts.

People see me from all over now. And while there is a level of danger to that, I mitigate it as much as possible. I take steps to make sure I won't be surprised by a client coming in and recognizing me. I vet everyone before they ever have an appointment on my books. I'm rarely a stop in and get tattooed kind of shop anymore. Hell, even when I am inside, if there's no daylight, then the doors are locked. Everyone needs an appointment, and I'm booked out at least three months in advance. It's good business. And it's safe-ish.

"Ruth, don't forget to call Gracie before she heads back to London," Lenny McKenna shouts from the open door.

"Go suck on a fire hose, Len. I don't need the reminder." We all turn and watch the resident grouch and the town gossip volley for words.

Lenny thumbs over her shoulder as she moves closer to our group. "My sister. Such a charming woman, isn't she?" She smiles. The woman loves sticking it to her sister.

"Lenny, to what do we owe this visit?" Vinny asks. Looking at his watch, he says, "You're about ten minutes too late if you had any plans to participate in the Q&A session."

She swats at the air in front of her. "Ah no, Vin. I have zero interest in asking rhetorical questions in front of an audience. I'd much rather tell you to your face what I don't like about your business."

She shifts her attention to me.

"Giselle, I need to know three things about tonight," she says with her hand slung on her hip.

I laugh. "Okay, Len."

"One, when you said bachelorette party, you meant like a girls' night out thing, right? Not a bunch of dicks swinging in my face?"

"Oh, honey, please say yes," Leo says from behind her. "I want to see pictures of dicks hanging in her face."

A literal cat snarl comes out of her mouth. "I was not referring to your OnlyFans page, Leo."

I raise my eyebrow at him. He waves me off and says, "Oh, please. I wish."

"If we're lucky, dicks will slap *some* places at the end of the night, but no, there is no plan for strippers. Jack made me promise." I roll my eyes, and Leo starts laughing.

Lenny nods. "Okay. Two, can I trust that you'll keep an eye out for Gracie tonight too? I'm her mom, so I don't want to crowd her. And I'm worried that she never goes out or has any fun when she's in London, so I want her to enjoy tonight. But will you do that, just in case I'm too drunk?"

"Of course, Len. She's my mini. I've got her back." Lenny smiles at me. She knows that I'd do anything for Grace. The girl has helped me out of plenty of shit over the past few years when it comes to my shop. The funny part is, I don't think her worry is warranted. I have a feeling Gracie goes out plenty when she's away.

"That was only two," I say.

"Three, I'm wearing my Crocs."

"That's not a question," I tell her.

"I know it's not. It's a fact. You and Everly can go right the fuck off if you think I'm wearing high heels. The last time I wore heels, I was marrying a man and trying to convince everyone that I liked dick."

"Jesus, Len." I bark out a laugh. "Wear your Crocs."

"That's what I said."

Vinny shuffles away, waving behind him. "I've reached my quota for the amount of times I've heard the word dick today. See you kids next week."

The sound of keys and heavy boots move from behind me, accompanied by a snort of air. Many might think it's a dragon dressed as a construction worker, but no, it's Henry. I peer over my shoulder and catch a glimpse. Dark hair cut tight. Just the right amount of facial hair, a little more than scruff, but not a full beard meticulously trimmed. The smell of pine and leather mixed with that crisp, cold hint of snow on the horizon annihilates my brain whenever I catch a whiff. It's ridiculous, really, that I can pinpoint those scents, but it's him. He invades spaces either with his stature or smell. It's annoying. Even now, his large frame moves toward the double doors, following out Vinny and Leo, and I have to look.

Henry manages to remain as delicious as ever. Granted, I can never say this out loud, but the man has improved with age. A few lines at the wings of his eyes and just a sprinkle of gray hairs that dance around his temples. Other than that, time hasn't slapped him like it does to a lot of men. He's still in great shape. I know he works out with Michael often, but I gather that most of his muscle comes from being so involved with his business. Perfecting outdoor excursions. Taking VIP groups on trails.

We've made good on our promise all of those years ago. When we do share time together, it's laced with just enough hatred to keep us behind the enemies' line, and never crossing over. It's an effort.

"Leaving so soon, Hanky?"

"G, I've learned by now that when you start throwing the word dicks around, it's my cue to leave," he says back, without turning.

It took a year after that night in the alley with Henry for me to let the idea of being nothing more than someone that he used to know really sink in. I kept up with insignificant hook-ups, and the need to quell a sexual thirst that, for some reason, is never totally quenched. Even now, I hook up with plenty of men, a few women here and there, but I still keep kissing them to a minimum. I don't want to forget how his lips felt on mine. I don't want to water down the memory by adding others. I didn't need therapy to tell me that I use sex as a way to feel close to people when I can't be completely honest with any of the relationships. But I stopped slut shaming myself years ago and instead, live my life checking off kinks like a tickertape.

I also remember the first time I saw Henry with another woman. A brunette who clung to him at the Sugar Shack after the family had done a day's worth of skiing and snowboarding. I did what I always do, meeting them for lunch mountainside and then drinks later. We all decided on a nightcap at the base of the mountain, and he went home with a brunette. That first time, it stung. Worse than I expected.

So, I stopped looking. He did too. There's a part of me that thinks he's still watching, even though it's not obvious. All these years later, and I still wonder if it bothers him the way it does me. The way I hate the idea of someone else getting to kiss him the way that I crave to.

Every November, Henry and Law make a bet about who can grow the most obnoxious mustache. In addition, every year, all I think about is how badly I want to go for a mustache ride. Not just make the joke. Though I do that too. This year, Law beat me to it.

"What do you say, G," Law says as he twirls the ends of his 'stache. "Save a horse, ride a mustache?"

Everly and Jack laugh uncontrollably, because we had just been talking about some of the new thoroughbreds that Asher brought home from his last trip out to Montana.

"Jesus," Henry grits out, standing to clear his plate.

Asher chuckles as he tops off everyone's glass of wine.

"Law, baby, all that chafing?" I nod toward his mouth and then look down at my lap. "The horse sounds like a smoother ride." I give him a wink and the table erupts into laughter again.

I reach forward and grab my glass, but as I sit back, I'm met with a warm chest. "Sounds like you've been settling for boys, G." Henry's voice sounds low in my ear, tickling slightly as he breathes. I dart my eyes around the table to see if anyone is watching at how close he stands to where I'm sitting, leaning into my space. "You should know what it feels like for your thighs to burn from scruff and your lips to be swollen from being worked over properly. Not going to get that from a smooth ride."

Everly catches my eye as Henry steps back, before I can respond with a joke or stab to offset his words. Dammit.

That's been the trend lately. He says something to me, and I lose my edge. We're either slinging insults or he's saying something that melts my insides. I don't know what's gotten into him. It's been years of keeping our distance, but lately, he's decided to provoke. Poke the bear, like I'm so used to doing to him. And I'd be lying if I said this bear didn't come barreling out of hibernation ready for her next Henry-sized meal.

I watched my best friend get completely bamboozled by love this past year and, for some reason, it's cracked my foundation. And lately, all I keep thinking about is how long it's been since I've been in his arms. Thoughts that are dangerous in practice and for my sanity. What better way to make careless choices and not overthink about the man I can't be with than to tipsily flirt my way around Everly's bachelorette bash tonight.

CHAPTER 22

Henry

I DIDN'T THINK I WAS A PATIENT MAN. BUT TIME HAS SHOWN me otherwise. At this very moment, however, it's becoming clearer that I've reached my limit. Nine years, life is different, but the way I feel about her has remained the same. Stubborn or stupid, I can't decide which is right. Nine years, and we've choreographed a simple dance around one another—pull each other in, and before we get too close, push away. Never too close, but never far enough to truly forget and move on. I'm not a saint, but I don't overindulge. I sleep with women occasionally. Most of the time, it happens after I've seen *her* with someone else, or if she's pissed me off enough. Fucking someone is less trouble than throwing punches.

The first time I watched her flirt the night away at one of our family events and leave with someone, I ended up in the back of Callen's police cruiser. I knocked a guy out who had said he'd skied better mountains. The guy wasn't even talking to me. It wasn't my finest moment. But I've learned. Instead of holding it in and ending up with bruised knuckles, I played her enemies game. We volley insults just enough to remain on the smarter side of our emotions. Anger versus want. Sarcasm instead of support. At least on the surface. She has no clue how often I've intervened, so that business owners along Main Street would stop instigating and finally consider Hideaway Ink a downtown staple. How Strutt's Peak's City Arts Council finally accepted her into their community. Small towns, if nothing, are welcoming to your face and brutal behind closed doors. If you allow it. And I didn't.

But for some reason, now, I've reached a stopping point. It wasn't any one moment or thing, but the reality that what I want, and what I can live with, has evolved. I watched my sister find happiness in ways she didn't even know she was missing. I see my dad make choices that always support the family. I live a good life, but I want what I want. And for the past nine years, I've been denying myself. She's been safe. Life has been quiet, with no issues with WITSEC. I've created programs with Agent Harper for other placements and there hasn't been so much as a peep from G's previous life. Nine years and no danger, other than the reality that I can't do this dance with her any longer.

So, I'm here, watching my sister drunk at the bar, along with her best friend. Pure joy radiates from every part of Everly after finding the person that makes her most happy.

"You're staring at her again," Michael says, as he leans against the same wall I've been holding up for the past twenty minutes. I ignore him. Out of everyone, he's the only one that's noticed more than what's on the surface between that maddening woman and me. "She'll probably go home with both of those guys tonight. You know that, right?"

I try not to flinch at his words because, yes, he's right. She doesn't hold back. She goes after the things she wants at that moment, and most of the time, it's in the form of some asshole. Tonight, it'll be two.

Turning my head, I look at my brother. His longer hair is pulled back into a knot, his facial hair looks a bit longer, and he's more fidgety than normal. "What's got you worked up?" I ask.

It doesn't take a genius to follow his line of sight too, and see the young brunette that's captured his attention.

"She's only back for winter break, and then she'll be back in London." I smile at him. "You should talk to her."

He looks back at me, lifting a brow. "You should take your own advice." Then he's right back to staring at Gracie McKenna. "And she's a kid, Henry."

"She doesn't look like a kid anymore. And I'm pretty sure she just had her twentieth birthday. Lenny wouldn't shut up about it."

A loud barking laugh draws our attention back to the bar. We watch as Giselle and Everly yell at each other to lick and suck on lemons.

Michael lets out a laugh. "Do you remember the Christmas after you broke off your engagement? The one with the lemon?"

Impossible to forget.

"The fact that something as trivial as not having lemons

could piss you off is insane, Hanky," G says as she pops a green
grape into her mouth.

*I was pissed because I needed lemons for two dishes I had
planned to make for Sunday dinner, one of which was her
vegetarian option, and our grocer had none. What grocery
store is fresh out of lemons?!*

"Why are you here right now? Ev is at the gym." I turn
back and start unloading the bags. "It's like the universe wants
me to have a shitty day," I say under my breath.

"Such a sourpuss." She starts laughing. "Right there. That
face you're giving me. It's like you just sucked on a lemon.
Sourpuss. Who cares, Hank. Improvise. Sometimes the world
doesn't work out how you'd like, and you have to find a new
way."

"Like you?" I bark back at her.

*She pops one more grape into her mouth and crunches it,
chewing with her mouth open. Obnoxiously. She says nothing
else, grabs a bright electric blue bag from the seat next to her,
and jumps off the chair at the counter.*

It was a shitty thing to say.

A handful of weeks after that, on Christmas Eve, a
night when I was feeling especially sorry for myself, and
the divergent paths my life had taken, we all decided to
open gifts before dinner. Dad hosts at the ranch, but I
usually do the cooking. Giselle had given out all her gifts,
even though Everly and Dad were adamant with her
about not having to bring gifts for everyone. It was her
first year joining us for the holiday.

G handed me a small bag, and inside was a single
Meyer lemon. She wrote "Sourpuss" on the rind.
Everyone had gotten a good laugh at that, in my honor.

What the rest of my family didn't know, and what Michael isn't aware of, is that later, that hilarious gift wasn't really the gift at all. It was the card.

Long after dinner, late-night hot toddys, and wishing everyone a Merry Christmas, I arrived back at my new place to find the real gift Giselle had bought for me. Waiting outside the door was a 4ft box labeled 'FRAG-ILE' with Italian post markings, but no shipper or return address. It wasn't a leg-shaped lamp. Though, I wouldn't have put it past her. Instead, it was a lemon tree. No fruit on it, but enough little white blossoms, just like the ones sprinkled behind her ear, that I had plenty just a few weeks later.

That damn pixie got me right in the chest with that gift. I knew it was from her. I had thanked her, sent her a text that night.

HENRY

You bought me a lemon tree.

Who is this?

You know who this is, Pixie. This sourpuss thanks you.

No clue who this is. Merry Christmas.

I still don't know why she sent it, but that lemon tree sits in my kitchen to this day, and every Christmas, just enough blossoms turn into the fruit that so often reminds me of her.

There have been times where we end up alone

together and don't realize it right away. I try to be the person to set it right and leave. But leaving those private minutes with her just keeps getting harder. After all this time, it should be easier. Every year, I have a weak moment when I like to tease her in some incredibly inappropriate way and push her to cave. Throw her caution tape aside and trust that I'd never do anything to put her in danger. But as infrequently as it happens, it does a number on me, and I'm left with an emptiness.

My life is a successful one, productive, happy even, but it's not fulfilling. I'm confident enough to admit it. My life feels like I'm just waiting for something. I've realized that something is a someone. And it's her.

The boom of the DJ changing the song brings my attention back from the past.

"We're like oil and vinegar. We don't mix," I say to Michael.

"Yea, but when you shake those two things together, like really shake them up, they do. And when they mix, it's pretty darn good."

Fucking Michael and his damn poetic moments.

"See ya later, man. I'm heading home. Give Jack an extra back slap for me. Great night, by the way. Law was right about the curated adventures. It's damn smart. Even yours, with the boozy sleigh ride. It's too slow for my speed, but I've got plenty of names who will want it, hands down."

I snicker at that because it wasn't my idea, the sleigh ride. That was G. All those years ago, when my brother asked her if she skied or boarded, she had a great idea and it never left me.

Law remembered it too. As much as my baby brother can still get under my skin, he's got great ideas and the persistence to make those ideas happen. A flex he's grown into. He managed to do it with Everly by pushing forward her designs for apparel into a substantial part of our business. She's moved it to her own company now, but it was Law who amplified it to the point of success. He's got a knack for this business. More than I do, and as much as people might assume I'll take the company over, it's more in his wheelhouse to let it soar.

I glance back one more time to Giselle, making sure she's not too drunk to deal with the guys that are pawing her at the bar. She's sober enough, clearly basking in the attention. It's not unwanted, but hands coasting along her hips and fingertips grazing her shoulders are my cue to leave. Get the hell out of here before I start swinging, because for some reason tonight, I'm in the fighting mood.

CHAPTER 23

Giselle

"LICK IT! I SAID, LICK IT ALREADY!" I'M KNOCKED BACK INTO the moment, too many memories clawing their way in my mind, but whenever I hear the word "lick," Henry Riggs is the only face I see. Damn tease. "Lick it, G! You're staring at that salt on your wrist like it's hypnotized you," Everly yells over the thump of the bass and the muffled sounds of the crowd. She's sweaty, her makeup shiny, and her hair looks like a hot mess under the short veil I made her wear.

My best friend in the entire world is shit-faced, and every moment of it is pure magic. Gone is the buttoned-up businesswoman who just started her own damn empire designing athleisure apparel and accessories. Instead, she's been transformed into a hilariously fun and very drunk bride-to-be. While she argued with me that a bachelorette party was stupid since she was, in fact, already married, I told her it didn't count since I wasn't at their ceremony.

Everly Riggs found the love of her life two years ago, and though she would tell me or anyone who asked that he came out of nowhere, the fact of the matter is, she put her want for it out into the universe. She was ready for that big kind of love. The kind that'll ruin you if it's not nurtured properly or found with the right kind of person. And Jack, well, Jack is an arrogant billionaire, but I like him. It took him a little while to figure his shit out, but after messing it up and working his ass off to fix it, he got to marry her. Lucky asshole. She's a damn catch. And I don't just say it because we're friends. Nope, Everly is the real deal. Like the best parts of every diva you could think of wrapped into a hot-ass package who would go to bat for any person she loves.

Goddess knows she's gone to bat for me countless times over the years. Even in ways she might not even know. The girl gave me more than a glimpse of a family; she invited me to dinner and made a permanent place for me there every Sunday and even during holidays. I folded into the Riggs family easily and with appreciation they'll never begin to understand.

But now, Everly has her new extended family with Jack. They decided to elope right before the holidays. They "wanted their vows to be for each other and the party to be for the ones they love." Her words. I was a little annoyed that I wasn't the Maid of Honor, not able to do all the traditional things like a bridal shower and rehearsal dinner. I've accepted the fact that those things are not in the cards for me, but I had hoped I'd be able to experience them through my best friend. The consolation is that we do get to celebrate. And if there is one thing the Riggs family can do with serious swagger, it's throwing a helluva party. In a couple of days on New Year's Eve, Jack and Everly are hosting a huge bash to celebrate their nuptials with everyone they love, and we'll do it while ringing in the New Year.

Tonight, however, we will drink until only bad decisions are fulfilled. We will celebrate my girl, all parts of her that are fabulous and fun. And tomorrow, we'll hate ourselves for self-inflicting such massive hangovers.

"Lenny! Lenny-fucking-McKenna, please tell me you are going to have another shot with us before we get up on that bar and show this place how to properly draw attention," I yell to the already very wasted town loudmouth. While she loves to stir the pot in Strutt's Peak, she's also one of those people that would have your back in a minute. Gracie is somewhere around here too, albeit quietly judging all of us in a corner.

"G, I love you with all of my heart, but I am not getting on that bar." Everly hiccup-laughs through her words.

"Fine, I need a better view of the delicious men in this place tonight anyway. Help me scope for a minute, and then I'll let you out of this." I'm lying. Her ass is getting on that bar.

"I spy with my little eye two guys wearing just the right amount of tattoos in the far back corner," Everly says.

"Oooo, I like this game." I take a look. There's one sizing up Gracie and the other gazing out over the crowd.

Everly and I look at each other. Gracie is only twenty and doesn't know how to handle that kind of attention yet.

"I'm on it. Talk to Lenny. I don't want to draw too much attention to this unless it's necessary." Everly nods and then makes her way down the bar. I move toward the tattooed boys and snatch up three shots from the shot-girl waitress on my way. I haven't seen these guys before, one with tightly cut black hair and the other with a longer blonde messy bun.

"Hello, boys! I see you've met my little sister. Full disclosure," I whisper-shout. "She's home on break right now and is not supposed to be drinking at the bar." I wink at Gracie and though she doesn't look too distraught about the situation in front of her, she does smile at me, maybe slightly relieved for another person to break up the attention.

"Where're you in school, beautiful?" the blonde Viking asks.

Gracie looks at me and then sits a little higher in the booth. "Just finishing up at Cambridge."

"No shit!" the Viking answers back. "England's fun, but is dreary as hell. If you ever want to explore beyond and find your way to Denmark, you'll need to look me up." I don't doubt he's being friendly, but I can only stare at him. The guy is clearly a good decade, if not more, older than she is, but the ever-charming Gracie just smiles and nods.

I interrupt again. "My best girl over there is getting married in a couple of days, and I know she'd love for me to head back and join her. What do ya say? Want to make some bad choices with me tonight, boys?"

They look at each other, eyebrows raised, as if I just asked them to fuck me in the middle of the bar, which, maybe later, but really, I just want to clear them from my little underaged darling, and see if they're the least bit entertaining.

The dark-haired one speaks to his friend, "Denne pige ser ud som en god tid." (Translation: this girl looks like a good time.)

"Bare se på hendes krop," (translation: just look at her body), the blonde Viking says back to his friend as I watch them both obviously rake their eyes around my body. I don't have to know the language to understand what they're saying, but I'm about to either blow their minds or embarrass them. Maybe both. Languages and my brain work well together. I pick them up quickly. Luna, my college roommate, was from Copenhagen and was the kind of woman I wanted to be. Fearless, totally fun and accepting. She was always a go-with-the-flow type of person, and I lapped up every bit of her culture and a bit of the language as well. I also lapped in between her legs a few times when the Zimas flowed too heavily. I smile, thinking about her. Life then was complicated in its own way, but nothing like what I had waiting for me years later.

I smile and hand them each a shot. Tossing mine back, I feel the burn of the tequila coat my throat. I lean into them and say, "Boys, Jeg har det godt, og min krop er bedre, når den prøver nye ting." (Translation: Boys, I am a great time, and my body is better when it's trying out new things.) I drag my eyes up and down their bodies. I'm nothing if not blatantly obvious about what I want out of a situation. They both just start laughing, partly in surprise that I can speak a little bit of Danish, and at what I'm demanding.

Two water bottles later, because I'm responsible like that, and after watching my best friend slur her words as she tells Jack's sister Kathryn how much of a catch she is, I'm content with continuing my fun on the dance floor. The Danes have been taking turns grinding up against me for the better part of Mary J. Blige telling me she's searching for some real love. And while I search for someone to satisfy every need, that's where the alignment of her words end for me. Right here, these sexy tourists with just the right amount of confidence are going to show me exactly where the reputation of nice Danish boys ends and their roots of being Viking kings begin.

Just as I'm about to shout dirty things into the ear of the dark-haired one, a loud whistle at the bar grabs my attention. I smile wide as I see Law Riggs, nice and drunk, standing on the bar, trying to gain the attention of the crowd around him.

"Gentlemen and all of you fine, *finnnnneee* women, I'd like to interrupt the evening with a toast." He raises a beer into the air and continues as Everly is laughing and looking up at him from the bar below. "Many of you know my sister, Everly, and her fiancé slash husband." He rolls his eyes. *Same, Law, same.* "I'd just like to say, I'm so proud of you, big sister, for all the obvious reasons, but for one big one that I'm sure will shock you." The seriousness of it falls away for a moment as he smiles wide at the crowd and continues. "I walked in on these two as they sucked face for the first time and while I thought I might go blind"—he looks nervous at his choice of words for a moment, looking toward the back of the room—"it was obvious from the moment they met that there wasn't anything anyone could do to stop these two unstoppable forces from colliding. Everly, you love unapologetically, soulfully, and continue to set the example of how it should be done." He puts his hand over his heart. "Jack. Brother, welcome to our family. Next rounds on me!" The crowd cheers and whistles with a few hoots following as Law hops down from the bar. A very drunk Everly is cry-laughing while wrapped in Jack's arms, and Law bear hugs both of them. I scan the back of the room, trying not to be obvious about who I'm looking for.

An arm wraps around my waist. I try to keep my mouth from smiling, but who I'm hoping it might be versus who it likely is hasn't registered with my tequila-soaked thoughts. As his mouth comes to my ear, I know by the smell of beer instead of Cognac and the lack of scruff. The blonde Viking asks if I'd like another drink or to get out of here. I shove my disappointment aside and force myself to remember why this is the smarter way to go. *Easy, forgettable, and just sex.*

"Giselle! Geeeeeeeee. Imma go home with my man now. You are my most favorite human." Everly grabs my face and drops a fat, wet kiss on my lips.

"Woman, if I knew the only thing I had to do for you to finally kiss me was to get you hitched, then I would have been pushing for it a long time ago." I smile wide at her and then wink at Jack, whose arms are draped around her shoulders.

"Mine, G," he says playfully.

"Always mine first, Jack. Don't forget that shit. But I love you too. Call me when your hangover is gone, my lovely!" I yell over Jack's shoulder to Ev.

Jack looks behind me at the Danes, and leans forward, asking, "You good here?"

I simply nod and watch as my best girl's bachelorette comes to a close. I can hold my own here, and I've wanted to work out some pent-up energy with these two tourists tonight. Maybe they'll surprise me with a nicely curved cock or a bit of an undiscovered new kink.

"What's the plan?" the Viking asks.

"I'm going to settle the bill. Meet me outside. I'll call us a car, and we can have a nightcap at your place. Where you stayin'?"

"A rental on Main," the dark-haired one answers.

"Excellent. Should I grab a bottle before we leave?"

They both nod in unison. If I'm lucky, these boys won't be as reserved when we get back to their place. Just as I turn to the bar, I notice the Viking smirk at his friend and lick his lower lip. It feels like more than a friendly vibe. Maybe my Danish acquaintances are familiar with each other in other ways? I could go for a great bisexual threesome.

My night seems a little more exciting now. Less about forgetting my mood from earlier and more about remembering a bucket list sexcapade. Vikings and swords swinging, let's go! I mentally clap myself ready as if I was just in a huddle preparing for a final quarter.

"Last call," is yelled out from the bartenders, and the pulsing lights drop a reality on everyone not drunk enough to go home with whomever they've spent the last hour flirting with.

Jack took care of our tab. And since the owner of the bar is a friend, and client, just having had his thigh tattoo of a rooster colored and shaded last week, it wasn't much of a negotiation to snag a bottle of Grey Goose and a lemon for the road. *Time for my Danes.*

The cold envelops me as soon as I step out of the double doors. They shut behind me with a thump and it knocks a bit of the buzz right out of my veins. My breath is visible, but the sidewalk is quiet.

Where did they go?

I look left and right down each side of the road. Nobody. Perhaps they started walking? There's no way they just left, not with what I promised. It's not until I keep turning that I see a plume of breath come off the wall behind me. My nerves kick up, and I'm immediately thinking about what combination of punches and kicks Mac from the gym would recommend at a moment like this. *Jab, cross, hook, rear knee? Or maybe a rear spiking elbow and run?*

"You looking for someone, Pixie?"

My nerves settle instantly. *Henry.*

"Oh, look, you've finally taken to lurking in dark alleys. I see that you're fully committed to the disgruntled perv I always knew you could be, Hanky."

"That was mean, G," Henry says as he pushes off the wall and walks closer. I forget myself for a moment and take him in. So much bigger than me, he fills out his parka nicely, and his scruff is perfectly manicured. "Mean, even for you."

He looks like the best kind of sexy man, the one that isn't trying. He just is. He takes care of himself; there's a level of perfectionism in his personality, maybe a bit of the Air Force that will never quite leave him. Whatever it is, it has me flustered. As usual. Nine years, and still, a moment alone with him has me overheated in the dead of winter.

"You and Ev didn't drink enough? You started this afternoon." He nods to the bottle and lemon in my hands. "Needed a full bottle as a roadie?"

"First of all, why are you keeping tabs? Second, not like it's your business, but my night isn't over yet. Adults tend to do things at night, but I understand how senior citizen status might keep you thinking that evenings end at sundown." I flick my wrists for him to go. "Run along. I'm sure there's something boring you're missing out on."

"You sure about that?" he chides, a smile spreading across his face. It immediately pisses me off and takes all my willpower not to smile back. When that man smiles at me, I'm a fucking goner. When it reaches the corners of his eyes and his resting bastard face is long gone, that's when he's most dangerous.

"Sure about what?" I scoff at him. "What did you do?" I grind my teeth together. "Did you just clit-block me?"

"If you're talking about the Harry and Lloyd look-alikes that were practically dry humping each other out here not five minutes before you came outside, then yes. I told them they can head to their place and that I'd make sure you got there safely."

"Un-fucking-believable."

Gah! And why does he smell so good? The cold

should have frozen my nose hairs by now. I'm annoyed I can smell him.

"I don't mess with your sex life. Stay the hell out of mine, Henry!" I need to get away from him before I do something aggressive like tell him to never speak to me again. I turn around to avoid any more interaction. The frustration is making me shiver. It's not the cold any longer; it's the adrenaline from a missed sex opportunity and the star of so many fantasies being the cause.

I pull the collar of my coat higher. "And while you're at it..." I turn around to continue my tirade, but I smack right into Henry's coat-clad chest. "Fucking hell, back off, you big lug."

"Can't do that, Pixie."

"Oh yes, you can. You have no say on who I choose to play with." I reach out and run my hands along the front of his jacket. "Or are you still sulking about never having your turn to play with me?" I pout, pushing out my bottom lip and looking up into his two-toned eyes. One blue and green, the other the color of the morning grass. I'm met with calm. The way he's looking at me isn't passionate or angry, but far worse. A stillness that's laced with unspoken truths that I'm far too much of a coward and cynic ever to slow down and hear. Immediately, I'm cloaked in regret. The proximity. The words. The feelings.

"I'm not sulking. Just waiting," he says softly.

It shakes me. Quiet words from this man are something I'm not equipped to handle. Combative and growly are much easier to navigate. I can word-spar with him all day, and none of it hits my soft spots, but when he speaks quietly, it calls attention to the idea that we shed our armor and have an honest moment alone.

"Waiting for what?"

"Not what. Who."

I flinch. I'm not sober or drunk enough to have this conversation. Why do this here? Why now? But those are questions I can't ask. I'm not able to hear the answer if I'm reading his body language right. The confident stance, leaning just a fraction toward me, keeping my eyes locked with his, and his breathing is even. Like what he's saying is just matter-of-fact and not against years' worth of hard-working avoidance.

"Your aunt coming to town for the wedding?" he asks, cutting the serious conversation away and moving on to something I can navigate.

"She's supposed to be here," I tell him. Bea stops in to see me every six months now. Less frequent in-person visits, more consistent with texts and virtual check-ins.

"Make sure she comes to dinner at my dad's place the night before. I'm planning to do ribs."

"Sounds gross to me, but I bet she'd be thrilled to eat whatever you're cooking."

I move down the sidewalk to my shop and loft. This is when I need to remember that being enemies is safer. Stop thinking about his specially curated meals and instead focus on the way he just ruined a sexual bucket list moment for me.

I know by the lack of crunching snow and the stillness of the night around me that he's watching me walk away. "Stop staring at my ass, Hanky. She only likes to be gawked at when a swift slap or grab is guaranteed to follow." I yell a bit louder as I move farther away. "And we have a strict hands-off policy. Remember?" I sing-song.

"I can't seem to forget, Pixie."

He's making sure I get home safely, and that part of Henry is the most dangerous. The one that cares. Where he looks out for me, making sure I'm okay. I don't dare turn around again.

"Enemies," I whisper to myself.

CHAPTER 24

Henry

"Just go with meeeeeee. You're always telling me you want to get out of here. To just pick up and go somewhere totally new. Why won't you go to London with me?" Law continues to badger Michael obnoxiously.

"Chop that." I throw a massive bunch of cilantro at my loudmouth brother. We're standing around my dad's state-of-the-art outdoor kitchen space. My dad doesn't cheap out on things. The pellet grill that can easily hold up to five full racks of ribs that sits next to the flat top grill would be the first thing to tip off a guest. Nah, Asher Riggs always aims high and then exceeds his own expectations. He's always exceeded mine. The kind of father you don't realize is incredible until you're well into adulthood. When my dad realized how much cooking pulled me out of the dark, how much I genuinely enjoyed cooking for Sunday dinners, he decided to revamp the inside and outdoor kitchens.

"Tell him, Henry," Law says.

I don't even look up from the grill when I say, "Tell him what? That you're a pain in the ass? That you're the worst person to travel with because you're like a dog. Constantly distracted by a movement. A woman. Hell, even any kind of food on display. He already knows that shit."

Michael takes a pull of his beer and laughs as he swallows. He tilts his chin up at me. A quiet thank you for having his back on this. Law is a pain in the ass all the time, but when he has his mind set on something, or worse, on something he wants *you* to do, then there's no getting out of it. He'll wear him down. He's done it to all of us.

"There is only one reason you want me to go to London with you, and I'm not fucking doing it. Pull up your up big boy panties and go on your own if you want to do this so bad," Michael says.

"Go where? Where we going?" Jack, my new brother-in-law, asks as he walks up to us.

"Hey, man, come help me flip this rack," I ask.

"I could have helped," Law says.

"No fucking way. You keep a three-foot radius from all the food until it's time to eat," I yell his way.

"It was one fucking time, Henry," he huffs out.

Michael laughs.

"One time too many."

"What'd I miss?" Jack asks.

"I dropped one plate of steak, *one* time..." Law yells out.

"It was a plate of Kobe beef for Dad's birthday, and

you dropped it and then stepped on it like a damn toddler," I say as Michael and Jack continue laughing.

It's taken Law and me a while to get to a place where we can joke around. It's taken time to really settle, for both of us to move on and start a friendship instead of just being brothers. A conscious choice to be in each other's lives because we wanted to be, and not out of obligation because we happen to share DNA. Plus, he makes me laugh.

Law brings one hand to his hip and takes a drink from his beer. "Jack, you wouldn't want to head to London for a long weekend with me when you're back from your honeymoon, would you?"

"You still trying to get someone to go to that sex club with you?" Jack asks.

"Fucking hell," I groan. "That's why you're hellbent on going to London? A fucking sex club?"

"I doubt your sister would be on board with me going. Unless I took her with me," Jack says.

"Bah bah bah, stop now. Okay. You're uninvited," Law yells, cutting off Jack's response.

"Where are we going?" Everly walks up, giving each of us a cheek kiss to say hello.

Law responds, "Nowhere. You're going on your honeymoon in like less than forty-eight hours."

Everly just smiles at our brother. Then she peeks over my shoulder to see the racks of ribs I have roasting on the pellet grill. "Smells good, Henry. Thanks for cooking for this crowd. I know it's a lot."

I kiss her forehead. "I'm happy you wanted me to do it. I'm going to leave these clowns to watch this for the last thirty minutes to go check the sides inside. Callen and David show up yet?" She nods. "How about..."

"She just got here," Everly says quietly and smiles.

"Who?" I ask, even though I know who she's talking about.

"She brought Aunt Bea. Do me a favor and be nice tonight, okay?" She turns back around to the rest of my brothers and says to Michael, "He convince you to go to that sex club yet?"

They all start laughing. Michael shakes his head and catches up to me. "I'm helping you inside. They're relentless."

CHAPTER 25

Giselle

"Ash, I love this place. Any time you need a house sitter, I'm your woman," Bea says.

Ash laughs and gives me a big hug. "Hey, kid. You look great."

"Thanks, Ash." I breathe him in. He smells like a campfire, and it cozies my senses. He'll never know how much I bask in it. The safeness of being welcomed into his family. "Okay, ya fox, what kind of drink did you make me?" I say as he wraps his arm around my shoulders, guiding us into the bar area of his ranch. The house is buzzing with more than the typical Sunday or holiday crowd. Asher is always one to entertain, but it already looks like full capacity. My skin starts to itch a bit. It's a lot of people.

"You okay?" Bea asks quietly as she leans into me. She knows that big crowds make me anxious. Too many faces to catalog and the ever-present worry that I'll recognize someone I don't want to see. From before.

"I'm good," I lie.

We shimmy our way through a few people I recognize.

Tildy from the diner; I wonder who's covering for her if she's not there. That woman is always there. I suppose when town royalty has a mini-wedding weekend, people put aside their norms and show up. Barney, from the town council with his wife, who always looks like she's chewing on something. Then, there's Merriam. She likes to knit booties for the hospital and the new babies born there. Too nice. I bet they have some distractingly kinky fetish. I can relate to that. The booties, not so much.

"I made a special drink in honor of the bride," Asher says to us from behind the bar.

"Nothing for the groom?" I ask with a smile.

"Of course. I love him like he's my own." Asher leans closer and says, "He's not a big fan of anything that deviates from Scotch or Bourbon, so I kept it simple and did a Scotch and birch beer. The birch beer was tapped from some of the trees on my property. Obviously."

I laugh. "*Obviously*. You know there's nothing simple about that?" He waves a hand at me dismissively. Gosh, I love this family. This silver fox especially. Always a little extra, but filled with so much love.

"There's Lenny. I need to ask her a few things about the fishing trip I'm planning this summer. I'm going to mingle," Bea says.

I look at her, a little surprised.

"What? I get a vacation too." She leans over the bar and snags a sparkling water.

"Nothing stronger, Bea?" Ash asks.

"This is good." She brushes off the question as she walks away. She'll never have a drink, always on the clock when she's here with me.

I watch her give Lenny a big-watted smile and they start chatting. As I look around, I notice there's a handful of Everly's staff in from New York's Après Eve office. All high-strung, but a damn good time after they warm up. They'll be the rowdy bunch I bet at the end of the night. I continue to scan the space. My current count is fifty-four people, minus the three Riggs boys and Jack. That'll make sixty people in total, if you add in me and Bea. Less than there will be tomorrow night, but still a full house. Even this massive place looks smaller with this crew and the fact there are long tables set up around the living room and dining space.

"Okay, here you go." Asher brings my attention back to his curated drink menu. "I decided it was only natural to do something with Everly's favorites, so I went for a cinnamon infused vodka, shaken with a maple apple cider and a champagne floater topped with a candied orange peel," Ash says proudly as he finishes straining the cocktail he just shook into a classic champagne glass. He tops it with the sparkling champagne and a twirled candied orange peel that's wrapped around a black pick.

"I appreciate your glass choice," I say as he pushes the drink toward me.

"Oh, please, I've listened to you two talk about the ridiculous design of martini glasses for years. I've caught on." He laughs, then proclaims, "No martini shall ever be poured into a martini glass in this house."

"They really are the worst. It's an instant spill," I say matter-of-factly.

Then, as I say it, someone catches my eye and I spill slightly anyway. The drink only coats my finger and thank goodness didn't dribble down my chin and onto my dress. My very expensive and probably way too over-the-top outfit. I look at Ash, who already has a cocktail napkin waiting for me. "Ninja reflexes for an older dude," I tell him.

"I'm not *that* old, G. And the other thing I've learned" —he moves from behind the bar and starts walking away, but before he does, he finishes his sentence—"brace for the spill whenever you two are in the same room." He nods toward the someone. Henry.

Goddess, he's stupidly hot. And he's walking in the room with slabs of meat, which should make me want to throw up, but I'm about a minute away from breaking out in a trundle-sweat from looking at him for mere moments. Navy blue dress pants that are filled out with thick thighs and a bubble butt ass that I have far too many fantasies about biting. The light pink, crisply pressed dress shirt is probably one size too small, because his arms and the way they're bent holding the tray of meat are practically begging to be set free. His scruff is perfectly manicured. As usual. And the sprinkling of silver around his temples looks like frosting on a deca-dent, dick-swinging dessert. *Nom Nom.*

The crowd starts catching on that it's time to eat and everyone moves toward the long dining tables set throughout the oversized room. This is the only time that this house has felt small. So many people.

Finally, I see my best friend through the horde. She waves at me and comes my way quickly. "Holy hell. We should have just done the reception tonight. I think most people are here anyway." She leans in and gives me a hug. "How's the dress? Too short?"

"No such thing. You look amazing," I tell her. And she does. Everly always looks incredible. Put together, flawlessly beautiful. She's wearing the hell out of a short white dress with a high neckline. Her hair is pulled up into a sleek ponytail, and it's topped off with some killer sparkling drop earrings. Simple and stunning, which is how she rolls. "Sit with me at dinner?"

"I was planning on it."

"Where did you get this?" She pulls at my skirt. "You look fucking incredible. This whole pink bandwagon you're on lately is perfection. And I love the earrings."

"It's a celebration. It called for champagne!" My rosé champagne bottle earrings match nicely with the bodycon bubble-gum pink skirt I have on. It's high-waist, so I paired it with a men's white-collared dress shirt that's been cropped. Only a sliver of skin shows, and with my lacy bralette underneath, I feel sexy, but not a spectacle. It's not my night. Or weekend, for that matter. Nope. Tonight and tomorrow are all about the best person in the universe, and the love of her life.

"Turn around. I need to see the full look," she says, and I do a little twirl.

I catch Henry's attention on me as my spin comes to an end.

Everly lets out a laugh. "You're too fabulous not to look at, but help me feel better. Please tell me you're wearing Spanx? I mean, your ass is always incredible, but I feel like there is magic at play here."

"I can't wear underwear with this. Are you kidding me?" I tell her. "It's all me, baby. Those workouts with Mac have officially lifted this ass a good two inches higher."

My eyes lock onto Henry. "No magic, just a little bit of discipline."

His gravelly voice interrupts. "Ev, you want to start making your way to the table? I think Dad wants to make a toast before we eat, and the meat has rested long enough now." He looks at me as he finishes saying it. My stomach does a flip, and I remember proximity. I'm standing too close to him.

"You heard him. The meat has rested long enough." I smile wide as I drag my eyes down the front of him.

Everly barks a laugh as she swats my arm.

"Thank you, Henry," Everly says, patting his chest. "G, grab your drink,"

I watch as Henry takes a full look at me from head to toe and back again. Meeting my eyes at the finish of his perusal. *Yeah, I know. Fantasy material right here, flyboy.*

"Too bad, Pixie," Henry says as he fishes something from his back pocket. He looks down at my lady bits region and then holds up a small, thin black remote, smiling. My stomach flips again, and it's like Cupid herself just shot an arrow straight to my coochie. Direct fucking hit, you crazy bitch. And then it clicks. Just like that, my memory drops back to last year's Riggs Annual Tree Lighting Festival and to what that remote controls.

I don't know if it's just the memory or the fact that I'm feeling a sudden urge of regret for not wearing a particular pair of underwear tonight.

CHAPTER 26

Giselle

WHAT IN THE EVER-LOVING KITTY CAT WAS THAT?! *I SHIFT MY stance. Maybe someone dropped something, and it made the floor thunder.*

It happens again. A pulsating beat. A quick zip as if I've put my phone on vibrate and tucked it into my underwear like a panty liner.

And then it registers.

The underwear.

After my last tattoo session today, my client decided to give me a fabulous present. She might be the newest transplant in Strutt's Peak, but she's an absolute doll, and she gave me vibrating panties. The newest elementary school art teacher has a side hustle, making some very scandalous and deliciously sexy adult toys. Instead of paying for me to cover up the name of her now ex-husband, we made a barter. I wanted a couple of new toys. She threw in the undies as an extra.

The part that doesn't make sense, though, is I didn't turn these on. Yes, I knew they vibrated, but I was only planning on playing a little if this evening ended up being a boring one.

"Here you go, Giselle. Vodka rocks with a sugared lemon wedge."

"Thanks, handsome," I tell the bartender. "Snag me a club soda too. I need to pace myself."

"You here by yourself tonight?" he asks.

Buzz, buzz, buzz, buzzzzzzzzzz. The vibrations cut off my attention before I can answer. I shift my weight again and try my hardest to hide my smirk. What the fucking fuck is going on? I dig through my small neon green clutch. Money, license, lip stain, and my apartment keys. Nothing else. No remote.

My underwear has been hijacked.

The bartender is still looking at me. He's cute. In a clean-cut, I like to iron my jeans kind of way. Not my type.

"Nope. Thanks for the drink." I slip him a fifty. "Please, any time I come toward this bar, have another one of these waiting for me?"

He nods with a smile.

I stare off into the sea of bodies and watch as my best friend stands across the room, schmoozing the crowd as she's so effortlessly used to doing. She runs the shit out of her family's business. I can see she's anxious to meet the guy she's been sleeping with here. Jack. The snack of a photographer that just came into town and barreled his way into my girl's universe. She looks refreshed and relaxed for once. And well-fucked. Maybe even happy.

I love watching people at this event. It's a perfect mix of local Strutt's Peakers and the pretentious out-of-towners. The town gossip train is here in full force, too. It's the auction that tends to bring the most scandal. Who will bid on which Riggs kid this year, and not to mention, once it's over, what will the winners do with them? Most of the time, it's an evening of drinking and whooping it up in a bit of luxury, but every now and then, there's something juicier. I feel the juice might be flowing this year, because each of the Riggs siblings, Everly included, is looking damn fine. One very growly enemy of mine, especially.

It happens again, but before I can move to the ladies' room and remove these magically inappropriate panties, Everly captures my attention and nods furiously for me to head to the table.

"Ladies and gentlemen, please take your seats."

In a span of what must be only a few minutes, I'm in my seat, and my vibrating panties have worked me up enough to soak them easily. I've decided I'm just going to lean into this. I can't get up now and take them off, and hell, I'm like two minutes from what might turn out to be a decent orgasm. Right in the middle of the opening speeches for this year's tree lighting and auction.

I look around the table, and across the overly priced centerpieces sit each of the Riggs boys, Law to my right, Michael, and then Henry. It is taking all of my wits not to look at him because the second I do it, this orgasm is going to have context. As much as I try to keep that beautiful asshole out of my mind, he shows up somewhere and then becomes the leading man in my every dirty thought. It's like a sickness. I need some kind of remedy, but until then, I'll avoid looking at him.

"What the hell, G? I'm trying to listen to this. Answer your damn phone or turn it off," Everly whisper-shouts to me.

"It's not my phone," I tell her as I stare ahead at the stage.

She's not satisfied with that answer, so she proceeds to lean over me and tell Law to answer his phone. I know full well that she's hearing the buzzing of my underwear, which right now are on what feels like an incline workout. Ebbing and flowing from a soft buzz to a punching bite. My body breaks out in goosebumps. I take a steadying breath and blow it out slowly, quietly.

Everly is getting huffy. She looks at me again, and I can't help but start laughing.

"Tell me that noise isn't coming from you," she says lowly.

"Oh. Oh. Oh," I whisper. A full-body flush takes over, and I can feel my orgasm readying itself. It's going to be a big one. My clit is being teased as mercilessly as Chunk in The Goonies. It's only a matter of moments. I need to get up.

Everly stares at me and shakes her head. "I can't take you out in public sometimes."

"I don't know where they came from," I lie. "Stop looking at me like this is surprising behavior! I need another drink. And to move around. Want something?"

She gets up with me, but is quickly distracted by Jack. She's been waiting for him to get here, and now that he's arrived, my friend is going to be occupied. Perfect. Attention away from me, so I don't have to explain myself any further.

As soon as I get to the bar, my vodka rocks and sugared lemon is waiting for me. I take a sip and look around the room. Most people are sitting at their tables while just a few are mingling toward the back. I watch as Everly, Jin, and Jack seem to get into some kind of heated discussion. I wonder what the hell that's all about. Looks like Everly's old colleague-with-benefits just met the new star of her porn show. Yikes. As much as I feel the need to come to my bestie's rescue to diffuse what-

ever bullshit is playing out on the other side of the room, I can't.

And then it hits me, with a massive zap and a prolonged buzz. The finale to the fireworks just began in my undercarriage, and I'm going to blow. There's no holding back here. I can feel it. I take a breath. Another. In through my nose, out through clenched teeth. Can I rush to the bathroom? Oh fuck. I'm going to make noise. Dear God, please be a woman and help a sister out here. I don't want to stop it, but if there was a way to mute it. Fuck!

I bite my fist. By some technological sorcery, it cranks up higher. How can this thing go higher? And that's when I see it. The source. The sorcerer of sorts. Henry Fucking Riggs.

"Oh. Muhgawd. Frshhhh. Hmmmm," pushes from my lips. I bite back the rest of the noises that are trying to escape out of me. Of course in the middle of a room, in a wildly public place, comes the most intense orgasm I've ever had handlessly. Or at least without the assistance of something I'm wielding.

When I blink my eyes open, I find Henry across the bar, leaning on one hand, watching me as if he's just seen the most magical show on earth. And in the other hand is a small, skinny black remote.

I march over, albeit on trembling legs. "Have fun with that?"

"Not as much as you did." He laughs, leaning in closely to my ear.

"That's probably the best orgasm you've ever given a woman." I look him up and down when I say it. Then, I throw the rest of my drink in his face, and as soon as he opens himself up to grab a napkin and wipe the vodka that's dripping from

his chin, I pull back, rotate my hips and give him a hook to gut.

"Ooomph," Henry grunts out an exhale and shakily says, "The fuck, Jizz?"

"Don't you ever take something like that from me again. You didn't have permission."

I storm out of the room just as Asher calls his kids on stage. I need to gather myself and let the spectacle that I just made die down before I can resurface.

CHAPTER 27

Henry

Today began calmly. The snow had just started to fall as I was walking Milo, but now, hours later, a small snow squall is happening outside my office windows and it's as chaotic as the clusterfuck I'm dealing with inside. To top it all off, now I'm running late. Of all days, vendors want to dish out problems and not solutions. Apparently, everybody worked over the holiday. And because my responsibilities at Riggs Outdoor have grown significantly, I'm the one who has to deal with it all.

"Listen, it's Winter Sports season right now, which means I need every vendor that was sold out on Christmas to tell me why I don't have backup inventory. I'm going to have high-profile customers coming in and they want to use the brands I recommend. I can't recommend what I don't have in inventory."

My phone buzzes in my pocket, and I know it's someone asking where I am. *Ignore.*

"Listen, I understand, but you're making this my problem, and it's yours, not mine. I can't help sell a brand if I don't have it. Get it here by next week or I go with someone else. It's that simple." I hang up and rush to wrap up a few more emails. The headaches from the success of the holidays began as soon as midnight struck and it was December 26th. That's what I'm dealing with more and more these days, headaches and spending far too much time behind a desk. Less time on trails and enjoying the outdoors, which was my main focus when Everly and I decided to pivot and work for my dad's company. Our company.

Now, since my sister had moved her own brand forward, it left our family business in a bit of an adjustment period. It's been a year of filling in for someone that had the largest role at this company. We've split her responsibilities, but even then, it's become overwhelming. Everyone assumes I want to fall into her role, eventually, take over for my dad as CEO, but the only thing I know I want is not that.

I can't think about any of that right now, though. I'm late and I still need to shower, throw on my tux, and be at my sister's house in time to help greet her guests for their wedding reception.

As soon as I hit send on one last email for the day, I'm jumping into my Wrangler and peeling out of my driveway. It's New Year's Eve and more than anything, our family, hell, the entire town, is ready to celebrate Jack and Everly tying the knot. The fact that they're already married threw everyone off, but I suppose it was romantic.

For this town, my dad, especially, it was a big hiccup. His only girl not having a huge wedding was the typical small-town gasp, but she's making it work in her favor. So, tonight she and Jack are hosting a massive New Year's Eve bash that doubles as their wedding reception. It's going to be a stacked event, but that's how we do things in my family. Always over the top and so memorable it's talked about until we throw the next one. My phone rings over the Bluetooth in my car, Michael's name popping up.

"Yo, I'll be there in less than fifteen minutes," I say before he can get a word in.

"That's nice, but you need to swing by the house and get me too," he says.

"Why aren't you already there?"

"I had to get in an extra workout today. Too much shit is going on in my head and I needed to clear it," he says honestly. That's one thing about my brother. He'll always give it to you straight, even if it's not the easiest to say, or hear.

"All good. I'll pull in your driveway in about"—I look at the clock on the dashboard—"six-ish minutes. Be outside. Ev is going to be pissed if we aren't there before other people start arriving."

As soon as I hang up, my phone rings again.

"Dad, I'm on my way right now," I say.

"I'm running late," he says.

"You live next door."

"And I'm not there right now. I'm running late. Are you there yet?"

"I'm on my way to get Michael, and then we'll be there. Where are you?"

"I just needed to wrap something up. I'll be there not too far behind you. Tell Law to calm down. He's already called the police station when I wasn't there an hour ago. Such a pain in the ass," he says.

Less than twenty minutes later, we pull into Jack and Everly's round-about driveway. Their house is massive. More space than I would ever want to keep up with. It sits on a ranch with property sprawling at least three miles in each direction. Technically, next door to my dad's ranch, though you'd never know since you have to drive five minutes or walk twenty to even see his place. Jack purchased the place from our family's friend in an effort to win my sister back. It worked. Or at least sweetened the deal. And the house is almost as over-the-top as my dad's. It turned out that Jack, though he came into town doing a job for our family business as a photographer and brand manager of sorts, was packing a massive financial portfolio of investments. He would never say it out loud, but my brother-in-law is a billionaire. And you'd never know it. He can be a real asshole if he wants to be, but to us, he's more than alright. And now, he's family. Needless to say, they're not going to spare any expense tonight.

They have a valet service parking cars, so I toss my keys to the young kid wearing the heavy coat and dress pants. "Make sure you come in to warm up after guests arrive. Don't stay in this cold."

He catches the keys and nods. "Yes, sir, Mr. Riggs. Hey, Michael."

I look at my brother, wondering how he knows this kid.

Michael nods. "See you at the wall on Monday, Jonas. No drinking."

My brother, for as anti-social as he can be at events, always makes time for the local high school and college kids who are interested in climbing.

This small snow squall this morning managed to drop just enough powder, so that everything looks crisp and fresh. As soon as Michael and I round the front of the car, we're met with a skulking Law.

"Um, what the fuck? Is being an hour late like the new thing?" Law says, standing on the porch, foot tapping away. "You know Dad's not even here yet. Good thing Ev and Giselle are tucked away in the guest house getting ready. Jack and the staff are the only ones in the main house right now. And that crazy agent of his, Luce. She fucking scares me. I'm pretty sure she just hired a hitman. I was eavesdropping. Maybe not. It could have been. Never again." He waves his hands around like he's stressed. Always so much drama with him.

I blow past my brother and into the house. It's bustling with people moving furniture, hoisting up chandeliers. It's only 5 p.m., and the place is decked out and ready for the biggest party this town has seen in a long time. The back of their house is a full wall of windows, and now, since it's winter, they've extended the outdoor tent to be connected. The massive tent is draped in dark velvets, green or blue, I can't tell from where I'm standing. It looks like a mess, but I can guarantee that it'll be flawless by the time the first guest arrives.

"Does it look like I care about the excuse?" I hear a loud New York accent bellow from the kitchen. Luce, who

Jack lovingly refers to as "Lucifer," is making a grown man cry right before my eyes. "You are supposed to have a ratio of one waiter per five guests and you're telling me people have called in sick? Not my problem. Figure out your solution or you do not get paid. And I will hunt you down myself after everyone has gone home to make sure your life is miserable if you are unable to figure this out. DO YOUR JOB."

I interrupt. "Luce. Looking as terrifying as ever." I move toward her and give her a hug hello. She's intimidating as hell, but what a force to have on your side. She's helped me out on a few occasions with some VIP requests that I had no idea how to make happen. Plus, she's been running the New York office of Everly's new apparel brand. She's practically family now too.

"Henry. You're late. I need you to go deal with Jack and the kid." I look down at her, thinking, *what kid?* "Benny. Apparently, Benny just got dumped by the woman he was with in Costa Rica for the past couple of months and he's"—she leans closer to whisper—"crying. I don't know how to navigate men crying." She looks at the waitstaff manager, who she was just berating. "Anyway, your suit jackets are up in the guest suite too. Please bring up Scotch or something to make it better while I handle this."

"On it," Michael says from behind me. He goes right to the bar cart and grabs a few shot glasses and a bottle of Crowne.

"Place looks great, Luce," I tell her as we move toward the grand staircase.

She waves me off and continues to unleash hell on

the few people within earshot who aren't moving fast enough for her. She's clearly the maestro here today. There're massive arrangements of white flowers shuffling in from the front door as we move upstairs. I hear glasses clinking, bottles of champagne opening. There's music being soundcheck from the back tented space. It's coordinated chaos, but it's clear that everything is being handled.

I double tap the door to the master suite at the end of the second-floor hallway, and hear Jack yell out to come in.

"She just said it was over," Benny, Jack's nephew, says as we step into the suite. He looks up and wipes quickly under his eyes.

"Hey, guys," Jack greets us.

We tell him the place looks great and move around the space to sit. There's a massive sitting area across from their bed and next to the ensuite bathroom. A wall of televisions, each playing an array of college football games, a spread of food, from wings to pizza, and a kegerator tapped with Strutt's Peak Brewery's double IPA.

Now that I see what's here, I regret doing anything today other than parking my ass right on that couch. Michael moves to sit next to Benny, and they speak to each other quietly as I sit beside Jack.

"You ready for the show downstairs?" I ask Jack.

Smiling wide, he says, "Of course." He takes a sip from his tumbler of Scotch. "Luce raising hell down there?"

"Of course."

"Okay, we've got about ten minutes to get our jackets

on, have a drink of whatever Michael brought upstairs, and then head down to finish what Luce needs before people arrive at eight."

"Benny, you okay, man?" Law asks. Michael gives him a look, as if to say, "why'd you ask that?"

"I'll be fine. Just a girl. Right, Uncle Jack?" he says.

"Until it's the right one, it's *just* a girl," Jack says. "Plenty more out there." He nudges his head toward the door. "Plenty more down there soon too. Let's have some fun tonight, yeah?"

Michael claps Benny on the shoulder.

Law pours out a shot for each of us, Benny too. He's not twenty-one yet, but that kid is more mature than the lot of us. "Cheers, my brother. To you," Law says. We lift our glasses. Then Michael says, "To us."

And with the flick of a shot glass, and the burn that glides down my throat, the night is ready to begin.

It's 8:30 p.m. and most guests have arrived.

I mingle around the room, grabbing a drink from the cocktail waitress.

When I look down at my watch again, it's 8:45.

I haven't seen her yet. I'm not going to pretend like I don't immediately find her in a room wherever we go, or keep an ear perked for her voice. I won't pretend that the way she looked at me the last time I saw her, when I held up the remote to her vibrating panties, that it didn't light me up. The look of desire, anger, and even need swirled in those big brown eyes of hers. I wonder if she kept them. Those panties were the boldest move I'd made in nine years.

Before that, it was only ever innuendos and antagonizing conversations. Every so often, I'd find myself in a moment when I'd consider throwing in the towel. Walking away from the responsibility of looking after her. Allow myself a chance at finding someone else. It would happen after seeing her too many days in a row, or if I watched for too long and spotted her happy with someone else. Those times, the reasons behind not being together faded enough, and I considered the extremes. Taking her in my arms or just walking completely away. But like clockwork, Agent Harper would do a check-in. And I was reminded of the entire situation. Reminded how much I'd grown even more attached. Cared more. Watched more closely.

The dumbest thing I ever did was follow these rules. Hers. Agent Harper's. Hell, even my own. I'm waiting and watching the clock for the arrival of a woman I shouldn't want anymore. Time should have pushed her out of focus. It should have, but it didn't. Instead, I watch the clock. I wait for her. I look for her. I still want her. And fuck, tonight feels like a good night to break some rules.

By 8:50, I see Everly, dressed in gold from head to toe, wrapped around Jack's waist as they talk with David Muldowney, and his son, Callen. I couldn't tell you the first thing about what kind of dress or hat thing Everly has on, but I'll never forget seeing the smile she's wearing tonight. She's never been happier. If there was anyone who deserved that type of happiness, it's my sister. She keeps us all together. Binds us unknowingly, whether through Riggs Outdoor or just the consistency of being woven into our lives.

"You're not going to believe this. Shelley Farley just showed up with the mayor. You believe that shit? She's still hot as fuck, but seriously, *him*?" Law gags. I bark out a laugh. "I need to get out of this town." He elbows me. "You know I hit that like a year ago, right?"

"Yeah. I know." She catches both of us looking at her and waves meekly. The catalyst, and she'll never know.

"Henry," David greets me. "You're looking good, son. How're things with your piece of the business?"

I shake his hand and Callen's as well. "Business is good. Peak season right now, so there's always a massive lack of sleep. We miss this one over here." I nod to my sister. "But Jack came swooping in with some great leads after he joined our board, and I'm genuinely excited to see things really start to take off." It's not the total truth, but business is booming, even if I'm ferociously treading water.

"How long are you in town?" I ask David. While he was a Strutt's Peak resident for the majority of his life, after selling his ranch to Jack, he decided to head to Canada for a while and try his hand at opening a restaurant in Calgary near Banff, right on Lake Louise.

Before I can hear his answer, my attention is pulled away. That feeling when someone is looking at you creeps up my back. I turn my head slightly to the right and my pulse rate jumps. I look around the tent, adorned with people dressed formally, laughing and talking. There's rich dark fabrics draped all around. The hundreds of chandeliers that hang above vary in size, but give off just enough light that the room glows with a dim warmth, almost as if the air is laced with flecks of gold.

I smile back at David. I have no idea what he said or what the conversation has shifted to, but I'm clearly distracted.

"She's somewhere around here." Everly leans toward me, speaking low enough for only me to hear. I look at her with a tight-lipped smile. My sister has paid closer attention than she should have over the years.

"If you'll excuse me." I place my hand on David's shoulder and smile. "Callen, let's hit the fat bike trail next week?"

He nods. "Absolutely."

I lean over and give my sister a kiss on the cheek. "You look incredible. Have fun. Save a dance for me."

"Behave," is the only thing she says as I walk away.

CHAPTER 28

Giselle

A ROOKIE MISTAKE. WHY DID I BOTHER WEARING underwear tonight? They're fucking ruined and I've only been here for twenty minutes. The moment I walked into the tent, I tried not to look for Henry Riggs. But I did. I'm trying to fool everyone else, but I think I have to stop lying to myself. I know why I look. I can't help it. Somehow, the man has burrowed deep into my veins. Every other pulse is a reason to stay away, but I can't ignore those pumps of blood in between the logical reasons, that instead, scream violently to see him and come close enough to touch him. I sound insane, but I'm aware of that too. The man, or perhaps lack thereof, has officially made me crazy.

But instead of him, I find Bea assaulting a massive display of meats and cheeses. After a quick check-in, I leave her to her own devices. She'll only stay long enough to be seen, to hold up her cover as my aunt, and then leave town again.

"You look like a fucking goddess, Giselle," Lenny McKenna says loud enough to turn a few heads in my direction.

"Thanks, Len. You clean up nice, too." I give her a kiss on each cheek. She always tends to lean more masculine in her clothing, and is wearing a full tuxedo with a white jacket.

"Gracie, just, wow. That dress, girl. That. Is. A. Dress!" I hold her arm out and make her spin for me. She fully embraced the New Year's Gatsby vibe and is wearing a flapper-style drop-waist dress with a low V-cut in the front that shows off insane cleavage. Gracie McKenna is definitely a grown woman. There are no traces of that awkward teenager any longer.

I talk with them for a few minutes. Gracie will help me with some things at the shop until she heads back to school at the end of January. Lenny tries to tell me all the gossip about who the mayor brought as his date tonight.

"I swear to all that is decent in this world that there is no way *that* man has the equipment to satisfy a woman of that caliber." She brings our attention to the Julia Roberts look-a-like draped on the mayor's arm. "I mean, look at that. That woman is a fucking ten. And Cliff is a hard four. There is not a dick big enough or personality golden enough for *that* man to score *that* woman."

"Mom, can you tone it down tonight?" Gracie interjects as she gives me an apologetic look. The kicker is that Lenny is probably one of the most solid humans I've ever met. Not to mention, she's spot on with the assessment.

"Len, you know it's not always what's on the outside. Who knows, maybe that ten is actually a two because she punts puppies for fun or has a taxidermy collection of insects," I offer.

Lenny deadpans and gives me an honest to goodness death glare. "G, shut the hell up. Cliff is in his late fifties and my guess is that redhead is easily just hitting her thirties. She could taxidermy *people* and I'd probably still be drooling over her."

Always a guaranteed over-sharer and nosy bitch.

I wave to a few friends as they make their way through the growing crowd. Mac, then Marie from the town clerk's office. I see Jin, Everly's business partner, and Kathryn, Jack's sister, but I keep away from that dumpster fire. Those two manage to drum up drama wherever they go.

I'd love to be drama-free tonight. And as I think about it, I still sweep my attention around the room. *Where did he go?*

Heading over to the massive bar, I order my favorite. Vodka rocks with a sugared lemon. Side of club soda. I suck down a water first. It's New Year's Eve, and this party is going to last well into the early hours of tomorrow morning. I plan to make this night a great one. The energy of the room carries this upbeat warmth. There's a smile tagged onto every conversation and each clink of a glass is laced with the unspoken promise for an exceptional evening.

I take a deep breath. There are a lot of people here, but I am not going to focus on that. Instead, I look around at the elegance of the food being passed, the velvet texture that's cascading from ceiling to floor, and the flicker of candles across every opening.

The band that's been playing has woven in some of Everly's favorite songs. Some play as intended, but then I recognize a few that are chart-toppers turned classical. Vitamin quartet-style.

The frenetic drumbeat on a high hat combined with the piano pulls my attention to the musicians. *I know this song.* As soon as the singer with her deep alto voice starts, I recognize it as Nina Simone's "Sinnerman." One of my favorites. It's about a sinning man who tries to hide from justice on his Judgment Day. While I don't think she was the original singer, Nina Simone's version is stunning. This singer sounds just like her. And before the song hits its chorus, which sounds like a poetic story where the Sinnerman has a choice: to face his judgement or he can run to the devil, that's when I find him again.

My devil.

The man who is my constant temptation.

Right now, frozen in place, he looks like something I should have. He looks like heaven, or at least some kind of divine intervention. Right now, I want that beautiful man across the room. If I lick it, it's mine, right? Oh hell, how I want to lick him.

"Goddamn, that man can wear the shit out of that tux," a loud New York-laced accent murmurs. An accent that used to cling to my words as well. But this voice belongs to Luce. Jack and Everly's henchwoman. That's what I call her, at least. I think the official title is an executive assistant or something.

I smile, but can't seem to look away. And without missing a beat, I just say, "Mine."

This is a picture I want to keep. Remember. He looks expensive and off-limits in that tuxedo. Classic black cut, crisp white shirt, black bow tie, and a black velvet jacket. His dark hair cut tight and gelled back on top, and sideburns that run into the manicured scruff along his cheeks, chin, and jawline. He's politely smiling. I can tell it's not a real smile, because the dimple on his cheek didn't cave. That fucker only comes out on special occasions, when he's truly laughing. Maybe I'll see it later. Tonight *is* a special occasion, after all.

"Huh," she tuts. That pulls my attention away from him, and over to her for a moment. She looks at me with her eyebrows pulled high and then back at the group we were both just shamelessly gawking at. "No shit? I really thought you two hated each otha. Go figure. I was talking about the one to his left. The Sherrif," she says.

I don't have the energy to correct her or spin some kind of truth that she'll actually believe. So I stay quiet.

Henry looks around for a moment, like he knows he's being watched. You are, big guy. *I see you.* Searching to his right, he drags his attention across the crowd, but I'm more in front of him than to his side. Before his gaze lands on me, Bea steps in front of my line of sight.

"Don't," she says.

I roll my eyes. "Give me a fucking break, Bea," I tell her, trying to seem unfazed. The energy I felt while looking at Henry wafts away. Bea has a habit of stomping the fire out quickly.

"Welp, kid, I'm going to say it anyway." I take a steadying breath and prepare for whatever warding off she's prepared to dish. She chugs down the rest of her soda.

"Nice," I say as she burps into her fist.

"Shut it." She points to my chest with her judgy, accusatory finger. "We have rules in place for a reason. There's a lot of history there, I get it. But it doesn't change the danger. I'm good at my job, because I plan thousands of steps ahead, and I'm telling you..." she pauses, looking over her shoulder. "There are too many flags. Do I need to list them out for you again? Think about his family. He's photographed, and often. I just saw a picture of him and his brothers in Forbes."

"You're wasting your breath here. I'm not interested," I lie.

"You forget I can smell a liar better than a fart," she says.

I scoff.

"But you need to start living. Find someone you can enjoy. You two need to stop dancing around each other, waiting for the music to stop because, kid, it's not going to stop."

"I am living. I'm not waiting for anything."

"You're in witness protection, not purgatory."

"Sometimes it feels like it," I mumble to her.

"Oh, G. No, honey. Out of anyone I've ever met, you deserve to find your happy. But that"—she looks over her shoulder back toward Henry, once more for emphasis—"that is complicated. Find something easy. Something that'll make you happy without the risk."

But easy sounds boring, and happy seems like an illusion.

"Bea, this isn't the place for this. I'm not equipped to handle this discussion right now. It's Everly's day. I'm just..." I don't know what I am right now.

"Hey. Look at me. You chose to stay here. Even after you knew he was here. I allowed that, but only because you promised me it wouldn't be a problem. Don't make it a problem." She moves away, guiding our discussion closer to the main house. It's clear she's ready to leave.

"You're not staying until midnight?" I ask.

She leans in, kisses my forehead, and says, "Nope. I have some others I need to check in on before the night is over. I'll talk to you soon."

I watch her leave, stopping periodically to say hello to folks from town who she's gotten to know over the years. It makes me smile. The woman doused me in truth a few minutes ago, but she isn't the cold cow I thought she was when I first entered the program. Bea really is the only person who knows all the parts of me. The details of what happened and the aftermath of it all.

When I turn back around, I'm met with a devilish smirk that reaches up and crinkles the corners of the most beautiful eyes I've ever seen. Henry stands less than ten feet away, squared off, hands in his pockets, looking every bit as royal as he acts most of the time. I stare at him, refusing to give him a smile. *Enemies*. It's an inner fight almost every time I see him because there's a part of me, the part I can't control, that wants to wave the white flag and dive into him. Because even on his coldest days, the ones when I'm a sarcastic asshole, and he's a quiet grump, I still want to cozy up to him. Lean into the warmth that he's burrowed somehow into my bones after years of watching me. Sparring. Waiting.

Listening to him talk about what trails are superior on our mountains and argue about how onion tastes different depending on how you cut or chop it. The safeness that radiates from his chest, unknowingly. Every day that I see him, it's enough to keep me pushing forward. And while all of that is a truth that I'd never speak, hell, I can't even believe I've allowed myself to think it... none of that is what I'm feeling right now.

Right now, I want to take a king-sized white sheet, wave the hell out of it, and then wrap us both in it. Preferably naked. The cut of his tux. The hands casually slung into pockets. The way he stands with an energy and superiority that most men couldn't even attempt to muster. My brain is short-circuiting. Or I'm just ovulating. Could be both.

He hooks his pointer finger at me and flexes it in a "twiddle-a-twat" or come-hither kind of motion.

And even though the condescending nature of it annoys me, my body is already moving toward his silent command.

"The hell you want, Hanky?"

He smiles at me like there's something funny I might have missed. He looked me over completely as I walked over, but he takes his time again to drag his eyes from my feet back up to my eyes. I feel his gaze languidly caressing my body, across my skin, and through my bloodstream. It sizzles right through me. I'm so affected by his observance of me that I'm almost waiting for words of appreciation or approval. I widen my eyes for a response to my question, but I'm met with silence and that stupid, sexy smirk.

"Well? Did you need something? I'm not sure if you're aware of the social gesture you just gave me, but it gives the assumption that you wanted something."

No response. He just stares back. Breathing loudly and basking in silence.

"Unbelievable. I don't have the patience to decipher your facial expressions or what could possibly equate your need to beckon me over to you like I'm some kind of eager pet," I say in a huff.

That gets him to laugh. "Shut up."

"Shut up?! That's what you're going to say to me right now. *Shut up!* There's something wrong with the way you think you can talk to women. It's like a man puts on a tuxedo, and we all, as the opposite sex, should genuflect, when really, it's just a suit with a dumb bow—" he cuts me off by grabbing my hand. His strong, comforting grip drags me behind him in the direction of the dance floor, through couples already moving and a few feet away from the twelve-piece band.

He pulls me around and into his arms, making my heart pick up speed. I bump into his chest as he wraps one arm around my lower back, the other close to our sides, clasping my hand in his.

"Yes, shut up. I was going to tell you to dance with me, but your big mouth wouldn't stop moving. So shut up, pull that fine fucking body up against mine, and dance with me."

What!?

But I can't even question what he just said, because my entire being has some kind of chemical reaction to his words. My temperature spikes. And the warmth feels good. An infusion that goes straight to all the parts that like attention. I step slightly closer, just like he demanded. Into his orbit. It's like the air that's around him is cleaner, easier to take in. Lighter and more freeing than I've breathed in a long time.

I should be doing the opposite. I should be reminding myself of the reasons why this proximity is dangerous. I should remember the words that Bea just spouted off mere minutes ago. But I can't. I *won't*.

Leaning in, he lowers his mouth next to my ear. "Can we just pretend that we don't know each other? That we aren't supposed to stay away. Just for the rest of this song? You looked too good in this dress. There was no way I couldn't touch you tonight." As he hovers along my neck, he takes a long breath in through his nose, like he's smelling the lemon blossoms that decorate my skin. His voice is low as he says, "You're lucky I don't drag you right out of here and taste you, Pixie."

I nod, enough that he can feel my hair brush up against his cheek. I'm aware of how close we are to one another. How anyone who is watching can probably see exactly what my body is doing. I'm fucking melting into this man. My legs feel numb and the only thing I want more than for him to keep talking in that low rasp in my ear is to remind me of how to be properly kissed.

I can't seem to find words. And silence isn't something I'm familiar with. He closes any gaps left between our bodies, so I'm flush against him. That's when I really feel him. How he holds me. But also... "Please tell me you have a water bottle in your pocket," I say with a smile. I know full well he's not toting around water to get his gallon in today.

He never flinches. Not even a twitch of his lips. Instead, he says, "I have a water bottle in my pocket. You thirsty?"

I lean in closer because we're talking about his cock, and I need him to hear me loud and clear. I have no idea what they're pumping into these air vents, but I have pure unadulterated lust pulsing through my body, and I want nothing more than to get this man in my mouth immediately.

"I'm fucking parched, baby." I look up, and finally, the dimple pops in his cheek.

CHAPTER 29

Giselle

"WHERE ARE THEY GOING?" I HEAR LAW SAY TO HIMSELF AS Henry pulls me through the doors. We rushed from the tent, and into the main house. If we weren't moving so fast, then I'd probably feel the small shivers that I know are running across my skin in anticipation. Perhaps even nervous energy that has nowhere to go other than forward. I don't dare look back to acknowledge it. Law's question or the fact that I heard it. Who knows what kind of need or truth would flash in our wake. If we're lucky, he's drunk already, and nobody else even noticed the way we danced. Or how Henry held me. Or how he's speeding me out of here, like if he doesn't hurry, I'm going to take back what I just said.

Spoiler: I won't.

The funny part is that it's usually him who has enough stamina to walk away, remember our agreement, and drop back into the roles we've cultivated. But the man is on a mission. Something finally snapped, and he doesn't want to think about the truths or realities. Maybe tonight we can be in a bubble. Tomorrow, we'll remember the reasons why this shouldn't happen.

With where my head's at, there isn't a single brain cell that would dare peek through and tell me this was a bad idea. There's nothing that would keep me from clinging to his hand and following him wherever he's willing to take me. I can't keep the smile from my lips, but I bite them just in case I look slightly insane to anyone that may see. "Where we goin', big guy?"

He doesn't answer, squeezing my hand instead. We walk with eager steps up the staircase and down the hall of the second floor. Henry nods at one of the security men in the hallway. Yeah, they know what's about to go down. I assume they're there to be sure people don't wander around the house. Kind of like what we're doing.

Henry pulls me into the room at the end of the hall.

"I don't get a bedroom?" I start laughing, because in all honesty, I don't care where we are. I want this man to hold me and touch me everywhere. The location of where that happens means less than nothing to me. But I also can't help busting his balls a little. It's too easy. And it's second nature by now.

I don't get words as a response. Instead, he locks the door and then stalks toward me. Not stopping, he takes off his black velvet tux jacket and drapes it on the counter as he moves closer.

I back up. The backs of my thighs brush against the vanity chair because I have nowhere else to go. Chills trickle down my arms with every step he takes.

"This fucking mouth of yours," he says in a low tone that might as well be the frequency that turns my clit to jelly because, like Pavlov's dog, this bitch is salivating at the sound.

"Can't decide what you want to do with it?" I raise my eyebrows in a taunting gesture.

"There's plenty I can do with it, but right now, I'm going to kiss you. Because as much as you piss me off most of the time, the one thing that pisses me off even more is the fact that nobody kisses me the way you do. And my mouth has craved yours for so long, if I don't feel your lips on mine in the next second, I'm not responsible for what might happen."

Well, shit.

He grabs me by the back of my neck, his fingers threading through my hair, and he pulls me toward his mouth.

"Then stop talking and kiss me already."

His plush mouth, with his full lips, skate over mine. The softness of his kiss catches me off guard, but only for a moment, because as soon as I part my lips and let my tongue glide out, the promised urgency and confidence return in abundance. The way we kiss each other is easy, setting a punishingly beautiful rhythm that's hard to forget. I'm lost in it. The way his lips move around mine, the way his tongue teases and plunders, it's filled with far too much emotion, and the promise that, if I'm good, I'll be able to feel them whenever I want.

I'm reveling in his moment, taking all I can get. In our bubble, all that exists are the sounds of my whimpering and his groaning. I've craved this so badly, and now that

I'm here, my energy feels replenished, like a full body charge for finally allowing who I've starved myself of for so long, to satiate me.

I feel the edge of the vanity pressing against the back of my thighs, just below my ass. Shifting myself up, I sit, and the movement bunches my dress. The coolness of the counter forces my eyes to open. Even up close, barely in focus, the man is breathtaking. His strong features are always stare-worthy, but with his strength and the way he's holding me, he's even more beautiful.

I brush my palm over his cock, up and down slowly. "I need to see it. I already know it's glorious. I've thought about what he looks like for far too long." He laughs as I start to move my fingers furiously, making quick work of his buckle. I'm a damn ninja when it comes to belts, buckles, and zippers.

Stopping my hands, he looks down at me and says, "I didn't drag you up here so I could fuck your mouth, G." That makes me raise an eyebrow. *Fucking liar.* And the way he says it makes me tingle. I don't normally tingle, but the promise of fucking my mouth versus me sucking his dick sounds like the best twisting of words. *Dirty wordsmith.*

Before I can call his bluff, he's dropping to his knees. Eye level with my chest now, he drags his hands over my thighs. I'm compact, but my hips and thighs are full. In his hands, however, they almost look petite. I am not, nor have ever been, a petite woman. He jerks my hips toward him, the movement pushing my dress up higher. My ass perches on the edge of the table, forcing my upper body to slouch back against the mirror.

"You look fucking incredible tonight," he says, looking into my eyes as if I'd object. I won't. I do look incredible. Hearing it out loud, though, from his lips to my ears, is a bit intoxicating. "But that's nothing new." He tilts his head to the right and places my legs up over his shoulders. He plants a kiss on my inner left thigh, pulling back when something catches his eye. I smile and almost giggle, knowing what he's about to read.

"Are you fucking kidding me?" he breathes hungrily, licking across the cursive lettering with its exaggerated curves and loops. Right where my hips crease, where my thighs meet the path to my pussy, is a statement I made him aware of all those years ago.

It's not going to lick itself...

If you're not close, it's hard to read, and many who have seen it haven't taken the time to really look, since the cursive makes it difficult to read at a glance, but not for Henry. Nope, my flyboy, at this proximity, pays attention to details. Which is why, when I inked this tattoo years ago, I hoped he'd eventually see it again.

"This is new," he says with a smirk. Another lick.

"Not that new."

He flicks his eyes back to mine. "This for me, Pixie?"

My face flushes with another wave of heat, and I smile. While every piece of art on my body is for me, that one in particular was always meant to be read by him.

"That's the sexiest thing I've ever seen." He nips at the same spot, capturing my skin between his teeth. It catches me off guard, and I yelp. *Dear goddesses of the universe, if I've ever deserved anything decent in this life, please let it be the orgasm about to happen.*

"I've had enough of ignoring what I want." He tilts his head to the left, kissing my right inner thigh. My breath catches. "Pretending like I hate you, when all I really hate is how I can't have you."

I'm so fucking turned on that my pussy is tingling in anticipation. His words spark every inch of me. They must knock me under some kind of spell, because I can't speak. I've lost the ability to form words. I can only watch. And feel.

"Tell me to stop, G."

Kiss. Nip. Lick.

"I dare you to tell me to stop."

I move my head from right to left. The universal signal for "no," but it must not comply because he is still looking at me, waiting for an answer. So I take a breath and gather what's left of my wits. No miscommunication on what I expect from this man.

"You had better know how to eat pussy, Henry, because if you're all talk and no show, then I'll die of disappointment." I give him the most alluring smile that I can muster, and he licks his lips. I've amused him with the challenge. "Don't you dare fucking stop."

He bites my thigh. But this time, I knew it was coming, and the pain from it sets a fuse, lighting up whatever hadn't already turned on in my body. My senses are primed, and I feel the warmth of his skin through his shirt as I wrap my hands around his forearms. I'm surrounded by the delicious smell of him, leather and pine; it always seems so masculine, but the scent ultimately makes me feel safe. And I never feel safe with anyone I'm with in this way. I never let go and allow myself to really free-fall into the moment, but in this one, I do. Without question.

The feel of his scruff against my thighs. His eyes on my very wet undies. I'm thankful this dress fits the way it does, because any tighter and I would have opted for Spanx. And while they do wonders, they're not the sexiest undergarment to rip off in a fit of desire. My Target-brand sheer black thongs aren't La Perla, by any stretch, but they still look hot as hell, albeit probably ruined after this.

He jerks my hips up even closer to his lips and I'm entranced as I watch as his face disappears from sight. I feel him nudge my clit ever so lightly. Such an over-achiever. The fact that on his first contact he finds my clit with barely any light, and while it's still fully covered, is a feat that deserves a standing ovation. I've had my fair share of men searching for it with a phone light and still missed. He exhales against my soaked panties, and it makes me crave friction. I want more. I *need* more.

"Henry. Oh God," I whimper. "Do that again."

Even saying his name turns me on. Friction or not, it's not going to take much to send an orgasm toppling through my body. Too much anticipation. Too many years of teasing, and far too many encounters that I've had to take care of on my own.

He bites me again, and this time it sparks a moan out of me. Before I can even ask, he's pushing my panties to the side and is moving just the tip of his tongue up and down, while flicking my clit at the finish of each drag. It's still a tease, and just as I'm ready to beg, he flattens his tongue and drags it devastatingly slow. Lapping up the arousal that greeted him at the beginning of his dirty promises. Oh fuck, I remember that tongue. I remember the pace. I want to send it a fruit basket and thank you note for still being a star performer. Well. Fucking. Done.

He pulls back to watch my face. If I had to guess, I probably look surprised. Needy for more. My mouth is slack and moaning at the loss of his warm tongue and cool breath. Two fingers push into where his tongue just fucked me, and I groan in response.

"Dammit, G. You're going to make me come just watching you get finger fucked, aren't you?" he says with a low gravel to his voice. The tone of it is erotic as all hell, while the accusation has me preening. His fingers pump in and out of me to the tempo of a waltz. Slow and steady, but building to something beautiful. Faster, and with purpose.

"Don't you dare come yet, Hanky. I still need to see how much of that cock will fit down my throat," I say, finishing on another moan. It makes him laugh. Hey there, dimple. Instead of a verbal response, however, he curls the two fingers that have now started to pick up the pace, hitting me in *my* spot. And I'm silent. I open my mouth to say his name or speak to any of the Gods willing to listen to this heaven on earth, but I can't. This man's fingers have managed to do the impossible and stifle my mind and my ability to speak. I can only feel. Bask in the warmth that's traveling across every limb. The low buzzing that settles in my gut, getting ready for something far greater.

His mouth descends back to where it belongs. He licks my clit, then kisses the hood of my pussy, and I think

I die a little. A small tremor rolls along my abs. A quiver. The man makes out with my fucking clit and then drives three massive fingers into me with orchestrated perfection. My orgasm doesn't crest into something poetic. No, it thrashes into my body and explodes from my lips. Both sets. The silence has ceased. And instead, I yell and moan while my body pulses around his fingers. My thighs shake and clench around his neck, beyond my control.

"Henry. Please," I moan.

"That's it, Pixie. Do as you're told and come all over my fingers. Show me how good that feels," he tells me, his mouth still against my pussy, still moving his fingers in and out slowly. "So beautiful. My name coming out of your mouth as you drip down my hand. That's it."

The movement mixed with his words makes my thighs shake again. Or maybe they never stopped. He buries his mouth into my lap, his tongue moving right above where his fingers are buried, and before I can say anything or even shift my weight, he bites my clit, and it causes a second wave to barrel through my entire body. I grip his hair with one hand and bite my other fist to stifle the scream tearing from my throat.

I don't know how I'm ever coming back from that.

"You taste so fucking good." He licks me again, and I'm so sensitive now I jump and giggle. All the imagination and vibrators in the world would never come close to replicating that.

As soon as my mind emerges from the fog of that orgasm, I look down to find Henry staring up at me with a smirk and eyes filled with complete lust. Perhaps even awe. He just made me scream and possibly see what an alternate reality could look like. My orgasm is all over his scruff and the filthy part of me hopes that he just leaves it. His reward for a job well done. I want to tell him that I've never come so hard in my life, but the thought is interrupted.

A knock on the door pulls our attention away from one another.

"Sir, just letting you know it's 11:55," the male voice from the other side says.

I sit up in a rush. All of a sudden sobered. "Fuck. We need to get down there. We can't miss the countdown. Everyone will notice we're not there. Especially your sister. FUCK!"

I've already hopped down from the vanity, now balancing on one foot to fully remove my thong. It's soaked and stretched out. She had a good run.

I'm too distracted to hear if Henry has anything to say in response. Instead, I search the room for my shoe. "Where the hell is my other shoe?!"

"Right here," he says as it dangles from his finger. I snatch it away and pull it on. "You stay here, I'll go first." But instead of listening to me and staying put, he follows directly behind me as I start to rush down the stairs.

"What are you doing?" I look back at him.

"I'm coming with you. If you want to countdown to midnight, then you're going to need to kiss someone to ring in the New Year."

I whip my head around to look back at him. *Is he serious? That can't happen. Not in front of everyone, and he knows it.*

"No. Nope. That's not happening. We aren't parading our hook-up around on your sister's night. No way."

We're still walking through the main room and past the kitchen before I stop to look at him again. Three minutes to go before balloons and confetti assault everyone on the other side of this space.

He says nothing. Not acknowledging what I've said, he pushes past me.

But before I can speak up once more, he stops his movement. His hands pause from opening the doors, and he turns to me. "There is no version of this world where you're so much as looking at another man tonight, never mind kissing someone other than me at midnight." He runs his hands through his hair and huffs in frustration. *God, I love pissing this man off.* "And I'm not kissing anyone else. Not when I can still taste you on my tongue."

Heat works its way across my cheeks. I don't want to kiss anyone else either. But I also haven't had any time to figure out what just happened. It may have felt life-changing, but the truth is that nothing has changed. I'm still me, and anything more with him is still off-limits.

"Those lips don't kiss, bite, or lick any other lips than mine."

There's nothing hotter than this man telling me what to do, claiming me. The feminist in me is fist pumping and hooting right along. Horny bitch.

He grits his teeth, voice deeper as he says, "I will not beg you to want me. I'm done playing this game. It's gone on for long enough. Now get your ass in that room."

I *feel* his declaration as he opens the doors to the party. I let him walk through without me, because I'm caught. There have been moments of weakness over the years. Stupid fights. Hell, even the promise and flirtation of what just happened upstairs, but never *that*. There's not a single place I'd rather be than in his dirty thoughts. And on his shit list. But the idea of being in his arms while others can see it makes it too real. A place that is bound to be a happiness that'll be plucked from me if the wrong people ever found me. Fuck, I still want it, though. It's been more than a decade. I've been smart. If I haven't been found yet, then maybe they've stopped looking.

When the roar of the crowd starts counting down from ten, it forces me to make up my mind. I take a much-needed breath and decide that it's time to finally go after the one thing I've been running from. I will go into that room with all the confidence in the world and kiss the ever-loving hell out of the man I want.

CHAPTER 30

Giselle

But neither of those things happen.

Two very opposite things happen instead, the moment I set foot back into the party. At first, I find Henry right away. The buzz of the crowd makes it feel like time slows down when I see him. Or maybe it's the counting down and yelling of, "Three... Two..." But I don't hear anything after that. Before I hear the number one, his eyes meet mine. My confidence is gone and in its place is a conflicting mix of calm and excitement.

People around us are singing that stupid New Year's song about old acquaintances being forgotten. The irony of those words. The old acquaintance I could never forget stands within reach. He gives me a smile, dimple out, and oh fuck, do I want to reach for him. But as soon as his lips twitch, and he steps toward me, time jostles back.

From slow motion into a body-quaking pace.

The movement of someone over Henry's shoulder

catches my attention, and my entire body freezes. My smile immediately lost. Every bit of calmness and warmth instantly drained from my body. Everything stops moving. It feels like I've stopped breathing. The flash of a neck tattoo, and a laugh that's been buried in my memories, barks out into the crowd, mere steps from where I danced earlier.

Henry must see my change in body language, because he moves quickly toward me. I can't say anything. Not even when he asks, "What's wrong?" He looks nervously into my eyes, around my face. Pulling me into his chest, he wraps his arms around my body. "You're shaking. What's wrong?"

Still, nothing comes out. I don't let go of him, even when he tries to pull back and move us off the dance floor. *Please don't make a scene.*

Bea comes up to our side. *I thought she left.*

She puts her hand on my lower back and leans into Henry. I hear her say, "We have eyes here. And I need you to get her out. Take her up to the master suite and I'll meet you there in a few minutes. Try not to draw any attention." He grips me tighter. "Now."

He speaks quietly. "You take her up there, Bea. It'll draw more attention if I disappear with her again. My brothers are watching me, and I wouldn't put it past them to make noise about this. Let me talk to Jack. I'll be three minutes behind."

Bea nods and pulls me out of Henry's arms. I don't register anything that's happening around me, only that we're moving with the intent to make it out of the open space, through the living room, kitchen, and up to Everly and Jack's bedroom. Every hair on my body is aware that I'm in danger. My stomach rolls. My hands sweat. My body knows that someone is near that isn't supposed to be.

I only remember a few clips of time once we make it upstairs.

Bea talking frantically on the phone. Calling in some of her agents to the event. Undercover in plain clothes so they don't throw off any red flags.

"Tell me, G, did you interact with him?" She sits on the floor in front of me with worry in her eyes. "Did he see you?" I can't even respond. I'm still frozen. Watching as if I'm out of my body. I hear her swear a few times and then Henry comes into the room.

I don't understand why she's talking to him like he's aware of the details. Why the man with the neck tattoo of a tiger's head is significant. Why it's caused this commotion. And all of a sudden, I'm worried about the rest of the family downstairs. "Henry. Everly. Everly needs to be safe." He rushes over to me. Looking me in the eyes, he pushes the pieces of hair that have fallen down behind my ears, cupping my face.

"She's fine. Everyone here is going to be okay. We need to get you out of here, though," he says, his tone laced with concern. It's not the Henry Riggs I'm used to dealing with. This version is calm, in control, which is nothing new, but the twinge of sweetness in his tone I notice. The same as his hands, which are shaking slightly. He's rattled, nervous even.

"I'm not. I can't leave. Bea, don't make me. Don't make me." I start hyperventilating. I'm not prepared to leave this all behind. I don't want to start over again. I can't. I'm not strong enough to leave another family in my wake. *My new family*. I didn't say goodbye to Everly. I can't just disappear again.

"Breathe, G. C'mon. In and out. Slow down. You're going to make yourself pass out. In and out. In and out," Henry keeps repeating, holding on to me.

It doesn't work and moments later, everything goes black.

I must have passed out because my eyes flutter open, and I see Henry hovering above me. I'm cradled in his arms. My head resting against his strong chest. His heart is beating faster than normal.

"She's waking up," I hear him say.

Bea walks over and looks at me, before saying to Henry, "Keep her safe."

Looking back at me, she says, "Hey, kid, I need you to take these and drink some water." She puts a pill in my mouth and then tips water up to my lips. I swallow. It tastes bitter. Before I can say anything, the room gets a little hazy again. I feel drunk, and I realize I've just drugged myself. *Shit*.

PART III
HIDING HER

CHAPTER 31

Henry

"Grand Cayman Traffic, Skyhawk Six Niner, five miles northwest, inbound to land. Left forty-five to runway one, inbound fields," I radio. I look over my shoulder into the back galley seat. She's still passed out. Whatever Agent Harper gave her must have been strong. G didn't move when we put her on the plane. She's barely made a noise since. And we've been flying for almost four hours now.

A goddamn icon in our town of strength and bravado is who she's become since setting foot in Strutt's Peak. But there was no trace of that tonight. Tonight, she was scared. The loudmouth who pours warmth over everyone she loves, and who spits fire and one-liners over the rest of us lucky assholes, was a shell of herself in a matter of seconds. I've never been angrier in my life than seeing her like that.

The radio crackles, knocking me out of my thoughts

again. "Approach, Skyhawk. Cleared for landing," the island's air traffic responds.

Around thirty minutes later, we land smoothly in the private flight field on the northwest side of Grand Cayman in the Cayman Islands. It didn't take much thought regarding where I'd take her. We had to move quickly, and Harper didn't want to take any chances of sending her to a safe house. Instead, her direction was to get her out of Colorado. It's easy to move fast when you know what you need. I'm a planner. And when someone is important to me, I don't cut corners.

A plane, a place, a plan. With a quick call to her connections, Harper had a small plane waiting. My brother-in-law, Jack, could help secure a place. The richest guy in the room will always have a place. Somewhere that didn't have a spread in a home magazine, or a spot that anyone would know about, and then he'd have a backup just in case.

Jack has properties all over the world. There are very few he keeps vacant, but I knew his place here, on Grand Cayman, was wide open. He was telling us about the renovations that had just wrapped up. The beachside paradise with every amenity anyone could think of, Casa Luna Portocalie. A wedding gift for my sister.

There's a Jeep waiting for us at the airstrip with the keys in the ignition and a GPS set with our destination. I round the back of the plane and grab our duffel bags. The warm air hits me like a swipe of Milo's tongue across my face; not exactly gross, but not the best feeling you want lingering for too long. I'm still wearing my tuxedo. I ditched the velvet jacket, but I'm sweating, regardless.

The humidity and nerves hit at the same time. I'm lucky we were able to get out of Strutt's; the prediction for heavier snow squalls could have kept us grounded. We're lucky we left when we did.

I have a satellite phone, and we'll be able to connect to our devices back home when it's clear. No one outside Agent Harper and Jack knows we're not in Strutt's Peak right now. It would look strange that the two people who seem to hate each other would abruptly leave a big family event together.

We'll sit tight. I know Harper will have a plan beyond my own. She's more than capable of handling this situation. I'm not some kind of secret agent to swoop in and kill the bad guy. I'm just the transportation. The lookout. The safety net. When it's clear, then we go back. Hopefully, without any repercussions, like relocation.

My gut sinks at the thought of her leaving. Needing to disappear. This is the short-term solution, so she can go back to her life in Strutt's Peak without any issues. It's her home. *Our home.*

A few minutes later, the GPS has us pulling into a massive villa. *Fucking Jack Deacon.* The sprawling villa in front of us is incredible. Brightly lit landscaping. I can hear the ocean breaking on the other side.

"What the fuck?" A groggy voice interrupts my assessment of the place. G sits up in her seat and looks down at her dress. "Why am I sweating? And it smells like the ocean."

I keep quiet and get out of the Jeep. At least she's talking now. The shock has worn off enough for her to see that we're no longer in the cold of Strutt's. I move around back and lift the bags out of the open trunk.

"We had to get you out of there fast," I say and move toward the front door. I tap in the code. I don't wait for her. I don't want to answer any questions until we're both inside, and I tell Harper we're safely tucked away.

The motion-censored lights in the main living space illuminate, and it's not lost on me that I'm in fucking paradise here. The massive room is cool and inviting. A quick assessment and I can tell almost everything in this house can be electronically accessed. Monitors embedded on surfaces and walls. Recessed lighting that activates with movement. I'm sure there's security, but I can deal with who has access to that later. The floor-to-ceiling windows along the far back wall mimic Jack's home in Strutt's. As soon as I walk closer, I realize they can be completely opened by the touch of a screen. I press two more, and a long rectangular infinity pool glows from under the water, then a bar lights up, then small white lights that outline the inside of a cabana, and then finally a daybed and umbrella that overlooks the small waterfall dropping water into the pool. I laugh, shaking my head, and under my breath, mumble, "Small place on the beach, my ass." This isn't a hideaway. It's a vacation resort.

A few hammocks are placed around the patio. To the left is a sandy walkway peppered with pathway lights that move toward what I can assume is the beach and ocean.

"Where are we?"

I don't answer her. Instead, I look around the living

room and take a seat on the plush couch. I'm so tired. Sitting was a bad idea.

"Henry! Fucking answer me. Now is NOT the time to be evasive. I need clear, precise answers. Starting with where we are, and how we got here." She's starting to freak out. And for good reason. Her world just tipped on its axis, and she couldn't do anything about it except buckle up.

"It's late." I look at my watch.

"I don't give a fuck," she spits out with slicing attitude. *Is she fucking serious right now?*

I turn my head slowly, reminding myself that she just had a big thing happen and practically shut down and then blacked out. "Tuck the attitude away right now." She opens her mouth to say more, but something stops her. Maybe my tone. It's clear I'm not in any condition right now to put up with her shit. "You needed to get out of Strutt's. Something happened, and your Aunt Bea asked that I take you out of town immediately."

"And you did," she says, brow furrowed.

"I did," I say, nodding my head once.

"Just like that?" Her eyes grow wide, waiting for more.

"Just like that." I clear my throat and look around the room. "This is Jack's place."

She nods slowly. Still catching up to what I'm telling her. "Oh God, Everly. Does she know where we are right now? She's going to think, oh fuck, what is she going to think?" She lifts the back of her hand up to her mouth. Worry is painted all over her face. She loves my sister, and it doesn't go unnoticed that she's more concerned about leaving my sister's celebration than about what happened earlier.

"Can we do this after I've slept for a little bit?"

Surprisingly, she nods and softly agrees. "Okay."

I pull myself up and move past her toward the hallway, where I assume bedrooms will be, but as I look around further, I notice only a few doors. One to a massive theater room, another to a fully equipped gym, one to a full photo studio, and the last to a huge bedroom. *Is he for real?* One fucking bedroom. In this huge ass house, one damn room?!

My nerves are shot, so I'll sleep wherever at this point. I toss her bag into the bedroom and drag my bag back to the open living space.

"You take the room. End of the hall. I have a few things I need to do."

I watch her hesitate, like she wants to say more. Ask more. But I mean what I've said, if I don't get some sleep, I'm not going to be able to function the way I need to while we're here. I hear the door close, and I finally take a deep breath. Relief runs through me. Knowing that she's out of harm's way, and I can make sure she stays that way.

I move outside to the pool and sit on the daybed. Who puts a bed outside? It would have been smarter to add one more to the *inside* of the house. I breathe in the salted air, trying to relax. It doesn't work, but it feels good to do it anyway. Pulling out the burner phone Harper gave me, I type out a message.

Landed and safe.

AGENT HARPER

> The problem here is under investigation. Sit tight. As far as I can tell, there was no recognition. The attendee was a coincidence. Vetting further. At least 48 hours. Keep a low profile wherever you are.

Two days on an island. Alone with G. We try to keep any time alone limited to less than ten minutes. I just had my head buried between her legs, my fingers and tongue thrust into her, working like fucking champions to hear her orgasm. I can still fucking smell her because there was no time to wash my face. And I'm enough of a goner for her that I'd probably have skipped it even if I did have time. I couldn't hold back any longer. I've reached my limit, which to be honest, most men wouldn't have lasted days, never mind years with the way that woman burrows into lives.

It's not lost on me that I threw in the towel on keeping a distance, and within minutes, she was in danger. I know it's irrational to think one had anything to do with the other, but the entire point of staying away from her for this long was in an effort to keep her safe. No connections to her old life. Keep her out of the spotlights that are sometimes shown on me and my role in my family's business. But it didn't matter.

Now we're here. How the hell are these forty-eight hours going to work?

I look up at the clear sky and laugh. This is not how I expected this day to end. "Please, whoever is up there, don't let *this* be what kills me." There's no way I can keep her at a distance now. She's going to have more questions when she wakes up, and the only one I can answer is why I'm here with her. The problem is, though, I don't know if she's ready to hear the answer.

A movement out of the corner of my eye has me jack-knifing up.

"I didn't mean to scare you," she says, looking uncharacteristically sheepish. And before I can get a word in, she holds her hand up. "I'm not asking any questions. I just..." She shifts her weight from one foot to the other. I lean my head to the side, trying to get her to look at me. When she finally does, she asks in a whisper, "Will you just lie with me? I don't—" She clears her throat, biting back the emotion that I hear shaking its way forward. "I can't be by myself right now."

I give her a nod and get up, following her down the hall and watching as she climbs into bed.

"I'm just going to use the bathroom. I'll be right out." It's smart to get out of this tux and maybe shower. Wash away the adrenaline that might keep me from sleeping.

It's less than ten minutes later when I come back into the bedroom. The light next to her side table is turned off and I only hear the faint sounds of the ocean. She's facing away from me, but I'm guessing by her slow and heavy breathing that she's fallen asleep. I quietly move to the bed and try my hardest not to jostle the mattress as I lower myself. I'm exhausted, but she needs to sleep. Her shock might have worn off, but I have no idea what she's going to feel like when she wakes up and tries to process everything.

I don't think twice about moving my body close to

hers and wrapping an arm around her middle to pull her closer. I take a deep breath, maybe in relief, or maybe just to finally settle. Holding her after what we just fled from, the crossed lines and dangerous pasts, it's exactly what I need. To be close to her. My pulse rate lowers. My eyes grow heavier. I breathe her in... lemons and sugar. The sweetness makes me smile, because she is sweet, underneath all of her bravado and jokes. She's the sweetest person I've ever met. It's just not obvious. You have to really look to see it.

It's not how I would have wanted it, but holding her like this, feeling her melt into my arms, it's a better ending to the day than I could have imagined.

CHAPTER 32

Giselle

THE HYPNOTIC SOUNDS OF STATIC WAKE ME. I STRETCH MY arms and legs out in opposite directions like a carefree cat. Taking a breath, in and out. I feel rested. But then it hits me. I realize, before I've even opened my eyes, that I'm not at home. The fluffiness of the bedcovers, the smell of leather and pine, coffee brewing, and the calmly quiet sounds.

I crack open one eye slowly, knowing the room is bright even behind my heavy eyelids. I'll be blinded if I sit up wide-eyed too quickly. As I open the other, the blur of sleep lifts. In front of me is a wall of glass that frames a modern paradise. Hammocks, a beautiful pool. *Is that a waterfall?* The sound of static isn't static at all, but the ocean. I hear waves pulsing and large swooshing every ten or so seconds.

Last night comes flooding back to me. Someone

holding me. Dancing. Henry's mouth. The thought of what we did worries me, and then the real panic rears in.

"Oh no," I whisper into my hand as it flies toward my mouth.

I remember. The tattoo. The voice. Henry getting me out of there. Wait, and Bea? They spoke like they had a plan for what was happening. I take a shallow breath. My chest feels tight and the air that I'm trying to pull in will only move so far before I have to push it out. The air is humid, but a steady breeze tells me that wherever we are, it's far away from the snow of Strutt's Peak. I'm safe. I think.

I'm up and out of the bed so fast that I knock my shoulder on the doorway.

"Motherfucker." *Dammit, that hurt.*

I pick up the pace as I move down the hallway, passing by a few other rooms without even a glance. I couldn't tell you what's inside, but this place is beautiful. Expensive. But it's at the end of the hall that has me stumbling to a halt. He's here. I blow out the breath that I was holding. He's here. I'm safe.

I furrow my brow, and the words are out before I realize it. "Why are you here?"

"Did you just call me a motherfucker?" he asks without turning around. "Rude. Even for you, G." He sways back and forth in front of the oven's stovetop. His tone sounds light, not the usual grumpy growl.

"What are you doing here, Henry?" I ground out. I hate not knowing what's happening.

"Making breakfast," he says in another cheery tone.

"Well, brunch, really. It's almost one in the afternoon. Local time, at least."

"Where is local time?" I ask as I move closer to his brunch spread.

"Cayman Islands."

I stop my path, looking around the room. "Fuck," I whisper to myself. I move to sit on the island stool and then stare at the food before me. Fruits and slices of bread are set out as if we've just stumbled into a resort's continental buffet.

"Now what?" I ask, loud enough to make him pause what he was doing. He doesn't turn around right away, though. Instead, he finishes stirring whatever he's cooking in the small pot.

He tilts his head to the side, acknowledging that he heard me.

Breaking the silence, he finally says, "We wait."

I play around with the idea of waiting. I try to work out what it is he's doing here right now, and the only obvious explanation is he was the only way I could get out of town so fast. He knows how to fly, and I needed to be taken out of the situation. Bea must have asked him to move me quickly. Why would she ask him, though? Why not another agent?

But as I sit there and try to work out the logic, I'm distracted by Henry's shirtless body. The now massive tattoo that runs slightly down the back of his left shoulder, but keeps going farther on the other side, down his chest and along the side of his torso. I'm a bit pissed I haven't done work on it. I see some feathered lines that could have been cleaner.

My eyes follow his well-sculpted back to a pair of low-slung gray sweats, cut off at the knees. My mouth waters. Could be the view, or the smell of apples and onions that are blanketing the room.

A French press is steeping coffee on the counter behind him. I hear the crashing waves colliding with the wind outside, and I'm just noticing now the sound of steel drums and guitar guiding Bob Marley's promises of every little thing being alright. *Touché, Bobby.*

Maybe some of that optimism is seeping through because I'm smiling right now as I gawk at two beautifully round and muscular ass cheeks gliding from left to right, flexing up and down. Does it make me a bad person that I want to slap them like bongos to the beat of the song? The song that will always remind me of him. This man is nearly impossible to ignore, because aside from the reggaeton Magic Mike show happening mere feet away, he's also cooking for me. He always cooks for me.

It doesn't go unnoticed that he makes me a vegetarian option at every Sunday dinner with the family. I never let myself swoon over it. I recognize that Henry is a people pleaser. That food is his way of doing that. Pleasing the people who matter to him. But with no one watching but me, I'm swooning. Hard.

Swaying his perfectly sculpted body, Henry Montana Riggs is in paradise, with me, making me brunch and humming. I watch for a few seconds more because, truthfully, I never allow myself to look at him for too long. Too many *what ifs* and *maybe justs* always circle my head when I stare for too long at this man. I've schooled myself into only brief visual assaults, nothing more than a few beats. But we're not in Strutt's Peak, and it would honestly be a crime against humanity not to appreciate the spectacular aura of this man. In those shorts.

Fucking hell, he's definitely going commando. The two dimples on his lower back are like little divots that deserve a celebratory kiss, marking the end of his back muscles and the beginning of that toned tush. I lick my lips. I'll definitely be using this material when I'm playing DJ Clitty Rubs later.

The clank of something being put into the sink startles me. Seriously, what's wrong with me? The worst possible thing that could have happened actually happened, and I'm thinking about sex. It's a new low.

I keep berating myself as I watch Henry scoop out a perfectly poached egg from swirling, boiling water. He places it on top of orange, green, and purple vegetables in a bowl. Then he repeats the same process with the second poached egg in a second bowl. He pushes one in front of me, turning around and searching for the utensil drawer, and giving me a fork a moment later.

I take a bite of crisp apple with salty, sweet potato, and the kick of onion assaults my tastebuds. *Geez, I will put anything in my mouth that this man makes.* I hum over the next bite. My eyes close.

"Good?"

When I open my eyes, I find him with a smirk. It's laced with satisfaction.

I just nod and shovel another forkful into my mouth. Truthfully, I'm starving. But really, it's completely possible I may just say something utterly vulnerable, like, *"the way you cook for me is a fucking art form."* Or, *"you're perfect."*

"What is this?" I mumble over a forkful.

He sprinkles a pinch of salt over the egg, then takes a pepper mill and grinds a half turn of pepper over it. "Give me the fork."

I pause and then hand the fork to him.

"You need to break open the egg, so the yolk coats this." He pushes his fork into the center of the egg, and a small gush of golden yellow spills over the vegetable hash. He pulls a small bite onto the fork and moves it toward my mouth.

"You're feeding me now?"

"We're alone too." He raises his brows with a wiggle. "You nervous?"

"Only if you've poisoned me."

"Shut up and put this in your mouth," he says as he stares at my lips and nudges the fork forward.

I smile and lift my eyebrow. "Tell me more." There's sarcasm laced in that statement, but I want to hear him say that again. Preferably after he loses the shorts.

He lets out a small laugh. "I've got plenty to fill that mouth of yours, G."

I open my mouth and take a bite. It's fucking heaven. The promise he just made is one I plan to collect on at some point in this life, but for now, I'll settle for this delicious meal.

He leans in closer so that I can't help but stop chewing. I stare at his lips while he says, "Stop overthinking." As I lift my eyes to his, my neck feels warm. My cheeks burn, and a rolling tide of excitement passes through my stomach. "Eat."

He passes the fork back and I take it. But not before his fingers brush mine in the exchange. That's all it takes for me to remember what I'm doing here right now. It's not the time to be flirting or whatever the hell *that* just was.

I clear my throat. "Why are you here?"

He looks at me as he digs into his bowl. "Why do you think?"

I drop my fork and it makes a larger clank than I had intended, but I'm not in the mood to make guesses.

"Why are you here, Henry?" I ask quietly.

"You weren't safe."

"And now I am?"

"You're safe here. With me, yes."

"Why are you here, and not an agent? Or Bea?"

He eats two more giant bites from his bowl and then turns to put it in the oversized sink. Everything in this place is exaggerated. The size of the space. The art hanging from the walls. The man in front of me. All of it feels broad and big. A bit overwhelming.

I wait patiently for more from him. But as I wait, I'm spending more energy keeping my feelings to myself. Like my emotions no longer have a lock. That the shock of running into my past, or it finding me, means I want to tell him everything. To tell him the details of what happened. How I lost everyone who meant something to me. How the broken bones, dislocated jaw, shattered pelvis, and all the bruises that followed were the easiest parts of it. How I cried so hard, and for so long, I don't think I have the ability to cry like that ever again. How I looked for him too. How I was worried that somehow he would be dead, because of me.

The piece I never understood between us. The part that I still don't know how to understand is why wouldn't he have asked more questions. How was it so easy for him to just believe that I wasn't some kind of criminal liar out to swindle him or his family out of money? I came to his town, granted unknowingly, but I was there with a new name, a new look, and his only response was that he wanted me. Oh, I'm such a fuckwit.

I pride myself on not being a fuckwit, but here I am. I never questioned why he just went along with being an arm's-length enemy. Why it wasn't a bigger deal to Bea for me to be connected to someone in Strutt's Peak? The realization must be written all over my face.

"Are you going to answer me, Henry?"

He ignores the question and walks toward the veranda. He pulls out an oversized phone and thrusts it at me.

"Read it."

AGENT HARPER

The problem has been addressed. Working through the clean-up now. Give me the rest of the 48 hours. Keep her safe, Riggs.

I push it back to him.

"That tells me absolutely nothing." I shift in my seat, starting to find nothing more than anger at this entire situation. At myself for not connecting the dots sooner. "I can't believe this. I'm so fucking stupid." I'm already up and moving to the other side of the house. Away from the smirk on his face. I need to breathe in some of this ocean air, otherwise, I might start kicking something. *Or someone.*

He raises his voice so I can hear him as I step onto the patio. "I met your Aunt Bea, or rather, Agent Bea Harper, two nights after I met you. Well, I should say after I met Giselle." I stop and turn around, eyes wide. Watching him and waiting for more. "We both know exactly when I met the real you," he says, dragging his hands through his hair. "She had an offer for me that seemed mutually beneficial." As he brushes right past me and walks toward the pool, I clench my jaw and fist my hands at my sides.

"She knew about my time in the Air Force. The accident. The injury. She also knew other things about my life that nobody really knows." *That* pulls my attention back to the present. "Things like how many times I showed up to the police station asking about your case. How often I called the detective assigned, asking for updates regularly. How I had a tree planted in Central Park in your memory. How I still flew out to Manhattan every couple of months and added to my tattoo every time I went."

I blink and try to digest what he's saying. We only knew each other for a night. Hours, actually. Why would he do that?

He takes a deep breath and looks up at the sky. A grounding breath, because what he's telling me is too heavy. "She didn't come at me with any hidden agenda or threat. Just with an offer to help her keep tabs on people she placed around Colorado in witness protection. I know enough people. I know the towns that nobody would think to look. I travel around for the family business enough to make stops and take the temperature of the areas she had placed some assets. It wasn't a coincidence that one of those people was you. Right in Strutt's Peak. You recognized me. She needed to play interference and find a solution."

I shift uncomfortably, knowing that his attention is focused on my reactions to all of this. I realize with a start that I'm still wearing the green dress from last night. Hiking up the length of the satin material so it's gathered at my hips, I sit on the side of the pool. I drop my feet into the cool, clear water. Then lower to my ankles. Then to my calves. The movement makes ripples as I drag my legs back and forth under the surface. It's enough to distract me from pouring too much into what he's telling me.

He drops down next to me and mimics the movement, gliding his feet into the water. I watch from my peripheral as he leans back on his arms, eyes on me. He's waiting. But I'm still not sure how I feel about any of this.

"I knew within seconds exactly who you were," he says, pulling a piece of my blonde hair between his fingers. "When she said the only way you were staying was if I agreed to work with her, then I knew there was no choice. It was to keep you at a distance and see you, make sure you were okay, or never see you again. Fate wasn't going to deliver you to my doorstep again. So I took her deal. Made the agreement with her, and you."

"What am I supposed to say to all of that?" I ask.

Because that admission... it's a lot. Way more than I ever expected. I pushed him away because I thought I had to, that it was the best thing to do. For everyone involved, but really, it was the least messy for Bea. We're so fucking stupid. Years. YEARS of pushing him away when I didn't want to, but I did it with the understanding that it was the smartest choice. The safest choice. But look at where I am. Where we are. We avoided nothing!

I've picked my feeling. It's anger. I choose anger.

I stand in a rush. It kicks up water, disturbing the infinity edge. "You know what I think?" I raise my voice. "I think you want to be the good guy. Always the good guy. Follow rules, swoop in, and save people, even when you don't want to do it. You couldn't be the hero in the Air Force, so you just do it everywhere else now. You do what you're told. You fly your planes to escape the obligations that were dropped into your lap unwanted. Well, newsflash, Henry. I'm not an obligation. I don't need your help. If you had been man enough to talk to me, and not Bea about all of this, we could have avoided—" I cut myself off. I'm trembling, on the verge of scream-crying from frustration. "*Years* of the back and forth when it didn't have to be this way. YEARS!"

Following my movements, he pulls his legs out of the water but doesn't stand. Instead, he sits there and smirks. He fucking smirks. Like I've missed the punchline.

"I don't think now is the time to start throwing around two-cent therapy sessions. You knew what I wanted from you. And you..." He shakes his head, still smiling like an asshole.

That's what throws my patience over the edge.

"I *what*, Henry?" I say, raising my voice. I have so many emotions rushing through me at the moment, but anger is the one I'm best at showing when it comes to this man. So that's what he's getting. My hands are moving as fast as my heart is beating right now. "My life was thrown into fucking shambles! And the only thing I'm told that will keep me alive is to follow the rules. Be someone entirely different."

He finally stands. A few feet from me, he watches as I unleash.

"Exactly," he says calmly. "You followed the rules. Did what you were told."

Hearing my words thrown back at me is brutal. Deep down, I know I'm being unreasonable, but the time wasted is ripping me apart. I can't stop shaking. "You want to just stand there and tell me that you looked for me, that you were looking after me. Trying to keep me safe..." I pause and move closer to him. "I'll never feel safe again. *Ever!* Look at what happened. I'm not the same woman you met in that bar. I haven't been her for a very long time, so stop thinking you feel something for me, when really, you haven't moved on from the idea of me. This is the clusterfuck of my life—"

I can't finish my rant because I'm suddenly moving through the air and crashing into the pool. That prickheaded sack of— I gulp a mouthful of pool water just before I break the surface.

I cough out water and suck in air. Instead of rushing out, I tread there, cooling off.

"You pushed me in the pool." I gape up at him.

"I did," he says seriously. A moment goes by, and he

lets a small laugh escape from the breath he was holding. "You needed to cool off."

He turns around to head back into the house. But before he makes it too far, I yell out, "I never asked you to ditch your own life and look after me. I don't want you to be the hero. This is my goddamn story. I'm my own hero!"

He doesn't look back, but he hasn't taken another step away either.

"You didn't have to ask. I made my choices. And I'd do it again."

He clears his throat, rubs his palm from the top of his head, through his hair, to the nape of his neck. Then, he starts to walk away.

Oh no you don't.

CHAPTER 33

Henry

THE WOMAN PISSES ME OFF MORE THAN ANY OTHER HUMAN on the planet. Even when I'm trying to tell her what she means to me. The things I've done and the lengths I've gone to in order to keep her hidden and safe. She still wants to fight me on it. Once she gets started on a rant, there's no stopping it. Especially when it comes to putting me in my place. Or trying to, at least. So, I pushed her into the pool.

Then, as soon as she breached the surface, I felt like a real ass. The woman has been through enough in the past twenty-four hours, and I should have known she was going to break down at some point. I just forgot that she's trained herself into believing that when I'm within fifty feet, all venom should be aimed directly at me. We're alike in that way; anger is always the first emotion. Hers just tends to be louder.

I grab two large white towels and move quickly back

toward the pool. I'm not trying to be a hero. But I sure as shit want to keep her safe. *"I'll never feel safe again."* That gutted me. If she only knew how hard it's been to watch her. Stand to the side and quietly observe. I've barely been living. Simply surviving from one snarky interaction to another. My breath hitches whenever I see her and I'm left waiting, just like Milo with his squeaking toy, patiently and eagerly, with whatever she's willing to give me. To not be able to hold her and make her feel even a fraction of what I feel for her. It's so much deeper than physical attraction. It's some kind of third-realm level shit when it comes to how my body responds to hers. I've been in a chokehold for too long. If she can't hear me, then I need to show her.

When my foot hits the living room tile, I stop dead in my tracks. Despite the humidity swirling around me, I'm frozen in place. Sweat forms on my upper lip and I get lightheaded at the sight before me. I'm a mix of anger and anguish, but a hit of arousal just came barreling through my body. My eyes dance around her skin. A body that I've only viewed in pieces. Never all at once. Never in full view. Not like this.

Standing across the room, just on the edge from where the house changes from inside to outdoors, my pixie stands wearing only a smirk and a sheen of sweat mixed with water from her toss into the pool. Droplets cascade down and around her curves, reminding me of the ski trails back home. Their chaotic movements opening a new pathway to either a drip off a shoulder, elbow, or nipple. Over the flare of her hip and thighs.

What I wouldn't give to lick up each drop. Explore every path.

Her long blonde hair is slicked back behind her as I catalog the map of her body. I know I have to blink, but if I do, this perfect moment and all of her vulnerability might disappear. My mouth waters and it forces me to swallow.

I never told my feet to start moving, but that's what they're doing. I can't stop. I've fantasized about this woman for longer than I can recall. I've never wanted to bite, fuck, slap, and snuggle someone more in my entire life. And in that order too. I feel slightly delirious as I stop in front of her.

I rake my eyes down her front, working into memory all of the parts I've never seen before. The curve of her tits and the small beauty mark on the underside of the left one. The way her hips take a sharp turn toward her belly button. Her bare pussy just waiting to be kissed again, and then fucked hard, and properly. I can't help it; I lick my lips at the thought. The taste of it, of her, coming back to me. My cock lunges in my shorts. The movement draws her attention down. Her smirk grows into a deviously bright smile as she stares up at me again.

"We have two days." She's breathing heavily, making her chest move up and down to a rhythm I want to mimic. "Two days, Henry. Without anyone we know around to ask questions. No explanations needed. No eyes or gossips. Just us. I'd like to finish all the things we've ever started." She raises an eyebrow in challenge. As if I'd pull back from this. From her. A better man would tell her to put clothes on. A good man would tell her she can't use sex as a way to cope with chaos. I'm not that good or too decent to begin with, though I am smart. Smart enough to know that if this moment slips away, I'll regret it more than any other moment of my life.

I move before she can say another word. I pull her into me as she pushes back, and we collide. Our mouths slamming together with a shared moan of relief. Tongues thrusting violently, teeth clanging, and her arms wrapping tightly around my neck. There's no holding back. We bruise our lips in a fight to feel every centimeter of the other's mouth. I can't find it in me to be gentle right now. I grip one hand around her neck, my fingers thrusting into her hair and tugging. Enough to move her the way I want her. Tilted enough for my tongue to swipe across her mouth and down her neck. I nip at her jaw while her fingers glide along my scalp with a whimper.

She's so much smaller than I am. Her thick legs, with their olive tone and soft skin, are so goddamn sexy to grip. And I grab them with force as I bend lower and lift them up. She locks around my waist, smiling into our kiss as our teeth clank for a moment.

Her bare pussy presses against my stomach, heavy breasts pushing against my chest, legs wrapped tight at my back, slightly shaking in my hold. Gripping her ass hard, I spread her cheeks as she grinds herself into me. I try to move us down the hallway to the bedroom, but as her mouth wraps around my ear, my steps falter with a groan. I push her against the wall, helping me hold her up, needing more of her right this second. The leverage frees my hand, so I can palm one of her breasts as she arches into me. Leaning down, I suck her hard nipple into my mouth. I suck so hard that she moans into my ear, urging me on. Turning me more into a savage for her than I thought possible.

"Fuck," she breathes.

I hoist her up higher on the wall and move my mouth to the other side. Licking around her nipple and swirling my tongue before I reward myself with a mouthful of her gorgeous tit. The noises leaving her throat have me ready to fully devour this woman. Every goddamn inch of her.

She snakes one arm around the back of my neck as the other grips my chin. Pulling back to look at me, she says, "I need you to deliver on the promise your eyes are always making." Her tone a sultry gravel.

I nip at her fingers and pull us away from the wall, farther down the hall. She stares at my face, both of us laced with need, but also so much more.

I laugh. "And what promise is that, Pixie?"

"That you're going to fucking ruin me."

CHAPTER 34

Giselle

My reflection in the mirror across from where we stand, or rather where he stands and holds me tightly against the wall, makes me smile wider. He follows my line of sight to our reflection, and that dimple on his cheek appears with a devilish smirk in its wake. As he turns us around, I drop my legs, my feet meeting the floor. He shifts my body, so we both face the full mirror, taking each other in. I'm completely naked, but from the way his eyes are dragging across my skin, I'm cloaked in confidence. My skin buzzes, needing to be touched however he sees fit.

"Look at how fucking perfect you look in my arms, Pixie," he whispers across my neck. Meeting my eyes in the mirror, he wraps one arm around my waist, pulling me tighter into his chest. The other hand threads up into my hair, tilting my head farther to the side, baring my neck so he can kiss me there.

The arm around my waist moves lower, ever so slowly. I watch in anticipation as it gets closer to my pussy, as if I can't even feel it, only watch to see when it'll get to where I want it. My skin's on fire as I watch first and then feel. A private show to something I've imagined for far too long. Right now, I'm at his mercy. And I wouldn't want it any other way.

When I blink, his other hand travels from my hair down the side of my neck and over the pulse that's working in overdrive. Then I watch with eagerness as he drags his knuckles through the lips of my slick pussy. That simple touch sending a full-body chill through me.

"You like watching me touch you, Pixie?" he whispers across my cheek.

Back and forth, he drags his knuckles, and I'm in a trance, watching and feeling. As my core tightens from the overwhelmingly light touches of his lips and hands, arousal drips down my inner thighs. I pull my eyes away and meet his gaze in the mirror. Moving his hand from my neck to my throat, his fingers trail up my chin, and his middle finger brushes across my puffy, and likely bruised, lower lip. I've never kissed anyone so hard in all my life. Our eyes stay connected as my tongue peeks out to lick the pad of his finger. He likes that because he adds his ring finger, softly moving them back and forth across my tongue and pushing them into my mouth. I suck hard at the same time as he uses his other hand to spread the lips of my pussy and thrust two fingers inside me.

We watch each other through the reflection of the mirror, as I suck on his fingers and feel him hard and grinding into me from behind. I moan around them as I see and feel him curve his two fingers forward and hit that spot inside of me that's pure, unadulterated pleasure. His jaw is slack as he watches and feels along with me, the air escaping his rumbling chest, caressing every kiss he leaves on my neck. The filthy sight of his fingers pushing in and out of me has unlocked an entirely new level of lust I hadn't known existed until this moment.

"Just like that, Pixie. Suck my fingers like you want to suck my cock. I can't wait to glide along this tongue, fuck this sweet tasting pussy," he growls and then pulls his fingers out and slaps my clit. Hearing his filthy words and feeling him dominate me has me ready to fall over the edge.

And he's not about to let up. If anything, his pace stays consistent as his fingers move in and out of my mouth. I coat them with saliva and suck as if it's a test for how well I can follow his direction. When he pulls them out and drags them over my nipple, I gasp at the sensation and sight of our reflection. He adds his fingers back into my pussy, and the intrusion pushes a moan from my lips. Using his free hand, he pushes down the waist of his pants. I feel him rub the head of his cock back and forth along my lower back.

I'm desperate for all of him as I turn my head and pull his neck toward me, crashing my lips into his. The urgency and need are back in abundance, and I've never wanted anything more than to feel him inside of me.

"Tell me you want this. G, tell me you want me to fill this pussy right now."

I moan at his words.

"Baby, fill my tight pussy with that big, beautiful cock right now."

"Fucking hell, woman," he groans. Dragging the head of his cock through my lips, he coats himself in my arousal. As he moves us forward, I lean on my arms, now against the mirror, watching as he teases my clit with his dick from behind. I moan with each graze, my hips lifting for more.

"I can't wait any longer. I need you inside me. I want to feel you stretch me, Henry." I barely finish speaking his name, because he listens. He fucks his cock into me hard and fast, taking my breath away. Groaning, he buries himself to the hilt, but he doesn't move as I clench around him. He's big, and he's giving me a moment to adjust to his size.

The moment he angles his hips, I know I'm not going to last. I'm going to fall apart as soon as he starts pulling out of me. I can't think of anything other than how good he feels. I open my eyes and see the edge he's balancing on in our reflection. I watch as sweat, or maybe water, from my hair drips down his shoulder, trailing down the length of his tattoo. Just looking at him is a fantasy, and now he's finally inside me.

He moves behind me like he's warming up a ride. Just a few pulls and pushes that are slow and sensual. Slow enough so I can feel how long and hard he is. Slow enough that I can feel my orgasm building, even more so with every moan we share. My body follows his rhythm and I meet the rolling of his hips. My eyes must have drifted closed, because moments later, they startle wide as Henry bites my shoulder. "That's it, ride me. Fuck yourself right on my cock, Pixie."

And I do as I'm told. I watch as he watches me from behind, and the look on his face makes me feel powerful. Beautiful. The way his expression changes as I slow my movements, twerk my hips backward, and tilt my pussy just an inch so I know he can glide in deeper. As soon as it happens, he breaks. Whatever was holding him back is gone. He meets my movements and drives into me, grabbing onto my hips with a roughened grip that'll leave marks later. I feel him harden more, and I know he's close.

"I knew you'd feel so fucking good. Fuck, Pixie, that's it. Squeeze my cock with your perfect cunt," he whispers, his tongue gliding up my neck.

There's no response. Those words just sent another wave of wetness around him that I can hear with every thrust. Moving one of his hands from my hips to my center, his fingers rub in small, purposed circles around my clit. Moments later, I'm falling over the edge into a complete, full-body orgasm. I feel it everywhere, from the bottom of my feet to the palms of my hands, up my back, and over my shoulders. My breasts press against the cool mirror and my pussy pulses with the beat of my rapidly pumping heart. My cunt grips his cock as I scream my pleasure, and seconds later, he moans. The loudest, most deep and guttural moan, as he spills into me. That sexy as fuck sound sucks whatever's left of my orgasm from me, leaving me trembling against him.

He pumps himself as deep as he can go, and I take all of it. Filling me exactly how I asked, sweat drips from each of our bodies. I pant, trying to catch my breath, my head pressed against the mirror. His breathing matches mine, fogging up our reflection. He rests his head between my shoulder blades, and then moves his hands from my hips and pussy to around my middle, holding me tight. He hugs my body with reverence. There isn't a single thing that will ever feel better than his arms around me. I don't care how we got to this moment, but it's sweaty, messy, and pure perfection.

Minutes pass as we lean against the mirror and each other, but just as I feel like my legs might give out from under me, I'm being lifted and draped over Henry's shoulder.

"Henry!" I shriek out.

"Not even close to done yet, Pixie," he says as he bites my ass.

Dropping me onto the bed, he crawls over my body. The weight of him is welcome and I smile as I look into his half-blue, half-green eye. As I reach up and touch his eyebrow, he leans into my hand.

"That was better than I imagined," I say, more content than I've ever been. "I've thought about that more than I'm even comfortable admitting, and it ended up being even better."

He smiles, big and wide, and then kisses me. His soft, full lips dance with mine so effortlessly, it's no wonder I'd kept my mouth from others. Why dabble with mediocrity when you've felt perfection? He moves his lips down my neck. Softly at first, and then as he meets my collarbone, he nips at the skin. I tilt my head down to watch as he draws a warm, wet line from one side of my breast, over my nipple and then across the rest of its swell. He doesn't stop there to play. He keeps going. Straight through the valley between both and to the other side. As if there was some kind of dessert he was licking up. It makes me feel entirely worshipped. Decadent, even.

I've always wanted to be savored by someone. Tasted as if I'm designed with layers of flavors that need to be discovered and then revered. He is probably the best cook I've ever met. He knows what to look for. How to taste and discover, and it's me that he wants to devour. Again.

Coming back to my nipple, he pulls it into his mouth, sucking on it until it peaks to his satisfaction. He runs the tip of his tongue over it, flicking it just enough so that the change in pressure drives a wave of renewed need through me. Moving one hand down my waist, he cups it over the top of my pussy and then flexes his middle finger so it brushes over my clit, making my body shudder, still sensitive from what just happened. His finger is coated in a mix of my arousal and his satisfaction. An erotic mess that I have every intention of repeating as often as our bodies will allow over the next two days.

I've had samples of this man over the years. Small morsels. Nothing like this. Days to play without repercussions. The urgent yet slow discovery of all the things we've ever wanted from the other. At the core of it, it's simply each other, though.

I've never allowed myself to think all of this, never mind act on it, but right now, what would it help to hold anything back. This may be all we get. And I'm gonna get it all.

Another lick pulls my thoughts back to the room. This bed. This man.

"I had no idea you were a boob guy," I say, smiling. He drags his teeth along my nipple again, making me yelp. "I do have great tits, though, so I get it."

He sinks another finger into me and curves it just right. The movement. The angle. Henry knows what he's doing. *Thatta boy.*

"I stare at your tits any chance I get. And they're fucking incredible."

Lick.

"They're sexy as fuck. You told me that once. A long time ago."

Lick.

"I've wanted to be buried in between them every time I catch a glimpse," he says as he moves his mouth lower. He moves his kisses toward the side of my body, the blank space of skin that runs from under the pit of my arm to where my ribs end. There's nothing special there other than the fact that I've never been kissed in those places. No ink there either. There's never been anyone to take the time to run their lips across my skin in places that aren't designed specifically for pleasure. Henry's mouth is running a canvas campaign along the untouched places of my body, officially securing every new spot as *his* in my mind. His perfectly curved fingers move languidly inside of me as he continues his exploration. One that's slow and intimate, completely different from what we just did, but equally sexy. My body is already buzzing with the promise of another orgasm.

I look down to watch, seeing his eyes closed, lost in

me. Tracking coordinates across my torso and down my hip and back again. His thumb makes small circles over my clit as his fingers continue to work in and out at a perfect rhythm to drive appreciative little moans from my chest. The rough animal and dirty promises did incredible things to me, but this version of him, watching him savor this, it's doing more than just turn me on. It's making me fall.

"Tell me how long you've wanted this," I say quietly. I'm not even sure why I would ask, but I need to hear his voice; otherwise, I'll crumble to the release he's teasing from me, and I'm not ready just yet.

He moves his mouth lower so that his lips hover just over his thumb. They stay there, the warmth of his breath making me fidget, trying to get him closer.

"That feels so good. Henry, you had better put that mouth on me," I groan out. I flex my hips and move them in sync with the way his fingers are diving in and playing me.

He laughs. I love making this man laugh. "Shut up and just enjoy this," he says.

Less than a second later, his tongue replaces his thumb as it licks my clit slowly, with just the right amount of pressure. I'm not lasting much longer. He continues to pinch and caress one of my nipples while his other hand and face stays buried between my thighs.

"Hen, that's too good," I whine. I don't want him stopping, but he needs to know this is like some sort of divine torture.

He adds another finger, and the fullness sends a quake through me. His movement speeds up slightly as he licks at my clit, and then practically makes out with the lips of my pussy. Pulling me into his mouth just long enough to feel suction and warmth before he moves on. I know he's as turned on as he's making me right now, because I'm learning that Henry is not a quiet man when it comes to sex. He groans into my pussy with every change in position of his mouth.

"Look at how pink and swollen you are for me, Pixie. Fucking delicious," he growls out.

Well, okay. I'll take that dirty talk and raise you a squirting good time, sir.

And that's all it took, apparently. Just a few dirty words and a groan from his gorgeous mouth to send me over the top and down into the valley of "holy fucking shit" and "don't you fucking stop." I yell out words, swears, perhaps even call upon whatever goddess might be listening, because my orgasm barrels through me, and causes my entire body to convulse. My pussy clenches his fingers like it just struck and closed a multimillion-dollar deal.

"That's it. Suck in my fingers, G," he says with an approving moan. "So wet for me."

In a haze, I look down at him just gazing between my legs. His hand still moving slowly, his chin and mouth glistening with my pleasure, and I'm entirely too impressed that he's messy and dirty. Exactly how I'd hoped.

I smile at him as he pulls his fingers out and wipes his face.

"So you've got some skill, Riggs."

He places his long middle finger into his mouth.

Then he sucks it clean so that it disappears to the knuckle. "Did you think I wouldn't?"

"Oh, I fucking hoped. But that—" I let out a laugh. "THAT was fucking magic Hank—"

He kisses me before I can finish saying the nickname that I know drives him nuts. I can taste myself still on his tongue and it sets me off all over again. I want to fuck this man so good. There isn't anything else in this world right now more important than reciprocating that same level of pleasure.

Pulling back from our kiss, still leaning over me, he braces himself on his forearms. He drags one thumb over my lips and down to my chin. "You're beautiful," he says.

"Oh, I'm aware." He smiles at my sass, and I press a quick kiss to his lips.

"And to answer your question. Since you asked so sweetly." He draws a line from my cheek to my chin, holding my gaze. I melt into the softness of his touch. "I've thought about this moment since you told me I reminded you of a Ghostbuster."

He brushes his lips against mine. "And then I thought..." he pauses, sadness flickering through his eyes for just a blink before he continues. "I thought you weren't an option anymore. So I tried to forget about the smartass pixie I damn near fell all over one night in a bar."

I try to keep the blurry tears that have formed from falling.

"And then when I saw you again..." His voice lowers to a graveled whisper before he kisses my lips again. The tears fall when I close my eyes. There's no need to try to hide any emotions right now. The man is lying on top of me, naked and handing over words that I've craved for more than a decade.

"You were sitting at the bar, and you laughed. You had been in Strutt's for about a month by then. It was a month, though, since I had seen you. Seen the ghost of a woman I thought I'd never see again." He pauses again, taking a breath, and if I didn't know him like I do, then I'd think it was just a pause to gather his next thought. But he's trying to hold back. "You threw your head back and laughed. Some joke between you and Everly, at the expense of a couple of douchebags that you both were flirting with that night."

I'm trying to flip my memory back to the night he's talking about. "I remember."

"That was when I knew I made the right decision. I couldn't marry someone else. I wouldn't let them relocate you. Never seeing you again wasn't an option I was going to allow. Once you came back into my life, there was no letting you slip away ever again."

He brushes his thumb across my lips, kisses them, and then finds my gaze. It's impossible to speak right now. "There was no way I could live without seeing you. Without knowing you were safe."

"We're supposed to hate each other," I say back, as tears track down the sides of my face.

"But we don't, Pixie," he says with a half-smile. "We play a game. We follow rules. But right now, we're in a big fucking time out and the only thing I want to do is fuck you, make love to you, do all of the dirty, kinky shit you've been taunting me with over the years, and then do it all over again."

I laugh. And our conversation has moved back to a place I feel comfortable, talking about some filthy fuck time with the sexiest man I've ever met. My chest is too heavy to think about more than that.

"We only have two days," I say with a frown I can't help. Lifting up, I bite his lip and then lick the tip of his nose.

"Two days to do all the things I've ever wanted to do to you," he whispers as he kisses my shoulder, his cock nudging my hip as if I've forgotten the rides I've just taken. My pussy is sensitive, but she's wet all over again. The bitch is ready with her park hopper, fast pass, sticker, ticket, and height requirement sorted. It's time to buckle up.

He moves his mouth down to the column of my neck, mixing kisses with licks and gnaws. His hands caress down my body as his fingers brush rhythmically against the sensitive space he just played, like a kid with a Casio. *Work that magic, baby.*

"Tell me you're on some kind of birth control," he groans into my chest.

I look down at him, the question sobering me slightly. It's not something I'd ever thought too much about. Anyone I've ever been with, they suit up. I don't know where their bits and bobs have been. The ability to get knocked up is not something I need to concern him with right now either. So, instead of saying any kind of moment-dampening truth, I opt to brush over it. The need to feel him inside of me again is all too consuming.

I nod, answering his concern, and then smile wide. "Henry, get that cock inside me right now, or so help me Godessesssssss—"

My demand is cut short because he started moving at my nod. The head of his cock pushes into me with ease. Between the attention his fingers were showing me and the way my pussy seems to spill for this man, the glide is smooth and salacious.

He holds himself inside of me. Buried deep, our hips meet, and I feel the dual sensation of pain and pleasure. I struggle with taking a breath. The intrusion needs accommodating, and my body is savoring the pressure. I would have thought I'd be ready for the size of him, but still, it takes me a moment.

I exhale a shaky breath a moment later. "I'm okay. You can move."

He drops a kiss onto my neck. Just that action sends another jolt of pleasure through every limb. I find his mouth and kiss him, our tongues meeting and dancing together briefly. Dragging his cock out of me, he looks down between us, making me whimper. But he wastes no time, slamming back into me with a groan.

I laugh after a moan escapes me. It's practically a giggle. I might be delirious right now. The mood he's giving me. The way he feels above me. The way he's watching and studying as his cock sinks into me, as if it's the best porn he's ever seen.

"What's so funny, Pixie?" he says, low and gruff.

"How much you're obsessed with me right now."

He mumbles something to himself, and then says, "You better fucking hold on to those sheets, because I'm going to fuck you hard now." He pauses, staring into my eyes with a searing look. "And, Pixie, you better not be quiet." Leaning his head down, he takes my nipple into his mouth, sucking hard and leaving a small bite as his mouth retreats.

"Now be a good girl and open those knees nice and wide for me."

And with that, he lifts himself up and leans back on his knees. With my ass resting on his thighs, he tilts my lower half upwards in one fluid motion, holding underneath my thighs to gain the right leverage. I lift my arms over my head and grab onto the pillows that have shifted behind me.

I watch him as he looks down at where we're connected. It's fucking addictive to see the lust, the want, the palpable hunger, painted all over his face. Just as I move my eyes lower to catch a glimpse of his sculpted shoulders, he slams into me. Tip to root, and my pussy grips his cock like it's found its perfect counterpart. That's how it feels. Like he fits me completely. Fully. It feels so decadently good.

He pulls back again, achingly slow. His cock drags out of me and my body protests. A small whine slips out.

He grins at me. "Tell me how good that feels."

He moves back into me with a languid push. He's playing with me now.

"It feels..." I say with an exhale.

Pulling out, he then slams into me. I can only yell, "Fuck!"

He's in control right now. I've given that to him and he's reveling in it. The way he's taking charge of what he wants. The way he owns every inch of my body, my pleasure.

I move one of my hands down my body, over my tits, and right to my clit. But before I can even brush it, he swats my hand away.

"Hands off, Pixie. That pussy is mine."

"Then don't disappoint her." I raise my eyebrow to challenge him. That seems to do it. The long game he was playing has fallen to the side.

Just a few words make this man detonate.

It's my superpower.

He hoists my legs higher. Lifts higher onto his knees, and with it, my bottom half, and driving into me.

Hard.

I nearly black out on the third thrust. But instead of tipping over the edge, he pulls out of me quickly, moves down the mattress, and covers his mouth over where we were just connected.

"Holy shit!" I gasp as he drags me down to the edge of the bed as if I weigh nothing. I don't know what this pixie shit is all about, but I'm not a tiny person. He's just so much bigger than most people.

He drives three fingers into me before I even know what's happening, and I moan, long and loud. His mouth clenches on me. Licking. Sucking. And with a growl, he bites my clit. I scream, and then I see stars. My mind hasn't caught up with the fact that an orgasm has blanketed my body. An orgasm that absolutely rocks my entire being. Everything tingles and just as I feel the thump of my clit, it registers that I'm being moved again.

He shifts the bottom half of my body, which is still

pulsating, and flips me over so that now I'm resting on my stomach. Chest heaving from the loss of breath to my lungs and blood supply to everywhere but my cunt. As I start to catch my breath, I smile, tilting my head back to look at him. He pulls my torso down so that my knees hit the edge of the mattress.

"Get on all fours," he demands.

Smack.

The slap on my ass makes my breath hitch for a second. Mostly because I wasn't expecting it, but before I feel the warmth or even the sting, Henry is rubbing the spot.

"I love your tits, but this ass is fucking perfection. I've been wanting to slap it so hard." He leans down and kisses the spot he smacked, humming. "Fuck, you're so fucking sexy."

It's not exactly poetry, but the man is making me melt. It's more words than he's said to me all year, if I'm being honest.

He grabs me. Possessively. An ass cheek in each hand as he pulls them apart so he can see every intimate part of me. I'm not a timid woman so I preen at this moment. He groans, and less than a second later, he's licking my slit. He finds his footing quickly. Tonguing it just enough so my pussy's fully engulfed in his flattened tongue and wide-open lips. He drags it up slowly and doesn't stop until he's gotten a full pass up the seam of my ass.

Why does that feel so good?

Gripping harder, he takes another swipe with his tongue. And just as my eyes drift closed to savor the wetness, to let go of anything left that would make me feel grounded or tethered to reality, Henry stands and thrusts his cock back into me. He pistons with such force that I'm barely able to stay steady. He holds himself deep and leans forward, draping his sweat-slicked body over mine, his weight pushing me down.

"That's it, Pixie. Take all of me like the good girl I know you can be." He nips my neck, the space right below my ear, kissing it again before moving back. Pressing between my shoulders, my chest meets the mattress, his one hand holding him up while the other grabs at my hip. "Ass up nice and high, G. You're going to come again before I fill you up. You understand?"

Dang, my baby is fucking dirty.

My head is nodding without thought. Hell, my body is practically saluting and "yes, sir'ing," with the way it continues to thrum with excitement at every word he grunts out.

"Fucking hell, Hanky, make me come, and stop talking about it."

Smack.

I let out a yelp. That's going to be a full handprint. That fucker smacked my ass hard that time. And my pussy is loving it. *Sycophant.* I'm ready to drown in my orgasm, but I have stamina, and I want Henry to tell me when I can succumb.

He grabs onto both of my hips and fucks me ruthlessly. The sounds of his thighs slapping my skin is the drumbeat to this torrid soundtrack. Snaking one arm around, he manages to reach my clit, pinching while his cock dives into me deeper. I'm barely hanging on. My heavy breaths mix with moans I don't recognize are being fucked right out of me.

"You ready to come for me?"

"So ready, baby."

His moan is what makes my orgasm unleash. A guttural moan of pleasure from this man is truly the sexiest thing I've ever heard. And if that wasn't enough, Henry breathlessly demands, "Come. *Now*. That's it." He sucks in an audible breath. "That's my girl. Take everything I've got." I clench my pussy, and he grunts with his release. "Fuck."

My mouth is dry. Ears hot. Face practically numb. My thighs are shaking. My lower abs are revolting. Quivering.

I should have passed out with the way he's worked me over, but I don't. His body is draped half on me and half on the bed. I love the weight of it. Quite literally, and figuratively.

My hair must be wild and in his face. Pieces of it are stuck to my neck and back. His hands rest low on my waist. Our limbs tangle in a chaotic design that is strangely comfortable. Every part of me feels so good, it's indescribable. Content in just being fucked by a man I've been fantasizing about for longer than I've been tattooing. He's finally infiltrated every facet of my life. Something I've worked tirelessly to avoid. But here, on this island, we can be exactly what we've wanted. Something important to each other. Something incredible.

"I'm going to need a minute." I can hear the smile in his voice. He's as happy as I am. I don't need to turn over to see it. But I want to.

I bark out a laugh. The man just fucked me three times. I'm going to need a whole lotta minutes.

I turn my body so I can lie on my back. We both adjust arms and legs, but he doesn't let go of me. Instead, he pulls me closer and nuzzles my shoulder. The tenderness of him right now is like shifting into a parallel universe compared to the rough fucker that just snow plowed my body.

He clears his throat and finally opens his eyes to look at me. I've been staring at his beautiful, full lips with the small white scar. But now, I get to see his eyes. A swirl of calm greens and that small splash of blue. *So beautiful.*

"You have some kind of tether on me, G. It's taken more energy to fight and stay away from you over the years. And I've tried. Geez, have I tried to stay away." I know he wants to say more, but I'm not sure I want to hear it. "I should call you a witch instead."

"You think I'm casting some kind of spell over you?"

There's a Nina Simone song that—

"It's like the Nina Simone song," he says, cutting off my thought. He smiles to himself.

I move my fingertips up and over his shoulder, tracing the dips and swells of his muscled back. His skin is soft and lightly tanned. A trait that the Riggs siblings are blessed with having. Tanned olive skin year-round. My olive tones like to wash out in the winter months. In the dead of January, I'm pale and look more Scandinavian now that my hair is blonde, versus the Italian Mediterranean blood running through my veins. Whereas he looks like a god.

"I'm so comfy, but I need to pee. And maybe shower."

He makes a noise to rebuke the idea and shifts his arms around my waist to hold me. "Go pee. I'll get us water. Then you get your ass back to this bed. I'm not done with you yet."

Moving his face into my chest, he kisses my right breast.

"I need to fuck you again before you get cleaned up," he says as he presses light kisses on my skin, brushing his lips against me. "Then you're going to suck my cock in that shower. And then I'm going to eat that delicious pussy for dinner by the pool."

"I like this itinerary, baby."

"Say that again," he says.

I laugh at the request. "I like your itinerary."

"Not that part." He pulls back from my tits and looks up at me. Vulnerable and sweet. Nothing like he's been with me over the years. At least not when anyone is looking.

I smile at this big, rough man. "Baby?"

"Yea. I like you calling me that."

I lean over and smile into a light kiss on his lips. "I like everything you just said, baby."

He shifts up and meets my kiss more fervently. His hands finding my neck and pulling my mouth toward his. The pressure of his lips mixed with the softness of his request has created an entirely new layer to this man that I couldn't try to hate ever again. But before I overthink the magnitude of any of it or freak out that this moment has a built-in expiration date, I pull back. I was only getting up to pee.

Don't lie, avoid the UTI. That's always been my motto.

And after that showing, it's necessary. With another quick peck on his lips, I hustle away from his body. If I don't move fast, I'll be lulled back into it.

"Be right back."

He pinches one of my ass cheeks upon my escape. "Hurry up. I'm not feeling very patient anymore, Pixie. Now that I've had you..." I shut the door to the en suite. Through the door, I hear him say, "I need so much more."

Me too, baby. Me too.

CHAPTER 35

Henry

THE SMALL BEAUTY MARKS ON HER BACK, PEPPERED HEAVIER around her shoulders and trailing down her spine, are like a constellation. There's no pattern to them, only the notion that her tiny imperfections mingle with the beautiful ink she's woven there. A few small hearts, a large vine that expands from one shoulder to the other, connecting colorful flowers.

I drag my fingers over them, tracing the artwork she loves so much. A canvas I've never been privileged to touch in this way. Until now.

My touch drifts lightly as if they're able to soothe her and satiate me. Today is almost over. The sun set a few minutes ago. She fell asleep about an hour before that. And while my body is tired, I'm afraid to fall asleep. I've waited for what feels like a lifetime to be with her, and now, I have her. It seems dumb to waste our moment on sleep. *Two days.*

I know it's what she said, but the truth of the matter is, and always has been, that I'm in love with a woman who will never allow herself to love me.

Two days. We said two days to work out this insane chemistry. Make sure she feels safe, cared for, and coveted. Then move forward. Move forward as if I've never felt her mouth on my cock. Forget how she tastes on my tongue. The way we kiss, or how she feels held in my arms. *That's* never going to happen. Forgetting. You don't forget the taste, the smell, the feel of the woman your soul craves. Everything else will be muted. Everyone will be less.

She moves and sucks in a breath. I can tell by her quiet, uneven breathing that she's awake. So I draw letters, numbers, and lines along her back. I don't say anything that I'm thinking. I get lost in the feeling of her smooth skin under my callused fingertips.

I draw the same thing over and over again. Wondering if she can feel it. Recognize it.

The room has gotten darker in the past few minutes. She must be hungry for actual food. I'm starving. And if I'm starving, then she's minutes away from getting *hangry*.

"Lower," she whispers.

"Here?" I move my fingers to her lower back just before the curve of her ass.

"Lower."

"How about here?" I drag my fingers over her ass and brush my knuckles up and down the crack, making sure I brush the lips of her pussy.

"Perfection," she hums.

"Hungry?"

"Don't you know me at all?" she asks and then rolls her body away so that she can face me. Propping herself up on her elbows, she smiles and says, "Of course I'm hungry."

"Why don't I make you some food?"

"Sounds perfect. I'm going to dip into that pool while you get started, and then I'll meet you in the kitchen."

Before I can lean in and kiss her, the phone rings, jilting us out of the bubble we've created, and dousing us with the reality of why we're here in the first place.

"Go for a swim," I tell her. But I know better.

"Fat fucking chance. This is my life, Henry. And I need to talk with Bea," she says, already throwing on a white t-shirt and pulling her long blonde hair into a knot on the top of her head. She grabs the satellite phone from the chair and answers.

"Bea? What's happening?" I can't hear anything from the other end. "No. You talk to me first, then I'll let him know you're on the phone. He's outside." She smiles at me. At her lie. She moves toward me as I pull my shorts up and on. Putting her hand up to her mouth, she kisses her fingers, and then puts them over my heart, over the words I've tattooed there for her.

You're killing me, Pixie.

Then she's dragging her fingers down to my crotch and squeezing, making me hold back a groan. Tapping my ass, she gives me a coy smile, then leaves and takes the call down the hall and away from me.

When I finally make my way to the kitchen, I listen to her side of the conversation, and I watch her like a hawk while I make us food. She's been on the phone with Bea for more than thirty minutes now, and I'm concerned that they're not making the kind of progress on the situation that should be expected.

I finish chopping the tomatoes, tomatillos, and cilantro. Dumping the full cutting board of vegetables and herbs into the onion, bell peppers, and jalapenos I've already finely chopped and minced. Gazpacho. To go with her favorite. Grilled cheese.

G finally walks closer to the island, and I can hear relief in her voice as she ends her conversation, readying to give me the phone.

"Bea, I understand." She looks up at me. I can't read what her eyes are trying to tell me, but she looks nervous. "I know. I've already heard this. You don't need to repeat yourself. It's a non-issue."

Me. I'm the non-issue.

She hands me the phone as she sits.

"Harper," I say as I tuck it to my ear.

"Riggs. Hell." Agent Harper isn't one to mince words, but she sounds exhausted. "You're cleared to come back with her. The situation has been taken care of, but I've warned her that she needs to keep a very low profile."

That hits me in the gut. Riggs is not a low-profile name. And neither is my role at Riggs Outdoor. I look at her as she chugs water from her glass.

"I need to know that she's going to be safe if I bring her back."

"The issue has been resolved. That's all you're allowed to know, Riggs. You don't have the clearance to know more. She has a full picture of the situation, but the only thing you need to know is that I appreciate your discretion. The way you jumped into action on this. It allowed us to do our job knowing you got her out of harm's way. And fast." Bea takes a minute and speaks to someone on her end. "You still there, Riggs?"

"Still here."

"I'd suggest coming back to town with her in the next day. Anything longer than that, your family will start to wonder where you both have been. I've already had to reroute some text messages from your sister. Those two talk way too often. I thought she was honeymooning?"

"She is. And, yea, they do."

"Don't push her, but she knows all the details of what happened here in the past twenty-four hours. Let her update you with that information. Listen, I want to make sure you know this too." She pauses. I know what's coming next. "I'm not an idiot. But I will ask that you put her safety first. That girl has been through too much to have to uproot her life again, but if things turn out that she's no longer safe in Strutt's Peak, I'm going to need to move her."

"Understood."

"Low profile, Riggs," she says again before hanging up.

One more day. I'll have her for one more day. I wait another minute to let that sink in. To tell myself one more day will have to be enough, knowing full well it won't be.

CHAPTER 36

Giselle

I CRUNCH INTO THE SALTY, BUTTERY BREAD AND THEN THE warm gooey cheese. The flavors are a mix of what must be a piece of soft goat cheese and some kind of herbed hard cheese that's been melted. A thin slice of tomato and maybe some honey hit the rest of my mouth, and I have to close my eyes. In all my life and my searches for the best grilled cheese, it's always Henry's that wins out and beats the last.

I wipe my mouth in between bites, just as he puts a small bowl of soup in front of me. He hasn't said much since he hung up with Bea. Usually, that's nothing new, his quietness, but after the shit-stain that has royally fucked my life, I'm surprised by his lack of questioning.

"It's chilled gazpacho." He leans back and reaches into the drawer across from where he's leaning on the oversized island. "Spoon."

"The person that I recognized is dead," I tell him as I take another bite of the salty goodness.

He squeezes a lime into both of our bowls and then looks at me. "Can I ask how that happened? And, I assume it's a good thing?"

He shakes a bottle vigorously and then draws a circle in oil over each of our chilled soups. I'm not sure why I find that sexy, but I do. I don't know where he got all the ingredients to make this, but in all reality, I don't care. This is exactly what I wanted without even asking. Without even knowing until it was in front of me. That's the level of attention this man has paid to me. How am I supposed to walk away from him? How do I pretend like I'm not wide awake now?

"Bea was able to identify the man and track him to the airport this morning. The idea was that they'd take him in for questioning about suspicious paraphernalia that would have been planted in his bag, but—" I can't hold out anymore; I need to take a bite of this soup. Once I do, I hum in appreciation. It's so fucking good.

"Henry, this is so good." He flashes me a big boyish smile and then digs into his bowl. He doesn't say anything. Instead, he eats and waits for me to say more.

I take another giant bite of the heaven that is cheese and bread and continue. "He wasn't in the mood to be questioned, apparently, so he pulled a weapon. Before he hit TSA too. I don't know where he would have put it if he went through the line, but that's moot at this point. Anyway, he tried to pull a hostage, but since the TSA agents were actually FBI, there was a whole shootout thing. And now he's dead."

I look up to find Henry staring at me with a spoon halfway to his mouth.

"That's not where I thought you were going with this. That's a lot happening at our small airport. Did anyone else get hurt?"

Forever the good guy. Of course, he's worried about his people. His town.

"Nobody. The news is reporting it as a drug smuggling issue, but that's the better angle. There's no way they want Mikhail 'The Tiger' Semenov, who's tied to the Russian Bratva, in the headlines, or being spouted from Dawn Danglewood or Mel Finnegan's lips during the six o'clock news."

He blinks, waiting for me to elaborate. He doesn't know the details. The magnitude of what happened. Who it happened to, and by whom. He only knows the grit of it. The outcome.

Now is the right time to tell him the big picture. It's time he knows the level of danger I'm still in and the magnitude of what happened all those years ago. He should have known this whole time while he promised to look out for me. If I had known...

"My pops was the best man in the world to me." I smile at the thought of him. His deep accent and the way he'd laugh. I can't hear it the same anymore, but I remember how it made me feel when I did.

"But by society standards, he wasn't considered an upstanding citizen." I take a sip of my water and put my grilled cheese down. "At the core of it, he loved me more than anything in the world, and that's all that ever mattered to me. But my pops made a lot of friends. Many friends that I came to find out weren't really friends at all."

I shift in my seat. Uncomfortable with the fact that I'm about to say bad things about the man that raised me and loved me unconditionally. Henry can sense it, so instead of standing there waiting for more details, he comes around to my side of the counter. Somewhere in my few sentences, the man found two glasses and a bottle of wine. He pulls my hands toward his body and up, moving us through the living space and veranda to the outdoor daybed.

As I sit, Henry pours. "Most of this, I didn't know until afterwards. The agents assigned to my case filled in a lot of the blanks for me, but I wasn't naive. Just the opposite, in fact." He hands me my glass of chilled white wine, and I take a sip.

Crisp. Light. A coolness to the warmth that surrounds us.

"You probably have figured out that I have a good memory."

Henry nods and takes a sip of wine.

"I can remember everything. More than eidetic, but not as clear as photographic. I can do dates, times, memories, connecting people to minor details. Mostly jobs and hobbies, or favorite drinks, but not necessarily faces. But I'm good with details. And numbers." I take another sip. "My pops was good with numbers the same way. I knew he gambled. I knew that money wasn't supposed to be in paper bags throughout the house. I knew that my uncles and my cousins were not really related to us. It was something we said, because we were close, but really, they were all people who worked for him. He wasn't in the mob, but he was as close to it as he could be without actually being in it. I think that's what made him more intimidating to people. Respected. But I chose to ignore the parts I didn't want to see."

"You said, Bratva. How do Russians play into that?" Henry takes another sip and then pulls my legs into his lap. The same way he did that night at the bar. Dragging his free hand up and down my ankle and calf, the touch feels comforting. Lazy and natural. I want to purr, it feels so good.

"Our neighborhood was a melting pot of families. We grew up in a close-knit five-block radius of people who were never supposed to be friends, let alone as close as family." I try to hold back the tears I know are just dying to swell to the surface. "My mom left when I was barely two years old and that left my pops with doing favors for people who would look out for me and keep me busy while he worked. He always said that we got a bum deal, but that I was the best thing to ever come out of his time with my mother. He'd say, "when life gave you lemons, that was life. Make the most of it, plant a lemon tree." I laugh to myself at how silly it sounds. "He'd call me his lemon blossom."

I watch as he realizes that the lemon tree I sent him years ago meant more than he even thought. A part of me always hoped for more with him.

"I guess you got that romantic streak from him, then," Henry says.

I shrug my shoulder, because maybe that's true, but there was nothing poetic about how he died. "He was a good man. Never the guy to forget unpaid debts or leave a promise unattended. He made sure that the people around us were taken care of financially. He worked numbers on tracks, at casinos, and within the trade routes he was in charge of at the time, and it caught up to him. A few threats that hit close, and he was working for the Italians, then the Russians. Hell, I think Bea even said he had a contact with organized crime in China as well. All of it was to line pockets. And he lined them well."

"So the wrong people knew he was good with numbers and they used him, but I don't understand what ended up getting him..." Henry pauses. The tears finally make their way to the surface, and my vision gets blurry. I blink to let them roll down my face. It's not worth the effort to hide any emotions. Not with him.

This is me.

This is my truth.

And likely, Henry will be the only person to ever hear it anyway.

"I think he mouthed off to the wrong person." I let out a laugh, then exhale heavily. "But it's not really clear. I could have walked in at the wrong time and escalated everything."

Henry glides his fingers up and down my leg in a soothing motion, encouraging me to keep going or just to remind me that he's here with me.

"My cousin, who owned the bar that I was working at the night I met you, wasn't really my cousin either. The loud Italians in our slice of the Bronx meant we were all related somehow. Nobody ever questioned it. He was an asshole, but he loved my father, and made sure I stayed out of the way most of the time. Those were the nights I'd end up doing shifts for him. In all reality, working that night kept me alive. And staying out with you." I shake my head and look up at the purple and pink painted sky, trying to keep the stream of tears from falling so quickly. "I should have gone home with you. If I had, maybe I would have never been there."

Henry leans forward and grabs my face, placing a gentle kiss on my lips. He leans back to look at me and wipes his thumbs under my eyes. "I'm sorry," he says.

"I came home, and I knew something wasn't right. The front door was open and though my pops was an early riser, there was no way he was up and out the door at that hour. I should have done so much differently. I walked into the kitchen, and he was getting beat up." I release a sob as the image of my father in that condition floods my mind. "I reacted. I grabbed a knife out of the butcher block and slammed it into the shoulder of the guy closest to me, and then went barreling at the other one." Sometimes I forget I did that. I smirk at knowing I left that fucker with a steak knife wedged into his muscle.

"I didn't account for whoever else could have been there. I put up a fight, but it wasn't enough. After a good showing, they had enough, and I caught a punch to the back of the head. It knocked me down, and too many kicks to my body and head forced me to black out. I have no idea how long I was out for. It could have been minutes, hours, but when I woke up, I was face down. Barely able to open one eye. I couldn't—" I take a shaky breath, tears streaming down my face and neck. "I couldn't move. I watched my pops bleed out less than ten feet away from me." I haven't thought about any of this for a long time. I stopped having to talk about it in WITSEC therapy sessions years ago.

"Cops showed up sometime after that. It wasn't until I was at the hospital two days later, and conscious enough, to understand what happened."

Henry shifts closer, threading his fingers with mine. He looks stoic, even a little angry. I'm afraid to tell him the rest, to be honest. It's not easy to say, and I can't imagine what it would feel like to hear from someone you care about.

"They didn't stop with my father. There were more than six people dead. My cousin, two uncles, the young couple that lived in the duplex next door. And my pops. Seven, if you counted me, which they did. Organized crime meant I wasn't going to be safe if I was reported as a single survivor. And that's what it was, organized. It never even made it far enough for me to testify. Most of the evidence didn't hold up in court, which meant plea deals and people out of prison too soon. There wasn't much left of my life after that night, so I stayed in witness protection. I'm not considered a high-profile, so I was able to pick where I wanted off a short list."

I finally look back up, connecting with green eyes and that pinch of blue that feel more like home than any place I've ever been. Even Strutt's Peak. I clear my throat, remembering that I want to get this all out.

"How long?" he interrupts.

I search his face, not understanding what he's asking.

"How long were you in the hospital?"

"Five days before they transferred me to their rehab

facility. Then another six weeks until I was able to walk out of there on my own," I say quietly.

He shakes his head and wipes at the corner of his eye. "What did they do to you?"

"Enough of a beating that it must have destroyed my father before they killed him. That's the part that hurts the most. Knowing he watched this hurricane of pain storm over me before he died. There's nothing that man did in his life that deserved that kind of cruelty. I'm still angry, even after years of therapy." I wipe the wet warmth from my cheeks. A reminder that no matter the emotion I tie to this part of my life, it'll always include pain.

Trying to brush away the anger, I continue. "I was unconscious for the majority of it. I woke up with most of my ribs broken. A surgery to fix the hole one of them punctured into my lung. A shattered pelvis, a hefty amount of internal bleeding, a broken leg, and dislocated shoulder. My face wasn't pretty for a while, but all of it healed. I should have died that day too, but I didn't. That fact isn't lost on me."

I blow out a breath, maybe one that I've been holding longer than I thought. I try to center myself from the heaviness of this conversation. The weight of what it means to tell him all of it. He leans forward, pressing his forehead to my chest. I listen to him breathe in and out. And then feel like I need to reassure him that I'm okay.

"I have a good life. A small life. That's nothing to be sad about."

"If I knew," he says breathlessly, as if the words I just spoke caused him to run fast and far, needing air.

He pulls back and holds my face in his hands.

Looking around my face, meeting my eyes last. The intimacy of it makes me feel uncomfortable, but not enough to pull away. I school myself to keep looking, because I want to. It's a moment that's important and I'm mature enough to stay in it.

"If I knew any of this, and then knew that piece of shit you recognized had anything to do with it, I would have killed him. I wouldn't have thought twice about it, either."

"Then we're both lucky he's already dead." I smile. He doesn't smile. He's not taking any of this lightly.

"Are there more? Are the others still alive?"

I wish I could tell him what he wants to hear, but I can't.

"I don't know. Honestly, if they were dead, I know I wouldn't be in witness protection any longer. But the truth is that they're part of something bigger. Something that, no matter how many die, or are behind bars, will never be safe for me. I know too much. I'm a loose end if they ever found out I wasn't actually dead."

I thought that if I ever was found, I'd put up a good fight. Kill the fuckers, but if New Year's Eve is a gauge of what would happen, then I'd be dead real fast. I froze. After years of therapy required by the government, and lessons in self-defense with Mac, I could barely breathe when I recognized that voice and saw that tattoo.

Henry must see the disappointment; I'm not sure I'd be able to hide anything with him studying me the way that he is. He lifts his gaze and pulls me close to his face. So close that the only thing I can look at, in focus, is his pouty bottom lip, and that beautiful white scar that spans the tip of his upper lip and disappears into his longer than usual scruff. Moving his hands from my face to my neck, he lowers my head so he can kiss my forehead. But before he can come back to my lips, I pull away.

I've opened myself enough for one night. Enough for a lifetime. I'm scared that if I show him anything else, say another word, that I'll never be able to walk away from him.

One day left.

CHAPTER 37

Henry

LAST NIGHT, AFTER SHE TOLD ME THE DETAILS OF HER story, the heavy weight of it, she fell asleep. I carried her to bed and held her for the entire night. There wasn't much that would have forced me anywhere other than that spot next to her. I don't remember falling asleep, only being woken up by her hands on my thighs and her mouth on my cock.

I fucked her slowly after that. It was the kind of morning you never forget. Wrapped up in the person you're enamored with and sinking into them as if it's the easiest thing in the world to do. We moved to the veranda, sprawled out on the daybed near the pool.

Now I get why this is out here. Smooth move, Jack.

I drag my fingers lightly around the cursive lettering that rests right in the crease of her hip. Then I lean over and lick the words, taking the suggestion.

"I can't decide if my favorite is the lemon blossoms

behind your ear that when I kiss them it makes you moan, or if it's this message meant just for me," I say, dragging my fingers around the word 'lick' again.

"You don't need to pick. You can worship all of my artwork," she says, smiling down at me.

We lie around in the sun most of the day, managing to touch some part of each other's body at every possible moment. It's perfection. Maybe it's the time limit. Maybe the way she opened her wounds for me last night and showed me every difficult part of her life. Maybe it's just the fact that, more than anything in this world, I want to be near her.

"What's it like to fly?"

"You've been on an airplane," I tell her without opening my eyes. Letting the warmth of the sun soak into my skin.

She jabs my side. "You know what I'm asking, Hanky. What's it like to fly? Be in control like that?"

I lean back against the pillows of the lounge chair. She lies on her stomach in front of me, half draped on my lower half.

"It's different now, but when I started, when I was training in the Air Force, it was scary as hell. But the good kind of scary. It pushed me, and I fell in love with flying. It made me feel important, and that I was something special. I liked the idea of doing something larger than myself, but the payoff was that it was such a high. Training the way that I was able to..." I push out a breath. "I trained at such a high level. It was such a small percentage who've ever done what I was able to do. But I also lost sight of my why. It was easy to get wrapped up in being the best. I think I wanted it so badly because I didn't have anything else I was good at, or enjoyed as much. And flying, I was fucking good at it. I still am." I peek over at her as she watches me with interest.

Clearing my throat, I look up at the blue sky.

"My dad is, well, you know Ash. Endlessly loving and naturally talented at everything. He's a lot to live up to. I don't see it like that anymore, but when I was younger, I had shit to prove. He doesn't think so, but Michael is just like our dad. Michael has his own shit, but he's exactly like him. Good at everything having to do with the mountains, completely aware, and the man loves so fiercely. He's quiet, intense, and just has this way about him that makes you want to earn his respect. Even as my younger brother. And then Law can be the chaotic idiot, but he's so damn likeable and kind. Everyone wants to be around him. He's always been like that. He's been talking people into doing shit they don't want to do since he was a toddler. He'll run the shit out of Riggs Outdoor someday. And Ev is one of the best people in the world. She's great at everything. She kicked all of our asses in every sport on that mountain. She was intimidating even before she went ahead and built up Riggs, and then started her own damn empire."

I look down and see G smiling up at me, laughing almost. I realize I'm smiling talking about them too. "It's true," she says. "They are all incredible. And so intimidating. But you're the same way, baby."

"I've always been easily annoyed. Most people keep their clearance. I don't put off a warm vibe, mostly because people are either idiots, or vultures." She barks out a laugh at that.

"I love our town, but everybody is always looking for an angle with my family. That's been the case, for as long as I can remember. When my mom left, women came out of the woodwork trying to be a stand-in. The hot single dad in town and they all wanted a piece. And then we got older, and I stayed bitter over all of it. People always wanted something. It pissed me off. And I was good at things... I'm not saying that I wasn't or that I'm not." I smile down at her because I see the face she makes at me out of the corner of my eye.

"I'm saying I didn't have something that was just for me. The Air Force, flying, did that. It was mine. And when it was taken away, I was—" I clear my throat and try to rein in where my head wanders. "I wasn't good."

I try to look her in the eye when I say this because it's a part of me that she may not even realize.

"When I met you, I was in a dark place over all of it. I was embarrassed to go home, knowing everyone would be talking about the accident all over again. At that point, it wasn't even clear if I could still be a pilot. I was cleared, legally, to fly privately, but I was nervous to try. And the work I put into the Air Force was fucking dust. I couldn't serve, and that pissed me off. All that time and money for nothing."

When I look down at her again, I notice her eyes shimmering. Reaching down, I touch her beautiful face, and she leans into my palm. I try to make light of it and say, "You asked what it's like to fly." I laugh. "Not all of that."

She smiles up at me, just letting me talk. Giving me the space to share what I want.

"I never thought anything would feel as good as flying. Seeing the sky at that height. It's incredible. It's not how I thought I'd be up there. But I still get to do it. And it's fucking spectacular.

I peek at her again.

"There are things that feel as good, though. Better, even," I say.

Lines have her brows furrowed, searching for the meaning of the words I just unleashed. I think we both realize that maybe I've stopped talking about flying and shifted things to be more about us. She leans forward and kisses my chest and then jumps up, pulling my arm forward.

"Swim with me, flyboy," she yells and then cannonballs into the pool. I laugh and jump in after her. I realize maybe she wasn't ready to hear that, but I'm not holding back. Not anymore.

We swim for at least an hour, or rather I swim, and she clings to me like a barnacle. We get lost in conversations about Strutt's Peak. The cold weather that'll stay until early May. The chaos that will be waiting for both of us when we get home.

We eat fruit, and she draws a tattoo design across my blank shoulder with a black marker that she found when we fired up the frozen drink machine. Two piña coladas later, a massive graphic of a plane similar to the one I flew here in, adorns my shoulder and upper arm. It's incredible.

"You were meant to do this," I say as I look at the marker in her hand.

She smiles and just says, "Yeah, I was."

As the sun finally moves down to the horizon, she asks about the winter events I'm missing while being here, and I ask how many tattoos she'll do this month.

"How many clients will you need to reschedule when you're back?"

She adjusts herself on the bar stool. "I'll have to push out ten clients, but that's—" She huffs, and I can pick up her shift in mood right away. "That's if I can even go back to my life."

Pushing her stool away from the bar, she says, "I need to go for a walk."

I give her a couple of minutes before I follow. I know where her head went, and I realize we've been so wrapped up in each other that she hasn't thought about what she's going back to. If she'll have to leave. That leaving and starting over somewhere new is always hanging over her, but now, leaving seems more possible.

My feet hit the sand, and she's easily twenty steps in front of me.

"I'm fine. You don't need to follow me," she shouts over her shoulder.

I give her the space she needs, but I'm not about to let her out of my sight. Not after hearing exactly the kind of trouble that could be looking for her.

I take a deep breath and the salty air clings to me. A constant breeze keeps my body cool, but the humid air hugs my skin. I can't decide if I like it. As much as this is paradise, I miss the crisp air of home. I don't want to think about what might wait for us there, but I miss the bite of winter after sweating all day. I love summer, but I know when it's coming, so I can prepare for it. This was a jolt.

The dark stretch of beach holds a different kind of calm than it does in the daytime. Waves and moonlight to my left, sugar-fine sand beneath my feet, and the warm glow of lights from the lines of villas to my right. I throw a few rocks that I've picked up into the water folding onto the shore.

Maybe I need the space too. Absorb what's happened between us.

When I look ahead, I see that G is a bit farther up, her long blonde hair being whipped around in the breeze. Legs and curves, highlighted by the moon. Even when she's prickly, she turns me inside out.

I hear music up ahead and laughter from a group of people. Steel drums popping off, the bump of an underlying bass, and a woman's voice singing. It must have caught G's attention too, because she stopped walking.

"I think it's a wedding," she says once I catch up, her eyes fixed on the commotion up along the lit pathway. We watch the crowd of people dancing. Celebrating. Lights strung above the dance floor, and small tables set up around the space flickering with candles. Without a word, she continues walking toward the party.

"Woah, where are you going?"

She doesn't stop as she looks back at me over her shoulder with a smirk.

"Stop walking, Pixie." I start following her. "No!" I whisper-shout, but as we get closer, I know it's no use.

The laughter and the music gets louder. She's already made up her mind. She's going to crash this wedding whether I go with her or not.

She slows down when she gets to the opening where the wall and bushes separate the property from the beachfront. I see her smile as she watches. If we're going to do this, then we might as well walk in like we own the place. As I come up behind her, I don't slow down, instead I grab her hand, lace my fingers around hers, and then take the lead, dragging her to the dance floor. Her smile as we move among the guests knocks me back.

I pull her body closer to mine and she turns around so that her thick, round ass nudges against my thighs, grazing my hardening dick. Leaning into her neck, I kiss behind her ear before saying, "One dance and then we're leaving, G."

A minute later, the band changes beat, slowing down from a calypso island sound to something more sensual with a Latin influence. Bongos and guitar that subconsciously make me roll my hips and erase any space between my Pixie and me. She leans her head back, dropping it to my shoulder, and says, "I love this. It feels, it feels so good with you. To be with you like this."

She turns around in my arms, and I swear it's like I've been slapped by the universe. I'm so in love with this woman, it's almost funny. As she loops her arms around my neck, she's so much shorter than me that I have to lean down to wrap my arms around her back. I smile and give her a quick kiss.

"Did you just say something sweet to me, G?" I smile, teasing her, as she leans her forehead against mine.

"If I say another sweet thing, you can't hold it against me, Hanky. Weddings make me mushy."

I nod, not wanting to say anything to get her to stop. I'll take anything she's willing to give me.

"You're the only person I always look for," she whispers. She leans back so her eyes meet mine. "I looked for you too. After I was in WITSEC. I tried cities near bases, thinking you'd stay on base or nearby." Her confession surprises me, and I'm not sure what to say. "There are a lot of Henrys who were in the Air Force. I gave up looking after I chose Strutt's Peak. I decided I needed to let go and really try to move forward."

I'm coated in her words. In the reality that she wanted to find me, even after everything she had gone through and was dealing with at the time. I feel relieved and angry all at once. Relieved that she felt what I felt, but so damn angry that it has to be so hard.

"Then there you were. Right in front of me. And I couldn't have you." She searches my face, hoping for some kind of response, but I'm at war with myself over this. Hearing all of it. "I still look for you. In a room. A crowd. On the gondola. I'm always looking for you."

She doesn't say anything after that. She just rests her head on my chest as we sway to the rest of the song. Tomorrow, we go back to our lives. A life where we can't be like this, but I'm not willing to accept that any longer. I need to figure something out, because there's no going back to how it was before. I'm different now. I can't unhear these words, not feel her like this.

I drag my arms around her waist tighter, and drop my head to her shoulder, breathing her in. She always smells like lemons and sugar, now with a little sweat and the smell of the ocean added in. When the song ends, she takes my hand to walk back to the beach. She yells, "Congratulations," over the buzz of the crowd towards the bride and groom who are mid conversation. They smile back at us, curiously, both trying to place who we might be.

We're down the beach long before they likely realized we didn't belong there.

She never lets go of my hand. I squeeze it to pull her attention away from her own thoughts.

"I want you." *Squeeze.*

She looks at me with a smile. She knows I mean it in more ways than one.

"Then let's hustle, Hanky." She pulls her dress over her head and throws it at me, taking off in a run toward the opening of our property. Her naked silhouette moves ahead of me as she laughs. I look up at the moon, pleading for more time. I'm not ready for this to be over.

Our two days are up, but I'm not going to give her up so easily.

I chase her down the beach, shove the heaviness aside, and instead I smile, knowing I have one more sleep until she'll try to hide from me again.

CHAPTER 38

Giselle

THE WATER ENGULFS ME AND WARMS MY SKIN FROM HEAD to toe. The breeze from the ocean left me feeling chilled. Or maybe it was the words that Henry left buoying between us.

I want you.

I've wanted that man for so long. I've wanted him so badly I tried to hate him out of my system, but it was inevitable, I suppose, that we would find a way to this moment. I don't think there was ever a scenario where I wouldn't end up beside him. Kissing him again. Feeling the way his body spasms, and the sounds he makes when he comes. That's my own personal reward and torture rolled into one. The way he holds me, though, that's the thing I never knew I wanted from him. I didn't know how easily I fit into his side. The place where my head rests right below his chin when he's holding me from behind.

How am I supposed to stay away from him ever again?

When I breach the surface of the water, I decide I'll get my fill tonight. I refuse to ruin what time we have left and make it burdened with feelings we have to tamp down. He stands above me, at the side of the pool, with his chest moving up and down, sucking that the ocean air, watching my naked body swim around in front of him.

He makes my body react in ways only romance novelists dream about. Sexy fucker. I almost want to be annoyed at how he pulls these reactions out of me without permission. The goosebump inducing, panty-soaking, feel it in my toes kind of reactions. Just looking him up and down, his wide stance and big dick energy vibrating off from his thick thighs to those strong, corded forearms. Goddamn, those arms are where fantasies begin, and the way he's looking at me and dragging his tongue over his lower lip is how they end. It's intoxicating.

I swim toward the shallow side, to a shelf with built-in chairs that lay half in the water and half out. Shimmying my body across one, I drape one arm above my head. I know I look fucking hot right now, and I'm going to play it to my advantage, because if there is one thing sexier than Henry Riggs and all of his man-meat glory, it's Henry Riggs turned on while he's looking at me.

"Lose the shirt, Hanky," I demand.

He doesn't miss a beat. He starts to unbutton the white linen shirt as fast as his fingers will allow. His eyes never leaving mine. When his shirt falls to the tiles below his feet, he drops his attention to my chest, legs, and then back to my face. It makes my body flush with anticipation, or maybe it's a promise. His eyes promise me exactly what I want, what I crave. *Him*. As he drags his tongue across his bottom lip again, his chest heaves up and down, anticipating my next demand.

"Show me how you stroke that big, beautiful cock of yours."

He walks closer so any more instructions only have to be said rather than yelled. When he stops next to where I'm perched, he widens his stance, eyes flaring.

"Drop those knees open first, and let me see that pussy."

Like the obedient bitch I am, I do just that. My knees butterfly open, and I tap two of my fingers on the hood. She's ready for the attention, eagerly awaiting his praise and his punishment. The water that skims my bottom half is cool compared to the heat of my skin. It draws goosebumps out across my arms and legs.

I feel dizzy as Henry unties his shorts, and they snake down his thighs. But I don't keep my attention on their path for long. He fists his hard, bobbing cock with harsh strokes. It's an insanely beautiful dick. How am I supposed to go back and forget how it looks? How it feels in my hand, my mouth, inside of me?

I move out of the shallow shelf of the pool, the need to be closer to him so strong, I'm splashing my way to him. It's not seductive any longer. It's urgent. He meets me halfway. I bite his nipple as soon as I reach him and then drag my tongue over it to soothe the ache I may have left. By the groan, it sounds like Henry likes a little nipple play too. I bend forward instead of dropping to my knees and wrap my fist above his. His cock is big enough that we can both hold on like it's the shifter to a damn fine ride, with room for me to still kiss the tip.

"God, Gia. That's it, kiss it."

I flit my eyes up to look at him while I lick and kiss the tip of his cock. My name, my real name, from his lips, makes me even more eager. The sight of our hands practically clasped while my mouth hovers over him has to be so fucking good to see and feel, and I can tell how much he's enjoying it. He moves his hand from the base of his thick cock to push my hair away from my face, gathering it at the nape of my neck and not letting go. I open my mouth and stick out my tongue. But I look up at him and wait for him to guide my head forward. He gets the idea real fast, thrusting his cock to the back of my throat.

"Look at you. Fucking my cock with that pretty mouth of yours. That's it, Pixie."

I relax my throat as he guides himself in and out. The way he takes control of my movements peaks my arousal. I can feel it dripping down my thighs. Moving my hands from the front of his thighs, I wrap them around to his round, tight ass cheeks. I pull him into my throat, but instead of pushing him out, I breathe through my nose and swallow. The moan he releases is one that I'll never forget.

That's right, flyboy, no gag reflex. A fabulous party trick that is right up at the top of my list of attributes, along with my immaculate memory and dashing personality.

I pull back to look up at him, and instead of protesting, he pulls me up. With his hand still wrapped in my hair, the other pulls me by the neck toward his mouth.

"You've ruined me. Nothing, no one, feels like you. I'll

do whatever you want, woman, be whatever you need," he says, voice sounding strained. He brings me closer to kiss him, the taste of him mixed with the eagerness of his tongue drawing a moan from me. Or maybe it's the praise I'm preening from. He swallows my moan, regardless, and playfully moves his tongue against mine. It's one of those kisses that doesn't make me want to move forward. I want to live in this moment with his beautiful mouth dancing effortlessly with mine.

He drags his thumb over the column of my throat, stroking it lightly as he holds me possessively. The way his hand is braced around my neck makes me feel enraptured by this man.

Before I can make sense of my weightlessness, we're moving inside. He's hoisted me up and over his shoulder. The move makes my stomach flip with excitement. I'm panting, waiting for him to manhandle the shit out of me. We dance between ownership. Taking turns to lead the other. It's the most fun I've ever had.

My wet skin and hair drip onto his legs. We leave a trail of water behind us, and for some reason, the carelessness of it, the fact that we're strutting around this home with nothing on but the promise of dirty, delicious sex, is making my toes curl.

Smack.

I feel his teeth take a bite of my fleshy ass. He licks the spot.

Smack.

He groans at the sound of it. I shudder as a chill runs through my body.

Bite. Smack.

"You'd better leave teeth marks, baby. If I can't bring home a t-shirt or a shot glass from a souvenir shop, then you damn well better leave a few reminders on me, so I know this was all real."

He tosses me onto the bed from over his shoulder, and I laugh as I bounce.

"This is real," he says with a smirk. "If I have to spend the next handful of hours making sure you never forget what it feels like to have me between those legs, then I'll do it." He pulls me down by the ankle, his body hovering closer to mine now. Leaning in, he drops a kiss above my belly button.

I always enjoy sex, but I never savor it. Imprint it to memory. The memory banks that I like to pull from frequently. This moment will be there. In that place, tucked away for when I need it most.

He moves up my body, licks across my nipple, and then drags his teeth along the swell below it, making me arch my back. "More of that, please."

"You like when I bite you, Pixie?"

I moan in response. And he drags his teeth back and forth across my hard nipple again. The same way I did to him by the pool. He licks, his tongue flicking and swirling, and just as I look down to watch, he bites, the twinge of pain leaving me squirming. I'm so wet, so ready for him, I'm aching.

Leaving kisses across my chest, he makes it to my lips. A penance, perhaps for biting.

"Too much?"

"No, baby." I smile and nip at his lip. "You're never too much."

He smiles his big, beautiful smile, the one that makes that dimple pop.

Leaning up on one arm, he grabs his cock by the base, looking angry and eager for what I can gather is its new favorite place. Henry double-taps it against my clit and the slapping sound mixed with the moan that just jumped from my throat is a filthy soundtrack I wish I was recording. Rubbing the head against me, he coats it in the arousal he's been working for.

He moves himself up and down from slit to clit repeatedly. I watch and writhe as he teases me. Never dipping in, just drawing nonsense, as if my cunt's the paper and his cock, the quill.

Tap. Tap. Tap.

His warmth and teasing are edging me closer to something perfect. I want it to end and continue all at the same time.

He leans forward and kisses me again, like he can't go long without touching my lips. His tongue glides with mine only briefly, just enough to wet our mouths, and make me moan again. This time, as he leans back, he sets one of my legs over his shoulder, holding his cock on the hood of my pussy.

Tap. Tap. Tap.

A scream escapes me as he finally pushes inside. He moans and sucks in a loud breath. I think he may have even blown his own mind, because he pulls back slowly, and then drives forward. Rutting into me as if he can't get deep enough. That pursuit hits a hidden gem.

"Oh my, my..." I can't catch my breath to say anything more. My orgasm waiting just off-stage to make her glorious appearance. For her moment. And that moment comes with enthusiasm. Henry shifts his weight, my leg still perched on his shoulder, and lies next to me. He fucks me hard and fast, pulling at my nipple, at my tits. I don't understand the physics of our position, or how I'm so flexible, just that it feels like every place that could offer satisfaction does. Then he pinches my clit as he thrusts twice more into me, and the exquisite orgasm that billows through my body overwhelms my skin in a thick, dark ripple. All-encompassing. Consuming me. I don't hear sounds. I can only feel him. And the way my body feels like it's discovered the warmest breeze, the coolest touch, a steady calm at the center of a chaotic, frantic storm at the edges of my grasp.

My heavy breathing is what I hear first when my ears turn back on. Then moments later, the guttural moan of my man reaching the same level of ecstasy that I just came from. He fucks my pussy with two more thrusts before I feel him pull out of me and splash his cum across my skin. My pussy pulses again as he drags his still-hard cock around.

"You're so beautiful, Pixie. This, right here. Right now, glistening with sweat and watching my cum drip all over you..." he growls. "It's fucking perfection."

I don't say anything. Instead, I drag my finger into the mess he's made. Drawing it in circles around my nipples. I watch his face as I'm doing it, and he just stares. With his mouth open, he watches the path of my fingers. No words.

The corner of his mouth tilts up. And his eyes flick up

to mine. I yelp as he pulls me up and scoops me into his arms. I laugh uncontrollably.

"Let's go, my dirty girl. Time to fuck me in the shower," he says as he carries me into the massive blue bathroom.

"No cuddling?!" I ask sarcastically, unable to stop laughing.

"No fucking cuddling. I need to fuck this perfect little pussy of yours again, so you don't forget how you owned me tonight."

CHAPTER 39

Henry

THE WATER FROM THE CEILING RAIN SHOWER TRICKLES
drops down our bodies while the jets on the sides douse
us with a steadier pressure. The water is cool enough to
keep us from overheating, but warm enough to allow us
to play in here a little bit longer.

I bend my head down so G can wash the soap out of
my hair. Her nails drag along my scalp, and my leg practically shakes involuntarily. I fucked her again as soon as
the water turned on and her legs wrapped around my
waist. It wasn't long, but the way she feels and fits me so
perfectly is impossible to resist. And I want more. I need
more. I want to touch her whenever I want. Kiss her
without permission. I want to hear the way she calls me
baby when my cock hits her just right. It had me coming
much faster than I would have wanted, but I can't help it.
Now that I've had her, I have no control.

She's bewitched me. The idea of never feeling her

again, in any way, sexually, or otherwise, is a reality that I can't accept. I rub her tits with soapy water and appreciate the way her nipples draw taut when I brush a finger across them. Her body responds to my touch, like our skin was meant to collide.

"How do we feel this good together," she whispers. I'm not sure if she's really asking or just saying it out loud by accident. She wraps her arms around my neck, which forces me to lean down. She's so much shorter than I am, and I love the way it feels to have her drape her arms around me. An intimacy that I've missed, apparently.

Instead of answering her, I just lean in and kiss her again. She doesn't want an answer, just confirmation that I agree.

The water cascades down our faces as I kiss her wet mouth, her chin, her neck. I suck on the spot that makes her melt into me. Right below her ear, where the line of lemon blossoms sprawls into her hairline. Her arms snake tighter around my neck, and I savor the neediness of her embrace. I draw lines, numbers, and letters across her back. Through the stream of cooling water.

She pulls back and takes my face into her hand, staring into my eyes, and the unspoken words she's telling me is all I need to know about how she feels. I kiss her in response, pouring the answers she craves into my lips and tongue in the only way that will make her feel comfortable. The only way she'll allow right now.

Without much maneuvering, I pull her up and into my arms again. She wraps her legs around my waist, and I push slowly into her pussy. I move us toward the shower wall. No words exchanged, just the movement of the water down our bodies and the driving force of my cock into her welcoming body. She clenches her legs tighter and I drop my head to her neck. The feel of her in my arms is almost more sensual than filling her. The way she drags her hands along my neck, her fingers in my hair, the way her tits feel against my chest.

"You're going to make me come again, baby."

"You wait," I growl into her neck. I want to come with her.

I rut into her deeper, my hips grinding into her body. I feel her clench and it pushes me right to where I want. Right before my orgasm shoots through me.

"That's it, baby," she says. "Please..."

I grind into her again, knowing the angle hits her clit just right, and she grinds right back. "Come for me. Now. Fucking come for me, Pixie."

By the third roll of her hips into mine, she does. With a roar. The woman fucking roars in my ear as if she's a damn lion. And the sound of it, of her, unleashing while wrapped around me in every way, sets me off.

My balls pull tight and seconds later, I come inside of her. I moan into her neck and then bite her shoulder; I'm so amped up. We pulse around one another. It's better than any flight I've piloted. Mountain I've skied. This woman is the best high I've ever experienced. It's the most complete I've ever felt. Being with her is the chaos and the calm I've been aimlessly and unknowingly searching for.

I know what the plan is. But how the fuck do I go back to my life?

"I know, baby. I know." She leans her forehead against

mine and takes a breath. Then kisses my lips so sweetly, softly. "I know."

We don't say what is hanging right there. The words that will snap us into the future we don't want to face. Realities we don't want to embrace.

The problem is, just because I don't say it, don't tell her, it doesn't stop them from coming or slow any of it down.

I love this woman.

I don't have her yet, but I will.

After the shower, she drapes her body over mine and falls asleep. I draw lines, letters, and numbers around her arms and across her back. I commit to memory the way she feels. The softness of her skin, the weight of her body atop mine. I try to stay awake for as long as possible because I know when I fall asleep, that will be it.

And that's when getting back to Strutt's doesn't feel like the end game anymore. Being like this, with her, no matter where, is.

PART IV
LOVING HER

CHAPTER 40

Henry

IT'S JUST UNDER A WEEK SINCE WE'VE BEEN BACK IN Strutt's. It's taken every ounce of willpower not to stop into Hideaway Ink to see her. Touch her. Hold her and see if she's okay. That's not who we are to each other when we're here, though. In Strutt's Peak, we avoid each other. We bicker and push buttons.

Does she miss me the way I'm missing her?

We got off that flight and Agent Harper was waiting in the hangar with two more agents. There was no kiss goodbye. There was no one last anything. I clung to her hand as I helped her down the ladder. The only thing she said before Harper came close enough to hear was, "I miss you." And I knew exactly what she meant because I already missed her too. It was two days, and I could touch her, talk to her, and kiss her, whenever and however I wanted. And that freedom was gone. I missed it. I missed her. Already.

The assumption was to go back to the normal we left at home. But our normal had changed. Everything's changed. So, I've started drinking over-priced coffee every day from Brews & Books, which is right next door to her shop. Something called a Bookish Cortado with oat milk. An espresso with equal parts oat milk, and a splash of burnt caramel. If my brothers saw me order this, I'd never hear the end of it. But it's fucking delicious. Never mind if they knew why I was really coming here.

Brews & Books' owner, Kathryn Deacon, also happens to be an extension of my family. Her brother is Jack, who I shamefully still owe an explanation to for hijacking his wedding gift to my sister in the Cayman Islands.

"Henry! I've seen you every day this week. Are you my new regular now?" Kathryn asks as I step up to the counter.

"Those cortados are too good. Plus, my brothers won't shut up about getting something called a Kouign-amann?"

She laughs as she takes a box out and starts moving to the pastry case. "They're pronounced *queen-amanns,* actually. And yes, my adoptive mom used to bake these all the time when I was growing up. I think they're the perfect mix of buttery and sweet."

A crash from the kitchen snaps both of our attention toward the noise.

"Excuse me. I'll be right back."

I look around the shop casually, in case my blonde pixie is lounging with a coffee somewhere.

"So sorry about that. Benny is finally back to help me

in the mornings, but I've only got a couple of high school kids for the afternoon and evenings." She rolls her eyes. "It's a learning curve, to say the least."

Something she says sparks an idea.

"Out of curiosity, how busy are you at night?"

"Depends. If I host an author event, that'll pack the place. But otherwise, it's pretty low key. I tend to get an after-dinner crowd here and there, but the morning and mid-day folks who need a jolt are where the bulk of my business tends to be right now."

She smiles at me as she pours the espresso into the brown to-go cup.

"I had thought maybe I'd extend the menu and do a dinner thing, but this year has been..." She shakes her head and then looks back to her machine as she steams the oat milk.

Kathryn has had a tough year. She found herself in rehab this past spring and then had to deal with her son leaving for a while to Costa Rica. She's a tough one, but even the tough ones need a breather, or maybe a partner.

The door chimes behind me as she secures the top on my drink. A small line forms as she slides the box of pastries my way.

"I know you've had a tough year, but I'll tell you one thing"—I look around the shop—"this place is really something. I hope you know that."

Her smile brightens. "Thanks, Henry. Means a lot."

"Make sure you and Benny come by one of these Sundays for dinner."

I head out of the shop with an idea, but it's interrupted both by the snap of cold that hits me and my phone buzzing in my jacket pocket.

> G
>
> I see you, creeper. Really getting into that coffee shop vibe?

I look up to find G standing with one hand on her hip and the other clutching her phone in her shop window.

> Who is this?

She looks down at her phone and then snaps her gaze back up to me. I smile at her.

> Your mortal enemy. Now be a good boy and stop stalking me. You're breaking the rules.

> That was never a rule.

I watch her smile at my response. This whole staying away from each other is going to royally backfire in both of our faces.

> See you at Sunday dinner?

I look up and nod. Her smile just hits me in the gut. I'm not sure I can do this. Whatever this is, it's not going to last long. Not when I'm one week in and ready to plow my way through that door and feel her mouth on mine. Kiss her senseless. The thought makes me lick my lips.

My phone buzzes, pulling my attention back down to whatever she's saying.

> What are you making? The only meat of yours I'll eat isn't on the menu.

That makes me groan, but just as I look up again, she's gone. And something that feels an awful lot like hope flares in my chest.

The wind picks up, a warm breeze compared to the cold that hovers around me. The overcast sky is promising more snow, and for January, that isn't anything new, but that warm breeze wasn't my imagination. Just like that playful text from her was more than just flirting.

It was an invitation.

CHAPTER 41

Giselle

"THERE ARE ONLY THREE REASONS TO USE THE WORD 'cream' and none of them include something sexual. I mean, people say it. I've read it. But the only time I ever really want to hear that word is when someone says, 'Do you want cream in your coffee?' Or, 'the best flavor of ice cream is cookies and cream.' It's never going to win me over to hear someone say, 'show me that cream.' I drag that last sentence out in a low voice to really give it the oomph it deserves. "I'm about ready to whip out some Lubriderm. That's where my head goes. Food or moisturizing. Never sex or getting off. So I'd say, unless it was delivered by a sultry voiced man or woman, it was a food related request. Were you, like, at a coffee shop or something?"

Michael only blinks at me. His arms are folded as he leans against the counter in Asher's sprawling kitchen.

I crunch down on a raw green bean and stare back. "What?"

"Giselle! Are you coming back in here with my limes or not?" Everly yells from across the room.

I look back at Michael. He's still blinking at me, not saying a word. Now, I wonder if I may have heard his question wrong. You know what, now that I think about it, he may have said green. Not cream.

"Michael…"

He shakes his head. "Nope. Not going to unpack that right now, G. I'll ask someone else." He walks away, and I'm left questioning what he could have possibly said.

I snag a few more green beans from the bowl and flick my attention out to the patio. Widespread shoulders and a bowed head, work hard on grilling some kind of meat. Henry's sweater can't be keeping him that warm out there. It's freezing tonight. I see a few flames kick up. Maybe he's warm cooking. Should I bring him a jacket? Why do I care? Oh, right. I don't. But then, I'm also not supposed to be remembering the way we fucked like damn porn stars last weekend.

"Giselllllleeee!"

"I'm coming! Jeez!" I yell back at Everly as I round the counter and move toward the bar across the room.

I plop an armful of limes on the bar top.

"It's a rude way for someone to ask or request how much you're willing to pay them," Jack says as he starts cutting the limes into wedges. "Who were you talking to that said, 'show me the green?'"

Light bulb. It was green, *not* cream. I feel like my job is done here. If I'm not making at least one Riggs family member uncomfortable, then it doesn't feel like a successful Sunday dinner.

"G, can you show up around 7 p.m. on Friday?" Law asks, as he sidles up next to me at the bar.

"What's Friday night?" Everly asks.

I dip a piece of lemon in the sugar dish. "Bachelor party."

"She's going to do tattoos for the bachelor party we've got coming in next weekend."

Jack comes up behind Everly and drops a kiss on her neck. "What's happening next weekend?"

"Big bachelor party. One of my boys is finally getting married," Law says.

"Is this the baseball player?"

Everly shifts, grabbing her drink. "No clue. He said, 'my boys.' I tuned the rest out."

"Yes, it's the baseball player! Want to come? There's going to be tattoos by our girl over here." Law starts ticking off more on his fingers. "There's a Bourbon and meat pairing that Henry's pulling together, a burlesque show for some entertainment, and I might try to see if we can do something a little boujee the next day."

"Don't say boujee," Michael chimes in.

"You will not judge, or your invite will be revoked."

"I didn't really want to go anyway," Michael says, lifting a shoulder.

"What!? Blasphemy. Your ass will be there."

Michael just laughs. "You invite Dad?"

"Duh. But he'll only make an appearance if he's bored."

I chime in, mostly because I'm curious. "Is Sheriff

Muldowney going?" I take a sip of water and then chase it with a sip of the lemon drop martini that's just waiting to be downed in front of me.

Henry laughs from the other side of the room.

"What's so funny?" I shriek back.

"You're not his type, G," Michael says.

I raise my brows. "I know. Just asking for a friend." I smile. Looking back at Henry, he's very obviously surveying the way I'm leaning forward on the bar. I watch as his eyes drag down to my ass and up my legs. He licks his lips.

Me too, big guy, me too.

Asher jogs down from upstairs. That man is a *DILF* in every sense of the stupidity of the word. The silver fox wears a three-piece suit at the office, but everywhere else, he's usually rocking some kind of chest-huggin' sweater and nicely fitted jeans that probably cost more than my rent. Today it's a chunky navy sweater and lighter washed blue jeans. Did I mention he likes to walk around barefoot? Even when it's fucking freezing outside.

"Daddy Riggs, you going to this bachelor party on Friday?" He smiles wide at me. "I've got the perfect tattoo for you," I sing-song.

"We'll see. I have a few things with the town council I need to work through, and that means buttering them up with some good steaks this Friday."

I pout and stick out my lower lip. He comes over and kisses my forehead. "I'll stop by this week at the shop, and you can tell me what tattoos you have in mind, kiddo."

That makes me smile. "Deal." As much as I joke

about Asher and all of his hotness, he really is like a surrogate parent.

"Time to eat yet? I'm starved."

"Could you not call my father *Daddy*?" Henry says close to my ear.

Where did he come from? It sends a ripple through my body. The man has been practically stalking me all week long, but I haven't been in a touchable proximity. I haven't felt his breath on my ear in well over a week now, and the reminder of what it does to me is like a Road Runner and Wyle E. Coyote run in. Always the same. A complete crash to my senses. And totally inevitable.

"Meat's resting. Ev, mind helping me with the rest of it?" Henry asks as he walks back toward the kitchen.

When I look up, I see Michael looking at me. He darts his eyes toward Henry. His stare, back in my direction, says one glaringly obvious thing. *He knows.* He tilts his head, a silent question. My face must give him what he's looking for, because he smiles and nods.

Dammit, Michael!

Dinner conversation is solely focused on Everly and Jack's honeymoon. The incredible time they had doing absolutely nothing. It has me thinking how similar our time away was. I shake my head, knocking that thought away. Similar, but not the same. Mine was an emergency, drug-induced kidnapping mixed with a decades' worth of pent-up sexual tension, while hers was the ellipses to finding and falling for who is sure to be the love of her life.

I bite into my grilled cheese. This one tastes like broccoli cheddar soup packed in between two buttery, crispy slices of bread. It's delicious. I don't realize I let out a moan when I take another bite, until I look to my left and see Henry staring at me. I watch his Adam's apple bob with a rough swallow.

I'd like to be bobbing up and down on his dick right now, if I'm being honest. He leans over and wipes a bit of cheese or something from the corner of my lip, and I smile. The simplest of gestures, and I want to melt all over him. The chatter from the room grows silent, and that's the only reason we both stop looking at each other.

"The fuck did I just witness?" Law gawks at us, still standing from his celebratory tirade from a minute ago.

Henry shifts and looks around the room uncomfortably. Clearly not sure how to play this. I look at Everly, and she's just smiling wide at me.

Shit.

It takes her two days to finally say something about the lip swipe scandal at Sunday dinner. Two days! Just when I think I'm in the clear, and she's forgotten about it, I'm blindsided. I'm sitting inside of Brews & Books when the text that makes my heart stop and brain reset, comes through.

EVERLY

When are you going to stop avoiding me and just tell me that you're sleeping with my brother?

Maybe if I ignore the question, it'll go away.

Can't talk right now. With a client.

Two minutes later, my best friend plops a spiked Earl Gray tea in front of me.

"I watched you freak out and then lie to me from the front window."

"I didn't freak out." I take a sip.

"Okay, then. When you're ready to talk to me about it, I'll listen. But I'm going to just say a few things, and you're going to hear me, okay?"

"I still don't know what you're talking about." I flick my eyes up to her. "But I'll listen."

"You're my soulmate, doll. It's that simple. You tell me as much or as little as you want when you're ready." She takes a sip of her drink. Likely, a Hungry Eye. That woman and espresso with oranges. It's borderline at the same level of obsession as me with lemons.

I wait, because I know she has more to say. Though a huge part of me is breathing a little easier, knowing that she's not upset about it.

"Henry has been through a lot of shit. He's tough. He handles it, but life, for some reason, likes to smack him around. So, I'd really love it if you'd go easy on him. Whatever it is. If it's just fun, then let it be that. If it's more, then just be careful with each other. I love you both far too much to see you hurt one another. But if I'm being honest, you've been so awful to each other over the years that any improvement is better than keeping the course you were on."

I don't respond. I'm not sure how I want to process any of this. Technically, Henry and I are supposed to be nothing right now. But I can't help but want to say, 'fuck that' and crawl right back into his arms, to that spot my head fits perfectly into below his chin and on his chest. I like the flirty text messages and the blurred lines, but talking to Everly about it makes it too real. And when I think about real, and what I can offer him, it wouldn't be enough.

I could never give him what he wants. I'll always be in WITSEC. I can't just be in a relationship. Be a wife. Give him a family. That's not something I'm able to do for anyone, especially not a man like Henry. If anyone deserves all of the things he wants, it's that man. I care about him too much to let him get stuck with me, and then realize too late it's not enough. That *I* wouldn't be enough.

So instead of addressing any of it, I let the air settle a little bit longer and then change the subject. Everly won't push. And I don't know that there is anything more to say.

"You need to let me raid your closet for the bachelor party on Friday night. I feel like I need to switch things up a bit. I'm feeling a little rock goddess meets slutty cocktail waitress."

Without missing a beat, she leans forward and says, "I have the perfect skirt."

CHAPTER 42

Henry

My sweat-soaked thermals are starting to give me a chill. It's been a good two-hour ride so far and Michael doesn't seem interested in slowing down any time too soon. The fat-biking trails are freshly plowed from the blizzard that came through a day ago, and he's loving it.

I take off my Oakley's and wipe my face down. The sun is bright and reflecting off the river. Mix that with the bright white snow and it's almost blinding. I can barely see the clear blue sky.

"Hold up," I radio over to Michael, who is a decent distance in front of me. The talkies built into our helmets were designed so our guides could connect with everyone as they move over trails. It's a safety precaution first, but it also allows less experienced patrons to get an overview of the valley they're riding through.

"I think there could be a stop here where each of the trails converge. A central location where we can set up a pop-up of sorts to refuel with something warm. Maybe a snack," Michael says while looking around where we've taken a break. It's a smart move and a simple addition that would bring in more revenue.

"Smart," I say, while taking a pull from my water bottle. I know I should think through the execution of this with him, but the truth is, I'm distracted.

"I could see if we can get one of those pre-fab airstream trailers to start. Something we could take in and out if needed. I feel like the zoning would be much faster too. Any electricity we'd need could be generator-run to start. If it makes sense for the rest of this season, then we can think about a more permanent fixture," he says, walking around the area.

The riverbank is about 100 feet from where we've stopped. The air always feels a bit heavier in lower elevation, but it's crisp and clean. Even though it's cold, the sun and temperature spike today melted a decent amount from the ridge, which means the river is high and loud. It's easy to be distracted by it.

"Tell me what's going on, man."

I look back at him. I'm not about to play dumb. Out of anybody, Michael notices things before the rest of us. And I'd never lie to him. Normally, I'd be thinking through the details of a business idea like this one, so a one-word answer is a flashing red sign to my brother that says *something's off*.

Michael laughs and then says, "Hen, I need to work out for at least another hour before I can call it a day, so you either tell me now or I'm going to obsess over it. And I'll just keep asking until you tell me, so,"—he shrugs his shoulders—"your call, but something is different with you."

I pull off my leather gloves and unclasp my helmet. I look at my brother with a smirk on his face, as if he already knows what I'm going to say. "Would it be too dramatic to say everything?"

"Only if it's not true. But you're not usually one to be dramatic. If you were Law, then I'd probably start laughing and keep riding, but that's not you, man."

He mimics my move, removing his gloves and helmet.

"I went ahead and fell in love with her. And now..." I rub the back of my neck and look down at my bike. "Fuck. Now, I don't know how I'm just going to pretend like I don't want to be with her every goddamn minute."

Michael's eyebrows raise as high as his hairline. I don't think he was expecting me to say love, maybe that I slept with her, but not this. Not love.

"We're talking about who I think we're talking about, right? Loud, talks too much, blonde, gets on my nerves, but somehow, I miss her when she's not around?"

I laugh at that description because it's incredibly accurate. "That's who I'm talking about." I blow out a heavy breath.

Michael squints at me when he asks, "Does she want the same thing?"

I laugh. "Yeah, I think she does. She's going to fight it, because she's a pain in the ass. But this isn't one-sided."

"But what if it is?"

I put my leather gloves back on, securing my helmet next. "Then it looks like I'm going to have to find out.

You're coming to that bachelor party tonight. She's doing the tattoos."

He laughs. "I really don't want to."

"I really don't give a shit. You're going."

I kick the snow that's caked onto my boot off, using the pedal, and start moving. "I'd rather avoid the drama. Can you just tell me how it went?"

"No fucking way. You've stirred the pot, and now you're going to be there for moral support. Or play interference with whatever douchebags are likely flirting with her."

"It's Law's friends, so likely all of them. We *are* talking about Giselle, right?" he calls out.

I look back over my shoulder as he rides up closer. I don't even need to respond. There wouldn't be anybody else. He knows that. Of all my family, Michael has witnessed it for years.

He yells back, "Because if she sees you, you bet your ass she'll be the one doing the flirting. That woman loves nothing more than to piss you off."

"No. Dammit. No," Michael says and turns back around toward the double doors we just walked through. I grab him by the arm. We spent the rest of the afternoon on the trails and then grabbed some food. I didn't know how I wanted to do this tonight, but waiting didn't really seem like an option. I've spent the past week stalking her and she knows it.

"You're staying."

The moment we walked through, I knew he wasn't going to be a fan of tonight, but if anyone could use some loosening up, it's Michael. I know he's not a virgin, but with the way he acts sometimes, he could be. I know for a fact he lost that on prom night, but he's not the guy to flirt and take random women home. That's our youngest brother's jam. Not Michael's. He never does unplanned or uncomfortable situations. For him, someone who thrives off of planning and structure to battle his anxiety and OCD, tonight is the antithesis of a preferred evening.

"I need you to stay. You don't have to do anything you don't want to do," I tell him. Looking around at the burlesque show playing out in the front where the bar is located is probably exactly what has him on edge. The tables are crammed with guys smoking cigars and playing poker. "I'll spot your buy-in. Go take those guys for all their over-inflated contracts."

He does a double take and spots the shortstop for the LA Dodgers, the starting pitcher for the Toronto Blue Jays, and last year's Cy Young Award winner. He'll find his footing fast among these guys. In truth, only a few of Law's college friends are asshats. The rest of his guys, the baseball guys and the few rugby guys who are here, are good people. Talking baseball is one of Michael's strong suits. As long as they talk shop, and not women, he'll forget to be pissed at me for dragging him to this.

The Blind Pig is a cigar bar at the base of the mountains of Strutt's Peak. Not too far from downtown, and at the beginning of the Strutt's gondola system. The place has a rich, speakeasy vibe, with an incredible number of brands of Scotch, ports, and Cognacs. It's the go-to after dinner, nightcap spot for tourists. But tonight, it's closed to anyone without an invite. Law rented the entire place for his best friend's bachelor night.

On the bar, two tables, and a swing swaying in the middle are burlesque dancers moving with the ebb and flow rhythm of "I Put a Spell on You" by Nina Simone.

I find her immediately. My body buzzes at the sight of her. It's as if the words to the song clicked into place, and the wild attraction that runs between us powers up. Wild braids that look like a crown on her head, with curls cascading down her back, she leans over a table tattooing someone. I stare at her profile. So focused as she moves. I've never been more envious of a piece of furniture watching her straddle the stool that her ass is perched upon.

A big hand claps against my shoulder. "Henry fucking Riggs. How are you, man?" Rodriguez, the man of the hour, interrupts my shameless staring.

Snapping out of it, I give him a backslapping hug. "You ready to finally get married? How long you two been together?"

He smiles wide. "I was ready the first week we met. But she needed time. And then you know the story; I ended up getting drafted. Life happened. All that shit."

"I get that." I look back at G and find her watching me now. "I definitely get that."

Rodriguez turns around to see where my attention is focused. He claps my shoulder again and leans in. "Come play some poker. Oh, and, Hen, everyone could have called that, by the way. Take it from me," he says while walking away, "don't be stupid and wait so long that she goes ahead and builds a whole life with someone else."

I never seem to make my way to her. Three more guys come up to me before I can move to the other side of the room. I end up betting at the roulette table. Only instead of just cash, they've added names to the wheel. The lucky winner gets Rodriguez's name and baseball number tattooed on his ass as the ultimate souvenir for the night.

When Sean King ends up being the unlucky winner, I'm pissed off, because I know Sean and G have some kind of history. The idea of her tattooing him again makes me see red. And before I even register what I'm doing, I've stopped in front of the tattoo table.

"Hi there," she says as she smiles. "You want me to tattoo you next?" Giselle asks as Sean lies face down on her table.

"Hen, how you been, bro?" Sean says.

I ignore him.

"I need to talk to you," I say to Giselle. It comes out with a bit more of an edge than I intended, but I'm not interested in seeing her touch Sean's ass.

Her eyes meet mine. She furrows her brow, questioning what's wrong.

"Sean, sweetie. I need to talk to Henry for a minute. I'll be right back," she says, moving toward the restrooms. Taking off her gloves, she stops short at the entrance of the hallway and spins around. Her eyebrows kick up, silently asking me to talk.

"What's wrong?"

"Cut the shit. You know what's wrong," I spit back to her.

"Is it that your good ol' buddy Sean is laid out on my table right now and you're afraid I'm going to tickle his pickle?"

I don't justify that question with an actual response. Even though she's partly right. But instead of saying that, I grab her hand and pull her fast so her body jerks against mine. Her eyes go wide, and she grins slowly, like the Cheshire Cat. She likes when I take what I fucking want. And I want her, with me, and away from anyone else. I want her in every way.

I lean in, and instead of kissing her, I move down farther and brush my lips back and forth against her neck. She melts into me and grabs my shoulders.

"Jealousy looks pretty fucking hot on you, Hanky."

"I don't want to watch you flirt with other men, G." I pull back and make sure she hears me. "I don't want to play games. I miss you. I miss the way we could be when it's just us. I want that. Here." I search her face for a reaction.

"No."

"What do you mean, no?" I bark back.

"It's not just us now. It's everyone in our lives. It's all my baggage. It's not *just* us."

I ignore her protest. If I'm going to lay this out, then I want her to hear all of it.

"The only thing I can think about since we've been back is you. I want you so fucking badly; I'm minutes away from kissing you in front of the whole room so they know you're mine, and then telling them all to get the fuck out so I can devour the rest of you." I rub my hand in between her legs, making her gasp.

I feel unhinged. I should have done all those things already, never mind just saying it out loud. She's searching my face, unsure of what to say, but her body's already answered me. The moment I said she was all that I could think about, she leaned in closer, her fingers gripped my shoulders tighter, and I watched her close her eyes with a hum. I nip at her neck and kiss behind her ear again.

She whispers, "Dammit," and then seconds later, she pushes me away. Shaking her head, she says, "We agreed. You agreed." She moves back toward the bar, and I can see the deep breath she takes, trying to steady herself.

"I take it back," I say as she keeps walking.

Her eyes water and the shakiness of her voice gives away exactly how much she doesn't mean the next few words out of her mouth. "It's done, Henry. That's over now. Just leave it."

None of this is simple with her. We can't just leave it. "You're not fucking anyone else," I yell after her. She stops mid-step and turns back around at that.

"Oh, is that so?"

"That's fucking so, Pixie. That mouth of yours." I nod down. "And that pussy. They're mine."

She starts laughing. Like I'm not serious. Like if I saw her with another man, I wouldn't end up with bloody knuckles and in the back of Callen's police cruiser again.

Without another word, she heads back to the party. There's a small smile on her lips, which she hides quickly, but I saw it. I've just thrown down some kind of fucked up gauntlet.

When I make my way back, I find a poker table with a

few guys, Michael and Law included. Michael's taking them for all their worth. I look over at the tattoo set-up, watching Sean rest his hand on G's leg under the table as she draws along his skin. I shake my head. My pulse rate kicks up, and I'm beyond pissed.

Because she's right; it's over unless I can figure out a way to make it work. I know the hurdles. My business shines too much attention on me. She's already taking unnecessary risks by being tied to my family in the first place. The only way I can avoid watching her with other men for the rest of my life is to find a way out of that spotlight.

CHAPTER 43

Giselle

It's been twenty minutes. Twenty minutes of obsessing about what the fuck they're talking about. About what's so funny. He's not *that* funny. I've watched his head kick back in laughter more than five times. She touched his arm at least three. And now, she's perched on the table in front of him in a proximity that is far too close. He's been flirting with a burlesque dancer for more than twenty goddamn minutes now, and I want to tattoo her face with permanent uneven eyebrows. She touches his chest, right where I know his tattoo lives. It takes every ounce of willpower not to yell at her and tell her to keep her hands off. *That's mine!*

I know it's not her fault, but I'm not thinking logically —or chicks before dicks right now. That's *my* flyboy. And it's not like I don't get it. I do, he *is* delicious. Anyone who would look around this room and not pick Henry first would have to be blind. Even with it being chock full of thirst traps and pro athletes. My bestie's hubs is hot as hell, too, but he puts off yellow caution tape energy that screams, "I'm taken." Hell, even Michael and Law are attractive as all get out, but Henry Riggs. *Sigh.* Henry Montana Riggs is something entirely different. When those mismatched eyes are focused on you, it's a whole new level of nervous energy mixed with wet panties and a twinge of aggression. It's like the greatest, full body cocktail that's been shaken and stirred to drive women insane. He's a sexual mixologist. I'm drunk on him, and that woman better step the fuck off.

I'm not even going to dive into the way he holds me when I sleep or how he knows exactly how much cheese is too much cheese in my grilled cheese sandwiches.

"What do you think?"

A hand squeezes my thigh, knocking me out of my internal rage campaign against that burlesque girl. I look down at the bear paw around my leg, and then back at its owner.

"Hands off, Sean baby. You had your turn, remember?"

I slap the last bit of wrap over his tattoo, and he sits up. "I couldn't forget, even if I wanted to, sweets."

I smile. Sean King is a giant ass, but he's a sweetheart at the core of it. We had a bit of fun a few years ago, but I like leaving the past where it belongs. No repeats.

As I think it, I look back to Henry. Except with him. I only want repeats with him.

It's taken me exactly ninety-two minutes of talking to myself, four blocks of walking, three pieces of American cheese, two outfit changes to feel like I've combined the right amount of "fuck me right now" and "I'm going to tease you until you explode" vibes. And a gondola ride to get my ass to his front door.

I knock quickly before I lose my nerve. I hear the faint sound of music playing from inside, which I'm surprised, because it's well after midnight now.

Maybe I should have sexted ahead?

The door pulls open and I'm met with a smiling Michael Riggs. "Why, G, what are you doing here?" he says condescendingly, like he's not surprised in the least to see me.

"I should say the same about you. Last I checked, you didn't live here, Mikey." I shove through the door. I already know by the cackling happening inside that there are women here. Not what I was expecting to find, but I can improvise.

"Not my name, but by all means, come on in," Michael says as he shuts the door.

When I turn the corner, I see a shirtless Henry Riggs chopping something next to the cooktop. With his back to me, he calls out over his shoulder, "Michael, who was it?"

I look into the oversized living room, its vaulted ceilings carrying the sound of laughter and a story that Law is overly animated while telling. They must have taken the last few standing from the bachelor party and came here for food.

"Gracie?"

"Hey, G!"

"What are you doing here?" I ask, surprised to see her here, of all places.

"The guys called for a Lyft, and I decided to help my mom out on a few shifts while I'm still in town. Henry told me he was making food, so I figured I'd come up." She peeks over my shoulder to where Michael is standing.

I shrug off my parka and walk it over to the side door, where the rack for winter gear is set up. Henry's gaze follows my movements as he whisks something in a bowl, and I don't dare look away. I came here for him and I'm not going to let a few people get in the way of what I want right now. I drag my eyes from the floor, where I notice he's barefoot, and up his body slowly, taking in the way his sweatpants hang carelessly low on his hips. I can't for the life of me understand why he's not wearing a shirt, but why question something if it's doing something good. I lick my lips and remember what his skin felt like to hold on to and drag my nails across.

"Her clothing line is my absolute favorite. There're a few of us that hunted down her boutique in New York on our last trip, and we must have bought out more than half of her inventory," the blonde on the couch says. Obviously talking about my girl Everly's clothing line. As soon as these women found out the last name of my boys, I guarantee they lit up like damn Christmas trees.

I watch as the blonde drapes her legs over Law's lap and laughs at whatever he's talking about. The woman on the other side of him, with short tight curls and bright blue eyes, leans on her elbow, listening intently, and doling out a hefty helping of "fuck me" eyes in Law's direction. That's when I notice she was the woman who had Henry's attention at the bar tonight. One of the burlesque dancers. She is beautiful, now that I look a little more closely, and now that she seems less like a threat.

I take a quick peek around to where Gracie and Michael sit, cross-legged and barely saying anything to one another. But Gracie looks like she's either getting annoyed or uncomfortable. Maybe both.

I walk closer to Henry. I haven't said anything to him yet. Words weren't something I was planning to deliver when I made up my mind to come over.

"What are you doing here, Pixie?" Henry growls out.

Ignoring him, I instead take another look around his body. His ass in sweatpants is a true gift. He watches me, and I know he's still mad about our conversation earlier, but quite frankly, he can be mad all he wants. I'm here to fold.

"I think you should tell everyone to go home now," I say as I round the island counter where he's making food. I drag my finger into some kind of red sauce, sticking my entire finger in my mouth and licking it clean. *Cranberries.*

He smirks at me. "Oh yeah? Why would I do that, G?"

His eyes follow me as I sit up on the counter next to where he's working on putting together a sandwich. He stares at my shirt, and I know instantly it was the right choice. An old band t-shirt I decided would do better if it showcased some of my assets.

"You here to tell me how much this can't happen, or how we won't work?" He lifts a knowing brow.

"Hanky, what happened to your shirt? Feeling left out, you needed to make sure the girls felt comfortable being practically topless in your home?"

He huffs a dark laugh and leans across my legs to grab the salt and pepper next to my hip on the counter. He uses proximity as warfare. But I can play dirty too. I mean, that was part of the plan.

"You didn't answer me, Pixie. What are you doing here?"

I don't answer, staring at the scar on his lip. I didn't like the idea of someone else feeling it the way that I have. I sit up taller on the counter, pushing out my chest just enough that the shirt I'm wearing rides a little higher, giving him a peek of two of his favorite things.

Law yells from across the room, dragging his attention away from my chest. "Henry, I'm so fucking hungry. Are the sandwiches almost ready?"

He ignores his brother, and looking up at me, he says, "Nice shirt. Since when do you like heavy metal?"

I pick up his phone and pull up Spotify, finding the song I'm looking for now that he's taken the bait. Before I press play, I make the suggestion one more time. "I think you should tell everyone to leave now."

He smiles and just shakes his head. Then he turns around to put a few bowls into the sink.

Alright, big guy. Let's see how fast you're going to change your mind.

CHAPTER 44

Henry

I SHOULD HAVE KNOWN THE MOMENT I SAW HER WALK INTO the house to kick everyone else out. She has no reason to be here unless it's to give in. I should have given one of my brothers the cue to cut out of here again when she took off her parka jacket. Once I spotted the Def Leppard t-shirt that she cropped so short you can see the under curve of her tits. I never knew how sexy that really was until I saw it. That little beauty mark on her left breast just peeking out at me, and I want to lick it to make sure it's really there.

She eyes the sliced lemon I have on the cutting board next to me. Then, hopping down, she looks in the cabinets above the espresso machine. Closing it, then opening the other. I don't say anything, just watch her while I finish plating the last of the sandwiches. She returns to the counter, puts the sugar bowl next to where she sat, and hops back up.

I look around the living room at the conversations still going on. I see Michael talking with Gracie, somewhat awkwardly. Law is flailing his arms around in some sort of story he's telling the other two women who came back here with us. But my survey stops when I feel her breath on the shell of my ear.

"Henry, I think it's time for everyone to go home now," she whispers, and then I notice her holding my phone. She taps away at the screen, and then seconds later, I hear the rift of an electric guitar across my sound system, throughout the house. "Fine. Have it your way."

"Step inside, walk this way..."

G raises an eyebrow, cranks up the volume, and then gives me one of her most wicked, sexy smiles.

Shit.

The bass kicks in, and then the vocals. You'd have to be living in a hole not to recognize the first few beats of "Pour Some Sugar on Me," but here I am, planted in place and staring. She kicks off her boots, stands up on the counter, and starts to sway her hips. As she bends over at her waist so that her ass cheeks are eye-level, I'm instantly hard. I don't notice what she grabs from the counter, just that she's about to dance on my fucking countertop in front of far too many people. This show was only meant for me.

"Get the fuck out," I say and look around at the room of people who are all watching my pixie move her body in ways I've never seen her do before, and my cock aches for it. Nobody moves, so I yell this time. "Get the fuck out. Now."

"Are you shitting me right now?" Law barks back. "I fucking knew it. I knew it!"

One look at my face, and Law throws his hands up and points at me. "I fucking knew it!" I flip him off, and then he motions for the girls to leave out the door. Michael and Gracie were already gone by the time the second request left my mouth.

I only hear the front door shut because my attention is back on G as she laughs and shakes up the bottle of soda water in her hands.

I shake my head, telling her she better not fucking spray me with water right now. And the moment I crack a smile, I know she's going to let it pour. The entire scene in front of me is some kind of 80s movie fantasy. G opens the cap, and the soda water sprays around the room, but she tips it so it douses the front of her instead of the entire kitchen, and I salivate at the vision she's created. She soaks her Def Leppard shirt right through, the fabric clinging to her breasts. It sprays across my skin too, barely cooling anything down because my blood is boiling, pulse thumping. I'm so worked up over the show in front of me.

The water drips down her stomach, and a steady stream makes its way to her black leggings. My pants are soaked, my head feels light, and I'm smiling at the sight of her. Her nipples are hard and tight, making the sexiest appearance through that scrap of a shirt. There's not a single person in the world that makes me laugh like this girl. And it's impossible not to laugh with her in this moment. She's ridiculous and so much fun. Something I didn't realize I wanted in my life until she breezed into it all those years ago.

I reach up and hook my fingers in the waistband of her leggings, rolling them straight down her legs. They're practically suctioned to her skin, leaving a trail of goose-bumps in their wake. She steps one foot out of each leg, and it feels too good to touch her again as I run my hands up her thighs.

"You're somethin' else, Pixie."

She keeps dancing and laughing as she looks down at me. I realize quickly she's not getting down, so I lean back and watch this live pin-up girl dance for me like a fucking professional in a thong and a soaked heavy metal t-shirt that's barely covering her tits. My body is pumping adren-aline through my veins, and I can barely contain the lust that I know is radiating off of me. My mouth waters as I take in her body. The way her hip kicks up as she sways. The way her waist stays still while her thighs control the movements.

I snag my phone from the counter and lower the volume,, my hands are shaking in anticipation. I have to touch her. My mouth is watering to taste her.

She finally sits in front of me, and as the music starts playing something with a lower tempo than Joe Elliot would ever allow, we stare at each other. Maybe both real-izing this isn't something we walk away from ever again. Nudging her knees apart, I settle between them. I drag my thumb around her bottom lip, then down to the column of her neck. So sexy, the way she swallows and gets turned on when I touch her like this.

"Hi." She smiles.

I take one of the lemon bits, and she watches as I glide the lemon through the sugar to coat it. Then I bring the thinly sliced piece toward her lips. She opens her mouth, but instead, I brush the piece around her pouty mouth. Coating them in the tart, granulated, and wet sugar.

"Hi." I smile back.

I lick her bottom lip, and the lemon sugar coats my tongue. When I pull back to look at her mouth again, she sucks her upper lip in her mouth for a taste. Settling my hands on her waist, I drag my thumbs under the swell of her tits. The feel of her skin is so soft, still damp, and I groan.

"Tell me you want this," I demand of her.

I lift her shirt, so I can finally see the rest of her. Rosy pink peaks that barely hid underneath the scrap she had on. I suck one into my mouth so hard it pulls a moan from deep within her chest. Then I pinch her other nipple just enough that she pushes her chest out farther, trying to meet my pull. But it's more than the physical want I'm asking for right now. I need to hear her say that she wants me. This. *Us.*

"Tell me," I growl as I tongue over the same path on the other side. The noises she's making have made me unbearably hard. There's no way I'm going to make it into another room. I'm fucking her in this kitchen. But not before she says it. Not before I see her mean it.

"I want you, baby," she says breathlessly. "I've missed you so much. Two days wasn't enough."

That's all it takes for me to let go. I pull her mouth to

mine, and we relish each other's lips in a kiss that I've wanted every single day since I've been away from her.

She pulls back. Out of breath, she says, "I want you so badly that I'm practically throbbing. You haven't even touched me yet, and I'm ready to come."

"You won't. You'll come when I tell you." I don't let her object, or play the game where she doesn't crave being bossed around a bit. Instead, I kiss her in a punishing rhythm, and her tongue meets mine with equal enthusiasm. She moves her hands down from around my neck and right to gripping my cock. Her touch is rough, but there's nothing soft about this moment. It's just the need to feel each other. Taste. Fuck. Savor. And then make a better plan. Because we couldn't last more than a week apart with the old one.

Her legs are wrapped around me so tight, and she tilts her hips up and down so that the heat between her legs rubs against my cock.

"Turn around," I growl into her ear, pulling her from the countertop.

A smile plays across her mouth. "Don't be gentle," she whispers as she drops her legs and turns her body away from me. The only thing she has on is a neon pink G-string; all it takes is a twist and tug to rip it, which I do. I'll play with her later, but right now, I need to feel her and fuck her the way she's requested.

I drag the head of my cock around the lips of her pussy, mixing her arousal with mine. My other hand grips her hips. She arches herself forward so that her chest meets the counter and her ass thrusts back. My skin touching hers feels so good. Slick from the show she put on and ready to be punished.

Begging me, she says, "Please. Baby, please. Don't make me wait any more."

I thrust into her hard and deep, reveling in her moan that matches mine. Fuck, this woman has ruined me. It's a privilege to feel something so good. My body buzzes with excitement and starts to unwind in relief from being wrapped within her again.

Pulling out to the tip, I watch as the drip of arousal moves down the lips of her pussy. And then pump halfway into her twice. On the third, I push all the way in until my hips meet her ass cheeks. I lean forward, wrapping one hand around the soft column of her neck, draping my body over hers. I don't think, I just react to every want pulsing through me. I move faster, fuck her harder, bottoming out on each thrust.

"More. I need more," she moans and pulls my thumb into her mouth, sucking off any lemon and sugar that may have been left.

I lean back to get a better glimpse of her ass as I thrust into her pussy. I know exactly what she's asking for as she bends forward and away from me.

"You're so damn sexy, Pixie. You take my cock so well," I tell her.

I run my thumb over her ass as I keep the punishing pace.

"You want my fingers here, Pixie?"

"Oh fuck, yes."

"Ask me nicely."

Without missing a beat, she listens and says, "Please, baby."

I'm not about to look for any kind of lube, so I suck my thumb into my mouth, coating it. I rub small circles around the muscle while I continue to fuck her, her hips pushing back for more. Pulling my cock out, I tease her with a shallow thrust, which she welcomes with a moan.

I lick my lips and then lean forward, spitting right where I want it, coating her with enough wetness to push my thumb inside.

"Oh, fuckity fuck. Damn it, Henry, fuck me hard. I'm so close," she whines.

I move my thumb in and out slowly as I thrust my cock into her pussy, harder and deeper. I know I hit her just right because mere moments later, she's screaming. Every profanity and name for a higher power escapes her lips. She throbs around me and it's taken every muscle in my body to hold back until now.

I come with a gut-deep moan. Every sensation in my body falls away from me and I'm met with an electric buzz across my limbs while I pump every last drop into her. I can barely hear anything aside from my panting and the thump of my heartbeat. She's still pulsing around my cock when I finally catch my breath. I slowly pull my thumb from her and then lean forward to rest my forehead between her shoulder blades.

"I might be dead. That was—" I blow out a breath. "That was so damn good, Pixie."

She starts to laugh. "Fuck yes, it was. Let's do it again," she says with a breathy giggle.

"I need a minute." I laugh as I pull back from her. My

cum dripping down her leg sets something off in me, and I'm starting to get hard again. I grab a towel from the drawer and wet it to wipe her up. She still lies there, chest down, ass out, and lifts her head as she watches me clean my mess. Her eyes flick down to my cock that has somehow fully come back to life.

"You sure about that? Your boy there looks like he's ready to go again." She stands up and turns around.

"You..." I point at her and laugh. "You are dangerous. You better start running, because wherever I catch you is where I fuck you."

She lets out a little scream as I pinch her ass, taking off and only making it as far as the stairs before I reach her.

"You're not getting away from me ever again, Pixie," I tell her against her lips.

She nods into my kiss and then says, "Don't let me."

CHAPTER 45

Giselle

THE *THWAP* OF A HAND SLAMMING AGAINST A DOOR JOLTS me awake. I wipe my mouth of the drool that was clearly happening as I slept face down in a fluffy pile of white down pillows and an overstuffed duvet. The craziest part is that this isn't my house. It's Henry's. His is the only man's bed that I've been in, where the thread count outdoes mine. I never want to get up.

Thwap, thwap, thwap.

The door. I look around the room. I'm alone. Glancing at my phone, I see a text from Henry that awaits me.

HENRY

Don't leave. I'm making you brunch. Had to run out to do something. Espresso machine is set, just press the blinking button if you can't wait until I'm back.

I smile. And then smile wider. I squeeze my eyes shut, smiling like a loon into the pillow.

"What the fuck are you doing?" I whisper to myself. Even if we ignore the rules laid out for us about staying apart, completely ignoring Bea's orders, that doesn't change anything. The only thing that's changed is that I've gone and officially become addicted to, not only him, but his dick. *Brilliant move.*

Thwap. Bang. Bang.

Right! The door. I look around the room and there's nothing of mine on the floor. I pull out one of his white t-shirts from the set of drawers on the other side of the room, throwing it on as I stop at the bottom of the stairs, weighing whether or not I should answer. I rarely answer the door in my own place, so I should probably just leave it.

As soon as I turn around to walk toward the kitchen, though, I hear barking. Three loud barks, and then the door bangs again. *Milo.*

"I know you're in there, Henry. Open the door." The shrillest of voices permeates the metal of the front double doors. *Denise.* His ex. The wildebeest. I forgot they still shared "custody" of their dog.

"Either open the door or—"

"Or what?" I open the door, cutting off her threatening tirade.

If I could bottle up the look of shock on her face right now and replay it every day, I'd consider it a satisfying morning ritual. But the satisfaction dies quickly as soon as she speaks, and I look down.

She laughs. "No way. I knew it. How long has this been going on?"

"What's wrong, Debra? You were hoping to lick my pussy first?"

"So crass, Giselle." She rolls her eyes and rubs her belly. Her very swollen belly. And I don't know why the sight of that bothers me, but it does. It hits me right in the chest. This atrocious person can do something I can't. "I'm not leaving Milo with you. When will he be back?"

"He's not here."

"Yes, you said that. Are you going to let me in?"

"Wasn't planning on it." I stand up straighter and glance back down at her bump. I know barely anything about being pregnant, but she seems like she's ready to squat out a watermelon.

Scratching Milo's head one more time, I grab his leash, and apparently his overnight bag, that she has dropped in front of the threshold. "C'mon, my furry prince." I look up at her, tip my head, and then shut the door in her face.

I take a deep breath as I walk toward the kitchen, then pressing the blinking espresso button, I pull out my phone. My fingers pause over the texting keyboard. What I want to tell my best friend is messy. She doesn't know about what's happened with Henry.

> Can Jack go a few hours without you tomorrow? I want to have some bestie time.

EVERLY

> Let's do the Hot Toddy Stroll downtown.

Perfect. Meet you at Brews & Books around 7.

See you then. Love you, boo.

I boost myself onto the counter. The same spot I got royally railed against last night, and the memory of it as I play it back in my mind makes my entire body flush with heat. Why couldn't the sex just be mediocre? If it turned out that all this chemistry we've been fighting against this whole time was a complete letdown, then it might make walking out of here so much easier. But I'm only kidding myself. It's so much more than physical with him. It always has been for me.

The realities of who I am and who he is, seemed less important last night when I had a raging lady boner, and far too much liquid courage. I missed him all week long and as much as I wanted to ignore it, I couldn't ignore him. The way he dragged me into the hallway. Said the things he did. But today, as I sip this insanely delicious espresso, the caffeine manages to shoot more than energy through my system. Not so much regret as it's distress at knowing how I have to let this all play out. If this were some kind of romance novel shelved at Brews & Books, I'd be the heroine trying to make a mess of something that could work, but I'm not a heroine. I'm fucking terrified. More broken than he even knows. Not to mention, the stats on being found again are far higher than they were before. I'm one bad decision away from being forced to relocate, not to mention, the potential of putting more people I love at risk.

I can't forget the fact that he wants a family, and I could never give that to him. My eyes water and that heaviness in my chest is back again just thinking about it. I smack the tears away, now pissed off about what was taken from me. Something I never even had a say about. The helplessness of it makes me resentful. Keeping relationships casual prohibits me from ever having to think about it. Or worse, telling someone, and seeing the look of disappointment on their face. The look of having to choose to stay or leave because I can't create a family.

I can't also forget the way his lifestyle and role at his company is way too public. It puts me in unnecessary danger of being photographed and recognized, which Bea has drilled into my head for years. She would never allow it.

Jumping down from the counter, I look around the room for my boots. I have to get out of here. I need to get my head on straight before I talk to him again. And that's not going to be today, so I'll do what I do best. I type out a text, keeping it brief, and cut out fast.

> Can't stay for brunch. Gotta get my day moving, big guy.

The bubbles bounce a few times, but I don't want to wait to see what he's going to say. Instead, I pull on my parka. It looks gorgeous outside, but when I opened the door earlier, it was fucking freezing.

My phone vibrates.

HENRY

Don't you dare leave, Pixie. I'm not
finished with you yet.

How do I respond to that?

With an ache in my chest, I splash water on my face
and find some soap to wash away any remnants of
makeup I had on from last night. Then I swipe an extra
toothbrush from under his sink and brush away the taste
of espresso and my reckless decisions.

I call a Lyft, hoping it'll be Gracie and not loudmouth
Lenny to pick me up, and then text him back.

Bye, baby.

CHAPTER 46

Henry

THIS MORNING I THOUGHT I'D WAKE UP AND JUST FIND more ways to pleasure the woman who has permeated every single one of my thoughts, but that wasn't what happened. Yesterday, I had a face full of blonde hair and a warm body draped on top of me. Snoring. Her mouth open, and a bit of drool on my chest. Even sleeping, my Pixie can make me laugh. *My Pixie.* But this morning, she wasn't there. When she left yesterday before I returned home, I realized she was starting to freak out about the words we said to each other. Her stubborn ass is going to fight this. In all of the years I've known her, the one thing I know best is that she's a fighter. She's going to fight me on this, on us. Which just means that I need to figure out how to make it so she can't. The fact that she wants all of it and with me, we would need a plan. Some things in my life, outside of her, need to change.

> You had better be at my house tonight, Pixie.

G

> I can't tonight.

> Whatever you're doing, you come to my house when it's over.

> It'll be too late. I have plans with Ev. I'm just going to stay at my place.

> You got away with that bullshit yesterday. I'm sleeping next to you tonight. I don't care if it's in your bed or mine.

> What bullshit?

> Whatever excuse you created in your beautiful brain as to why you weren't shaking underneath me last night. Or screaming my name in the shower this morning.

She doesn't respond to the last text. She's working up to pushing me away again.

My Jeep struggles to make it up the rest of my dad's driveway. Late last night, a few more inches of snow fell, making it so that a clean coat is draped over whatever had melted. The sun today will melt just enough to create a good layer of ice. Not the most ideal board, ski, or bike conditions, but also nothing new in Strutt's Peak.

As I hop out and nearly bite it on my way to the front door, I recognize Callen Muldowney's cruiser parked off to the side, in front of the garage. He's been having coffee with my dad more frequently lately. I'm not stupid; there's only so much the town Sherrif would need to discuss with someone from my company, and anything important enough would happen at the office and not at my dad's ranch. But the reality is, I have no idea what kind of relationship they have. It could be the fact that Callen's dad and mine raised their families next door to one another. Both without partners. For years, we'd be at David and Callen's ranch as often as we'd be at our own.

I give a shout as I walk through the front door. "Dad, you here?"

"Kitchen," he yells back.

I make my way through the great room and around the corner to the kitchen. A space I'm very familiar with since I tend to spend more time cooking in it than my dad ever does. Callen sits at the counter, holding a cup of coffee in full uniform, and greets me with a big smile.

"Callen." I give him a handshake and back slap.

"How you been, Hen? Haven't seen you for a bit."

"Busy, trying to plan out the rest of the season. You know this time of year is chaos, whether we have everything planned out or not."

My dad grabs a mug from the cabinet and brings it over to me, along with the French press. "Getting fancy with the French press now, Dad?"

He leans in and kisses my cheek. My dad is never one to shy away from affection. Even as a teenager, he would wrap us in unwanted hugs and always welcomed us home with kisses on the cheek. Physical touch, signs of affection, are his love language I learned as I got older. But after football practices, getting a backslap and a smooch from your dad was next-level embarrassing in front of the whole team. Now, I lean into it. Asher Riggs is the best kind of man. For me, a sounding board. A reminder to be the kind of man I want to be.

"The coffeemaker is broken and the new one I ordered doesn't get here until next week. Callen brought over this thing. Not bad, but way more complicated than pressing a few buttons." He laughs, taking a sip of the black coffee he just topped off in his mug after pouring mine. "But it's good." He winks at Callen.

"Alright, I've gotta start my shift in a little bit. Ash, I'll talk to you later," Callen says. He stands and puts on his sheriff's hat. It's still a bit crazy for me to see him wearing it, considering how much trouble he used to get in when we were younger. "Hen, always good to see you, man. You let me know when you all want to do some sparring again with Mac. I could use some new partners. The regulars are starting to be predictable." I don't miss the way he brings his attention back to my dad.

I sip my coffee as Callen makes his way out.

"I didn't think you'd be busy this morning so early, I would have called first if I'd known," I tell my dad. He bats the air, as if to say, "don't be silly."

Watching and waiting for me to tell him what I'm here about, he leans on his elbows across from me. I didn't know exactly what I was going to say, but now that I'm here, I'm nervous to disappoint him.

"Hen, it's six-thirty in the morning on a Sunday. Whatever it is, you can tell me, but I know you're not here just for a cup of coffee and a visit."

I laugh. I blow out the breath I must have been holding, and look at my old man. The funny part is he doesn't look old. Just the opposite, in fact. Happy and thriving. He went our entire lives without having a partner through it all and he never complained about it. My mother left him with four little kids, and he just made it work. Even now, I wonder if he thinks about moving on with someone. If he feels like he missed out. He looks content, but I would give anything to see him with someone that makes him smile the way that I've been doing since the Cayman Islands.

I look down at my hands. Anxious to tell the one person I never want to disappoint something that will, at some level, disappoint him. Or at the very least, make his life harder.

"I need to step away from the business."

He smiles and nods, as if he was expecting it.

"What's changed? I thought you liked what you're doing."

I clear my throat. "It's not that I've stopped liking it. I just have new"—I search for the right word or words—"priorities. And maybe even a new perspective on what I really want to be doing every day." I take another sip of my coffee and lean back in my chair, a little less anxious now that I got that out.

"You know I wasn't ever looking to step in as CEO."

He nods in response. He's known for years that I never wanted that role. It was always Everly primed to take his spot when he was ready, but when she left last year to tackle her apparel line, everyone just assumed I'd be the one to step up.

My dad comes around from the counter and tilts his

head for me to follow him. He leads us down into the lower level of the house. A space he's converted into one part wine cellar and the other, a state-of-the-art movie theater. The spiral staircase that leads down, carries a chill as soon as we hit the midway point. He flicks on the lights and the entire room of wine illuminates. Every cubby that holds a bottle of wine, and the oversized wine barrels spread throughout the center, all glow with a warm light from underneath.

Every season, he hosts a small wine tasting with friends from town. Some who are regulars and others who are lucky enough to get an invite. Ash never does anything small, so the wine tasting ends up being a full evening of wine and food pairings. A few of which I've helped him host when he couldn't fly in a Michelin-Star chef, because of weather or conflicts.

"What's your plan? I know you, Hen, you wouldn't be telling me this unless it's something you already have a plan for," he says. I watch as he walks down to the far end of the wall. He pulls out a bottle of white and then moves to the other end and pulls out a bottle of champagne.

After I tell him my thoughts about cooking. Turning my love for that into something I could make a living doing, he smiles wide. He starts spit-balling concepts with me. Ways to cut the overhead until I decide it has success potential. He lights up about all of it. I don't know that he was ever this excited when I asked to join Riggs Outdoor.

I nod at the bottles he's holding. "What are those for?"

He holds up the bottle of white wine. "She likes this one best." And then he holds up the bottle of champagne.

"This one is the perfect floater for those limoncello smashes she always asks me to make."

"Who?"

He gives me a death-like stare. "I'm not stupid, Henry."

I just laugh and shake my head. "How long have you known?"

"Kid, give me a break. You've been in love with that girl since the first time you laid eyes on her. Awkward, since when you met her, you were engaged to someone else, but it's about time you both got your heads out of your asses."

If he only knew. But that right there is Asher Riggs. Really the best parent anyone could ask for and the kind of friend you always hope sees things for what they really are.

"It was also going to take something big to get you on a different path. I'm just glad that it's with Giselle. She's already family." He rubs the back of his neck, realizing something he hadn't maybe considered. "Does Everly know?"

My sister. Hopefully not a hurdle. I puff out my cheeks to blow out a breath. "Depends. If the rumor mill works as fast as I think it does in this town. Then, yea, she knows."

"What aren't you telling me?"

I pause, because there's a lot I can't tell him. Plenty, in fact, but the most relevant is that I'm about to change my life, and the woman who is the catalyst for it has no idea.

"She's not really one to commit. You know this about her. I think for as long as she's been in this town, I couldn't tell you a single person, guy or girl, who she's considered long term."

"But you think she wants that with you?"

Well, fuck, when he puts it like that. "I don't know, Dad. I hope so. It's going to take some time, but if I know her the way I think I do, then I'm thinking she wants *this*. Wants a life with me." I have to laugh at the next thought. "But she's so stubborn that she's going to fight me on it, regardless."

"Good." He claps me on the shoulder. "Nothing worth it ever comes without a little pain in the process. And she's worth it."

We make our way back upstairs, some weight on my shoulders lifting.

"Speaking of pains in the ass, your brother is going to be shocked about all of this. You think he'll want to take my spot in a few years? Michael has been very clear he doesn't want to touch it with a ten-foot pole. But I think Law could."

"Dad, are you kidding? Law will shit himself if he ever hears you say that."

"Like a *good* shit himself?"

"When is shitting yourself ever good? I don't think there are categories for that." We both laugh hard and while I can't wait to hear that conversation, there are a few people I need to talk to before I can move forward with my own plans.

"Think they're going to be pissed I'm leaving now too?"

"Let me ask you this, were you mad when Everly left?"

"Not at all, but I also didn't know how much would be dropped in my lap once she was gone."

"Leave that piece up to me. I can offset that. But your brothers only want what's going to make you happy. I think they'll be surprised, but not mad."

I hadn't planned on doing this today, but I might as well rip off the band-aid. Time to tell my brothers what's going on. "Thanks, Dad."

He claps my shoulder and then says, "Don't keep that girl waiting. You two have already taken long enough."

I give him a longer hug than usual. I know this is going to put more pressure on him, maybe even prolong any retirement plans he started thinking about, but I know my dad. He'd never say it. So I hold on a little longer.

"You might want to have a talk with Kathryn over at Brews & Books. Jack mentioned she's a bit overwhelmed with the longer hours. Maybe there's something there you two can work out." He waves his hand in front of himself. I know he's trying not to overstep, but when it comes to business and his kids, my dad likes to over-stride. "Just a thought. I know she's busy tonight with the Hot Toddy Stroll, but it might be worth you stopping in."

I give him a smile and a nod. I'm not ready to discuss much more yet, but I've already had the same thought about that space. I planned to have a discussion with Kathryn later about how we might be able to fix each other's problems with a mutually beneficial solution. And now's as good a time as any.

CHAPTER 47

Giselle

"Benny, Benny, Benny. You got hotter. I didn't think it would be possible, but you did. You went ahead and turned yourself"—I tweak my voice to do a British accent—"into an eleven. You go to *eleven,* now."

He doesn't get it. I'm met with a smile, but a stare as if I'm a bit crazy.

"Anyway, that Costa-Rican life treated you well?" I ask.

He smiles at me, and it's not lost on me that the kid has a little crush. I mean, I don't blame him. I am a catch. If I wasn't hung up on the oldest Riggs sibling, then I would consider showing this little pup a few things about satisfying a woman. He *is* over eighteen now.

"It was an experience," he says it with a twinge of exacerbation. But a beat later, he follows it up by saying, "You know, Giselle, I'm always on the hunt for a life lesson. I had a couple when I was down there." He smiles wider. "I'd be down to learn a few more, now that I'm back home."

"No." Everly leans forward. "Benny! She's got, like, fifteen years on you."

Everly elbows my side. "Ow!"

"Plus, you're going to tell me all about the man that's finally making you breakfast." She quirks her right eyebrow high. This bitch already knows what I'm going to tell her. If I had to guess who told her, it was likely Michael. It's always the quiet ones that gossip first. *Fucker.*

"Benny doll, maybe in another life. I can feel a good cougar coming to show you *all* the ways." He laughs.

I look around the menu again at the hot, spiked drinks. They really do have the best twists on favorites here. "We'll take two Hot and Filthys." The spiked raspberry hot chocolate comes in an oversized mug rimmed with dark chocolate and skewered dark chocolate-covered raspberries as garnish.

The menu at Brews & Books has a long roster of drinks with a romantic twist on the names, and a tweak *or twerk* that manages to make them all delicious. Since it's just next door to my tattoo shop, I've tried almost everything. The evening drinks are my favorite. A little spike done right. The Hot and Filthy is part of their Hot Toddy Stroll specialty menu. A yearly event that gives everyone permission to shop local while drunk. Also, one of the reasons I don't stay open for it. Too many people overindulge in the hot toddys by the time the strolling part is underway. Every shop has their own version of a hot drink, some spiked, some not, but Brews & Books has the best options, obviously, since it's their business.

"You read my mind," Ev says, and then pulls out her wallet.

"Nope. On me," Benny says. "Uncle Jack says you don't pay when you come here. He covers whatever you order."

She smiles. "Your mom here tonight? I want to say hi. I haven't seen her since your uncle and I got back from our honeymoon." She drops a twenty into the tip jar.

"Yeah, she's around back with your brother, actually. They've been talking back there for a while now. I'm sure she wouldn't mind if you interrupted."

"Henry?" she asks, and he nods.

Great.

"Ev, let's just start the stroll. There were a few pieces at Leo's boutique I wanted to snag before the crowd gets heavier." I leave out the part that I'm not ready to see Henry in public. Let alone him engaged in conversation, or whatever, with another woman.

I give Benny a wink before we head out.

The door chimes as we walk through it. "That kid is still ridiculously hot. I don't care if that makes me a cougar or what." I take a sip of my drink as we start our walk. Tart raspberry and sweet chocolate coat my tongue. The shot of vodka and splash of Kahlúa, give it that extra oomph. It's a little bit of heaven and the first thing I think is, *Henry would love this.*

"You know, I think she has something going on with Jin," Everly says after she sips her drink.

"Who?" I ask. Even though I already know.

"Kathryn. I think Jin and Kathryn are secretly seeing each other," she says. "So whatever you're starting to get salty about over there, just stop. She's not into Henry. And I guarantee he's not into her either. According to my dad, my brother is making some adjustments. Maybe he's here about that."

"What kind of adjustments?"

Everly shrugs her shoulders and says, "I don't know exactly. You should probably talk to him."

I stay silent. I wasn't sure how this conversation was going to go tonight, but it seems like I'm not fooling anyone. And apparently there's more going on that I don't know anything about. And *that* pisses me off. The idea of not knowing what's going on in Henry's life or just being that last to know.

"What are you implying?" I blow on my drink and take another sip as I side-eye my best friend.

"Oh, fuck off, G. I've known something has been brewing between you and Henry for years." She laughs and raises her voice. "Years! I didn't think I'd have to hear about it from Michael when I was doing squats this morning, though."

"That gossipy little bitch!" I start laughing. Of course it was him. Everyone tiptoes around him and his bullshit, but he's the first one to spill the tea. *Payback is a bitch, Michael.*

The air is cold, but I've lived here long enough to know how to dress for a night out in this weather. Between the layers, my fierce furry boots and a pompom snow hat paired with the hot drink I'm sipping on, it's going to get toasty the second we step inside one of these storefronts.

I pull open the door to Leo's boutique. Greeted by one

of my favorite people, he hugs both of us, and then brings us to the front case to show the accessories that just arrived in stock.

Everly tries on three bracelets before she can't help herself any longer, and asks, "Are you going to tell me anything, or do I need to just assume you're not going to hurt him, and it'll all be fine?"

"What makes you think I'd be the one to hurt him?"

"Oh, I don't know. Maybe the fact you're highly allergic to commitment. That you don't believe in monogamous relationships." I give her a look. One that says, "don't throw my own bullshit at me."

"What?! You've told me since the first moment we met that any man or woman who wants to sleepover is blacklisted from your cooch!"

I did say that. I even remember where we were when I said it, but that's beside the point.

"It's complicated, so I'm trying not to overthink. Okay, I'm failing at that part. But yes, I'm doing the dirty with your brother." I squint at her and wait for a reaction. Maybe she'll read my body language, as if this isn't as big of a deal as it actually is. Even though it's a big fucking deal. I'm damn near in love with the man.

"But, you hate him." She takes a sip of her drink. I can see how she's working it out in her head. "Oh my gosh. New Year's! You both disappeared after the ball dropped and then you were very weird and short in your texts to me all week long."

I don't say anything, because I try my best not to lie excessively to her about things that need to remain a secret.

A secret from her is better than an embellished lie. I hate both, but I love her too much to put any kind of additional danger in her path. New Year's Eve was close enough. And, not to mention, she's not totally wrong in her assumptions.

We walk up to the counter to pay for the few things we've managed to choose from the case. "Leo, baby. Everything in here is gorgeous," I tell him.

He waves his hand at me. "I just put out the pieces you both chose. They are my favorite." He points to the earring and bracelet set that Everly selected. We chat for a few more minutes about the apparel of Everly's he just ordered for Spring.

Once we're back in the cold, we make our way farther down Main. More crowded now, we decide to snag a bench to finish our drinks.

"Are you really *not* going to tell me anything more?"

"Can we pretend it's not Henry for a minute so I can gush?" I ask.

She enthusiastically nods.

"I have been officially fucked the way the universe had always intended. It's so good. I know, I know, don't make that face at me."

"Fine. Keep going."

"I've never come so hard in my whole life, Ev. And I've done it a lot. Like a lot, a lot. But everything that man does drives me insane. And it's not even that kinky. It's just hot, and it's like if he isn't fucking me, or licking me, or touching me in some filthy way, it's not enough. My whole body buzzes like there's a live wire somewhere every time he's near me. I don't understand it." I stop talking fast and furiously with my hands and finally look at my best friend.

She smiles. A big, wide, stupid grin.

"And he's just so easy to be around. He can be so grumpy and dick-headed, but I forgot how easy it is to just talk with him."

"Wait, didn't this just start? What do you mean, you forgot?"

Shit. I backpedal. "Just that I didn't realize he'd be like this. Like, I can just talk to him without having to try too hard. It's easy to be with him. You know what I mean?"

She stares at me for a minute, nodding slowly.

"And I've always been attracted to him. I mean, look at him." I smile at her because she makes another stink face. "But when we're alone, just the two of us, it's nothing I was expecting. But it's easier to breathe. He makes me feel protected. I don't know... this all sounds ridiculous when I say it out loud." I shake my head and try to tamp these feelings down a bit.

"You're in love with him," she casually says as she sips her drink.

I scrunch my nose at her. Hearing it out loud makes me want to shove it back in her mouth, like someone who shouldn't, might hear. But I don't correct her.

"Holy shit. G, you love my brother!" She scrunches her nose, mimicking me, and then covers her mouth like she's just discovered the most awesome and awful thing all at once.

"No. I am absolutely not in love with him." *I'm fucking lying.* If it wasn't for the visit from Denise, the very knocked-up wildebeest, then I'd probably be planning to see him after this. Text him back and tell him to meet me in my bed, but seeing that woman, doing something I can't, did more than sober me from our situation. It shook me. At my core. And I'm trying really hard not to let those feelings unravel me completely.

"You're going to marry him," she sing-songs. "Are you going to have babies with my brother. Holy shit, you are!"

That statement knocks me sideways. "I'm not. I can't, even if I wanted that. Which I don't."

My vision blurs, and I realize quickly that I've just let a truth slip out that I never had any intention of sharing. With anyone.

"Hey, hey, hey. Why are you getting upset? I'm so sorry. I got carried away." Everly drapes her arm around me, and I lean on her shoulder and let a few tears fall.

"We were never even supposed to happen, Ev. I can't be what he needs, not in the long game. I can't even *have* kids." I look up and shake my head at her, telling her I don't have any desire to go into the details. And like my total ride or die, she doesn't push. "He wants all of those things. A family. I know he does, but that's not something I can offer. Not in any traditional way, at least. So for now, we're making things complicated, and I don't know if I'll come out on the other side of it whole, but well, here I am. Now you know."

I wipe the tears that are still falling and look back at her. She wipes my nose with her sleeve. "That was gross. You didn't need to do that."

"Shut up. I got you," she says.

We sit back on the bench and look up at the sky. So many stars. So many more than I ever saw in my old life.

"I promise not to disappear," I tell her. She looks at me curiously. "When things fizzle out with me and Henry. Or when one of us takes it too far. I promise I won't disappear or ruin this. Ruin us."

She smiles at me. "I know, boo. Just have fun, then. I know Henry could use some. Make him smile for me, yeah?"

I nod. Damn, I love this woman. They broke the mold when they made her.

"Can we play the game where you pretend it's not your brother and I can tell you what really made him moan the other night? I feel like Jack would be into it."

She just starts laughing, "Dammit, G, this is really a whole level of compartmentalizing that I wasn't prepared for tonight. I'm going to need more drinks."

CHAPTER 48

Henry

"Skyhawk Six Niner, three miles southwest, inbound to land."

"Roger that, Skyhawk. Permission to land," air traffic control says over the radio. A quick but frequent stop just thirty minutes north from Strutt's Peak and into Wyoming. Just over the border in another small town where one of Agent Harper's assignments has been placed undercover. Next door to Diamond Peak is a massive ranch that deals in cattle and bison, where I can land my small plane easily. Aside from a good landing spot, one that I'm welcome to use, I can check in with the old man who runs the place.

"Good to see you, sir." I shake the old timer's hand. It's been a few months since I've seen him, and he looks more weathered than my last visit. I'd imagine eighteen-hour days working on a ranch at seventy-nine will do that. The thing he doesn't know, or maybe chooses to ignore, is the fact that we share a last name.

Buck Riggs is my grandfather, who doesn't speak to my father, and chooses to ignore the fact that Asher Riggs has a big bold life just a state away. Far enough from the rancher life that he was supposed to inherit. It's not a secret in our family. Our father and grandfather are estranged. The details are murky, but when my father refused to take over the family ranch in Montana, my grandfather sold the ranch and then relocated to Wyoming. My guess is the rancher in him couldn't retire, and stay away from what he did for his entire life. This ranch, in Wyoming, has been functioning for close to twenty years now, but it's nowhere near what the Riggs Ranch in Montana once was. Or so I've been told.

I couldn't tell you if my dad even knows that his father is in Wyoming now, but he chose to leave the expectations and judgement from his old man a long time ago. Both of them never made an effort to be in one another's lives, so I have to assume they both would rather let it lie. It all makes me appreciate the relationship I have with my father even more.

I stumbled upon this place shortly after I started flying again. I needed an emergency landing. Air traffic control directed me to the open fields of the ranch. The old man approached me with an attitude and a shotgun, but once he introduced himself, it was too hard to not look a little deeper. I kept coming back for odd jobs. He asked that I'd keep an ear out for ranch hands or when he needed extra brawn for bringing in new cattle. He was always looking for folks who wouldn't mind some hard work. A few from witness protection have taken jobs here, and it works out for everyone. Buck doesn't ask questions. Agent Harper knows the connection, and she couldn't care less as long as her people are tucked away.

"What brings you here, son?"

"I wanted to see about some bison, actually. I'm opening a farm-to-table pop-up restaurant, and I want to source everything local from Colorado and Wyoming. Thought you'd be my guy for meat."

"I don't know what the fuck a pop-up restaurant is, but you're welcome to buy from the best."

After we settle up the details and delivery, I give him a good, firm handshake. I always try looking for any similarities between him and my father. Him and me. But, aside from the jawline and maybe an appreciation for dealing good business, there isn't much. Over the years, I think I've learned I don't want to find too much. Just enough to know he's okay. I respect my father and know that he left for a reason and didn't look back. But I also couldn't look away once fate dropped me right into my grandfather's field.

By the time I make it back in the air and land on my airfield, it's just after 9 p.m. Not too bad considering I put in a full workday today, flew to another state, secured a decent agreement for farm-fresh meat, and already have a roster of additional farmers I'm meeting with over the next few days. Sourcing locally, a well curated menu and a pop-up spot could be just the right amount of commitment I'm willing to make right now. I can't help but smile. My ideas are finally coming to light, and it feels good.

My phone buzzes.

G

I told your sister about us.

And what did she say?

Your loudmouth brother had already told her. Apparently, my private show at your house was what gave it away.

Does that mean I get to see you tonight? I miss you.

Now how am I supposed to say no when you say shit like that to me?

I'm smiling down at my phone, distracted by how much I've wanted this with her, when a familiar voice interrupts, "I figured I'd meet you in person for a status update, Riggs. It's been a minute since the fiasco on New Year's."

"Agent Harper." I nod and move to shake her hand.

"So it's true, then?" she says, lighting up a clove cigarette.

I keep quiet. I hadn't planned on addressing this with her before I spoke with G about it. Up until that text, I thought I was going to have to convince her that we can make this work. That I'm making changes so that it can work.

"I leave you two alone for two days and you do the exact thing I warned you both not to do," she says.

"Harper—" But before I can say anything else, I register what she just said. "You told her to stay away from me?"

"Yes. And I told you the same. You have a history. A small one, but you kicked up enough dirt when you were always poking around, asking questions. And then you went ahead and started a brand where you and your family are on magazine covers and gossip sites. Your youngest brother is all over TikTok too, supposedly." She shakes her head in annoyance. "You're making my job really fucking difficult, Riggs."

"With all due respect, fuck that. We kept our distance. I looked after her the best I knew how, and someone still found her. Her past surfaced and we could only react. And that had nothing to do with me. So, when it comes to making your job harder or not following your direction, fuck that."

I rub the back of my neck, trying to tamp down my anger right now. I'm pissed off she was put in any harm's way, but I'm just as angry that it didn't matter how much we kept ourselves practically miserable by staying away from one another. She was still compromised.

She takes a drag of her clove. "I don't want to have to relocate her."

"Then don't."

She takes another drag and stares a minute longer, but I need to make sure she hears this.

"This isn't a fling. I'm in love with her. I have been for years, but I'm not going to put her in unnecessary danger. I'm making adjustments to my life, so I can guarantee that. It may be your job, but it's my life. And she's the most important person in it. I'm not going to make your job harder." I give her a leveled glare. "But I'm going to make sure you do it better. What happened on New Year's is unacceptable. If she's in danger like that again, I need you to move fast. And I go with her."

She doesn't respond. She just glares back. Not many people, I imagine, tell Agent Harper what to do.

A good minute passes. She finishes her clove, then stamps it out right on the floor of the airplane hangar.

"Remember what she's been through. She lost everything that ever mattered, and then picked her shit up and made a small life for herself. She's made friends. Built a business. Hell, it took her years to get the people in Strutt's Peak to consider her a townie. I think that bitch, Ruth DeMaio, still gives her shit. Make sure you make her life happier, not just more complicated."

As soon as I nod in agreement, she changes the subject back to the couple of placements I just did status checks for in both Harmony and Laramie. I have the closest thing I'm going to get in the way of an approval, now I just need to convince my girl.

CHAPTER 49

Henry

IT'S BEEN A COUPLE OF DAYS SINCE I TOLD AGENT HARPER that I was in love with G. I still haven't said it outright to her yet, but I need to tell her about the plans I've been making. That my life is about to take another turn, and hopefully this time it's in the direction that allows for us to be closer. Be what I want and what I know she wants deep down.

The door chimes when I walk in. She's sitting at the front desk with Gracie, talking through some kind of program on the iPad. She doesn't look up until I say, "You've avoided me for long enough now."

Her eyes flit up and I see a pink creep across her cheeks.

Gracie tries to hide a smile by eating a handful of Skittles.

"I have to prep for my next appointment, Henry." She moves toward the back of the shop. "Grace, you can head out. Let's talk about that program next week before you head back."

"You bet, G." Gracie smiles at me, grabbing her bag from behind the chair. She stops next to me before she leaves and says, "She missed you. Don't let her get away, Henry. She's been a totally different person since New Year's."

I nod and give her a smile. The door chimes again behind me, letting me know she's left.

"Stop trying to avoid me, Pixie," I yell, so she can hear me from the back.

G comes back and starts setting up her materials next to her tables. "I'm not avoiding you. I just was giving you space."

"Don't want space."

"Fine, then I was giving myself a minute to figure out what the hell I'm doing," she says, still not looking up at me. Focused on charging her tattoo gun and wrapping it in grip tape. "I just don't think this has a long shelf life. I mean, the sex is..." Looking up at me, she shakes her head when she sees my face. Then she's speaking again before I can finish her sentence.

"Stop smirking at me like that. The sex is insane. You know that. But we just don't want the same things and great sex doesn't change why we can't work."

I drag my fingers along her shoulder, and it gets her to stop trying to multitask and focus on the conversation I want to have with her. "I quit."

Her brow furrows in question. "What?"

"I'm not working for Riggs Outdoor any longer. I knew I needed to make a change after we came back from

Grand Cayman, for us to make this work. To be together for real. And I remember something you said... well, lots of things people have said to me over the years, and trying to do something I love seemed like the best place to start."

"Wait, what? What do you mean? You *quit*?"

"I've already started sourcing and planning. The start-up capital I need is coming from some of my savings and then my father and David are backing the rest as an investment. I'm opening a pop-up restaurant in the evenings, just a few days to start, at Brews & Books," I tell her, but before I can continue, she interrupts.

"So you're just going to be a chef and open a restaurant?" she asks, taken aback by all of this new information.

"Yes."

She rushes past me, and under her breath, I hear her say, "Of course. Just open a restaurant. Fucking rich people."

"Are you annoyed?"

"I don't know what I am, Henry. You're telling me I'm the reason you're blowing up your life, and that's a lot of pressure. Are you sure you even know what you're getting into? I mean, we had sex a bunch of times. Does that mean you should upheaval your life? It sounds—"

But I cut her off before she can say anything more. "What, G? What does it sound like? Romantic? Stupid?" I take a breath because I'm going to try not to get too worked up at her freakout. "It's necessary. I want to be with you, and the life I have, the role in my family's business, is one of the reasons I can't be. So, I'm making adjustments so that I can get what I want. It was also time for me to find something that would make me happy again. The business wasn't doing that for me any longer, and life is too short to stay working in something you don't enjoy if you can change it."

"What makes you so sure that I'm what you want? That you'll feel the same way in a couple of years?"

I smile at that and realize she's not annoyed. She's nervous this isn't what I truly want. She still doesn't get it.

"Pixie, you're it for me. There's not a single thing I wouldn't do to make you mine." I pull her closer to where I'm sitting now. She stands in between my legs, and I grip her chin, bringing her closer to my face. I want to make sure she hears this, loud and clear. "You take whatever time you need to let all of this sink in, but I'm going to do everything in my power to make this work for us, you hear me?"

She nods. Then the door to the shop chimes again.

She tries to look at who came in, but I don't let her chin go. I can see there's so much she needs to say and work out as she looks into my eyes, but now's not the right time. "I hear you," she says, and then turns around to greet my brother Michael at the door.

"You guys need me to come back?"

G walks closer and smiles back at me. "Nope. I'm all yours. Hanky was just leaving."

"Benny, will you make me one of those Earl Gray drinks that G likes before you head out?"

"You bet, boss."

Telling G about my plans of building a pop-up dinner spot at Brews & Books was just a piece of the puzzle. In truth, my life needed to adjust if I wanted G to be a real part of it. But couple that with how I've been feeling restless at work, and it all made more sense than I ever thought it could. Now, I'm starting something new. Something that's for me. We made a lot of great things happen at Riggs Outdoor, but all of it was expanding on something for which my father had already laid the groundwork. It wasn't mine. This is mine, whether it succeeds or not. When I saw that Kathryn had been overwhelmed with the long hours of the coffee shop and I was already toying with the idea of an exclusive dining concept, it was just about moving forward and not overthinking. Now I'm working every moment I can to bring this restaurant to fruition. It also doesn't hurt that the spot is right next door to Hideaway Ink. Closer to my girl.

MICHAEL

There's a 50/50 chance I end up with a dick on my thigh instead of a mountain.

She seem off? Maybe pissed too?

I don't want to know what the hell you two are doing, but next time, can you make sure I'm not on the books for a tattoo before you have a huge relationship conversation?

> You're her last appointment. Make sure she gets back to her loft when you guys are done.

Yeah, no problem.

"Henry, you've got a delivery. Here's the Earl Gray latte. You want me to bring it to her?" Benny shouts from the back door of the store, moving toward the kitchen.

"Thanks, Ben. I'll do it." I make my way to the back and meet the delivery driver, signing for the meat and vegetables that have come from Wyoming, and then start prepping for this weekend's first tasting group.

I've decided that I'll use this time to perfect my menu for spring and reward my friends and the business owners who own shops all along Main Street. If the next two weekends go well, and I can work out any issues, then the place will be ready to start taking reservations. If it's good enough, it'll build buzz. I want the place to have a speakeasy, exclusive vibe. Booked out reservations for tourists, and walk-ins only for Strutt's Peak residents.

"Henry! You back there?" Jack shouts as he makes his way toward the kitchen.

"Hey, man, what are you doing here?"

"I've got a few business partners, some colleagues too, who are going to be coming through over the next few months to check out some mountain sports. Michael is trying to build out his summer excursions. We thought it would be cool to set up some exclusive dinners. Give them a real taste of the full Riggs experience." He leans against the industrial sink, canvasing the spread of goods that were just delivered.

Jack joined the board for Riggs Outdoor when he married into the family. He's already made some smart connections between his artist gallery patrons and the small companies that service outdoor sports accessories. When Everly stepped away to do her own thing, Jack stepped in. He and my dad are making smart moves.

I chop away at the kohlrabi and fennel. Smiling, I ask, "And?"

He grabs a handful of the blueberries from the bowl they're soaking in. "And nothing, that's what I wanted to ask. If we can get a few groups on your books for April and May."

Chop. Chop. "Yea, but you could have called or texted that. What else?"

He laughs, scratching his jaw. "Ev wanted me to see if I could do some digging." He shifts, because Jack and I don't typically talk like this. In fact, there was a time not long ago when I punched him in the face and threatened him to get his shit together about my sister. We keep things mostly about sports and investments. There was when I asked him to use his Cayman Islands place and not ask questions, but other than that, we don't dive deep into feelings.

"She already knows, probably more than she wants." I laugh and grab the box of frozen bison from the dry ice container. Running the water, I clean out the sink and start unwrapping the meat.

"Is it serious?"

I laugh and so does he. "Yeah. It is."

He nods. And a beat later, he says, "The Lakers have a pretty good shot this year, yeah?"

"That's rhetorical, you know that."

My phone buzzes on the counter twice.

My hands are wet and covered in juices from the meat I'm separating, so I leave it.

"Want to hit Mac's pads class tomorrow morning?"

He doesn't answer with my phone bouncing and buzzing again.

"You want me to check that for you?" Jack asks.

"Yea, just let me know who it is," I say as I run the water to rinse my hands.

"Agent Harper?" he says. "She keeps texting. It says: 911. Compromised."

My stomach sinks. And before I can grab my phone from his hands, I hear screaming from next door, followed by the loud banging of something or someone hitting the wall.

"Fuck!" I shout as I rush out the back door and run as if her life depends on it.

CHAPTER 50

Giselle

MICHAEL RIGGS HAS HAD THIS TATTOO SCHEDULED FOR more than six months now. I've told him that I can fit him in sooner, but every time I have a cancellation, he tells me he needs the time to decide on the design. Pain in the ass, but he's grown on me. I think because he's the only one left in the bunch who I can still make uncomfortable with what comes out of my mouth. But today, I was relieved to see him. I wasn't ready to hear what Henry was telling me. How can he just change his life like that? He doesn't know all of the facts yet, and now he's making huge life adjustments for someone that he doesn't know the full picture about.

"You okay?" Michael asks, interrupting my thoughts again.

"Yes, I'm okay." I shake off the chaos happening in my mind for a minute and focus back on Michael. "What's it going to be, Mikey? Finally decide on a big banana and cherries for your lower back. A nice bright tramp stamp?"

Ever the serious one, he doesn't even crack a smile. "Not funny. Also, not my name," he says. "You sure you're okay? You look kind of scared and angry all mashed together."

"Do you think that's the right thing to say to someone who's going to spend the next couple of hours tattooing something on your body? Permanently?"

I raise my eyebrows at him as he sits in the front of my shop. "Okay, let me print out what I drew for you. Show me how big you want it."

He stands and lifts one leg of his basketball shorts, showing off his thigh. One thing about Michael Riggs, the man works out diligently, and it shows. His thigh is a lump of muscle. It's going to hurt like a bitch to tattoo it. I smile at the thought, because I'm a dick like that.

I turn on some Nina Simone, because that woman can croon in my ear for hours. She's also been giving me inspiration lately with some new designs. Plus, I can't help but think about my Sinnerman. Ugh, how do I navigate this with *him?*

A few minutes later, and we've decided on the size of the vector design of the ridge that mimics the one in Strutt's Peak. I wipe down his thigh and start to shave the dark hair away so that the surface area is clean and prepped.

I hear my phone buzz from the front counter, but I don't want to take off my gloves and have to re-sanitize. So I ignore it. As it is, the size of this thing is going to take at least two hours tonight just to outline properly.

I watch as Michael texts away on his phone.

My phone buzzes again.

Michael is not one of the chatty Rigg's kids, that's for sure, but I thought he'd at least talk to me while I was doing this for him. I'm not even certain he likes me all that much. He's more prickly than Henry. But then again, both of them are far bitchier than Everly and Law. They both have this don't fuck with me vibe, and most of the time, it comes off as rude. Henry can turn on the charm when he needs to, but Michael chooses to keep up with the asshole vibe ninety percent of the time.

The door opens in the front of my shop, and I curse at myself for being distracted and not locking it up when I got started with Michael. I don't do walk-ins and there's no more appointments set for today, so that means I need to turn away anyone who's thinking they're getting a piercing or ink on a whim.

From the tattooing space of the shop, I see two guys walking in.

"Give me a sec," I tell Michael. "I need to tell these guys I'm not doing any more appointments today."

I remove my gloves as I make my way over, and I'm hit with the smell of black licorice. I never liked the smell, but something about it this time, mixed with cigarette smoke, makes me instantly nauseous. My stomach has that sinking feeling.

"I'm not taking any walk-ins tonight, gentlemen," I say as I take in the two men hovering in the lobby of my shop.

The taller of the two smiles at me with a tilt of his head, as if I've met him before. It doesn't register right away that I have, not until he turns his neck toward his friend, and I see the top of a lion's mane peeking out of his leather jacket. I suck in a breath and freeze instantly.

I look at his friend, shorter, with jet black hair. He removes his leather gloves, and a bear claw tattoo shows on his left hand.

Lion.

Tiger.

Bear.

The smile that creeps along his mouth turns my stomach. The tall one starts to speak, and I blink, only watching his mouth move, but no sound comes out. They step closer to me, and the proximity turns my ears back on.

"Saw your sign lit up. Our flight doesn't leave until after midnight, so we were thinking of adding a little ink. Kill some time," the one with the bear claw tattoo says.

I swallow, but my mouth is so dry that it makes me cough. I do my best to stand tall, try to hide the nervous energy that's thrumming throughout my body. "Sorry, boys. Like I said, I'm not doing any more appointments tonight."

Moving toward the front desk, I try to put space between us. As I turn away, the one with the lion tattoo moves closer and says, "I like the flowers. Bright and loud. I'm partial to keeping mine black."

"What are those?" the bear accusingly asks as he juts his chin out toward me. He points his finger at my neck.

And without thinking, I answer, "Lemon blossoms."

The moment the words leave my lips, I regret them. My eyebrows jump. And the realization must register all over my face. I look to the Lion and back to the Bear. *Fuck.*

"I've seen ones like it before. What'd you say your name was?"

I try to smile, but I don't know what my face actually does because I'm on the verge of tears. I need to get away. "I'm so sorry, but I have to get back to what I was doing. I'm not doing any more appointments ton—"

"I remember you," the lion says in his thick Russian accent. He turns his head to the side to study me, maybe trying to remember that night a little more clearly. My hands start to shake, and my body has broken out with a sheen of sweat that coats my face.

"The Italian's daughter." He shakes his pointer finger at me. "We left you in a pool of your own blood, couldn't find a pulse. How did you survive, Su-ka?"

"So you are what Mikhail found," the bear says as he stalks closer to me. I don't move. If I move, they'll grab me, and the only way I can get out of this is if I play along, and then run.

Mikhail? The guy from New Year's Eve. The Tiger.

"We thought he was going to a New Year's bash for some billionaire who had taken photographs of his model girlfriend. Then, to my surprise, I found out that he had an altercation at the airport and somehow ended up dead. It all seemed strange." He shifts, scratching his chin. "Mikhail didn't do drugs. He would never carry drugs. If we smuggle, we ship, we never carry," he says with a *tsk tsk.*

"Did you kill my brother, Su-ka?" the lion asks as he pulls a switchblade from his jacket pocket. He's intimidating at his height, but I see his hand shaking. I swallow my fear and start to pay attention. He looks gaunt, sickly skinny. Not at all built like a lion. He looks high or strung out by the way his pupils are blown wide, almost entirely black.

"You're supposed to be dead, Su-ka. What are you doing breathing right now? The last time I touched you" —the bear reaches out and drags his fingers along my jawline—"you were barely conscious. Just how I prefer my women." Another wave of nausea runs through my body at the thought of this piece of shit touching any part of me.

The knife the lion holds drags up my chest, between my breasts, and up the column of my throat. He stops the blade at my chin. "I think we will have fun tonight, Su-ka. You didn't learn your lesson the first time,"

A laugh bubbles out of the other one standing far too close to me.

"Your father did. Yes, he certainly learned." The strung-out Lion tilts his head again, studying my reaction. I don't give him one, instead I pay attention to his words, both of their actions and proximity.

I won't let them hurt me again. I won't let them hurt my *family*. If they leave here, they will. And I can't allow that. I haven't survived this long just to be terrorized. The adrenaline that's running through me turns into something else entirely. It's not nervous energy any longer. It's survival. Protection. Because one thing is for certain, I will not freeze this time. This time, I'll fight.

And everything after that decision, is a blur. A movement from behind the man leering so close to my face, draws my attention away. Before it even registers, I hear a crack and then a blood-curdling scream. The man who crowded behind me is down. *Michael.* He moved fast, stepped behind the Bear, and kicked out his leg with what must have been powerful by the sound of the shrieking.

The knife that rested on my chin slices at my skin. Deep. I feel blood pour from my face as I lurch back. I touch my chin, but it's too painful. As I look up, I see the man with the bloody knife look toward Michael. And I snap. *You won't hurt anyone else.*

Remembering what I've learned from Mac in self-defense, I crouch low and drive my shoulder into his gut, knocking the wind out of him, and my momentum works in my favor. I run forward. Moving at full speed and we don't stop until we hit something hard, likely the wall. He yells and I sprawl. His hips hit the floor first. Then his ass. My body laid out flat, chest down, hips on the floor. Toes curled so I can pop up fast. And I do. I lift up and drive my elbow into his groin. His shirt lifts just high enough that I can see that his stomach has already been peppered with bruises. Perfect. A paint by numbers guide to where I need to punch.

I have no idea if Michael is okay. *Please let him be okay.* But I can't look around, my focus needs to stay solely on the man I've managed to get to the ground. I slam my elbow and fist repeatedly into his Monet of blacks and blues. He barks out a yell, and moves his arms to get me to stop. But that's my opening to attack where I need to.

Bad move, asswipe.

I turn my body and sit on top of him. With his head

now uncovered, I drive my fingers into his eyes and push. He screams and flails, trying with whatever he has left in him to get my body off of his. But I don't budge. My legs are locked onto him, and I keep driving my fingers inward. A blood-curdling scream escapes him. Or maybe it's me, but I'm not stopping until he stops moving.

I don't know when it happens, but I'm being lifted off him from behind. I keep screaming.

"G! Baby! Baby, I've got you. I've got you," a deep soothing voice shouts in my face.

Henry.

I can finally focus. Henry.

"Henry," I cry out.

He drapes his body around me as my chest heaves. Looking at my face, he moves the hair from my eyes as I sit cradled in his lap. I don't know how I ended up here, but I don't care. I grip onto him. He rips his shirt off and holds it to my chin, where I can still feel blood flowing. It hurts. Burns. My teeth chatter, keeping time with the rest of my trembling body.

I hear the screeching of tires from the front of the building, but I don't want to look anywhere other than at him. "It's okay, you're okay," he keeps saying. "I have you. I have you. You're safe, baby." He keeps the shirt pressed firmly to my chin, his strong, comforting arms wrapped around me. I still can't take in a full breath, my chest cramping as I shake uncontrollably.

A movement over his shoulder catches my attention. Black shirt, dark hair, bloodied face. The lion. He moves toward us, his knife pulled back, cocked and ready to do damage. "Henry! No!" I scream.

I hear Bea shouting from the front of the room at the same time. Henry looks back and sees what's coming. He drapes himself over me, squeezing me tighter against his chest, trying to shield my body from what's happening around us. I can't see anything with my face buried against him.

Muffled grunts and yelling agents get louder. With the popping off of gunshots, I'm pushed backwards farther and forced to the ground. Henry's full weight on top of me now, unmoving. My heart stutters.

"Henry! Henry!" I try to push him, but he's heavy. I can barely move him. "Fuck, baby! Talk to me!" I can't see his face, with his head buried in my neck as he grips me. I don't know what hit him. What knocked us down. No, no, no, no, no, please be okay. "Baby, talk to me!"

I can't lose him.

"I got you, Pixie," he says in a whisper. "I'm fine. Just got the wind knocked out of me." He coughs as he sits up, never letting me go, taking me with him. He pushes the hair out of my face and tilts my chin back.

I can't do anything other than look around his face. The white scar on his upper lip, one green eye, one green eye swirled with blue, scruffed beard, furrowed brow. It's all there. He's okay. I thought for just a second he wasn't. That something terrible had happened.

"You're okay. You're okay," I keep repeating, tears pouring from my eyes. He smiles and pulls me closer, kissing my tear-soaked lips. I wince, because it hurts. "I thought you were shot, or that knife hit you in the back... I just thought—" I can't even finish without crying harder.

"Look at me. Look at me, Pixie." Henry leans his head lower to meet my eyes, so I'll stop freaking out.

I take in a ragged breath and stare into those perfect swirls of my favorite colors. "You can't be anything other than okay. You hear me, Henry Riggs."

"I hear you. I'm okay." He looks around the room and yells for a medic to come over. "Fuck, you're bleeding badly."

I touch my chin, the pain from being sliced on the face barreling through. I finally take in the room around me.

I see Michael sitting hunched over on the floor, talking to an agent. A lifeless body next to him. *The bear.* Michael saved our lives. He just reacted. He was a complete force. He usually rolls his eyes at me, and most of the time, vacates the room when I enter. But he didn't leave. He didn't hide. He fought for me. The man just killed someone to keep us both safe. I hiccup a cry.

Medics come into the space, followed by Sheriff Muldowney in plain clothes, who's speaking in hushed tones with Bea and another agent. A few minutes later, Bea rushes over as she barks orders at three additional agents who are already taking pictures and laying out the crime scene. My shop. The heavy drapes are pulled closed, keeping the aftermath away from prying eyes that might be walking by Hideaway Ink tonight.

Henry won't let go of me, and I don't want him to either. I grip onto his forearms.

It takes an hour to get cleaned up by the paramedic, and then stitched up by the plastic surgeon that Bea called in from two towns over. They don't want anyone heading into the hospital tonight.

"I won't let go until you tell me," Henry says.

We watch Bea and Sheriff Muldowney speak with Michael next. His hands constantly moving. Rubbing his neck, cracking his knuckles, raking them through his hair. He isn't emotional like I am. Michael doesn't usually have a tell. You have to look closely. And right now, he's freaking out. The magnitude of this, it's already jilting, but he doesn't have the backstory. That this wasn't just two scumbags trying to attack a woman. That it's so much more.

"Will she tell him the details? He deserves to know some of it," Henry says from behind me.

"I don't know what she's allowed to say, but I'll tell him. I'll tell him everything. He deserves to know that what he did—" I pull in a jagged breath. I try to bite back the emotion that I just managed to rein in for a moment. "That I will never be able to repay him for it."

"Are you going to be okay if I go over there for a minute? I want to be sure he's doing alright," Henry says, kissing my temple as I lean into him.

"Yes, go."

Henry squeezes the hand he was holding, kisses my knuckles, and says, "I'll be back in a minute. He looks over toward Jack just as he lets go of my hand. An unspoken agreement to keep me company, I assume.

"You okay?" Jack asks as he leans against the table I'm sitting on.

I nod. "I am. Or, will be, at least."

"This has to do with the Cayman Island trip you and Henry took suddenly?"

I nod again. I watch as Henry talks with Michael. Henry's hands gripping Michael's shoulders, speaking closely, reassuring him the best he can.

"What does Ev know? Because despite what that agent over there told me, about this being a wrong place, wrong time situation, I know that's total bullshit."

I look up at him, swallowing hard. "Nothing. She knows nothing about my past. About what brought me here. It was always safer for her *not* to know."

He nods and looks down, thinking about what he's going to do. Or say next.

"Your story to tell, G. Not mine. I'll take my cue from you and her brothers on what they want to disclose. If her not knowing is the safest thing, then that's my choice. She's my entire world, which means making sure she's okay is the only thing that matters to me."

"Jack, at this point, it's safer if she knows everything. I would like to be the one to tell her, though."

He nods again and gives me a tight-lipped smile. "I'm going to see if they need anything else from me before I get out of here."

Bea comes back to where I'm perched a few minutes later. "You need to get some rest. You're going to do those therapy sessions again. No excuses." I smile as she points at me. "I shouldn't be surprised that you're my biggest pain in the ass these days." She waves off one of her agents. "I'll be over in the morning to talk through where we stand." Bea nods to Henry. "He's taking you home."

My stomach drops again, a shiver of dread running

through me. *Fuck, I don't want to leave Strutt's.* But there's a nagging feeling that she's going to recommend it. I look around my shop in shambles. Broken glass, body-sized dents in the drywall, not to mention the blood splatter.

I hop down from the table and move toward the back of the shop where Henry and Michael sit talking. Henry hunched over, elbows on his knees. Michael mimicking his position. He's been peeking up at me every few seconds. I think he's nervous to lose sight of me right now. They both watch me as I get closer. Henry stands and pulls my hand into his and then sits back down, placing me in his lap.

"Michael." I blow out a big breath and do my best not to start crying immediately, clearing my throat. "You saved my life tonight." His eyes dart to mine. He's so hard to read, but he needs to hear this. "If you weren't here with me, I'd be dead right now." I wipe the tears that have tracked down my cheeks. Henry wraps his arms around my middle, and I feel him rest his head on my back. He holds me tight, and it's exactly what I need. He always knows what I need.

"You did pretty good there. More than held your own. Knocked that scrawny one right into a wall. Then you unleashed hell on him." He laughs, breaking up the heaviness. "You gotta tell Mac. He'd be proud of you." I give him a tight smile and nod.

"You okay?" I ask, searching his face for the truth. I watch as his hands shake slightly, his knee bouncing with anxiousness.

"I'm not sure yet. I killed someone tonight. And yeah, it was self-defense, but that, that's not something I'd ever thought I'd have to deal with, so..." He clears his throat to stop the shaking of his voice. Henry grabs Michael's shoulder, and I lean over, wrapping my arms around Michael's broad shoulders. He leans in and hugs me back. I can feel him inhaling a few deep breaths, before he says, "This is so fucked, but I'm glad I was here. You're family, G. Can't let anything happen to you. It's what family does. We protect each other."

I burrow my face into his neck. I don't think he'll ever know how much I needed to hear that. Those words at that moment. *Family*. I try not to cry too hard.

"Do you want to stay with us tonight?" Henry asks him, bringing us both back to the present. I'm pretty sure we held on for a solid couple of minutes there.

"I'm going to have Callen drive me to Dad's. But I'll call you in the morning."

The exact thing I was so scared of ever happening, happened. And it put my new family, the people who I've grown to love so much, in danger. There's a part of me that will carry that guilt forever. The idea of exposing them to anything that could harm them isn't something I'll ever stop trying to make sure never happens again.

"Let's get you home," Henry says as he stands. Without thinking twice, I move closer to him as he tucks me underneath his shoulder. *Home*. The question is, for how much longer.

CHAPTER 51

Henry

I HELD HER ALL NIGHT LONG. I DIDN'T SLEEP. I COULDN'T. I just traced numbers, letters, and lines along her back, and down her arms. I'm exhausted, physically and emotionally, but there are too many scenarios playing out in my mind about what could have happened if my brother hadn't been there, or if I wasn't right next door. I can't lose her again.

She's been awake for a little while, but I think we both just needed to lie here and absorb one another without words. The sun starts peeking through the drapes of her loft, and the muffled sounds of businesses opening on Main Street echo from outside.

"I can't have children," she whispers with her back to me. She doesn't say anything else. Instead, she nuzzles into me, waiting for a response. I sit with that for a minute. Something I haven't allowed myself to really think about for a long time. Kids. A future, with her. I've been so focused on the immediate next thing, that anything beyond that, doesn't even register for me.

"If you're telling me that because you don't want to keep any more secrets from me, then I'm happy you told me." I wait another few beats before saying more. "If you're telling me, because you think that's going to change how I feel about you, or what I want with you, then you haven't been paying attention, Pixie." I smile as I say it, because the truth is, she's telling me for both reasons.

She turns over so that now we're facing each other. So beautiful, even with a bandaged chin and bloodshot eyes. I swipe a tear that's moving across the bridge of her nose.

She looks around my face before saying anything, but I know what's coming. "What do you want with me, Henry?"

"This. Your trust. Mornings with you in my bed, wrapped around me. I want every minute that you'll give me."

She drags in a shaky breath, eyes watering. "I want that to be true." She looks down at my mouth, then to my chest where she's fidgeting with her fingers. "But you want a family. I know that you do."

My stomach clenches, thinking this is why she's held back. Why she's been pushing me away the past week.

"I can't give that to you. You don't get that if you're with me."

She tilts her head back so she can look me in the eyes again, letting out a shaky breath before she continues.

"I don't need you to be the good guy right now, baby. I need you to be brave enough to walk away from this if you need more. If you need that with someone, I want you to have it."

"If I wanted someone else, Gia," I pause and sit up, pulling her up with me. I wrap my hands along her jawline and rub my thumbs along her cheeks. "If I wanted any of that, I would have had it by now. If it was just about moving my life forward, then I would have. But the thing is, you're the only one I've really ever wanted. And no matter where I've been or what I've done, you're my anchor, Pixie. No matter what adventure I choose, I want you on it."

She closes her eyes. Her expression relaxing in what seems like relief. "You said my old name again," she whispers.

"I'll call you whatever you want, Pixie. I love you. You have to know that by now. That I'm so in love with you." Now I have to take a second. I look up, trying to keep the glassiness in my eyes from falling. "Being able to say that to you, hell, Pixie, that's more than I thought I'd ever get."

She lets out a cry and smiles so big, my chest warms. I know she feels it too.

"I'll tell you every day. Every single day, Henry. I didn't know how to say it, how to keep myself grounded, and still tell you that you're everything to me. And then everything happened last night. I thought I was going to lose you. Lose us. And I would have never told you how seeing you every day kept me moving. The hard days, when I was missing my pops, or feeling lucky to be alive, you would show up somewhere and I'd feel relieved, safe. Just the idea of you close, even though we couldn't be anything to each other, it's made my life infinitely better."

"Even when you were pissed off at me?" I laugh. "Trying to hate me?"

"Especially then." She pinches my arm. "I never could hate you. I tried, but it wouldn't stick. You made me so mad sometimes, but I mostly hated not being able to kiss you." She smiles, leans in, and kisses me. As she moves her body closer, legs rubbing mine under the covers, I pull her tighter against me. I love kissing this woman.

She pulls her mouth back just a fraction from my lips and says, "I love you, and I'll keep on loving you for as long as you'll let me."

I've never felt such a sense of joy in all of my life, as I do hearing those words from her lips.

She closes her eyes again, scrunching her nose. "That was really fucking scary to say." Tears trickle down her cheeks and into her mouth, down her neck. I kiss her lips softly. "Ow." She laughs. "My chin hurts so bad." I kiss her forehead and she shifts up and over, just enough on the bed to get onto my lap, wrapping her arms and legs around me. We hold each other tight, breathing together, sharing this moment, and feeling lighter for it. I could have held her like that all day, but a loud knock on her door knocks us out of it.

"It's Bea." She wipes her face. "She's going to want to do a full debrief and statement today. I need to figure out what the options are right now," she says as she moves into the closet.

"I'm staying," I say as I pull my jeans up my legs.

But just by the way she looks at me as she pulls her hair up into a knot on the top of her head, I know what she's about to say. Every fiber of my being wants to fight her on it.

"You're going," she says. "I need to talk to her on my own. It's going to be a while too. Please, go see Michael. He's going to need someone to keep him company after the adrenaline of last night finally wears off."

Before she starts to move down the stairs to get the door, I grab her elbow and pull her back to me. "I love you. You hear me?" She nods with a devilish grin dancing along her mouth. "I go where you go."

She searches my eyes, registering what I'm telling her. She doesn't get to leave. Not without me.

She kisses my lips softly and whispers, "I love you, Henry."

Those words from her turn me upside down all over again, spreading a warmth through my entire body I didn't realize I was so desperate for, until now.

With a wink, she says, "See you later, baby."

CHAPTER 52

Giselle

I'VE DIED AGAIN. AND WOKE UP IN HELL. I MEAN, THIS MUST be hell, because shoveling shit in a cattle pen on a farm is not the life I imagined I'd be living. I'm not some cute farmhand either with cut-offs and cowboy boots. Nope. I'm in heavy coveralls and rain boots because I'm in literal shit. I chose a place that promised blue skies, but the only blues that are consistent these days are the world's oldest pair of Wranglers attached to this salty asshole who has a mouthful of chew, and an even bigger attitude problem.

"You're slower than my son was when he was eight years old, for Christ's sake, woman. And that boy was slow as fuck back, then."

"Excellent parenting skills you must have had."

The old son of a bitch blows his nose in the most disgusting rag of a handkerchief and keeps talking. "They told me you'd be here to help me for a few months, not cause a larger pain in my ass."

"It's all that meat you eat that's making your ass larger, old man," I yell back. "You might want to be nice to me because I'm the one hauling a heavy as fuck shovel around here. I wouldn't want to swing it your way, and accidentally let it hit you on the way back." I smile my most obnoxious smile in his direction.

He laughs.

It's been eleven weeks, six days, and thirteen hours since I've been in Wyoming. The worst place in the universe, and with the devil's decrepit grandfather, who just barks orders at me. As if I'm really here out of my own free will to do work for him. No way. This shit was forced on me. Literally, as I look around where my feet squelch every time I move them.

"Last day, kid. Why don't you finish up and go get clean."

I tilt my head back and shield my eyes from the midday sun. "I'll finish your death chores first." I give him a smirk. I'll miss him. I hate him, but I'll miss him.

"You could come to visit, you know," I say as I rake out another section.

He leans on the fence, staring at nothing, maybe even thinking about it, but he gives me the answer I was expecting. "Too much to do here."

I don't push. I'm not one to force an issue, especially when I don't know the whole story. Buck Riggs is not the kind of man to divulge much, but I know he's lonely. I feel for him, but my loyalty will always lie with Asher. That eight-year-old kid he so lovingly referred to as "slow as fuck," is the man I've come to adore. Who treats me like one of his own. It's not my place to try to fix something that may be better off broken.

About four hours later, I'm packed and finally ready to return to my life in Strutt's Peak.

Back to him.

I had two choices the morning that Bea came to see me.

Relocate with a new identity, or find some patience and wait it out.

I chose to wait it out. Patience wasn't something I've ever had, but I liked my life, and I was willing to do anything to hang on to it. That also meant I had to leave for a short while and allow any repercussions that were going to happen, happen, and be out of the fray if they did. There could be no contact of any kind. Bea would gauge how to handle the details of where I was, and to whom. Essentially hand my life over again, and hope to every goddess in the universe, from Beyonce to Gaga, that it would be enough. And that the men that found me were not still tied to the organized crime they slithered away from.

I followed all of the rules. Well, most. And now I get to go back.

There's always going to be a risk. The number of people that were connected to my pops was vast, and all of them were dangerous in various ways. But as far as the men that murdered and destroyed my life, they're all dead now. Flight logs, facial recognition, and electronic footprints were erased and reconfigured, placing The Lion and The Bear in Vegas instead of Colorado for anyone who looked. They have names, but I'd rather not add them to the memory banks. Them disappearing from Vegas would cause far fewer questions if people inside their organization cared to ask. And if they did, there wouldn't be any reason for them to come looking for me. As far as the U.S. Marshalls and FBI are concerned, my case is closed. There's no one left to put behind bars for the crime that happened the night my pops died. Me staying away from Strutt's for a little while was simple due diligence. Something Bea wanted to do, just in case.

I've sketched more tattoos than I'll ever be able to put on skin, but it's kept my mind busy. Over the past few months, I've lived with the bare minimum, and it's allowed me to remember all the things I've taken for granted. Like desserts that aren't pie. Buck Riggs only believes in pie, apparently. I've had every flavor I ever knew was possible, and while that's nice and all, I want to eat German chocolate cake after the gooiest of grilled cheeses. I miss Henry's cooking. I miss all the parts of him.

And in a few hours, I get to see him. Figure out life with him. Beg him to make me grilled cheeses and desserts... for as long as we both shall live.

Bea won't tell me what's happening in Strutt's. Only that they've let the rumor circulate that I'm visiting family out of state. And most importantly, she demanded that I don't contact anyone. Everly is likely short circuiting. I have to assume Henry would have told her at least part of what's happened. I'll fill in more of the details over time.

I step out of the shower and wrap the sorriest excuse

for a towel around my body. Really, this should be a hand towel. It barely covers me. I pull it tight and tuck it between my boobs. My skin is still slick because there is no air conditioning in the farmhand apartment. An apartment is what Buck calls it, but it's a damn shed. And not the cute she-sheds on Pinterest or HGTV. Nope, nothing like that. We're talking wood paneling for days, and everything creeks. It's a creepy wood box on the edge of his farm that could easily be the inspiration for the next Evil Dead movie.

After getting ready, I rub my hand on the mirror. "Yup, perfect!" I lined my lips with my crushed berry lip liner and then filled it in with my favorite matte red lip stain. I haven't worn makeup while I've been here unless I'm taking selfies with my burner phone. Selfies which I've perfected in getting the right angle. I take one more shot of well-curated cleavage and a pouty, red-stained lip in the frame to remind my flyboy what's coming back to him.

Bea said no contact, but she wasn't specific, so I send Henry some sort of dirty pic daily. He never responds, likely because he's following the rules, but I know he's getting them.

I miss Strutt's Peak and its blue skies. I'm itching to get back to my business. I miss my best friend. I miss having a decent coffee with more options than black with sugar cubes. I want to tell Ruth DeMaio to shove it in another town meeting regarding whatever complaint she might have next. And I miss Henry. I miss him most of all.

I pull out my burner phone to fire off one last dirty picture text, and now, it's time to go home.

CHAPTER 53

Henry

SHE LEFT. AFTER I TOLD HER THAT WHEREVER SHE GOES, I go. And she still left. I planned to be where she was, no matter what, after that night. There wasn't a single thing that would have kept me away, except not telling me, and leaving anyway.

She told me she loved me and then disappeared. I spent that morning with Michael, working out, walking Milo, trying to sweat out our feelings from the night before, but when I came back, she was gone. There was no note or text. Her phone was left behind, along with most of her things, including me. To say I wasn't in a good place for the following eighteen hours after that would be a grand understatement.

It took an entire day for Agent Harper to seek me out and assure me that she would be back. More like, Harper couldn't take me anymore after I sent a decent amount of spiraling texts that took a turn toward threatening. I may have said something like, "I will hunt you down," to a U.S. Marshall. Not my finest moment. I was too out of my mind with worry to think Harper would have placed her somewhere I knew. But Harper caved and told me. I should have known she would send her to Wyoming. Sent my Pixie to rough it out for a little while with Buck. I'm sure Harper got a good kick out of that. G, not so much.

Then, two days later, I got a picture text of an insanely sexy underboob with a very specific beauty mark, and what was left of my worry, settled. I knew she was okay. Harper told me as much, but hoping she was coming back to me wasn't enough, until I heard from her, saw a piece of her.

Every day for the past three months, I've received a close-up picture of a curve, crease, or series of body parts from my Pixie. I'm not allowed any communication with her while they wrap things up with her case, so I enjoy my daily pics, and keep planning for when she's back. Spouting a simple lie to business owners along Main Street who noticed the shop closed, or the need to reschedule her clients, has been fairly easy. But after everything that had happened, it was impossible to keep any of the truth hidden from the rest of my family.

So with their promise to keep it quiet, I told them all about G. Who she was, how we really met, what happened at her tattoo shop, and that she had to disappear for a little while. She would have done it herself if she had been here, but I was tired of keeping up the lie. I didn't want to do it anymore, not with them.

"It was her? All along?" Everly had asked, glassy-eyed,

as I helped put all the pieces together. "Oh, Hen, it's an insane level of fate. You realize that, right? I can't believe it's her." She hugged me tight and cried at the reality of what I was telling her, that her best friend was the woman I searched for, the one she hoped I would get over, the same woman who she knew that I had fallen in love with over the years. All of it complicated, and worth it.

"Well, it makes a ton more sense now," Law had said as he rested his hand on his chin, shaking his head with a grin. "You cockblocked me for a decade, and I thought it was because you just wanted to be a dick about the Shelley Farley thing."

Michael had gotten the full picture the morning after the incident in her shop. He needed to know who those men were, what they were capable of, and what they had done. Any remorse he may have felt, I'd like to think, would have eased, knowing all of it. The fact there was more to our story wasn't news to Michael. He always picks up on more, sees more than the rest of us.

"Henry, I've got this. I can wrap things up here. You go ahead and get out of here," Benny says as he strides back into the kitchen. Now double in size, with the proper stoves, ovens, and refrigeration, since I needed to make my piece of this business successful. "I've already prepped for the coffee shop in the morning. I can handle what you have left here."

"Thanks, Ben." Normally, I wouldn't take him up on it, but it's Saturday night, which means it's the last night this week that my space is open. I keep Sundays for myself, so I can still do dinner with my family.

The word-of-mouth, reservation-only, dinner pop-up that I host out of Brews & Books is only available Thursday through Saturday nights. While the coffee shop bookstore hybrid has a romantic, lighter style, my side of things that extends into the back of the space and spills outdoors, offers a deeper, darker feel.

Black metals, ash-colored wood-top tables, luxurious leathers, and warm, oversized lighting fixtures, carry the speakeasy, Gatsby-like vibe that I wanted. It can only be found through word of mouth. And not so easily accessed. But if anyone from Strutt's Peak talks about *The Lemon Tree*, they know who owns it, and where to find it.

My menu is seasonal, food choices are pre-selected during the reservation process, and curating meals for people has become as much of an obsession as my new profession. I've always loved cooking for my family, but this has unlocked creativity I would never have guessed I actually had. I have plans to study with some guest chefs who Jack is planning to fly in during the off-season, and maybe someday, it'll be something even bigger. But for now, it's everything never knew I wanted.

I jog up the flight of stairs and I'm just about to step into the loft when my phone buzzes.

EVERLY

The movies on the green kick off tonight. Come and meet us down here.

I'm beat. I'm just going to call it a night. I'll catch you at dinner tomorrow.

I toss the phone on the bed and hop into the shower.

From my new workplace to my front door is less than a five-minute walk. I shouldn't say *my* front door. I've been staying in G's loft since she left. Every time I left and went back home, it didn't feel right to be there. I felt closer to her by being in her space.

The woman has way too many plants to keep up with, and her kitchen made no sense when I found underwear in the drawer next to the stove and a bag of vibrators under the sink, but I expected nothing less. It's a great-looking space. And I've made minor tweaks since I've been here. A few upgrades she'll appreciate when she's back. Plus, it's convenient for work now.

The rainshower splatters water down from the ceiling while I rest my head on the hunter-green subway tiles. One of the small projects I've completed to supe up the bathroom. There was no way I was going to shower in the clawfoot tub she had. I almost fell getting in and out of it multiple times. I had to practice chest-level knee lifts just to avoid slamming a shin into the edge. So, with the help of my brothers, we did some renovating. I bought the vacated loft next door on a whim so we could bust through part of the walls and make the space bigger. I can't wait to show it to her. It's a 50/50 whether she'll swoon over it or kick me out.

I grip my cock, thinking about my girl and that picture she sent to me earlier tonight. Those pouty lips and lick-worthy tits. I flex my wrist. It only takes a few harsh tugs before I'm already teetering on the edge of a decent orgasm. The truth is, as much as I enjoy every inch of her body, I probably miss talking to her the most.

She's the only person who can really make me laugh at any time of day, no matter where we are.

But right now, as I'm getting ready to paint this wall with my cum, I can only think about how good her pussy is going to feel gripping my cock when she's finally home. I rub my balls while I make quick jerking movements along my shaft, just imagining all the places I want to tease and fuck— "That's it. Fuck, G," I groan and spill. It's a short-term solution. I'll be half hard again in a few minutes.

I step out onto the heated tile floor and turn on the room fan. When it's on high, I can air dry while I brush my teeth. I have expensive taste, but I don't flaunt it. That's the rest of my family. I lived off of an Air Force salary for years, but I've been smart with money since. I made good money working my way up the ladder at Riggs Outdoor. I've watched and learned from my father, and now my brother-in-law. I spend on the things that are little luxuries. Heated floors and not needing to towel dry my body are just some of those things.

I throw on a pair of mesh shorts and t-shirt, noticing a ton of texts that went off while I was showering. All from my sister. *Shit.*

EVERLY

You're like 50ft from the green. Just come down here and eat popcorn with me.

Law ditched me for some woman who he said has "big cougar energy"

> C'mon. Otherwise, I'll just be on this blanket alone…

It's just after 9:30, and the movie has likely already started, but she's right, I'm a few steps away, and there's no reason not to keep her company. I throw on my shoes and grab Milo's leash.

"C'mere, boy. Let's go hang out with your Auntie Ev for a little bit." He barks back as if he knows exactly what I just said. *The goodest boy.*

I hit the sidewalk, and there's a big crowd spread out across the lawn of Strutt's downtown green. An oversized outdoor movie screen on the farthest side. The movie's already started, but I hear Milo bark excitedly before I can text Ev to find her.

"Henry Riggs, that devil dog of yours was in the dog park again this morning," the shrill voice of my least favorite DeMaio sister bites in my direction.

"It's a nice night, isn't it, Ruth?" I say, purposely ignoring what she said.

"He was chasing my little sweetie pie," she says while petting the white curly-haired poof in her arms. "Honestly, if you're going to utilize the dog park, please keep your mutt in the large dog side, and not the space for the small dogs."

I breathe through my nose and take a calming exhale. In all honesty, I have no idea what she's talking about. Milo doesn't go to the dog park unless I take him, which means he got out somehow and then, by some miracle, let himself back inside. He's smart, but I doubt he's mastered opening the door on his own.

"Sure thing, Ruth," I say, trying to brush her off.

"It's Ms. DeMaio to you, Riggs."

I keep walking. "Have a nice night," I yell over my shoulder. "You crotchety battleax," I mumble under my breath.

I scratch my old boy's rusty-colored hair. "Are you chasing the ladies in your old age, Milo?" I laugh and then pull out my phone.

> Okay, where are you?

I look around from the edge of the lawn, not spotting my sister.

> EVERLY
>
> Closer to the back. Just start walking, you'll find her.

Her?

As I move through the crowd of people sprawled out on blankets and lawn chairs, the screen grabs my attention.

"Why worry? Each one of us is carrying an unlicensed nuclear accelerator on his back," Bill Murray says sarcastically on screen as he creeps along the New York City Public Library.

Ghostbusters.

A smile takes over my face instantly. Something tells me I'm not going to find Everly right now. I look around the lawn, trying to spot wildly long blonde hair and bold, colorful tattoos that trickle down both arms.

"Looking good, Hanky," I hear from behind me,

where I was just standing. "You really know how to fill out those short—"

I cut her off as I whip around and rush into her, wrapping my arms around her waist and lifting her off the ground. Her arms circle my neck and squeeze, holding on so tight as she lets out a contented hum against me. I lean my head back to look at her beautiful face. I missed those big brown eyes on me. The energy and feelings have always been there, but the love that's grown for her billows all around me. I feel blanketed in it. Lucky.

"Hi." I move my arms up higher, and she locks her legs around my waist. I tuck a piece of her blonde hair behind her ear.

She smiles. *God, I've missed that smile.* "Hi."

"I missed you, Pixie," I whisper to her, leaning into her and taking a deep breath. Sugar and lemons. I could lick her up right now, but instead, I opt for a kiss just under her ear.

"Missed you more," she says as she leans in toward my mouth and nips at my bottom lip. I pull her head closer to capture her in a kiss I've dreamt about for months. Her mouth parts, welcoming my tongue to dance with hers. A small noise escapes her, and I savor it.

Hoots and hollers pull our attention away from one another. Milo joins in, barking.

"It's about time, you two!" Law shouts. My dad claps and whistles while Everly wipes the tears streaming down her face as Jack holds her from behind. Michael whistles and claps in unison with a few other onlookers. He looks genuinely happy, an emotion I haven't seen from him much lately.

I feel her lips on my neck again, ignoring the praise around us.

"As much as I want to finally watch this movie with you, I'm going to need you to get real rough and dirty with me, stat," she says into my neck, with that sexy voice of hers. The one that tells me that was not a request.

"I love you all, but we're not staying for the movie," I say while putting her down. G wraps Everly in a big hug, and they talk quietly for a minute. I give Jack a handshake and backslap hello. My dad does the same and follows it up with his words of wisdom.

"You better get out of here before G and your sister end up ditching your ass for their own version of trouble," he says.

Overhearing their laughter, and the mentioning of drinks and dessert, has me moving toward my girl.

"Henry! Henry, okay. Fine!" she concedes as I throw her over my shoulder and carry her back to the loft. I slap her ass, and if we weren't making a spectacle in the center of town with an audience, I'd probably bite it too.

I quicken my pace. "C'mon boy," I yell behind me with a quick whistle to get Milo to follow. He trots behind me, holding his own leash in his mouth. We make it across the street, up the stairs, and into the loft. It's not fast enough, because I need to hold her, fuck her, tell her how much she means to me. And in no particular order.

When I finally put her down, she starts laughing. But her laughter dies as she starts to move around the apartment, looking at some of the changes. "Oh my gosh, did you move into my loft?!"

"You left. I told you I was coming with you, and you

left." I lift my shoulder to shrug. "So, I live here now." I head into the kitchen and snag the homemade bottle of limoncello from the freezer and a shot glass. I pour one out, shoot it back, and turn to move back toward her. "Made you your favorite. A little alteration, but I think you'll like it."

She laughs again, sitting on her green velvet chair. She must think of the same memory as I do because I stop in my tracks, and my cock gives me a nice jolt in remembrance, genuflecting to the queen on her throne. She drapes her left leg over the arm of the chair and slouches back. The smirk on her face is filled with dirty promises. I pour another shot and saunter back to my goddess. When she brings the glass to her lips and tilts it back, I damn near come in my pants. There's really nothing quite like the confidence and sex appeal of this woman.

"You added Cognac," she says. Licking her lips, she adds, "I like it."

I kneel in front of her because, really, there isn't any other place than I'd rather be than on my knees in front of her right now. She moves her fingers to my face, tracing along my forehead and down the bridge of my nose. I close my eyes, relishing in her touch. The softness of it, the meaning of it. She moves her fingers toward my mouth, tracing my upper lip.

"I love this scar," she whispers. "For the longest time, I wondered if I'd ever be able to look at it as close as I am now. If you were with someone else, I wouldn't be able to trace it with my fingers, or stare at your blue-green eye without getting into a fight with a woman who would never appreciate them as much as I do," she says.

I put the shot glass and bottle down next to me. Moving closer, I grab underneath each of her thighs to bring her body closer to mine.

"No more leaving," I tell her as I lean down and kiss her beautifully puffy lips.

"No more leaving," she agrees and kisses me again.

I pull her bottom lip in between mine, taking my time with her mouth.

"Kissing you feels like your mouth was only ever intended for mine," she says in a whisper. She nips at my lower lip. "I could never really kiss anyone else after I felt what yours was like."

That admission sparks something primal in me. I yank her legs up as she leans back, kissing the inside of her right thigh and then the left. An offering. Respect, because I'm about to worship every inch of her body. The warmth that resides mere inches from my face is an altar I've been praying at for longer than I think I've even realized. This woman has had a hold on me in every way that matters.

There could never be anyone else.

"Well?" she says, a smirk taking over her face as I look up. "It's not going to lick itself, Hanky."

I can't help but bark out a laugh. I pull her thighs closer, resting each one on my shoulders. As I breathe her in, the smell of her lights every last part of me that wasn't already on the edge of burning. I practically growl out a hot breath right on her pussy. The black leggings she's wearing are a barrier to what I want right now. The stitching at the center grabs my attention. So, instead of lifting her hips to slide these off, I use both hands to grip on either side of the seam and yank it hard and fast. They rip right down the middle. I only hear her yelp in response.

"Oh my fucking hell. I loved those pants," she says with a shaky breath. And before she can say anything else, I push aside the neon yellow thong that's the last piece of material keeping me from tongue fucking her.

"Yes! Holy shit, baby. Lick that pussy. Goddess, I've missed your mouth."

"Mine," I growl into her wetness.

I lick and suck every inch of her cunt. There's not a single place that isn't drenched with her arousal and my urgency to taste it all. When I flick my eyes up, I see her watching me, biting her lip and pinching her tits through her tank. The lust in her eyes revs me further. I suck on her clit with long pulls and flex my thumb into her. It's just enough of an intrusion to push her closer, but not enough to get her there. I want her begging for my cock. I need to hear her plead for it.

"Yes, baby. Fuck, I'm fucking yours," she moans.

I keep the same pace. I fuck her with my thumb and tongue her clit. I know it's getting her nice and close, because her thighs are starting to shake, and she's stopped talking. It's one of the few times she's quiet, when she's on the verge of an orgasm.

I smile into her pussy. It's impossible to stifle it, knowing I'm going to see her unravel in minutes, and own every inch of her pleasure. But instead of continuing, I pull back.

"You're going to take my cock and you're going to thank me for it. And then, Pixie, you're going to come all over it. Do you hear me?"

"Baby, I love you, but my God your mouth—" And the praise cuts off as soon as I bury my cock inside of her. In one fast thrust of my hips, I'm balls deep, and it feels so fucking good that I'm already moments away from coming.

I pull back out slowly and hover, with just the tip at her entrance. "Didn't you hear what I said? I want you to come all over me right fucking now, G."

She opens her eyes and smirks. "You do know that a request like that is only asking for a woman to fake it, right?"

Chuckling, I push back into her hard and fast three times, knowing exactly how to get her there. Then I pull back out on the third, dragging so achingly slow, wanting to feel every bit of warmth she's willing to give me. Her breathing picks up faster, her head tilted up, mouth open.

"Clench my fucking cock with your pussy and don't let go. Do you hear me, Pixie?" I groan as I push into her again. And she does. *My good girl.* She practically chokes my cock as she grips me. And as soon as I move, pulling out again, she's screaming.

I can feel her pulsing, and it breaks down whatever reserve I had for holding my own orgasm. I roll my hips into her repeatedly, because for some reason, I want every last drop of my cum as deep as it'll go inside of her. A kink or a want that I've never once thought about, but the idea of painting her inside and out keeps the release buzzing through my body.

My body slumps over her, and I rest my forehead on her chest. Both of us breathing hard, coming down from the high those orgasms left in their wake.

"Please, let's do that again," she says as she drags her fingers through my hair. I laugh, feeling drunk on her. On the love we just made, on the idea that I can do this with her whenever I want now.

I can feel the wetness start to drip from where we're still connected, so I lean back and grab my t-shirt from the neckline, pulling it over my head. All of that happened so quickly, we didn't take our clothes off. I use it to wipe up just enough so that the disaster on this chair is left to a minimum.

Leaning forward, I bite her right nipple through her shirt, and she lets out a giggle. "I missed you so damn much."

"Me too, baby."

Hearing her call me that drives a chill across my shoulders and down my arms. I don't know why it sets me off the way it does, but that word from her lips is the equivalent to scratching behind Milo's ear. Speaking of my furry boy, I let out a small whistle, and he comes trotting down the stairs to where G and I are draped on each other.

She looks around the loft, and I see that she's finally noticing a few more things that are new. First, the cut-out that breaks the wall from this loft to the next, and then her attention shifts to the front of the room toward the floor-to-ceiling windows that overlook her strip of Main Street.

She sits up, asking, "You've really been staying here?"

I don't answer her right away, instead, I stand, lifting my shorts back up, and make my way to the refrigerator to grab us waters. I'll let her take in the things I've done since she's been away.

"Where're my sketch books? And cups of markers?"

I lean against the counter and crack open the water, still silent.

She jogs up the loft stairs and shouts from the top, "Did you just move in? What the fuck, Hanky?" She moves farther into her bedroom space, her mumblings getting quieter, so I move closer to the stairs. "I don't remember you asking," she shouts again. A few minutes later, as she moves around the upper level of the loft, I hear, "There's no way that I'm sharing my closet with you. It was already too small to even be called a closet to begin–" Her voice cuts out. That's when I know she's found one of two upgrades in that space. I see her lean over the railing. "Did you... There's a whole room that's a closet up here. Where?... How'd that happen?"

I smile and start walking upstairs.

"You moved into my house," she says, still in shock, turning around. In that moment, when I finally take in the look on her face, I have a flash of "oh fuck, this was stupid."

"You left. So, I just went for it. I'm in this. I want this."

She holds up her hand to silence me. *Shit.*

"You moved into my house. You apparently went ahead and made massive renovations to the space. You decided all of this on your own, while I was away!"

"If you're not happy, then—" She holds her hand up higher, and I stop talking again.

"You're not allowed to make life-altering decisions without me anymore. You understand?"

Anymore.

I nod, trying to stifle the smile that's ever so slowly creeping out. She looks so serious; I'm on the verge of pissing myself right now, and smiling is my nervous tick at the moment.

She narrows her eyes at me and says, "My sketching stuff needs to go back to where I had it. Other than that, you did good, Hanky." Then, she smiles. "I will promptly be moving all my things in that room that is supposed to be a closet. You're also bringing your espresso maker, because my coffeepot is shit compared to that thing."

I walk a little closer, wrapping my arms around her again, and she kisses my chin.

"I love you," I mumble into her neck. Right under her ear, in the place that drives her crazy. "I love you so fucking much, G."

"You've told me, baby. In so many more ways than words. I remember every single time, too." She stands up on her toes, closing the sliver of distance still barely between us, and kisses me with reverence. Her beautiful mouth meets mine, and I feel a sense of relief wash over me. The fact that we finally get to do this. Be in this together. Fight and fuck. Love each other. It's an indescribable feeling. One that, long ago, I resigned myself to believe would never happen for us.

"I need to try out that shower," she says as she lets go of my neck and leans back. She drags her hands toward the hem of her shirt and lifts it off.

She turns, and just as she crosses the threshold to the

bathroom, she damn near kills me again when she says, "Hanky, there is one thing I'd like to change."

"What's that, Pixie?" I ask with a smile. Because who knows what the hell she's going to come up with.

"I want your last name."

EPILOGUE

Giselle

I'VE BEEN BACK IN STRUTT'S PEAK FOR JUST OVER TWO weeks now, and life is pretty fucking delicious. It took a few days to get back into the flow of work. Hideaway Ink is as busy as usual. My clients were thrilled to be back on the schedule. But I've decided to only do tattoos in the late afternoon and evenings now. I try to keep most of them booked from Thursday through Saturday, so that mine and Henry's work life is synched. The rest of the days, and our mornings especially, we spend together. I'll fit in a piercing here and there, and I still take classes with Mac at the gym regularly. And of course, I spend plenty of time with Everly. But most of my time is spent with my flyboy.

He's been drawing on my back for an hour now. I don't even know if he realizes he does it. Every night and every morning, he glides his fingers around my skin in lines, letters, and numbers. It's so relaxing that I don't ever want him to stop. Two more drags across my back, and then I'll turn over, and then go brush my teeth so I can kiss his beautiful face and mouth good morning. He drags his fingers from left to right, always restarting once the sequence is complete. I figured out what he was drawing on me that first night we'd slept together. On the island. I think I was already aware that I loved him by then, but the movement of his fingers and what he drew on me was the piece that made me realize there was nobody else for me. I was always meant to have him.

"You've drawn the quadratic formula across my skin countless times, but the question I have for you, sir, is do you know what it's used for?" I turn over, and I'm met with the sexiest, tired face with wild bedhead.

He curls a piece of my hair around his finger and moves it behind my ear. Smiling a lazy morning smile, he says, "Yeah, Pixie. It's used to make you fall in love with me."

"Well, it worked."

I move my hand to his face, but as I lift it, I notice something that wasn't there before. I tilt my head back to get a better look, smiling in awe as I do. On my left ring finger sits a beautiful emerald cut diamond attached to a brushed matte-black band. It's exactly what I would want if I had ever thought about what I wanted. But the truth is, I never allowed it.

"Take my last name if you want it. The rest of me is already yours, Pixie."

I don't know when I started crying, but as I kiss him and drape my body on top of his, I hear small sobs break loose from my throat.

"What do you say? Can I have you forever?" he asks as he wipes the tears falling down my nose and cheeks.

I sit up slightly to look at the ring again, then back into his beautiful eyes. *Damn*, this man. The greens and the splash of blue. I memorize again the lines of where his scruff meets the smoothness of his cheeks. The white line that brushes his upper lip. All the parts of him that are imperfect, but when you put them together, they make up the most incredible face I've ever seen. And that's not even the best part of him. I put my hand over his chest, right where his heart beats. *The best part.*

"The truth is, baby, that I want all of it. Your name, your family, a life with you. Whatever that might look like for us." I look down at his lips. "I want to kiss you whenever I think about your mouth." *Kiss.* "I want to fight with you." *Kiss.* "I want to make up with you." *Kiss.* "But mostly, I just want you to cook for me." I kiss him again, laughing. He pinches my sides, causing a fit of laughter, and the very graceful flailing of my body. I twist away and jump from the bed.

"Get back here, Pixie. I need to fuck you to seal this deal," he tells me with clenched teeth.

Well, how do I run away from a request like that? I jump back into the warm bed, and he curls his body around me.

He asks, "Are you happy?"

I bite on my already puffy bottom lip and run my fingers over his scruffed jawline.

I nod. "You're not so predictable, after all, Henry." I pause and look around his face.

"What are you thinking?" I ask.

"That this is how it was always supposed to be." He rubs his nose against mine. Soft touches that feel like so much more with him. "Me and you, Pixie."

And as mushy as it might sound. Or as serendipitous as it may seem. It's our truth. Henry is my anchor. My constant, regardless of the adventure. My safe place. My home. The piece of my life's equation that, at its root, was always meant to equal us as a pair.

Quite plainly, he was always meant to find me, try to hate me, protect me, and irrevocably, love me.

Henry

"You do not *have* a girl. I'm your girl, Henry. Your actual girl is a tattoo artist, which means, that's what's happening." She's so frustrated by this topic, it's kind of priceless. "You will not be getting tattoos by"—she pitches her voice up and uses air quotes as she says—"*your girl*, unless that bitch is me!"

She looks up from chopping the garlic. It's impossible not to laugh at how mad she is, but I'm trying.

"Stop it! This isn't a joke, Hanky. You will only get tattoos from me. Or"—she points the knife at me—"you may wakeup with a very enthusiastic dick tattooed on your face one morning."

I bark out the laugh I was holding. "Oh please, you would not do that."

She raises an eyebrow and cocks her head to the side in an extremely frightening way. My balls actually clench and draw inward toward my body. A chill runs down my arms. As much as we tease each other, there's still something lethal about *that* look. All men have seen it at some point or another. Just enough of a reminder that women truly run the world and they just allow us to co-exist.

"Fine. I don't have a girl. You're my girl from here on out," I concede.

"Exactly."

The braciole has been slow cooking in the sauce for most of the day, along with a few pieces of hot sausage and the meatballs I finished prepping this morning. I made her coffee and brought it to her in bed while I rolled them. She told me all the ingredients that her Nonnie used to put in her recipe, and then I added a couple more for my own spin. When I asked her if she just wanted to do it, she told me there was no way her hands would be rolling around that much meat unless it was the kind of meat that dangled between my legs. So, I listened to music and prepped dinner in our kitchen bright and early. And then I went upstairs and made love to my fiancée.

Days like today are the ones that you live for. The kind of days that you remember fully. All the details and nuances, because it's a day that means something special to only you. That's what today is for me.

"Is it dry enough yet?" G runs her fingers over the hanging pasta that she rolled out and cut a little while ago. Long, thick cuts of fettuccine.

"Yes. It's good," I say as she leans over the island and kisses me.

"What about the sauce? You want to taste it, see if it needs anything else?" I ask.

She drops the spoon and sends me an annoyed look. "Gravy."

"What?"

"It's gravy, Hanky"

"It's sauce, G. Gravy is brown."

"The fuck it is. Do NOT let this be the thing that destroys us." She points between the two of us. "I am Italian. We call it gravy where I'm from. Which means that's what it's called. Capiche?"

I scrunch my nose at her, but it's not worth the wrath. "I'll call it whatever you want, Pixie." I turn around and move fast enough to snag another kiss on the lips. I pull her by her belt loops closer to me as she leans back, playing mad and trying to keep her mouth from mine. "I'll call it cream if you want." I laugh.

She hits me. "You will not! That word has a very specific time and place. Now is not one of them."

The small swatting movement lets me in closer so I can kiss her again. Even in a kitchen filled with garlic, onion, and Italian spices swirling around us, all I can taste on her is sugar and lemons. *My sweet and tart girl.*

"Oh, for fuck's sake, everywhere I go these days, I'm walking in on people making out," Law says as he comes into the kitchen.

We brought everything to my dad's house for Sunday dinner.

Opening the refrigerator, Law says, "I still think you should have opted for the younger one in this family, G."

He wiggles his brows at her at the same time I chuck a piece of bread at his head.

"Watch it!"

He throws his arms up. "Hurry up, I'm starving," he laughs out. Running his hand to the side of his mouth, he whisper-shouts, "G, if he misbehaves, I'll take his seconds. I don't mind being a pinch-hitter."

"Get the fuck out, Law," I bark at him.

G yells as he leaves, "I'll take a glass of whatever's open."

She grabs a hefty pinch of salt and throws it into the boiling water meant for the pasta.

"You gonna misbehave, baby?" she says as she leans in and bites my shoulder.

"Watch it, Pixie, or I won't make you dessert later."

She raises her eyebrows.

"Can I be your dessert later?"

I turn around and wipe my hands on the towel that hangs over my shoulder. Pulling her into my arms, I kiss her beautiful lips. I move my mouth to her neck and bite just under her ear, grazing my teeth against her skin. I can feel the goosebumps pluck up on her arms.

She makes a small moan.

"You better stop making those noises, or else I'm going to make you my meal instead tonight. They can all fend for themselves while I devour that pussy of yours."

Another small moan escapes her mouth. "That sounds like a challenge."

"Just a promise."

She moves her hand to grip my hardened cock in my

pants. "Don't push me, Pixie," I say as I lick her neck again.

A loud clang hits against the countertop. "Come the fuck on, you two!" Law yells as he moves back into the room. "You wanted wine. I was gone for like two minutes. Crap on a cracker, it's like if I'm not getting any, everyone else is."

She laughs, and I smile at her as she takes a sip of her wine. A few minutes later, the fresh pasta is cooked, the meat and *gravy* are ready to be served. We all gather in the dining room, my entire family present.

I clear my throat to gain their attention, but before I can say anything, I'm interrupted by G grabbing my hand. I pull it to my mouth to kiss it, and I realize that this is the moment I've wanted. To be able to tell my family, who mean more to me than anything in this world, that I'm going to marry the love of my life.

The movement stops my dad and Everly's conversation about the pool that she and Jack are planning to put in next summer. Jack and Michael stop talking with Law about the UFC fight they just watched.

"We're getting married," I say proudly.

She leans in, kisses me, and then looks around the room. "I'm going to be a Riggs!"

The squealing and hugging that explodes between G and my sister is louder than the hoots and hollers from the guys. My dad gets up, and with tears sparkling in his eyes, he wraps his arms around me. "Make every day count, Hen. Let her know every day how much she means to you. And don't ever let her go."

"I won't, Dad." *I won't.*

Giselle

"That's not...it's not possible, Ruth," I hear Henry say from the front door.

Great, my least favorite Strutt's Peaker has decided to knock on our door on a Monday morning to bother us with what is likely another complaint. My guess is it's the new potted plants I've packed with boxwood trees and black lights and put out front. It's not October yet, but I love Halloween, and in my opinion, it's never too early to start decorating.

The door closes, and I yell from our bed, "Everything okay?"

A big, hairy lump nudges up against me. Milo likes to snuggle in bed in the morning. He's too big to sleep with us, but I give him some time every morning with extra pets before Henry takes him to the dog park. The wildebeest stopped asking for him to go back with her after she had her baby, and honestly, I was relieved. I never thought I'd love routines, but the lazy mornings we have together always start with sex and end with dog snuggles and coffee. I mean, really, what is this life?!

Henry jogs up the stairs, looking a little distracted. "I have something to tell you. And I'm not really sure how it's possible, or even what you're going to think, but..." He stares at Milo. And then points at him when his rusty-furry head pops up to stare at his dad. "You," Henry says, pointing at Milo. "You've been a bad boy, haven't you!" Milo tilts his head and barks back.

I sit up, looking at him curiously. He makes his way over to the bed and plops down. "Well..." He blows out a breath. "Ruth seems to think that Milo is going to be a daddy."

I bark out a laugh. "What?"

"I guess we'll see in a few months, but her little princess is expecting puppies, and the only dog she's been around lately is Milo."

"Milo!" I look at the old boy. "Were you getting busy with that little poodle? You know what? Good for you! After years of being stifled, I'm sure you just needed to let loose a bit," I say as I scratch the scruff of his neck.

"He's been getting out, but I'm still not sure how. And Ruth found them. In the back of her yard, well, being *friendly*..." He starts laughing.

"I know how he's been getting out." Henry looks at me, waiting for more detail. I hadn't thought about this until now, that perhaps Milo would have found it.

"There's a crawl space under the stairs that leads right to the back courtyard. It was one of the things that made me feel more at ease here, like a secret escape, if I needed it. Granted, it's like right near the front door, but still." I laugh again, shrugging. "I guess Milo found it."

We both pet Milo before either of us says anything more. I'm anxious to hear what he's thinking, because he did just start a business. I'm as busy as ever at Hideaway Ink and growing the level of awareness, and in turn, clientele. Who would have time for a puppy? Milo is such an easy dog. Partly because he's really the sweetest boy, and partly because he's older. He craves walks and attention, but nothing even close to what a puppy would need.

Training, constant playing, and lots of space. Most days, Milo sits at my feet in the tattoo shop, and then for the days that he wants to move around a bit more, he'll go for walks with Henry to The Lemon Tree. He'll stay for prep, and then come back to the loft right before Henry opens for dinner service.

That does leave three days a week open for time, though. I wonder if we could do it. If we'd want to grow our little family in that way.

"I know it's not the same," Henry says, looking up at me, tucking a piece of hair behind my ear. *I love it when he does that.* "But we're already really great dog parents. We could add a puppy to the mix if that's something you'd want."

My eyes well with tears before I even realize it. Having children isn't in the plan for us, but the idea of a puppy sounds like our own version of a little family. And that concept makes my heart so happy. I'm nodding vigorously when I say, "I want. I definitely want."

...Just before Christmas, on the cusp of one of the largest snowstorms to come barreling through Strutt's Peak in a decade, we welcomed home three new members to our little family. When Ruth called in early November and told Henry that she was at the vet and her princess just gave birth to three male mini golden doodles, and that he was paying for all of it, I was almost certain I saw tears in his eyes. The man is never short on telling me how he feels, and showing it in a roster of ways, but Henry Montana Riggs does not get choked up very easily. Apparently, when his fur babies are concerned, all bets are off.

It seemed only appropriate that we named our littles after some of the greats: Egon, Winston, and Venkman. Henry likes to call them his little ballbusters, instead of Ghostbusters, but really, the way that man smiles when he sees them as soon as he walks in the door, or the way that he talks to them like they're going to say something back, it's so swoony. I've basically just started wearing panty liners regularly.

It's never simple between the two of us, but the fighting and the compromise are worth it. We piss each other off, but we always get over it. We can stay up late and laugh for hours. We can sit comfortably quiet together. He takes me on frequent flights. I get to see my blue skies up close and talk to my pilot the whole time. Watching him fly a plane is an entirely higher level of sexy that makes me instantly horny, but I think he secretly knows that too.

I think this version of his life, the one he didn't expect, the one where he gets to fly, gets the girl, and all the pieces in between, is the one that was always meant to happen.

And while the life I've built in Strutt's Peak is damn fine. The fact that I've built anything is mind-blowing most days. Hideaway Ink is my art come to life. A chance to change up what's old or turn it into something exciting and new. But even the hard work and the pride I feel toward my business is the extra, just the frosting. There isn't anything better than being a Riggs. Henry gave me something that I thought I wouldn't have ever again. A family. There isn't a day that goes by when I don't look up and thank all the goddesses of the universe for it.

We have that easy kind of love. The kind that doesn't make you worry or overthink. The kind that lets you breathe. Smile. Fight and argue, but know it'll turn out okay. Live confidently. Grow together.

Henry was a force that barreled into my life out of nowhere. An attraction, a connection, that was so heavy I couldn't have escaped it. And I really tried. For over a decade, we fought it, but in the end, we couldn't hide from each other anymore. It's a beautiful life. Being part of a whole. A piece of a formula that equaled happiness. A blue, purple sky after a storm. The anchor to a new adventure. A life where there's nothing to hide from when it comes to that person, and where fighting, pushing, protecting, and loving each other every day, is the peak.

THE END

I hope you enjoyed Hide and Peak!
Michael and Grace's love story is next in
The Sneak Peak

My Best Friend. Young. *Tempting*.
She bid on me at my company's charity auction and won. Back then, she was too young, with hearts in her eyes and her whole life ahead of her. That's how we started, and after all this time, she's become my best friend.

Being a single dad of twins and running Colorado's most

successful summer sports company requires control and focus. Both of which are slipping through my fingers.

I just crashed her date and watched her kiss another man. The whole time her eyes were on me.

Now, she's living in my house, nannying my kids for the summer, and saying she wants to "explore" things that drip with the kind of filthy curiosity that I crave.

I don't want her to have anyone else, but I know it'll change us if I take what I want. And, if we destroy our friendship it'll ruin me. Or worse, end up breaking my kid's hearts and hers.

ALSO BY VICTORIA WILDER

Jack & Everly's Story

Michael & Grace's Story

A SIP FROM BREWS & BOOKS

THE HOT & FILTHY

Ingredients

- Hot Cocoa Mix
- 8 oz of hot water
- 2 oz of Vodka
- 1 oz of Kahlua
- 1 oz of Raspberry simple syrup

Optional:

- Dark or semisweet chocolate for melting
- 3-5 frozen or fresh raspberries
- Whipped cream
- Dark Chocolate shavings

1. Using raspberry jam or what had been straining from your raspberry simple syrup, coat the rim of your mug. Dip the coated rim mug in dark chocolate shavings.

2. Mix the vodka, Kahlua, and raspberry simple syrup in a shaker.
3. Mix the hot cocoa mix and hot water in your mug
4. Then add the vodka, Kahlua, and raspberry syrup from your shaker last.
5. Give it a stir and top it with whipped cream, chocolate shavings, and chocolate-covered raspberries.

Raspberry simple syrup:

1 cup fresh or frozen raspberries, ½ cup sugar, ½ cup water, and a pinch of salt. Combine and simmer on stovetop for 15 minutes. Strain and store in the fridge for up to 2 weeks.

Chocolate-covered raspberries:

5-10 fresh raspberries to use as a garnish/treat. Melt your favorite chocolate (semi-sweet, milk, or dark). Skewer 2-3 raspberries on a straw or toothpick, and dip them into the melted chocolate. Pop into the freezer for 20 minutes to harden.

A Hot and Filthy is best enjoyed with your bestie while spilling whatever tea is brewing. If your friend isn't available, I'd suggest flipping back to Chapter 33 for some extra steam...

ACKNOWLEDGMENTS

Thank you so much for reading Henry and Giselle's story. By the time I had hit the halfway point in writing Peaks of Color, I knew that Henry and Giselle would be next. I had no idea until I started writing, how crazy it would be to get to their happily ever after. Thank you for taking the ride with them.

There is an incredible community on Instagram of readers who consume romance books passionately and who fantastically support others. To all of you, I am so grateful. I'd like to give a shout-out to a handful of some very incredible women in this community whom absolutely impacted this story. Lauren @romancensass, Sara @playlistsandpaperbacks, Adi @HopelesslySmutty-Reads, Amy @CoffeeandBookObsessed, and Dominique @Sugaaaaadigsbooks. Whether it was through random chitchat, their excitement as they read, or gorgeous pictures they posted, which in-turn, inspired scenes, I thank you. You are all so fabulous!

Thank you to my beta readers and my girlfriends, whose constant excitement about these stories keeps me feeling like I've hit the friendship jackpot.

To the FAA crew, you all inspire me without even realizing it. A special thanks to Nick, Roger, Alex, and Will for letting me creep on Thursday's wrestling and Jiu Jitsu class so I could accurately portray a damn good fight scene.

To my sisters, who are woven throughout the relationships of the Riggs siblings, thank you for cheering me on. Blair, you are my forever sounding board, the most epic cheerleader. I will never be able to properly repay you because: how can you put a price on the time and genuine excitement you've given me during all of this? Thank you, seester!

Mom, you're the kind of main character energy that every writer needs in life. Thank you for your constant excitement and for always being ready to talk romance books with me.

Dad, I know you didn't read the book. And you know what? I'm totally fine with that. Please don't. Thank you for your neverending support and for blindly selling the heck out of these stories to anyone whom will listen.

To my hubs, there are never enough words, but in our lifetime, I hope I can say at least a fraction of the ones that let you know how much I appreciate you. Your actions are always louder than even my loudest words, and while writing this book, I needed every single one of them. Thank you, my love.

To my editor, Mackenzie, I am so damn lucky to have you as my guide. You pushed me with this story, and I'm so happy you did. These two are really something special. Thank you for your constant positive energy, creativity, and the real talk I absolutely needed along the way. I can't wait for what's next!

ABOUT THE AUTHOR

Forever a hopeful romantic, author Victoria Wilder writes contemporary romance with deliciously witty and wild characters. Her stories range from small-town swoon-worthy men to fiercely powerful families and lead characters whom aren't afraid to ask for what they want.

She's an east coast girl, always chasing the next season and living it up with her husband, two kiddos, and dog, Linus. When she's not reading or writing, you'll find her training at a kickboxing class or finding an excuse to sink her feet in the sand at the beach.

She believes in the power of a great story. That words have the ability to change the trajectory of your life.

instagram.com/authorvictoriawilder
tiktok.com/authorvictoriawilder
bookbub.com/authors/victoria-wilder

Made in the USA
Columbia, SC
28 June 2025

60037115R00307